THE LAST CIRCUS ON EARTH

First published by Brio Books in 2020

Brio Books
PO Box Q324, QVB Post Office,
NSW 1230, Australia

www.briobooks.com.au

Cataloguing-in-publication data is available from the National Library of Australia

978-1-925589-98-6 (print)

978-1-925589-99-3 (digital)

Internal design and typesetting © Brio Books 2020

Cover illustration and design by Roy Chen

Dedicated to Brenda

THE LAST CIRCUS ON EARTH

B.P. MARSHALL

'By the pricking of my thumbs,
something wicked this way comes . . .'
Macbeth, William Shakespeare

Book One—
United Counties of
England, 2070

Chapter One—Beware the person with nothing to lose

My name is Blanco. I belong to Mister Splinter's circus. I do the murders.

I hate murdering people. When I was a daft twelve-year-old, I asked the Gaffer if I could look after the elephants instead but he said everyone had to do what they're good at, and I was a born murderer. I mumbled I'd murder *him*. He just belted me over the back of the head. 'We all got our place in the scheme of things, Blanco. Yours is to do what you're soddin' told.'

Six years later, I'm a soddin' expert, trudging through some stinking village in the dead of night to the next job.

In the dark of another unfamiliar house, my bare feet slide soft on the wooden floor, hardly stirring the dust. I move toward the bedroom door. I freeze as a feather-like touch brushes my ankle. A cat, coiling around my leg, looks up at me, lit by the flickering lectric streetlight coming through the window. He's a friendly old moggie, a bit moth-eaten, keen for a smooch and a feed. I scratch his head and step past.

The open doorway lies ahead, through which I see a guttering candle in a glass jar beside a bed. I creep to the door. The old geezer is dozing, but only just. As I get to the bedside, his watery eyes slowly open. I stop and wait in case he thinks it's just a dream and falls back to sleep. Instead he focuses on me, frightened but calm.

'I've got nowt, lad.'

'I know,' I say.

He guesses what I'm there for. He sighs, then manages a small, sad smile. 'This is me done, is it?'

'It won't hurt none, I promise.'

Puzzled, he looks me up and down—a strange, tall, skinny lad with paper-white skin, bone-white dreadlocks and dark eyes. 'You look so young. You're just a child.'

'I in't never been a child, mate.' I sit on the side of the bed and pick up a framed photo of the geezer's family. 'Happy-looking bunch.'

He scowls. 'It's an old photo.'

I pick up a fading photo of a dog. 'Nice. Looks like a wolfhound.'

The geezer smiles and reaches for the photo, wistful. 'Irish wolfhound crossed with I-don't-know-what. I called her Daisy. Got her off one of your lot as a pup.'

'Beautiful mug on her. She looks like she'd run all day too.'

'Could she ever. I'd take her hunting in the woods and fields.'

'Much game about these parts?'

'More now the forests are growing back after the last big wildfires. We did alright—a bird here or there. A bunny if we were lucky.'

'She looks too sweet to kill anything.'

The geezer's eyes mist over, focused on the past. 'She could run them down like a champion, but she was hopeless at the end. I'd catch her up and there she'd be, lying down beside some exhausted rabbit, licking its face like a mother washing its pup.'

A tear rolls down his cheek. 'Did my grandchildren pay you to do this? So they could get my money?'

I nod, and carefully hand him the neatly folded handkerchief, discreetly holding my breath. 'Here you go. Have a blow in that, eh?'

The geezer takes it and wipes his eyes and nose as I keep up the patter. 'There's nothing like a happy dog to warm the cockles, eh. And she looks happy alright.'

'She was the happiest creature on this Earth.' The geezer sniffs at the kerchief, sleepily curious. 'Vanilla. Nice.'

I give him a smile. 'I bet Daisy never left your side, am I right?'

'Never. She'd sleep on the bed, sit by my feet, walk with me everywhere.' The geezer's eyes are closing as he murmurs. 'I'd just have to look into her face and it'd bring a smile to mine. The happiest, sweetest, most loyal . . .'

The geezer falls asleep. I carefully take the kerchief and put it back in its case, wafting the air about with my free hand so I don't gas myself. The cat jumps up on the bed to find out what's going on. ''Ullo, puss,' I say, and give it another scratch before I suffocate the old man with a pillow.

In the geezer's kitchen there's some meat in a big stone jar, so I give that to the cat, thinking it might not get fed again for a while. I take some bread from the bread bin then walk back to the circus in the dark, chewing, trying not to think.

Sometimes, just before I do people, they'll look at me like I'm doing them a favour. Some might be ill or dying, but all got guilt preying on them. They tell me things. Things they done during the Collapse. Bad things.

Sometimes I hear them out, sometimes I don't. I got enough stuff I don't want to think about.

I hate murdering people. I'd do a runner but even if the Gaffer didn't catch me, where would I go? How could I survive outside Mister Splinter's Magnifico Cirque du Amusementes, in a world where being a freak gets you killed; where they stopped burying people after the first few billion deaths, and there's barely room for what's left of us.

Our giant Russian witch, Baba Yaga, says we're all wanderers on this blighted Earth—our hearts full of hope, our souls full of dreams.

I dream of death.

Mine.

Chapter Two—An hour of play discovers more than a year of conversation

When I got back to the circus, I was roped in to be Lecturer for the 10 pm freak show.

I put on the white lab coat to play the part of a 'scientist' reminding all God-fearing peasants of the Horrors of Science, then trudged past the queue of punters to the trailer steps, where Kongo the Ape Woman, wearing her grey 'Failed Experiment 41G' smock, loomed over everyone. 'Alright, Blanco?'

I stopped thinking about the old man and his dog, managed a nod, then went inside to check everything was ready. I made sure all the curtains were drawn across the 'cells' as I slung the unloaded rifle, 'to prevent escapes', over my shoulder. Then I opened the door for the punters to enter our dimly lit 'High-Security Freak Enclosure'.

Once they were all in, and the door was closed, I began the usual spray in front of the first curtain.

'Salaam, and welcome, lays and germs. Everyone make room, please. Let the kids and shorter folk come in front so everyone can see our first exhibit in the Horrors of Science—the science I too am a victim of, and now study in order to help the less fortunate.

'A warning—the creature you is about to see is so horrible I cannot predict the reaction it might cause in them with a delicate constitution.

'Before I pull the curtain aside, I'm required to warn you by law that this lady, for lady she is, is confirmed by all legal science to be the ugliest woman in the world. No mirrors are allowed because if Baba Yaga, The Witch from Siberia, sees herself, she can go into a rage so great the iron bars here might not hold her back. Imagine living with yourself, ladies, if you looked like this . . .'

I pulled back the first curtain, and behind the iron bars, Baba Yaga's misshapen bulk was sat on an old plush chair, dressed in her usual rags, knitting. Her 'cell' was made up to look like a fine lady's boudoir. Missing from the dressing table was the mirror, but the walls held a few framed prints of beautiful women through the ages to help remind the thicker punters of the ideals of feminine beauty.

The gasps of horror came, as ladies clutched the arms of their menfriends, appalled by Baba Yaga's size, lumpy potato-shaped nose, ropy lips, and crumpled ears protruding from her thick, grizzled black hair. Even sitting down, Baba was as tall as most men. Her gnarled hands, muscular and deformed, looked too big to be knitting like she was. She give the punters a shy smile, her tombstone teeth luminous with some green gunk from the makeup cupboard.

I kept up the patter, getting ready to segue to the next freak and keep this group moving. 'Baba Yaga was captured after locals tried to frighten her out of the village by holding up mirrors. What a tragic mistake, ladies and gentlemen, because they drove her insane with fury. She went on a rampage, causing injury and mayhem to innocent folk. Now, safely confined in this lab, Baba Yaga tries to make amends by knitting clothes for any orphanages what we pass by in our travels. I hope you'll all offer a prayer that she might one day be forgiven—though, truth be told, some will think this poor cursed woman has been punished enough.'

I drew the curtain on her as I launched straight into the next spray. 'And punishment is what Erik the Eel knows all about. God knows what Erik done in a former life, but it must've been pretty bad to be born not only without his hands, not only minus his arms and feet, but also his legs. Prepare to be shocked, ladies and gentlemen, for Erik, the human eel!'

I pulled back the curtain, and there was Erik, lying chest-down on his padded platform, immaculately dressed in vest, suit jacket, and the stumps of trousers, his big curly-haired head arching up to read a newspaper through his spectacles, his 'cell' made to look like a living room. He looked up, blue eyes shining over his grand moustache, his Austrian accent crisp and cheerful. 'Good afternoon, ladies and gentlemen, I'm Erik.'

'Please say "hullo", folks,' I whispered. 'His Excellency Erik von Hildebrandt is a Prussian nobleman and former scholar of the science what has so cruelly caused his deformities.'

A few in the crowd greeted Erik, who nodded back. 'I hope you don't mind if I smoke?'

One of the lads pulled out a tin of cigarettes and offered one to Erik. ''Ere yer go, mate.'

Erik just smiled. 'Thank you, young man, but I prefer to roll my own.'

The punters watched, astonished, as Erik used his lips, tongue, chin and nose to extract a cigarette paper, fill it with tobacco, and roll a cigarette while I kept up the patter.

'I know what some of you is thinking, and I refuse to answer any questions about whether or not Erik has been spared the removal of *every* appendage. That is for God, Erik and his wife to know.'

I got the expected confused looks. 'That's right, folks, Erik is not only conversant in over a dozen languages, and holds degrees from universities in six European nations, he is also a happily married man.'

At which point our pretty lead acrobat, Julietta Fazio, entered through the back, dressed like what we thought a sexy Prussian 'wife' might look like, holding a plate of what looked like freshly baked scones. Her smile turned to a convincing display of surprise as she saw the punters. 'Oh, I'm so sorry.'

'That's alright, my love,' said Erik. 'We have visitors.'

'Please don't let us disturb you, Mrs Hildebrandt,' I said. 'I was just lecturing our neighbours from this lovely town about Erik's accomplishments.' Here I turned and winked at some ogling lads at the back.

'And clearly, given Erik has a beautiful wife like Mrs H, we have the answer to that question we can't ask.'

Erik had his cigarette rolled by then, though admittedly not all the lads in the crowd were looking at him as he finished his trick by lighting it. As I slowly closed the curtain, Julietta brought her 'husband' a scone, bending over to give the punters a healthy dose of cleavage.

'And as we allow the happy couple some domestic bliss—and you men ask yourselves a few private questions what shouldn't be uttered with ladies present—I have to warn you the next resident of our community is going to shock you. I know you think you seen it all, that nothing can shock you no more. But I'll be honest, folks—our next freak does stuff what I can hardly bear to look at. In fact, my best advice is to look away from this piteous creature. Spare yourselves the nightmares of the things what he does. Ladies and gentlemen, I give you . . .' I paused to shudder. 'Dislocato!'

With the punters primed, I opened the curtain to reveal, behind the bars, a darkened cell with just a square mat in the middle of the floor. On it was skinny, brown Dislocato, standing on one leg, eyes closed, dressed in a loincloth, his left foot resting against the inner thigh of his right leg.

I lowered my voice to a whisper. 'Hush now, folks. He may look like just another rare and exotic Hindoo fakir standing there like that but, when he starts his horrible transformation, you'll be lucky to hold on to your lunch. Please keep your screams to a minimum, as it disturbs some of the other freaks.'

Slowly Dislocato raised the foot resting against his thigh, and stretched the leg out and up. The punters winced as his foot rose until it reached the side of his head. Then it slid around his neck until the back of his knee rested there. Sinking down to sit on his skinny bum, he brought the other leg around to his left side. Where an ordinary man's leg should stop, his kept going. Finally, it was wrapped around his waist.

His arms snaked through, around and under his legs, turning himself into a single knot. Then he stopped, the only movement the slow rise and fall of his breathing. The punters held their breath—was this it? Then there were a subtle movement of one of Dislocato's shoulders—which was now where no shoulder should be—and a faint, muffled click. There was another sickening snick as his other shoulder dislocated, then two louder ones as his hips did the same. I winced. No matter how often I see it, that sound makes my skin crawl.

Dislocato, apparently in the deepest of trances, was now a knotted bundle of skin and bone, unrecognisable as a body, his head atop the pile. Then, without warning, his eyes snapped open.

There were screams and yelps from the punters, as Dislocato stared at the group, unblinking.

Then he did the really horrible bit.

He slowly opened his mouth, wider and wider. You could already see both sets of his teeth when, with a soft pop, his jaw dislocated, his mouth opening in a hideous gape guaranteed to give you nightmares. On this, I slowly closed the curtain, whispering to the now shocked audience. 'The truly sinister Dislocato will also perform amazing feats of twistology during the Grand Show in the Big Top, starting in half an hour. For now, I urge you all to remain calm. Our next freak cage holds not just one but three creatures.'

I began to open the curtain then paused. 'I wonder, ladies and gentlemen, just how brave you are.'

One of the cheeky lads snorted. 'Brave enough ter laugh at whatever you got in there.'

I smiled. 'It seems we have a *real* man amongst us. But is he courageous enough to enter the cage?'

The lad kept his grin—just. 'No bother, mate.'

'With a blindfold?' I added.

The other lads urged on their friend, who had no choice but to tough it out. 'Why not?'

I drew him to my side, and whipped a silk scarf around his eyes as I kept up the patter. 'The creatures you is about to see are only half-human. On a remote island called Tasmania, an evil scientist ground up DNA from humans and animals, whacked them in test tubes, zapped them with rads, and went home to bed. The next morning, three of them tubes had something in them. You are about to see the results, as this brave fella calmly allows himself to enter their lair.'

I pulled back the curtain to reveal a single chair behind the bars.

'Now, let's go inside and make you comfortable, eh? You should rest before you tests your courage.' I paused, feigning concern. 'Are you sure you're still up for this? Just say you is scared and I'll take the blindfold off and let you stay safe with your pals.'

'I'm fine,' said the punter, dogged.

'Good man,' I replied as I opened the barred door. 'There's a comfortable seat here. Rest your bones, eh?' I sat him down and stepped back to the door, where a rope hung down. 'I'll release them now. I don't know which one will come out first, but at the first sign of trouble, I'm out of here.' I pulled slowly on the rope, and a wooden grate, painted to look like iron bars, lifted up at the back.

I whispered to the crowd, 'Your friend is a tough one. Just sitting there, not worried about a thing. Not worried about what's going to come through that gate back there.'

A pink fleshy limb appeared, without a hand or foot on the end, spider-like. A few in the audience gasped.

'Blimey,' I muttered, acting worried. 'It's her. Good luck, lad.'

Hearing me 'escape', and the door slam shut, I knew the only thing keeping the lad on the chair was pride. Then he heard a rattle—could it be a deadly malformed monster? It's Lobby shaking a maraca out the back, but the boy on the chair was ready to bolt. Then he heard the intake of breath from the punters as Spider Susy crawled through the grate, hissing through her teeth for effect, and looking around as if for suitable prey. Susy walks on all fours, her truncated limbs splayed out to the sides with her head up, moving slowly. What's normal for her looks sinister to others, like she's 'stalking'.

'Jesus,' muttered one of the lad's friends. 'Is that thing dangerous?'

'As long as he keeps perfectly still and shows no sign of fear, he'll be fine,' I replied. The lad was malarial with fear as he heard Susy approach. Then came a strange wet, clacking sound, and Lobster Boy come through the grate, wearing only shorts, his skin painted red, his stumpy little foot flaps slapping the ground, his arms raised and clapping his 'claws' together, apparently looking around for fresh meat.

The crowd murmured with worry, especially when Susy and Lobby started sniffing around the lad in the chair. One touch from Lobby's fleshy 'claw' and the lad yelped, jumped up, pulling the blindfold off as he leaped at the door—which I pretended to have trouble opening.

The second it opened, he squeezed through, and I slammed the door shut as the lad calmed himself, staring in mixed shame and horror at Lobby and Susy.

I grinned, joke over. 'It's alright, folks, step closer and I'll introduce you to Susy the Human Spider, and Lobby the Lobster Boy—half-boy, half-lobster.'

Ready for her part of the act, Susy went to a pad of paper, picked up a pencil with her mouth, and began sketching one of the girls in the audience. Lobby swapped a grin with the still-trembling lad. 'Need a haircut, son?' Then he clacked his claws as the lad backed away.

'Where's Penguin Girl, Lobby?' I asked him.

He looked around, his voice gentle. 'Come on Penny, come and say hullo.'

The crowd leaned closer as Penny stumped her way out. Penny's a double gimp—not only did she get partly formed arms and feet like her brother Lobby, she was also born without much in the way of a brain. In carnie-speak, she's a pinhead. Which means she's got no legs to speak of, flaps for feet, longer flaps for arms, and a small pointy head topped with a fuzzy ball of ginger hair. She's daft as a brush but always wears a happy smile. That, plus her big buckteeth, she's welcome relief for the punters. They all smiled as she waddled over, grinning, her top teeth spilling out over her tiny recessed chin, flapping her arms. She loves attention, does our Penny.

'It's alright to let her stroke your arms, folks,' I reassure the crowd. 'She's very friendly, is Penny the Penguin Girl. And, as you can see, Spider Susy is doing a portrait of a beautiful young lady in the crowd, which can be purchased for a very reasonable price after the show. Lobster Boy is available to give haircuts—with a pair of scissors and all appropriate tools, sterilised and clean, in the gentlemen's salon at the end of the midway, next to the halal kebab stall.'

The rest of the show was a blur. Mathematico played Bach on his tiny lectric keyboard and did lightning-fast calculations using his fingers, as punters tried to beat him using a calculator. Elasto stretched his neck skin over his face, made a kilt of skin out of his stomach and back, and did amusing things with his prick and balls for a men-only showing. Methuselah told the punters a soft, sad story of the history of their town that had them silent with awe as they saw the past through his eyes. Our most boring 'performer', Povero Cristo, simply hung, nailed to his cross, in what looked like—and was—genuine agony, while his assistant and disciple Guido the Gimp collected and sold vials of his blood as good-luck charms. Humbolt the Human Art Gallery proudly displayed his tattooed paintings, copied from the ruins of some Old Londonne gallery. Ezekial Scamp—the Man with Two Faces— chilled the punters' blood as he turned, very slowly, to reveal the other side of his face, bulging and twitching. Skeletor just had to 'smile' to have them all gasping in horror.

Then Kongo waited at the blow-off to loom out of the shadows, scare the proverbial, and collect 'donations' for the freaks' 'ongoing care and rehabilitation'.

I was hoarse with talking but didn't care. I had to hurry and prepare for my act, and all the fucking pain that went with it.

Chapter Three—Where the scythe cuts, no more fairies

I n the dusty eucalypt forest outside New Londonne, I was enjoying the smells of the warming trees while collecting firewood with Baba Yaga. Like a big bear wearing a dress, Baba reached up and gripped dead branches, used her weight to snap them off, then tossed them toward me for chopping into firewood.

I enjoy these moments of escape from the prison of the circus. And, with Baba Yaga to protect me, I didn't feel no fear from the locals.

I love forests. The air is sweet and, for a while, I don't have my nostrils filled with the circus stench of shit, piss and burning sugar. I can let my mind drift and marvel at the little birds what come to collect the insects we disturb doing our work.

Sometimes I see deer or wild dogs or foxes. Sometimes our eyes meet and, for a few heartbeats, I feel a cool kinship with another outsider—an outsider what locals would kill without a thought. With most days in south England reaching into the thirties, the mornings were gentle, the breeze still cool and soft on the skin.

I was thinking all this airy-fairy shite when Doctor Po rode up on one of the motorbikes, his long legs and knees sticking out, ornate oriental robes flapping behind him. 'You, Blanco. Come with me.

We go to next town and make arrangements.'

'What do you need me for?'

'Mister Splinter say I must teach you the art of negotiate.'

'After last time?'

'He say this time you watch me, and learn. And don't make sad face.' Po mocked me in a deep voice: '"I am Blanco. I come from unhappy circus that make everybody miserable—please tell everyone in your town to come and have bad time when we arrive."'

I scowled, but Baba Yaga nodded. 'Po is right,' she growled. 'You think like a Russian. You need to pretend you is like happy normal English boy. Make the smile.'

I didn't feel like smiling, especially at a bunch of suspicious townies who aren't sure whether to shoot us or let us set up. I sighed and handed my axe to her. 'A man must put grain in the ground before he can harvest.'

'Good boy,' murmured Baba Yaga. 'If you smile, maybe a pretty girl see you and smile back, mm?'

'Yeah, then her father and brothers will beat the shit out of me.' I sat on the back of Po's bike. 'Will you be alright by yourself?'

'You think anybody give me trouble?' She straightened her back, the axe hanging from one strong arm, her broad bulk towering over us, swathed in a neck-to-knee dress of layered cloth and hessian, her lumpy face wrinkled and brown as a walnut.

I smiled. 'Only a madman with an army of madmen would give you trouble, Baba.'

'Damn bloody right,' she replied.

Po rode us slowly through the trees over the rough ground until we reached the track. Then we puttered past locals carrying sticks and logs, deflecting their wary looks with a cheery wave.

Finally, we reached the highway. As Po dodged potholes, horses, donkey carts, bicycles, tractors and the occasional lectric truck, I began to relax. For a while, I didn't have to do nothing but hang on and watch the river of humanity flow around us.

It was early spring, and the sun was already warming us. The rains had come at last—flowers and grasses covered the crumbling road edges, and the forest was bright with new colour. The air smelled clean and medicinal from the eucalypts and pine, and there was a faint tang of the sea coming from the south-east.

We passed rickety roadside stalls, and my mouth watered at the smoky aroma of grilled nuts and strips of meat. Travellers wealthy enough to sit and take their leisure enjoyed the passing parade, as the stallholders' children brought them tea and snacks.

An entire family could exist on the proceeds of a well-placed and well-defended stall but, as I looked at the dust around them, at the wire and tin barricades, the fenced pigs and the chickens on the roofs, I wondered how anyone could live in just one place and not go mad.

The Gaffer once told me circuses are like sharks, what die if they don't keep moving and feeding. That was us alright—moving, feeding, robbing and killing. We were surviving, true enough, but there was bugger-all joy in it. If there's a god like they say there is, what the hell is he doing sitting up in the clouds letting the likes of us get away with murder and mayhem?

We slowed to get through a tangle of traffic, stalled by a broken-down cart. It belonged to a family, their possessions piled high. The father was shouting at the children, and I saw him pick something off the cart and throw it onto the roadside.

It landed with a yelp. A puppy.

I got off the bike before Po could stop me, and picked up the wounded dog. Then I handed it to Po, and headed toward the man.

'No!' yelled Po. 'Blanco! Stop—it was accident!'

'It wasn't no accident,' I muttered. The man saw me coming, and the look in my eye. He was scared, but squared up to me.

'Oi, you. I dinnae want trouble.'

'Too late,' I said. Then I saw the fear on his wife and kids' faces as they looked at my pale murderous mug. I turned to the man and spoke softly like Baba Yaga does when she's *really* angry. 'Don't. Ever. Hurt. Animals.'

The man was no fighter. He swallowed, edging a trembling hand toward a machete tucked beside his seat. 'We're no fit for feedin' oor-selves, let alone a wee pup.'

I gave the machete a glance then looked back at the skinny Scot, so he knew I didn't give a shit. He pulled his hand away. 'Keep the dog,' he said. 'Might be a meal in it, eh?'

I imagined what he saw. A freak. A traveller. Moving from place to place was something he was forced to do, but I did it for a living. My cold anger, and my ragged clothes shielding my too-white skin, told him I had less than him to lose. He looked down.

I give him a final dead-fish look. 'A real man don't yell at kids neither.'

'Whatever you say, son. Good as gold, eh? Nae harm done.'

I unclenched my fists and pointed at his right arm. 'Should you harm another animal, may that arm wither, and your will to live do the same.'

After this fake Gypsy palaver, I gave him a solemn devil sign, knowing this lowlander peon would probably have nightmares about it. Then I walked back to Po, who was sweating. 'Come, Blanco. We go now. Quickly.'

I took the whimpering pup and sat behind Po, noticing others had seen me lay the curse. In some places, it's enough to get you killed. Po eased the motorbike through the scrum until we were clear. Then he sped up, checking and rechecking the mirror for signs of pursuit. I didn't care. I just looked down at the pup, a mongrel with sad eyes and a leg that bent the wrong way, feeling her pain like it was my own.

Chapter Four—It is easier to milk a cow that stands still

P o stopped the motorbike outside the town walls of Rayleigh and wheeled it toward the watchtower gates.

'Get rid of dog,' he muttered. 'We need to look like professional performers, not Gypsy bad persons.' He indicated a rickety wooden minaret looming over the town walls. 'If anyone ask, you are strict Muslim.'

'I'll watch and listen, Doctor Po. As instructed.'

Po sighed and give up on me. We nodded to the guards, got thoroughly searched, asked for directions then walked the bike through the gates and barriers, a few rifle barrels tracking our progress. It was a short distance to the mayoral office, a rough two-storey shanty built from assorted bricks and stones—the reassembled wreckage of several buildings.

We were parking the bike as a bald, red-faced brick of a man walked out the doors with a slim, blond teenage boy and a couple of big lads with guns. We guessed this was the Mayor, so I stayed by the bike as Doctor Po gave an impressive sweeping bow, his gold-embroidered robes flashing in the sun. 'As-salaam Alaikum, your Worship, and a good morning to you, sir.'

The Mayor looked at Po, wary. 'Wa Alaikum salaam. And who might you be, sir?'

Po cleared his throat and used his best English. 'I am Doctor Po, here to represent Mister Splinter's famous organisation to great and mutual benefit of this beautiful township and ourself.'

'Oh, aye, and what line of business might you be in?'

'Our enterprises are many and varied, sir—but our primary business is the spread of happiness.'

'Drugs and alcohol then, is it?'

'No, sir. While it is true our organisation has a professional chemist in its number, and can supply medications for many purposes, we offer only to entertain, amaze and instruct the wonderful people here.'

'A circus?'

Po stood straighter, the definition of pride. 'We are Splinter's Magnifico Cirque du Amusementes!'

The Mayor frowned. 'Have I heard that name before?'

I hoped he hadn't. Po quickly continued. 'Undoubtedly you have, sir. We are the cleanest, happiest circus currently travelling the Allied Republics of Britain and Europe. We have entertaining and educational sideshows, also an incredible display of distorted humanity that will encourage prayer in all who see them, clowns who will bring laughter, and daredevil acts that will bring gasps to every family member.'

Po continued, but I'd heard it all a million times. I felt along the pup's hind leg. It was a plain break with no broken skin, and just needed straightening. She barely whimpered as I did the deed. I tore a strip from the fraying hem of my shirt, took a straight stick from a pile of kindling, split it with my knife, and fashioned a splint for the pup. Then I became aware the blond boy was standing close, watching me. The Mayor was also looking at me with interest. 'What's your lad doing?'

Po's smile didn't falter, even though I could see he was annoyed with me. 'Blanco is preparing to hand this stray dog to the authorities, as is required by the relevant laws, so it may be destroyed, thereby preventing the spread of disease among the wonderful communities we visit.'

'It looks like he's fixing it,' said the blond boy.

'I am,' I said. 'She has a broken leg.'

The Mayor pushed past his guards and looked at my work which, if

19

I say so myself, was tidy. 'Neat job, lad. We could use a few like you at the clinic.'

Po was suddenly at the Mayor's side, smoothly seizing the opportunity. 'I myself am a qualified medical practitioner, and our circus boasts one of Europe's finest surgeons. Blanco here is also a fully registered nurse. Splinter's Magnifico Cirque du Amusementes can deliver a baby, repair a broken limb, and comfort the dying with one of our proprietary medicines.'

The Mayor looked at me, at my face, and I looked back. Unusual. Most avoid my eyes and avoid me, but this townie was sizing me up, man to man. He nodded. 'Can you sew up wounds and all?'

Before I could reply, Po was talking. 'Such stitches as would make a seamstress proud, sir. Blanco can sew a wound so there is never a scar left behind.'

Clearly not trusting anything Po said, the Mayor looked to me for confirmation. I shrugged. 'I sew clean. Clean means less infection and a smaller scar.'

The Mayor nodded, then turned to Po. 'Your lot can come by. To the south, there's a fallow pasture with a well. You can stay one week there at five pound a night.'

'Thank you, good sir,' smiled Po. 'We'll provide such entertainment as will fill the hearts of all the good people here.'

'And empty their pockets no doubt. I don't mind that, but I won't hold with any thieving, drunkenness or rape. Any of your people step out of line, my men will step on you. If you provide us with some medical assistance—and no quackery, mind—we'll pay you for it and be grateful. Am I understood?'

Po was solemn. 'Mister Splinter is as honest as the day is long, and enforces sharia to ensure no untoward behaviour occurs. Our good name is everything to us.'

The Mayor nodded and turned away as Po bowed low. The teenager gave me a cheerful nod, and trotted after the Mayor, who I guessed was his father.

'He's gone,' I murmured, finishing the splint.

Po straightened, brushing dust off his pigtail. 'Why you interrupt negotiation with filthy dog and sewing and registered nursing? All you have to do is not look like disgusting Gypsy bad person. Instead you make the one-man show.'

'It got us the gig, didn't it? They need doctors, so you can pretend to be one, and the Professoré can cut people up and sell his poisons. We'll be a bleedin' hospital for them and sting them every which way.'

Po ignored me and started up the bike. I tucked the pup into my jacket. 'How many towns we visiting today then?'

'Only here. This shit-hole is last stop before we go to Port Rochford and sail to the continent.' Po glanced back at me with a grim sneer. 'Then we take the Haute Route to the big hoo-ha.'

Happy to remind me I was going to die soon, he turned and snicked the bike into gear. As we trickled through the crowded streets back toward the town gate, I sneaked looks at pretty girls, and tried not to think how it would be to finally die in front of hundreds of travellers and freaks at 'the big hoo-ha'. The only happy thought was imagining the Gaffer's frustration at losing 'an investment'. When the time came, I hoped I'd have enough strength left to close my hand while leaving the middle finger raised.

Chapter Five—Some think they are done, when they are only beginning

Baba Yaga cradled the pup, unimpressed. 'What you want me to do? Boil or roast?'

I sighed. 'Keep her safe while I'm doing my act. No cook, no eat.'

'Why you keep? Is dirty dog. Gaffer will be angry.'

'I'm not telling the Gaffer—Mister Splinter don't hold with no dogs. If you don't want to look after her, hide her with the freaks.'

'You are still child,' she sighed. 'A man does not have dog except for eat or guard.'

'Daisy can learn to guard Jumbo and El Grande.'

'Dog have name now?'

I thought of the old man I killed. 'A dog's got to have a name or you can't call them to you.'

'You don't call. You whistle,' she grumbled, but I noticed she was holding the pup with a gentle hand and stroking its belly.

I smiled as I walked away. 'And give her some milk or food, eh Baba?'

'Maybe I throw her in pot and make witchy spell to sell to stupid peoples.'

I looked back from the door of my trailer. Baba Yaga's head of wild hair was bent forward, her lump of a nose hovering above the pup, her lips turned up in what might, in a normal, have resembled a smile.

After my act, I went back to my trailer to stitch up a tear in my arm from one of the hooks. I can't get stainless steel hooks no more so I'm reduced to polished iron ones, and they sometimes catch as they're coming out.

The Gaffer stuck his sour-faced head in the doorway. 'Oi. Outside.'

'I'm fixin' myself.'

'You were sloppy tonight or you wouldn't be stitching. Do it after.'

I saw Strombo the Eunuch looming behind him. Strombo, the Gaffer's human pit bull—a two-metre pillar of hairless muscle, capable of bending steel bars without having to trick them first. I was in for a beating. I finished a stitch, tied it off and snipped the loose thread, reckoning haste wouldn't make Strombo take it any easier on me. I stood and stretched slow so I didn't split any healing wounds open again. Then I sauntered to the doorway like it was no bother getting done over.

Strombo pulled me off the top of the trailer steps with one swift arm, sending me stumbling to the ground. I pulled myself in to protect my face and balls, but Strombo reached down and pulled me onto my feet, whispering in that high voice of his, 'Splinter wants yer.'

My guts churned with fear. What the hell had I done? I give Po some lip but I didn't harm the negotiations. Was it the dog? Splinter's a full-blood Gyppo, and I knew they got a thing about dogs being filthy, but even so. I tried to sound like I didn't care. 'What's he want?'

The Gaffer gave me the sort of smile Strombo does before he pulls the head off something. 'Dunno. But it's time you got what's coming, boyo.'

The Gaffer is Mister Splinter's enforcer, circus bandolier and shift-boss. Except there isn't no shifts. Twenty-five hours a day, eight days a week, we're either working or we're drinking amphetamine-laced vodka so we can go on working. He also negotiates deals with locals as we maim and pillage our way through whatever fair land we're in.

Gaffer and Strombo pushed me into the shadows between the trailers. I thought about running, but this world don't tolerate anyone without a well-armed family or tribe behind them. Loners are killed or made slaves. Freaks like me do even worse.

'Bury me standing, thanks,' I muttered. 'I been kneelin' me whole bleedin' life.'

When we got to Mister Splinter's trailer, I expected to be pushed to the space below his window so Splinter could look through the curtains to make sure the beating was done right. Instead, the Gaffer pushed me onto the steps. 'In you go.'

I froze.

No one but the Gaffer, Po and the Professoré have seen Splinter face to face in a very long time. The thought of seeing him proper made my skin crawl. I spend all day with the freaks and see nothing but the people they are, but Splinter was a different kettle. He got modifications back in the old days. Mods what went bad when the rads were off the scale. I glimpsed part of him once—an arm poking through the mosquito netting, the flesh knotted like a tree wrapped in parasitic vines. A rigger what stole money off us was being punished in the usual spot, and this bolt of blue seemed to come out of Splinter's arm at him. The rigger slammed back into the wheel of a tractor, and died right there and then. When Splinter's arm pulled back into the window, a gust of wind lifted the net, and I saw the edge of his face in the shadows. What I saw wasn't human. If the devil ever came calling on Mister Splinter, he'd be there to ask for his face back.

I looked at the Gaffer, defeated. 'Just do it. Just kill me.'

He give me a level look, like he's angry I took something what was his. 'Get inside or I'll make you watch while Strombo does over your favourite Nightingale.'

Nightingales is what we call the girls the Professoré kidnaps and converts into singers—singing is all they can do after he's done messing with their brains. It killed me to think of Strombo hurting any of the Nightingales, but especially Moineau.

Moineau can't talk but she sings like an angel. Sometimes I think I see a flicker in her eyes, like there's a person still in there somewhere. The Professoré tells me there's not. It's all dead in her brain, he says. Like it is inside me, I thinks to myself.

I turned and knocked. The door opened. It was dark inside, a thin curtain dimming some tobacco-coloured lamplight at the far end of the trailer. My mouth went dry, my voice a croak: 'Mister Splinter? It's me. Blanco.'

The Gaffer pushed me into the trailer, then pulled the door shut. It smelled bad, like rotting fish and Professoré's chemicals. I heard a hoarse whisper. 'Come to me.'

I walked forward to the ragged curtain, seeing a darkness within the half-lit shadows on the other side—a rippling mass that spoke again, 'Come.'

I stepped around the curtain. Splinter's profile was lit by a dim yellow lamp, the bulk of him hidden in shadow. I looked down at the floor not wanting to see more.

'You have been practising for the Great Feat?'

'A little, Mister Splinter. Everything I do is practise.'

'It is not enough. You must have complete control of your body and mind, or you will die.'

I fell silent. How much pain would I be forced to go through before the end?

'What. Speak.'

'I don't understand what the Great Feat is for, Mister Splinter. Me and some others will walk into a lake in some remote mountains, and whoever don't drown will be declared winner. Why?'

'Endurance is just the tool to test the concept,' he growled. 'Evidence. Invaluable data.'

'For what, sir?'

There was a hesitation. 'To prove you are the best of your cohort.'

'Why do competitors have to be tested in a way sure to kill most, if not all, of us?'

He arced up. 'We do not have time to trial slowly. Learn to command yourself, to endure, and quickly. We will reach the Convergence of Travellers in three months. If you do not want to die there, you must master the Great Feat.'

I gave up. 'Yes, Mister Splinter.'

There was a long silence. I felt he was reading me like a book. Finally, I heard his soft whisper again. 'Do you *want* to die?'

Part of me wanted to lie, to say no. Part of me couldn't lie. In the end, I said nothing.

'Ah,' he sighed.

I saw movement, and risked a look. A ravaged, muscular arm pointed to a small table, where some old books were piled. 'Those are yours to read. Take them.'

I was more confused than ever. 'Thank you, Mister Splinter.'

'You've nothing to thank me for. Read, think, and learn, or it will go ill for you.'

I nodded, but in truth I was defeated already.

Mister Splinter must have sensed this. 'What have you been told will happen if you successfully perform the Great Feat?'

I recited what had been drilled into me. 'If I am the one to survive, our circus will be declared the foremost, and we will win great riches.'

'That is what you were taught. It is a lie.'

Startled, I looked up. Now my eyes were adjusted to the light, I saw him proper for the first time. Leaning forward, Splinter's great head and thick neck sat on broad shoulders, rippling arms gripping his mechanical throne, fleshy muscles standing out where no muscles should be, bulges that made him seem like a creature of pure violence, ready to explode. I looked away.

'If you perform the Great Feat and survive,' he rumbled, 'you will be declared King-in-Waiting.'

My brain jammed. This made no sense. I was no one—a freak; thieving, murdering, scum. The Traveller King was revered and feared as a wily old warrior who wielded enormous power around the world throughout the secret society of the Confederation. All I could think was Splinter had gone mad with all the mods what was done to him. I didn't know what to say.

Splinter creaked in his seat, his burning eyes ripping into me like a blowtorch. 'It is you who will save or condemn us.'

'But, why?'

'Because I am dying.'

I was briefly rocked. 'Why me?'

'Because I made you.' He leaned back into shadow. 'Because you are my son.'

Chapter Six—Only
the bad don't sing

After I left Mister Splinter's trailer, needing the company of people I could trust, my feet took me, still carting Splinter's books, to the freaks' trailer.

During the freak show, the bars we put up are real. To the punters it looks like we're keeping them safe from the freaks, but it's really the other way around. Some punters spit, some wave Bibles or Korans and babble on about God's punishment. Some want to touch the freaks or want the freaks to touch them. Some get angry for reasons I never been able to work out.

Normals are the *real* freaks.

After they're all gone for the day, we slide the bars out of the way and stack them against a wall so there's space to sleep and socialise.

Inside, there was the usual fug of smoke and murmuring chat. Vodka and cigarillos were being passed around at the end of another long night, so I wasn't noticed at first. Penny and the Nightingales— the three pretty ragdolls, Moineau, Princess Mirela and Poupee—were on the floor curled up against Baba Yaga, a stolid, potato-munching mountain of hessian and muscle.

I sat on the floor just inside the door. Lobby waddled over on his flapping stumps, a bottle tucked under one arm. 'Chuckles is here at last! The party can begin.'

I don't usually take more than a sip to help me sleep, but this time I took a big sour mouthful and hung on to the bottle. Lobby's smile fell off, replaced with concern. 'Oi, what's up with you then?'

I shook my head. Lobby offered me a crooked smile. 'Need a hug, eh?' He looked down at the flippers ending both arms, acting dismayed. 'Bugger. How about a slap around the chops instead?' It was an old joke between us; he's the gentlest gent alive, our Lobby, but I couldn't smile, I couldn't think, I couldn't feel.

Lobby gave up on me and rejoined the others to bellow a verse or ten of 'The Good Ship Venus', mainly because it drove our money boy, Mathematico, mental.

Math is a strict Muslim lad from North Africa, skinny, nervous, and as black as I am white. He hates swearing, blasphemy and anything to do with sex, so the poor bastard's been in hell since the moment he got sold to us.

When we got him, Math was a little wobbly-headed twelve-year-old, continually counting things, putting crooked things straight, and avoiding people except if they were playing music or giving him maths puzzles to work out. Now he mainly just does the accounts and avoids everyone.

Lying beside Math was Erik the Eel. He wriggled over to me, arched his upper half up so I could take the cigarillo out from under his moustache and he could look at the books Splinter gave me. He muttered in his thick German accent. 'Zis is not your usual literary diet, Blanco.'

Erik nosed and chinned his way through the pile, noting the titles. '*The Art of War* by Niccolò Machiavelli, *The Art of War* by Sun Tzu, *Consciousness Debunked: World Cognitive-Neuroscience Congress 2048*, *Complete Essays of Francis Bacon*, *Non-Lethal Security Device Overview Two Thousand and Forty*, *Meditation Can Heal* by someone called Sri Bobo.' Erik looked up at me. 'Zis requires explanation, young sir. Do you intend to read these or sell them?'

'I have to read them.'

Spider Susy scuttled across, intrigued. 'Any pictures?'

Susy paints portraits, mainly copies of people she fancies from books and old magazines, using a fine brush held between her lips. None of her pictures show anyone with hands or feet, or wearing clothes. Got a filthy mind, our Susy.

Erik arched up again, so I replaced the cigarillo in the corner of his mouth. He turned to Susy. 'These books are for men who lead armies, not for artists like you, who paint them.' He wriggled back to his mat, frowning. 'I can only wonder why Blanco needs to learn from them. Is he going to war?'

Methuselah, his tall bony back against the wall, creaked his head in my direction. 'Blanco is always at war, though mostly with himself.' This was Methuselah's idea of a joke. Flakes of dusty skin fell from his cheek as it twitched into a pale smile. 'The most interesting of the books is that of . . .' Methuselah coughed, his language, as ever, educated and 'proper'. '. . . Francis Bacon—one of the few men in history who make me proud to be an Englishman.'

'What is it about?' asked Erik.

'The art of science—the sciences being the finest fruit produced by human minds.'

Susy looked at me, sceptical. 'Science is filth from old days. Why's you need to read that stuff?'

'Mister Splinter told me to,' I murmured. 'Read and learn, he said.'

At this, the trailer fell silent.

Baba Yaga shuddered. 'You see Mister Splinter? In his trailer?'

I attempted a smile. 'He said I have to perform the Great Feat and save you all.'

Baba Yaga growled. 'Great Feat is stupid. What for you get killed?'

Gaunt and red-eyed, Povero Cristo whispered from where he lay on the floor, recovering from his night's ordeal. Guido, his constant companion, listened, then turned to me. 'The Christ, he also ask why you martyr youself.'

'I do what I'm told,' I shrugged. 'Every night I mutilate myself. In my spare time I kill people and train to kill myself in the Great Feat.' I took another pull on the bottle, not caring that I'd been told to keep the news to myself. 'Splinter's dying, by the way. Or so he says. He also said he was my father.'

Everyone looked at me like I was mad.

'Could this be true?' murmured Erik.

'Dunno,' I replied. 'Can't see the family resemblance myself.'

Then I noticed Moineau seemed to be looking at me, and her hands weren't resting limply in her lap like the other Nightingales' were—she was cradling and stroking Daisy.

'Moineau?' I couldn't be sure, but I thought there was a flicker of something in her eyes.

Baba Yaga looked down at Moineau. 'She like the doggy. Is nice. Maybe I don't cook her after all.'

I crawled across to look at Moineau more closely. 'Has anyone ever seen her doing anything other than sing or just sit there and wait to sing? I think she looked at me, like a normal. Just for a second.'

'Wishful thinking, my boy,' muttered Erik.

'But she's petting the dog. She never does nothing on her own.'

'She probably don't know she's even doing it,' said Susy, thoughtful. 'It's just instinct. Like when you step on a roach and it keeps waving its legs.'

I looked into Moineau's blue eyes but there was nothing—just her sweet, tragic, divided face, one side damaged and sagging from the Professoré's surgery, the other as beautiful as sunshine at dawn. I sighed, and leaned into Baba Yaga. 'Make them sing, Baba. Something happy.'

Baba Yaga started singing some old Russian tune. Soon Moineau, Mirela and Poupee were improvising harmonies like songbirds. I was on the good side of Moineau's face. Watching her sing was looking at all the things I wanted—peace, calm, contentment. The freaks softly joined in as they drank and smoked and gave me the odd wary look. The song was beautiful, but it just made me sadder.

The trailer suddenly shook as the obese pear-shape of Humbolt squeezed through the door, followed by Elasto and Ezekiel. Though he was bringing bad news, Humbolt clapped and rubbed his hands together with enthusiasm. 'Alright, chaps—we've got trouble. We need to scarper.'

Everyone started asking questions, and Dislocato and Skeletor, asleep under some blankets, raised their heads at the ruckus. Between them, Madam Tracey the clairvoyant rolled her rotund bulk upright, sending her stick-like bedmates tumbling away from her. 'What the effin' 'eck is it nah?' she snarled.

'Some young gadjo female had her throat cut,' Humbolt replied.

Elasto nodded. 'The polis are doon at the entry askin' th' riggers aboot it.' He looked around and found me. 'Wis it us?'

I shook my head, apathetic. 'Not one of mine. Anyway, what do they care about another stiff?'

'This one was someone's daughter,' said Ezekiel. 'Nasty, it was, and we been here long enough to qualify as suspects.'

'Fair enough,' said Madam Tracey. 'I can't fink of no one more suss than us.' Which was both accurate and honest, considering Madam Tracey read palms, wrote blackmail letters for the illiterates, and altered people's wills to her clients' advantage.

I stood, shrugging off the weariness. 'We'd better get packing then.' With a last look at Moineau's beautiful lopsided face, I slipped out into the pre-dawn dark. It would be six hours of solid, sweating labour before we were ready to pull the pin on a town whose name I couldn't even remember. When I heard Lobby rousing us on with more verses of 'The Good Ship Venus', I joined in.

Anything to stop myself from thinking.

Chapter Seven—A good answer results in a better question

worked in the dark, pulling pegs and retrieving ropes by touch and memory. The circus was part of me—I knew to the inch where everything was, how it was fixed, and how it was best unfixed to be stowed proper. I made note of ropes what needed braiding and canvas what needed stitching. I stayed away from where the polis were still talking with the Gaffer and the Professoré.

I noticed there was someone lurking, using the dark and the vans and whatnot as cover. I wasn't too bothered. We get lots of lurkers, mostly kids curious about the freaks, sometimes perverts, sometimes men looking for money or trouble. As dawn began to break, whoever it was thought the better of getting caught, and slipped away.

My best didikai, Tog, came by with some bacon-and-egg sarnies. Being a dwarf, he had to reach high to pass my half up to me. 'Keep an eye out, mate,' he warned. 'Could be trouble brewing with the Committee. I heard them saying your name.'

That news wrecked any appetite I had. I chewed and swallowed, thinking it through. 'Maybe it's time I do a runner,' I suggested. 'Now Siberia's stopped burning, there might be work and a safe place for me there. I speak some Russky and a bit of Chinese. I got some mechanical skills. I could bluff my way.'

Tog had heard it all before. 'Whatever you say, Blanco. You in't going nowhere.'

'I don't like the idea of saying goodbye to you, mate, but how can I stay? I'm good at what I do in my act, but there's a reason they call the Great Feat "great"—it's feckin' impossible. Pain's one thing, but why should I die 'cause Splinter says to? And why should I believe that evil old sod when he says I'm his son?'

'Do you look like him?'

'If I looked anything like that monster, you'd run screaming. Trust me.'

Tog stood, chewing the last of his sandwich. 'I'd better get my big babies hitched.' He paused, serious. 'If you ever did go, I'd go too 'cept I can't leave them. I can't trust anyone to look after them proper.'

'I know, mate. Jumbo and El Grande is lucky to have you.'

Tog went off to hitch his elephants. Then, as I was hefting another roll of canvas onto the back of a tractor, the Steering Committee appeared. Tog was right—I had trouble.

The Committee is the Gaffer, the Professoré, Madam Tracey, and Mala and Milosh. Strombo was there as the muscle—after all, someone has to hold the victim while the others do their thing. Mala and Milosh were the ones to watch out for though. They might be five-foot-nothing but they is old-school travellers with a German sense of humour and the fish-eyed courage of nutters. They do the knife-throwing act plus they caper about as backup clowns. Trust me, them smiles is strictly painted on.

'What's up?' I said, discreetly eyeing possible escape routes.

Madam Tracey jabbed a finger in my chest. 'What's this about you bein' 'is son?'

'How would I know? It's what he told me.'

The Gaffer leaned against the tractor, casually blocking an exit I was seriously considering. 'What else did he tell you?'

'He said to read them books, learn them, and perform the Great Feat so I could save the circus.'

The members of the Steering Committee swapped loaded looks, except for Strombo, who just stood there itching to punch someone, preferably me. Milosh give me the fish-eye. 'And then Splinter, he tell you he is dying?'

34

It's generally easy to be scared by someone what's six-foot-six like Strombo, but Milosh and Mala got knives so sharp you wouldn't know your head was separated from your neck till you heard the thump on the ground. I nodded and kept it calm and polite. 'That's exactly what he told me. He didn't say what he was dying of, or how long it's going to take. I assume the Professoré might have the score on that kind of detail.'

'I remove his growths, and I supply him with the drugs and chemicals he asks for,' said the Professoré, ice-grey eyes glinting through his steel-framed spectacles. The Prof was being modest. Give him a scalpel, and a body what's still kicking, and he'll turn it into something what might live long enough to scare the bejesus out of you.

He give me a filthy look. 'He has never mentioned this dying business.'

Madam Tracey turned to the Gaffer. 'What about the other thing? Could Blanco be the son?'

The Professoré looked away, taking a sudden interest in his nails as the Gaffer studied my face. 'Who knows? I brought women to Splinter way back when. A few survived, some had babies, but the women were whores so the sprogs could've been anyone's.'

Madam Tracey persisted. 'Did Splinter 'ave favourites? Ones he kept around?'

The Gaffer frowned in thought. 'No, but now I think on it, how we got Blanco was different. Splinter made us stop in a village on the coast of Normandy. This was when Splinter wasn't bad like he is now. He said it was to pick up supplies, but then he goes off by himself to the local knock shop. He brought this one back with him. He told me he bought Blanco because he looked strong.' The Gaffer looked at me like a farmer appraises a bullock outside the abattoir. 'Got him from a woman we knew as a prossie back when we was touring the North Country— Gussie was her name. Apart from being on the drugs, I remember she was a clever one, an' I know Splinter liked some talk before he did his thing. It strikes me the timing is right too.'

My fists curled. 'You know my mother? You know where she is?'

'Want to send her a love note?' he sneered. 'She was a whore, mate, and she sold you for drug money. Anyway, she could be anywhere by now. My bet is six foot under.'

I reined in my anger. 'I know what you lot want, and you can have it. I don't know why Mister Splinter said what he said, but I don't care nohow. I in't going to be king of nothing, and I in't going to be saving no one's neck but my own. If and when he dies, this circus is all yours.'

There was a moment when I could see the same thought run through all their minds—they was thinking they should do me in and make sure of it. I spread my hands, indicating my skinny arms. 'Look at me! Can you imagine me taking on you lot because suddenly I think, "Oh, yeah—I feel like taking over this here enterprise and turning into my good old dad"? "Just call me Mister Splinter Junior, if you please."'

This guff was off the top of my head, but they knew I wasn't suicidal enough to take them on, ever. They also knew for definite that I didn't have no ambition neither. Things visibly relaxed. Mala even managed a thin smile. 'It is a wise boy who knows his limits. Stay alive and, who knows, one day you might meet girl and find happiness.'

This was as much a threat as it was a promise of hope, and she knew I knew it. They started to walk away but I grabbed the Professoré's sleeve. 'Prof—a question.'

He stopped and gave me a wary look. 'Yes?'

I drew him aside. 'The Nightingales. Have any of them ever come back? To proper life, I mean. Thinking like a normal.'

'Why do you ask?'

'I was just wondering.'

He sighed. 'About Moineau.'

More than a few of the jobbers and layabouts around the circus saw my usual frown turn upside down when Moineau drifted into our foul orbit two years previous. She strolled by me as I sat on the steps of my trailer polishing and sharpening my equipment, and time seemed to slow down. I could see she was a user, but she was pretty in a way that stopped people in their tracks. Her smiling dial was like a flower in the sun, turning light into happy. Just looking at her, she give my heart a jolt and jammed my brain and made me suddenly yearn for something I didn't know what. Happiness? What the fuck was that?

I was about to walk over and introduce myself when the Professoré lured her in to score whatever drugs he thought she was after. Then I heard her scream. Strombo stopped me going in but I knew what was happening. Me and the Professoré never got along since. I think about killing him for what he done to her.

'I thought she looked at me last night,' I said to the Prof. 'Almost a proper normal look. Plus she was cuddling the puppy. That's what you call "purposeful movement", innit?'

The Professoré frowned, thoughtful. 'It is.'

'Could what you done to her brain heal up? Could she get normal again?'

'Anything's possible. Let me know if you see any other changes. I might have to work on her again.'

I clenched my fists, suddenly braver than I had a right to be. 'No, Prof. No more work.'

The Professoré had power in the circus where I had none, but he must've seen something in my eyes that made him think again. He shrugged it off. 'It's remotely possible she could be healing. Neuroplasticity is a marvellous thing.' He started walking away, then paused. 'You should consider one thing, however.' He gave me an evil smile. 'If she *were* to regain consciousness, she'd become fully aware of who you are and what you do. Will she like you or loathe you?'

He continued walking. We both knew the answer.

Chapter Eight—It's better to have a dozen enemies outside the tent than one inside

By late morning, we started rolling out—a slow-moving caravan of tractors, trucks, trailers, horses and the elephants. We kept to the dusty back roads, avoiding any more attention than we already had.

I sat with Tog on the driving seat of the Fazio family's trailer, behind El Grande's big arse. Tog says the elephants love towing the trailers, and any other work he gives them. It seems mental having Tog be elephant-wrangler, him being so tiny and them being so big, but Jumbo and El Grande don't care he's small. They love him, and for good reason. He'd pull a knife on anyone who so much as looked at them the wrong way. When he wakes them up in the morning, them elephants smile and reach out with their trunks to touch their human. You can see the love in their eyes.

In the window above us, the Fazio girls, Julietta and Alessia, were doing their makeup and ignoring us freaks, at least they were until El Grande farted. Then me and Tog were laughing like drains, and them girls couldn't pull the window shut fast enough.

The Fazio family do highwire, acrobatics, burglary and prostitution. They in't freaks, so they think their shit don't stink compared to us lot.

Tog pulled out one of his 'religious relics' to finish carving the details. Every now and then, he'd look up at me with a shy grin. Eventually I frowned and said, 'What you on about then? Who give you the happy pills?'

In reply, Tog hooked a thumb over his shoulder. I leaned out and looked back along the caravan to where Baba Yaga was sitting at the front of the trailer being towed by Jumbo. She was feeding the Nightingales. I noticed Moineau still cuddling Daisy. I turned away and scowled at Tog. 'Don't you start, you bleeder. The Professoré says even if she does come to her senses, she'll do a runner.'

But Tog only grinned and sang, 'Blanco and Moineau, sittin' in a tree, K.I.S.S.I.N.G.'

'Hilarious, Tog,' I muttered. 'A big round of applause for our newest clown.'

Farshad, the Afghani cook, came pedalling alongside on his bicycle, his long black moustache trailing either side of his face. 'Good morning, gentlemen—breakfast is served.' Still pedalling, he reached into the basket on the handlebars and passed me a small loaf of fruit-bread.

'Thanks, mate.' I tore the loaf in half and gave Tog his share. 'Any news?'

'Only about you. Is it true?'

'You can tell anyone what asks it don't matter if it is. The Steering Committee will run this place if Splinter dies, and that's fine by me.'

Farshad kept one hand on the bars and gripped the side of our trailer so he could stop pedalling. 'You should be having more ambition, Blanco.'

'What for? To run this freak show? Do me a favour.'

'This freak show is our home. We are family.'

'Weirdest family I ever heard of. We is a mob of con artists and murderers.'

Farshad shrugged off my bitter tone but I noticed Tog's face fall. I patted him on the shoulder and put on a high voice. 'Still, at least I have my lovely son, Tog here. Apple of my eye, he is.' I leaned down and give him a big kiss on top of his head to make him squirm, then turned back to Farshad. 'What's the story with the polis? Are we in the clear?'

'Assuming you're not doing any extracurricular work, then the murders are nothing to do with us.'

'I thought there was only one. Some local girl.'

'Apparently young women from the area have been killed.' Farshad let go of our trailer and pedalled harder. 'Take care, my friend. Keep only those you trust to your back.'

'Making me a human shield for them behind me—nice one, Shad.'

Farshad smiled and cycled on up the line to make his next delivery. I looked at Tog, who was chewing bread and checking his handiwork on the relic. 'Another splinter off the holy cross?'

Tog shook his head. 'Noah's ark. A bit of the plank from up the front where it curves.'

'If you glued together all the bits of Noah's ark you've carved, you'd have the whole bleeding boat.'

But Tog had stopped smiling. 'Will you do it? The Great Feat?'

I looked at Tog's earnest mug. 'Is you worried I will or worried I won't?'

'Both.'

'Truth be told, I don't know. I don't want to think about it. Maybe I'll steal all that money what you make selling fake holy relics, and run away to Tasmania.'

'Where's that?'

'Dunno. Some island in the Pacific, I think. Near where New Zealand used to be.'

'What's there?'

'I heard it's all forests and bears and wolves and dwarves like you.'

'Really?'

'That's what I heard. It'd be safe there. No polis, no wars, and especially no bleedin' circuses.'

We reached the pastures outside Rayleigh by mid-afternoon. Then we got word Splinter was ordering us to open that night.

We were pissed off about that. After an early start and a big day on the road, it was unfair we weren't getting a rest day. This kind of barnstorming makes us tired and hungry, and in no mood to paint on smiles and do a show. It's good strategy to take your time setting up—the yokels love to watch a circus grow from an empty field. It gives them time to get excited and, more to the point, collect their pennies so they can spend them on us. Instead, we'd be opening for a tiny audience with bugger-all spare change in their pockets, and hoping word of mouth would bring the rest of the mugs in the following night. Still, with the Gaffer and Strombo standing there, whips in hand, orders is orders.

I was helping the riggers when the Mayor's blond son shows up.

I nodded, polite but friendly. 'Hullo, mate—we in't quite set up yet. How about you come back with your friends about six o'clock tonight, eh?'

The kid's accent was posh. 'My name's Tommy. I saw you with the Chinese chap yesterday.'

'How d'yer do, Tommy. I'm Blanco.'

'Did you fix the dog?'

'I did. She'll be right as rain in a few weeks.'

I looked back to my work but he didn't take the hint. 'Can I help?'

'Thanks all the same,' I replied, 'but we'd be in trouble if you broke a finger hammering things.'

'I wouldn't let you be in trouble. I'm the Mayor's son.'

I kept an easy smile on my face. 'Seems like a nice chap, your dad. Very decent to us, I thought.'

Tommy scowled. 'He just wants you to cheer people up so they stop thinking about the elections. If the sheep are happy, they'll vote him back in.'

'Well, that's politics, I suppose.'

I looked back to my work but Tommy continued. 'Plus my dad wants you to fix up his soldiers. We had a skirmish with the Wickford Puritans and a lot of our chaps sustained injuries.'

'I'm sorry to hear that, mate.'

'Call me Tommy.'

I kept up the cheerful palaver. 'Tommy it is then. I tell you what, seeing as you're a diamond geezer, mention my name when you come along tonight, and you and a friend can come in for free.'

'I haven't any friends, but thanks. I'll see you later, eh?'

'Get ready to have your socks blown off, Tommy. You in't seen nothing like our show before.'

'Okay, see you.' He wandered off, hands in pockets.

I felt sorry for him. He seemed a bit gormless, and it was tough a kid his age didn't have friends.

It was getting dark as I walked back from the town with supplies, cloaked and anonymous in the crowds making for the circus. It seemed locals were so hungry for entertainment they rustled up the readies on no notice. Good—the sooner we took their money, the sooner we could be someplace else.

I approached the bright lantern-lit entrance, where Mala and Milosh were doing the bally, drawing in the gadjos by juggling machetes and so on. Humbolt was pacing up and down in front of them, his tattooed chest on show, bellowing his pitch into a mike with that plummy voice of his. 'Step right up, ladies and gentlemen! Step right up! Everyone's a winner at Splinter's Magnifico Cirque du Amusementes. We have games with prizes for all, challenges for the bravest amongst you, the terrifying freak show, and finally the ultimate in thrills and excitement—the stunning acts of the big top. You will gasp! You will scream with fright! You will pray to the One True God that the performers will survive the heart-stopping feats they attempt to perform tonight . . .'

I nodded to Tog, who was up on his box taking the entry money, and walked through the gate and down into the broad avenue of the midway.

To either side, the sideshows were up and running. Canvas stalls with colourful painted banners were already two-deep with mugs queuing to give their money away, as Humbolt's voice carried through the still evening air. 'Do you dare visit the horrors of science in the freak show? Be warned—no one with a heart condition or a nervous disposition should attend. Ladies, especially, may find merely seeing the freaks is too much to bear. Also be warned, those to whom bare, naked flesh is an abomination should stay away. Though every one of our exhibits has been converted to the One True Faith, and tended to by our resident imam, the educational nature of this exhibit means that bare nakedness, in all its sin, is fully on display!'

Fragrant smoke wafted from Farshad's pretzel and kebab concession, his moustache freshly waxed and pointed. I paused to hand him a bottle of wine from my sack. He'd need it; he'd be stuck where he was till we closed at midnight. He nodded his thanks as he set out the first savoury batch of kebabs over the coals, the scent of rosemary and sage making my mouth water. I nodded back. 'Kushti crowd, mate. We'll make some dinari tonight.'

I walked on, Humbolt's voice following me from tinny speakers strung up with the lights. 'Dare to see Erik the Human Eel, a creature so extraordinary you will scarcely recognise him as human!'

At the next stall, Binh was running the Wiffle Ball and the Duck Pond but, because he's Vietnamese, all the local low-lifes assume they can ask him about buying drugs. Because they do, he does. He don't do small talk, so I handed him his rice and beans and walked on.

Humbolt was keeping up the grind. 'Can any of you stomach seeing the extraordinary Elasto, the most elastic man in the universe, pull his own face clean off his skull?'

At the shooting gallery, Dognose Dabir, the mechanic, was 'proving' to passing punters that the air rifles weren't gaffed, by firing them with deadly accuracy at the targets. Then the cheeky devil give passing male punters a casually challenging look as he smoothed his moustache, and smiled at the ladies. Lads being lads, they sensed the challenge and quickly handed over cash for the rifles. I passed him a parcel of food and bottle of wine wrapped in paper. I didn't stay to see their growing incomprehension as they kept missing, and kept paying, over and over, to prove their manhood.

Humbolt's pitch boomed out again. 'You will see the oldest man on the planet, Methuselah, who is proven by independent medical verification to be over one hundred and ninety-six years old!'

Past the tiny maglev ride, full of tiny screaming tin lids, Baba Yaga was in her carpeted tent, almost filling it with her looming bulk as she laid out potions, charms, amulets and the crystal ball on a tiny table. I put some food down as she looked up, curious. 'Where is little dog?'

I undid the top button of my jacket so she could see Daisy, sleepily peering out at her. 'I'll pass her on to Moineau before I go on,' I replied, turning away.

'Don't get hopes up.'

I gave Baba a flat look. 'I don't hope for nothing, Baba. Hoping's a mug's game.'

Outside, I slipped away from the lights and noise of the midway, squeezing between the trailers. I stopped quick when I spotted the Gaffer and Strombo in the shadows ahead, talking with some sweaty local. The Gaffer stood there, guns akimbo, while the gadjo nervously waved a wad of cash about and made his request for our less advertised services—getting someone dead or abducted or poisoned or whatever. The Gaffer does the nodding with these sorts of deals, but when he's going for the closer, he'll look up at Splinter's window, get a signal, then take the client's money before telling them to sling their hook. The mark will slink away, looking like they just ate medicine they isn't sure will cure or kill them.

It'll always kill them. Guilt does that—eats away at you till one day it makes perfect sense to end it all.

So as not to scare off the client and his cash, I backed away to take another more difficult route through guy ropes and pegs, as Humbolt's voice carried across the incoming crowds of happy yokels. 'Look, if you can, upon the most dreadful sight imaginable—Skeletor, the Living Dead! Turn away in disgust as Dislocato, the man with rubber bones, tortures his body into shapes Allah never intended!'

His voice dimmed as I walked around to the freaks' trailer, now sporting a colourful illustrated banner that hinted at the horrors within.

I pushed past the *Closed for Feeding* sign, opened the door and entered to find them all making final preparations for their acts, putting up the bars to the 'cells', set-dressing, and pulling curtains into place. I smiled at Kongo, who was brushing the Nightingales' hair. Despite her muscles, spinal deformities and all-over body hair making her look like a gorilla, she's a very good hairdresser. I gently eased Daisy, still sleepy, out of my jacket. 'Is it alright if I leave Daisy with Moineau?'

'Of course.' She paused to pinch a flea from the thick hair on one of her arms. 'I hope you don't mind, but I borrowed the book on meditation. I thought it might help with the anger management.' Kongo is a lovely woman, but she does have a temper. I seen her knock out a geezer with just one punch—right through his truck windscreen.

'You take as long as you like with it. I'll read the other ones first.'

'Cheers, Blanco. I was glad they didn't kill you. The Steering Committee, I mean.'

'Thanks, Konnie. See you later, yeah?' I laid Daisy in Moineau's lap, and watched as she began to stroke the dog. I couldn't tell if it was just reflex, so I just whispered, 'Thanks, Moineau. Back after my show.'

I walked out into the night and headed for the big top, only to have a shadow bounce out of the dark at me. 'Hey.'

I tensed, whipping out a blade, but, as he moved into the light, I saw Tommy's grin. I pocketed my knife, annoyed, but managed a smile for the kid. 'You got in free alright?'

'I did. Thanks.'

'Great. Okay, have a good night, eh?'

I turned away and slipped into the back of the big top, lit a lantern, then took it to the corner where my gear was waiting. I was laying it out when I realised I was being watched. Tommy had followed me in, clearly interested in my hooks, blades, broken glass and bed of nails. 'You use that in your act?'

'I do, but we don't let punters back here, okay? Out. Now, please.'

'I just wanted to see everything. What are the hooks for?'

'Come to the show and you'll see for yourself.' I ushered him out. 'Don't want to spoil the surprise now, do we?'

'Alright. I'll see you later.'

'Yep. Away you go, mate.' I watched him disappear into the shadows, then went back inside. I stripped off my top, applied the medicated creams, then painstakingly cleaned and oiled every single hook and blade that would soon be sticking in and through me.

Another show, another night of excruciating pain.

Chapter Nine—All warfare is based on deception

The trick to my act is there is no trick. The only question it raises in the punters' minds is how much pain I can stand. No one can believe one skinny, ghost-white teenager can endure being hoisted by hooks through his flesh, smash bottles on his head, stamp about in broken glass, headbutt bricks or any of the rest of the act.

I was taught to read at a young age. It wasn't so I could read fairy-tales or vampire stories, or learn about the world, or actually enjoy myself—no one cared enough about me for that. No, they give me anatomy books to read, and I had to learn everything in them or cop another beating. Point to any bit of me, and I can name it in Latin or English, from the epidermal layers through the fascia to the internal muscles and organs, all the way through the bones to the matrix where blood cells are made.

That's how I know, for example, where *not* to stick the six-inch hatpins.

When I came out for my act, Tommy was in the front row, studying me with interest as I kicked off with a not-even-slightly funny variation on auto-da-fé—hanging myself with my dreadlocks. Now, don't get me wrong, interested faces in the audience is fine—better than yawns or cruel smiles—but I'm used to awe, horror or pained amusement. Tommy studied me like he was thinking of having a go right after.

When I called for a volunteer to 'help' with the bed-of-nails routine, Tommy was the first to raise his hand, but our head mechanic Barrelmouth Bashir's other job is to be my ringer, and it was him I chose, apparently reluctantly, as he pushed through the crowd. I acted like I was trying not to look worried as Barrelmouth made the most of his girth, pushing out his stomach and waddling as if carrying more weight than he did. The punters got the impression that if there was a trick to my act, then something had gone wrong. I added to this by making my movements less certain, while Barrelmouth did his drunk-village-idiot act.

I caught another glimpse of Tommy, who remained intent. I showed the punters the bed of nails, let them touch it to see the nails were real. I laid it down with exaggerated care, getting it perfectly level as if my life depended on it, checking and rechecking so Barrelmouth had time to 'sneak' another drink behind my back. This heightened the audience tension, as they assumed the event was slipping further out of my control. I briefly 'prayed' and lay myself down.

Barrelmouth hammed up his drunken bloodthirsty pleasure at the horror to come, then blearily wobbled across toward me. I put up a hand to stop him, adding a tremor of fear. 'Slow down, mate! You need to take care. I want you to raise one foot, place it on me, then *slowly* bring your full weight onto me. On no account hesitate, stumble or step too quickly.'

The crowd cringed as Barrelmouth hesitated, staggered, appeared to have second thoughts, then too-quickly stepped up onto my stomach and chest, looking worried for the first time, as if convinced he was going to kill me in the process. Cue the amazed gasps as the punters and Barrelmouth realised I was somehow coping with the pain and *not* dying. I copped a quick look at the audience and saw Tommy nodding to himself, not in the least surprised.

Even with the next routine, when I was suspended by hooks, and women and children were screaming or crying, and the men just looked sick, Tommy was unfazed. He studied the arrangement of ropes, pulleys and hooks—and me, a spider helpless in his own web.

When I started the finale with a hatpin through both cheeks, and one through my tongue, he didn't flinch. Another two pins, one through each upper arm, then one each through my feet. Then, another two through my palms. Then the last pin. I acted thoughtful, as if wondering where to put it. The crowd, already appalled, turned uneasy. Mostly. A few hecklers called out suggestions, most of them rude, but none expected what came next. I placed one end of the pin over my heart, and there was a sudden hush - was I bluffing? With slow determination, I pierced the skin, allowing a drop of blood to collect and roll down for effect. *My God*, they think, *he's going to do it. He'll kill himself.* I held my breath and 'concentrated' with closed eyes, as if anticipating my end, then pushed the pin right in. Then I stood still, pin inserted through my heart, and swayed very slightly. *My God, he's going to fall! He's killed himself!* I opened my eyes, acting pained, prolonging the uncertainty. A long pause . . . then I removed the pin, sighing with apparent relief to find myself still living.

The removal of the rest of the pins produced winces, and the uneasy applause quickly died away. The ringmaster, the Gaffer, ran on to do his spray, and the clowns—Spod the junior mechanic, and Mala and Milosh—entered on tiny bicycles, pedalling frantically but moving slowly around the ring in a slow-motion chase, Spod holding a bottle of vodka to himself, pursued by the other two—the 'joke' being they could walk faster.

After a last glance at Tommy, I disappeared into the dark behind the canvas as relieved laughter swelled at the clowns' capering.

I cleaned myself up, then my instruments. This part is as important as the prep. If I stuff up anywhere along the line, I can die of septicaemia.

'Hi.'

It was Tommy. I managed to stay polite. 'Mate, I told you already.

No one is allowed back here. Especially not when I'm cleaning up.'

Tommy didn't move. 'I couldn't work out how you did it. That last pin must've gone right through your heart, unless it's a trick.'

'It's not.' I gestured toward the tent flap. 'Now, if you don't mind, hop it.'

He paused by the exit. 'I've seen other circuses, but they always do tricks that are totally obvious. Your act impressed me.'

Something about this kid's enthusiasm started to creep me out. 'Cheers. Good night.'

With a final, cheerful, smile, Tommy left.

I was still wrapping my gear when the Gaffer came in. 'Got a job for you.'

'Already?' I was tired and fed up.

'It's an easy kill. The party concerned is in the audience. After they head home, you do them, and make it look like a botched robbery.' The Gaffer pushed me toward a small, discreet viewing flap in the inner canvas. I peered through it, scanning the crowd. 'Who am I looking for?'

'Number eight post, two seats to the left.'

I sighed, dismayed. 'It's a woman.'

'Red top, flowery scarf, middle-aged piece?'

'She's young.'

'Ish. I'd do her, if that's what you mean.'

Something inside me twisted, painful. A decision vomited up out of me. 'No. I'm not killing her.'

'You bloody are.'

'No, I bloody ain't.' I didn't care no more. This was it. I was ready to die.

He grabbed my throat, and I felt a knife prick my belly. 'You listen to me, pal,' he hissed. 'You been gettin' ideas above yer station and don't think it in't been noticed. Splinter anointing you his son an' heir don't mean nothing—you do what we tell you or you won't be heir to nothing but worms.'

Strombo appeared. The Gaffer grimaced. 'You was right, Bo. He's toey.'

Strombo reached outside and pulled Moineau in.

I sagged, powerless. 'Go on. Do me. Stick it in. You know you want to, you prick.'

'I would but it's inconvenient, see? Instead, I gots to keep you alive because we gots to be makin' a livin', which means you do what you're told and the little songbird won't have her brain reset by the Professoré, alright?'

He let me go and stepped back, enjoying the defeat on my face. After a moment, he and Strombo walked out, leaving me and Moineau. I looked at her damaged, vacant dial, wondering if she could see the tears pouring down my ugly mug. I wiped my nose on my sleeve, slung my gear over one shoulder, and gently guided her out and back toward the trailer. 'Why did she do it, Moineau?' I whispered. 'Why did my mum sell me for a handful of drugs? Was it me? Was I such a horrible kid? Was I born a murderer?'

There was no answer. There never would be.

Chapter Ten—He that is master of himself will soon be master of others

When the show was over, so I led Moineau back to their trailer. Inside, bars and props stacked out of the way, Kongo and Baba Yaga checked her over, concerned. Even Madam Tracey was uneasy. 'The Gaffer didn't 'urt 'er, did 'e? You did the right thing?'

I give her a look. 'What do you bleedin' think?'

Madam Tracey had the grace to look guilty. 'You're a good boy really. We all know that.'

'I murder people for money and I'm a "good boy"?' I walked outside and went to my trailer to pick a weapon and the knock-out drugs.

Years ago I got the Professoré to make some chemicals up for me. I have to be careful not to breathe it in but, if I do it right, the victim smells a whiff of vanilla as I press the pad over their face and they pass out. They're asleep when I switch them off.

That's what I call it. I'm 'switching them off', I tell myself. Like turning off a generator. No pain, no drama, they're just switched off. No harm done.

'No harm done,' I slur into a bottle afterward. Except someone's been murdered, leaving their friends and relatives to grieve for the rest of their lives. Still, a tola of opium and I feel no pain. No effin' harm done.

I watched the woman in the scarf through the flap in the canvas. She was enjoying the last of the show. So was her kid. When I saw she had a kid I wanted to top myself then and there, but I don't have the courage, plus Strombo or the Gaffer would do the killing instead—or worse—so I was back with no choice.

She was with a man who didn't seem to be enjoying himself. He fidgeted in his seat like invisible people were poking him with sticks. He sweated. He kept looking at the kid. He kept looking at his watch.

He'd be the client, then.

I wondered if I could talk her into paying more to do a hit on her husband who ordered the hit on her. I'd get a beating for breaking the contract, but I'd bring in money so I'd survive.

I thought that scenario through. 'Hi, I'm a murderer. Would you mind trusting me, giving me a great deal of money, allowing me to kill your husband—who is, by the way, a sack of shite—and then not mentioning any of this to anyone?'

I wondered if I could do the hit on him, then run away with the woman and the kid, keeping us all safe. How would that play? 'Hi, your husband, the man you chose to father your child, wants you dead, so how about you, the kid and me—a man who murders people for a living—how about we kill your hubby and run away to someplace safe?'

The show ended and, with my hood up, I joined the punters as they filed out. They were happy enough, chattering about the bits they loved the most, Julietta Fazio's amazing trapeze act; the bit they hated the most, my act; and the bits that freaked them out, Spod's mesmerism routine and Mala and Milosh's clown interludes.

Outside, in the dusty cool of the night, the crowd streamed home toward the town, smaller groups turning off onto roads and tracks leading to surrounding farms.

Just ahead of me, the husband was holding his wife's hand, and appeared to suddenly 'remember' he'd left the kid's favourite toy under the seat back at the circus. In a fake happy voice, he grabbed his kid's hand, told his wife to walk on and that they'd race back and catch her up. He and the kid ran back toward the circus before she could protest. She sighed and carried on.

The crowds thinned, peeled off in pairs and groups, and then she was alone in the semi-dark, holding a faltering wind-up torch, the woods closing in on both sides.

She only had a second to hear me and turn before I grabbed her and pulled her into the woods, my hand over her mouth. I pitched my voice low so no passer-by could hear, and calm so she might calm down too. 'Listen to me. Listen and be quiet and you won't get hurt.' She stopped struggling, breathing fast, probably swinging between panic and thinking through her next move.

'I've got bad news and good news,' I whispered. 'The bad news is your husband paid my boss to have you killed. The good news is I hate my boss and I'm not going to do it. But you need to find a way to get yourself somewhere safe tonight. You cannot go home and you cannot go to the militia. If you do what I say, and do a runner, you'll live and find a way to get your kid back. If you tell anyone, someone I value will die. I'm going to let you go to prove I'm telling you the truth, okay? When I let you go, I'll answer any question, and explain anything I can. I will not harm you in any way, okay?'

I got a tiny nod. Whether she believed me or not, she seemed to figure she had to play along.

'Great. Please don't scream or carry on. I'll tell you everything, alright?'

Another tiny nod.

I released her. She sprang away, but she was the plucky sort and pulled out a small knife. I put my hands up. 'It's okay, lady. Just stay calm, alright?'

Before she could say anything, I heard a matter-of-fact voice behind me. 'Are you going to rape her first?'

I whipped round, pulling my blade out. It was Tommy, who pointed over my shoulder. 'Look out!'

As I turned back, I saw the woman was running. Tommy sprinted past me into the trees and jumped on her back. By the time I pulled him off, he was looking proud. There was a knife in her back, and she wasn't moving. 'Whew,' he grinned. 'Close one. Lucky I was here, eh?'

Chapter Eleven—When the music changes, so does the dance

To stop it looking like a contract killing, I rifled through her clothes for jewellery and cash. She had neither, not least because she was a poor, struggling woman whose husband had decided he'd rather marry his sixteen-year-old cousin or whatever. Then I laid that poor woman down under some bushes, numb with self-loathing.

Through all of this, on a post-kill high, Tommy only stopped wittering on after he realised I wasn't going to clap him on the back and commend his quick thinking.

To avoid being seen, we walked silently back to the circus through the woods. By now, most punters would be home and tucked up in bed—except for the husband who'd be pretending to be worried as he contacted friends and family to ask about his missus. Then, alibi firmly established, he'd contact the militia to tell them his wife was missing. Cue the gruesome discovery by mushroom-hunters or woodcutters in the morning.

I couldn't understand why Splinter authorised this job. Circus arrives, murder occurs. Gee, what a coincidence. The local Sherlocks would be all over us like sarcomas on a prossie. As for which way my new pal Tommy would jump when questioned by his dad's men, I guessed he'd choose the option of being star witness at my trial. I imagined his cheerful face in the crowd as they put the noose around my neck, giving me two thumbs up for whatever trick he imagined I'd pull to escape death.

'Are you angry with me for some reason?' he finally asked.

I kept my thoughts to myself. 'I was just wondering about that knife you used. Mind if I have a look?'

Tommy handed it to me. In the light of a quarter-moon I could see and feel it was steel, good quality from the old days, kitchen usage.

'Should I throw it in the canal?' he asked.

'No.' I handed it back. 'You should take it home, clean it carefully, and put it back in the drawer.'

'Right. Of course. Obvious when you think of it. In the canal, it's potential evidence. In the kitchen drawer it's not.' He beamed at this valuable new trick of the trade.

I ground my teeth and kept walking.

Tommy hurried after me. 'I suppose you have a right to be annoyed. I should've explained first.'

'Explained what?'

'I'm your new apprentice. I want to learn how to do your act and how to be a murderer.'

I stopped and looked at his dial. Nothing but enthusiasm.

Time for a think. Option A: kill the mad fuck and spare the world the mayhem he's undoubtedly going to cause. The downside: he's the Mayor's son, and us circus types are still the obvious suspects.

Option B: politely put him off with some guff. Downside: I had the feeling he wouldn't take rejection well, and I could imagine him getting snotty enough to tell Daddy he saw a horrible bad man in the woods with white dreadlocks and a big knife.

Option C: welcome him aboard as my apprentice, then deal with him somewhere quiet and well away from here—during our upcoming Channel Sea crossing, perhaps. Downside: me, yet again, killing someone.

You'd think I'd be past caring about killing, but I'm not. The pain has grown with each death, like a shard of glass in my guts. That pain I could no longer drown with the physical pain I put myself through in my act. Guilt was killing me as sure as some minging great cancer. I could almost feel the lump of it inside me, in my chest, gripping my heart and squeezing.

But why was I like this when others didn't feel nothing but pleasure in other people's pain? Why did it hurt to think about disposing of a monster like Tommy?

'What makes you think I'm a murderer?' I asked.

'I've been following you, watching,' Tommy replied. 'You nearly caught me a few times but then I realised you knew I was there and you were actually letting me in on everything. I imagined you thought if I'm good enough to stay hidden without getting caught, I'd make a good murderer.'

Part of me was intrigued. I'd never met an actual psychopath before. 'Murdering people is wrong,' I said. 'You know that, right?'

'The only "wrong" is being weak. Never *show* weakness, never *be* weak—that's what my father taught me.'

'Your father isn't a murderer.'

'He has people killed. Well, he gets his men to. Anyone who threatens our town or our interests.'

'So why hitch your wagon to my one-man act?'

'I want to learn to be strong for myself. I don't want to rely on other people to kill for me; I want to do it myself. "If you want a job done well, do it yourself"—that's another thing my father taught me.'

'If you respect your father so much, why not stay and help him out?'

'Because I hate him and I hate this place.' Tommy shrugged. 'Besides, I can only go on killing here for so long before they realise it's me.'

'Sorry?'

'So far I've just killed whores, but I want to branch out to kill lots of other people—people who insult me, or short-change me, or just look at me like they're better than me. You don't look at me that way. I trust you. I trust your abilities.'

'It's you who's been killing young women.'

'Only six so far. I see them walking around, pushing out their breasts when they see some man they want to do it with. It's disgusting.'

I held down the bile at seeing myself reflected in this sick animal, then tried another approach. 'Okay, well, the thing is I've decided murder's against my religion. I'm going to do penance and read the Koran and the Bible till I'm forgiven. No more murdering. Which is why I can't take you on.'

He looked at me, trying to read my face. Then he smiled. 'I get it. You're testing my resolve. Wait.'

He fossicked in his back pocket, and pulled out a small leather bag. He loosened the string and emptied the contents onto his palm, proud. 'See?'

I'm about the worst kind of human being you could hope to meet, but I was sickened. In his palm lay six teeth. Six little white trophies.

It decided me. 'I'll ask the Gaffer. If he says yes, you're in. If he says no, that's it, okay?'

'You will ask him.'

It was almost an order. 'What did I just say?' I growled.

'It's okay.' Tommy nodded, earnest. 'I trust you.'

I stabbed a finger toward the town. 'Go home, make sure no one sees you, clean that knife and put it back. Also, even if you don't sleep tonight, get up at your usual time and pretend you've had eight hours.'

'Easy. I sleep like a baby. Always.'

Of course he slept well. Hence the rosy cheeks and happy smile all the day long.

'Good. Go.'

He nodded and slipped away into the dark.

I'd stopped feeling guilty about killing him. A mid-Channel swim was too good for the prick.

Chapter Twelve—You can't hide a cat in a sack; its claws will show

The Gaffer was waiting when I got back to my trailer. 'Well?'

I acted surly because that's what he'd be expecting. 'Job done,' I muttered.

The Gaffer handed me a few coins. 'See? Do what you're told and everyone's happy.'

I took the coins, casual. 'Oh, and the Mayor's son. He wants to sign on with us.'

Gaffer was uninterested. 'Really.'

'I told him no but he's still keen.'

'Any talent?'

'He's a cunning little rat. Been watching us for days, listening in on talk he shouldn't have.'

'Like what?'

'You talking about contract murders, for one.'

The Gaffer's jaw set, and his eye twitched.

'He's fine about it,' I shrugged, acting like I was too stupid to think it was an issue. 'In fact, he thinks killing people would be great fun.

You'll laugh at the next bit—he asked to be my apprentice.'

'He wants to do your act?'

'And the rest. He knew all about the job you give me tonight.'

'The Mayor's son knows we topped some bint?'

I enjoyed seeing the Gaffer's eye twitch, but I kept a straight face. 'Like I said, he's a little rat.'

The Gaffer seethed. 'I want to know exactly what he knows, and exactly what you told him.'

I told the Gaffer only what I needed him to know, and made it look like I wasn't selling him on taking on Tommy.

He was thoughtful. 'We should try him out.'

I faked surprise. 'You're joking. No way I'm having him as my apprentice.'

Which made the Gaffer realise that was exactly what he wanted me to do. 'You're taking him on,' he growled. 'Makes sense to have two of you what can do the murders. He's young, so he can be trained.' I acted sullen and cowed, making the Gaffer's mouth twitch in his thin-lipped version of a smile. 'Deal with it proper or we'll have the Mayor's militia on us,' he added.

'Yeah, whatever,' I said, sounding defeated.

'Splinter thinks you got talent but we know better. You is meant for taking orders, not giving 'em. Tell this boy we'll take him on two days after we leave here so his dad doesn't think to chase us down.'

The Gaffer left me to get some kip, but I wasn't ready for sleep.

In a nervous funk, I went to the freaks' trailer. In the familiar and comforting fug of smoke and old sweat, Humbolt and Methuselah were still up, talking softly over a pipe of opium-laced tobacco. Penny and the Nightingales were piled asleep beside Baba Yaga, Daisy curled on her lap. I gently picked Daisy up and held her to my face, smelling her puppy smell, feeling the softness of her ears.

'Where you disappear tonight?' mumbled Baba Yaga in a sleepy murmur.

I sat beside her and told her everything. Then I sighed. 'I can't go on like this, Baba. But I don't have the courage to top myself. Tell me what to do.'

'Close your eyes. Let Sleep be the Mother of Counsel. In the morning you will know what to do.'

I nestled down in the pile of blankets. I couldn't be sure, but I thought Moineau's eyes were slightly open and looking at me. I smiled but she didn't smile back. I closed my eyes, hoping Baba Yaga was right and I'd wake up dead.

Then, in the morning, everything changed forever.

Chapter Thirteen—Sparrows fight as hard as eagles

The sun was barely up, and I was peeling spuds by the kitchen campfire with Farshad, watching Daisy limp about scrounging for scraps of meat Binh was accidentally-on-purpose dropping for her. Humbolt strode up like he was coming onstage for his dramatic-hero-saving-the-damsel routine. 'Oh, Romeo, Romeo—wherefore art thou Romeo?'

He looked around in that hammy way actors do, his hand shading his eyes, then pretended to spot me. 'Ah, 'tis you, young Romeo. Arise! Your Juliet awakes!'

'Yeah, bravo, Hummer. Bleedin' Shakespeare, innit.'

Humbolt dropped the act. 'Seriously, dear chap, she's with Baba—your Juliet has awoken.'

'Make some sense, pal, I need an actual excuse to get out of doing KP.'

'Moineau—she's regained consciousness.'

You could've knocked me down with a proverbial. Farshad took my peeling knife and pushed at my elbow. 'Go to her. Apprise yourself of this miracle.'

I stood and followed Humbolt in a daze, aware others were also crowding in toward the freaks' trailer. The doorway was a crush of people, but I was pushed through them all and was suddenly inside. And, suddenly, there she was.

Holding Baba Yaga's hand was beautiful, lopsided Moineau, surrounded by the smiles of the other freaks. The enclosure fell silent as they saw me, and Moineau turned and locked her gaze with mine. Her eyes sparkled, her cheeks were flushed, her lips were red, her straw-coloured hair shone—and then she spoke in a voice she stole from an angel. ''Ullo, you big murderin' bastard.'

I froze, boggled. I'd lived with Moineau for two years, knowing her only as one of the Professoré's freaks with a singing voice what made me happy, or unlocked my cold, black heart to let me cry all the way to the bottom of whatever bottle I was drinking. Was this some new evil trick the Professoré was playing on us all? On me?

She cocked her head, puzzled because I was just standing there like a big pillock. 'What's wrong with you? In't you 'appy to see me?'

Baba Yaga saw I was in shock, and pulled us away from the crowd and out the back door. 'You two go for walk. Talk each other, da?'

Baba let us go with a push toward a path leading up a small wooded rise. 'Go. Talk.'

I was still stunned as we walked side by side up the hill overlooking Rayleigh, me wondering if this miracle could be real, and thinking how filthy and disgusting I was when next to me was an angel.

Moineau touched my hand. 'You alright?'

I nodded but I couldn't look her in the eye. 'I'm glad you're better.' It was all I could manage.

Moineau stopped me 'What's up, Blanco? I come good. I'm alright now. You been so decent with me, I thought you'd be happy.'

I finally got courage to look in her eyes. 'It's you? Really you?'

'Who else would I be?'

'I dunno. You could be some program the Professoré stuck in you.'

'I in't no program, you big bollocks—I'm me.'

'You been awake all this time? Since you was with us?'

'I started hearing and seeing about a year ago. Maybe a bit longer. It was like a dream, knowing I was awake, but I couldn't do nothing. I just watched everything and did what I was told like a bleedin' robot.

And the whole time, you was there being nice to me, and everyone else. I liked you. A lot.'

Her smile. It was full of sunshine and flowers and . . .

I heard a yip and looked down. Daisy was there, limping and looking expectant. Moineau picked her up. 'As for you, you little mongrel, I fucking *loves* you.' She looked at me again, and then my heart, it jammed up in my throat or whatever, but I could see this thing in her eyes, this feeling, like what Tog gives me when we is drunk and we says how we loves each other, but this was more than that.

I didn't have a clue what to say or do. I never had no one look at me like that before. I read about people who love other people, and I seen other people in love—but it just didn't make sense. I'm nothing. I'm filth. I steal stuff, follow orders, kill people, and think about topping myself. Who could love that? Answer—no one, ergo this look from Moineau wasn't love. I looked away. 'I have to get back. I'm real happy you woke up, Moineau. It's great, but you'll need to do a runner so the Professoré don't get his hooks into you, so let me know when you're ready and I'll help. Money, weapons, whatever you need.'

I walked back down the hill, feeling like I'd just kicked Daisy.

Making my way through the trailers, keeping my head down, I got back to the campfire, picked up my knife and started peeling again. I could feel Binh and Farshad swapping looks.

'Not a word,' I growled. 'Not one bleedin' word.'

After breakfast, which I couldn't eat because I was sick thinking about Moineau's imminent departure, the Gaffer sent me into town with Doctor Po and the Professoré. In the barracks, a dozen wounded militia were going septic. The Mayor ordered them to keep the screaming down to a dull roar, and we started work.

The Prof and Po did their thing, chopping off any bits what was too far gone, then I closed up with my world-famous stitchery. Them soldier boys was tough. I showed them the needle, told them what I was going to do, then started sewing. Not a murmur from any of them. Tommy drifted in and acted like he never met me. He strolled about, inspecting everything, watching the Professoré fixing bones and doing his usual rough surgery.

The Prof and Po aren't big on the after-care side of things, so I told the big lads how to make sure the wounds didn't go bad. Them gadjos didn't like a scruffy freak like me giving them advice. One of them muttered to the Mayor, who turned to me. 'None of this is that Gyppo magic carry-on, is it?'

It was more a statement than a question, but I figured that word of me laying a curse on that Scottish peon might've got around. 'No, Mayor,' I replied, looking honest as the day is long. 'My mum was a registered nurse before she went into the nunnery, and she taught me some of the old ways. Spider webs and honey got plenty of the antibacterials what will keep them wounds healing up.'

The Mayor studied me, then nodded and give his men a stern look. 'What he says goes. Understood?' Cowed, they accepted their lot, casting wary looks at me.

'My son tells me you helped him out last night,' said the Mayor.

I managed to stay calm, scanning his face for anything he wasn't saying. 'Tommy, isn't it?'

'It were nice of you to give him a free ticket.'

I managed a tight smile. 'He seemed like a decent lad. Us circus-folk aren't all bad, Mayor.'

Which was when some geezer ran in, puffing. 'Mayor—there's been another murder. John Cox's wife. They found her in the trees near Bull Lane.'

The Mayor scowled, thoughtful. 'She's a bit older than the other murdered women.'

'Aye, by ten year or more. Knifed, she was. In the back. She were coming home from the circus.'

'Where was John?'

'He'd gone back to the circus with the boy to find a toy or summit.'

'Who the hell would kill a good woman like John's?'

'Mebbe same one what killed t'others. She weren't raped.'

All eyes was on us circus-folk, none of 'em friendly. The Mayor give me a hard look. 'Any of your lot might do this?'

'No, your Honour,' I replied. 'We heard a woman was killed but, if there's more, you're looking for a psycho.'

'I'm thinking there might be some in your circus what fit that description.'

Po and the Prof were looking nervous. I give the Mayor a straight look. 'I'd be lying if I said we were pure as the driven, but we work too hard to carry drunks and madmen.'

I was being as honest as I could, and he could see it. Finally he nodded, thoughtful. 'We'll like as not be talking with you all about it anyway.'

'Fair call,' I shrugged. 'Mister Splinter's ill, but the Gaffer will help you out.' I was about to suggest he look in his own backyard for a dodgy fuck, but Tommy came back, acting shocked. 'I heard there's been another murder.'

'Aye,' said his father. 'Some bugger's got militias in three counties running about after him.'

I saw a flicker of satisfaction cross Tommy's face. I turned away and kept stitching.

When we got back to camp, Baba Yaga wasn't happy. She grabbed the back of my coat and marched me aside. 'What you do to Moineau? She say she like you and you throw back in her face?'

'I don't even know her, Baba. Plus now she's back in the land of the living, she needs to be out of this place quicker than you can say "corrective neurosurgery".'

'She not go. She stay.'

I was stunned. After what we done to that poor girl, how could she stay another hour with us? 'The minute the Gaffer and the Professoré hear about this, she'll have her brain rewired. You should've told her that and all.'

'You tell her.'

'I bleedin' will, Baba. I don't want her nowhere around here.' I looked around to check no one was listening. 'Especially with that psycho Mayor's son going about the place.'

'See? You try to look after her. You like her too.'

I scoffed. 'You been reading too many of them Russian folk tales, Baba.'

I left Baba, determined to do the right thing. I found Moineau in the freaks' trailer getting the other Nightingales ready for their first show of the day. She clocked my grim dial, uncertain, but still happy to see me. ''Ullo, you.' She left what she was doing and came in close and personal like. 'You found somethin' nice to say to me?'

I backed away till I hit the door, determination wavering. 'I come to make sure you do a runner.'

'I in't runnin' nowhere, sunshine.'

Why was she smiling at me?

'We're the people what kidnapped you and done your brain in. What about your family?'

'Dead. You lot is my family now. I loves Baba, I loves these two Nightingales and most of the freaks. And I got feelin's for you an' all.'

'I'm a murderer, you daft bugger. I'm worse than a murderer—I kill people for money.'

'I know you, Blanco. I know you good. I been watching, and I seen how you look at me sometimes. But you never pawed me, or worse. You was kind. To all of us.'

'I'm not kind, I'm evil. Look at the trail of dead behind me. Case bleedin' closed.'

'If you got to know me, you might like me too.'

I tried another tack. 'You can't stay, Moineau. It's not safe for you here.'

'No, but I got you and everyone protecting me. I'm safer here than I am out there. Oh, and me name in't Moineau anymore. "Moineau" is French, and I in't French. From now on, me name's Sparrow.' She leaned forward and kissed me. 'So stick that in yer pipe and smoke it.'

She turned back to help the Nightingales, leaving me standing there like a village idiot. I wondered how the feck I was going to keep her safe . . . then I realised she'd kissed me.

Deep inside my guts, some part of me seemed to move, to change. It hurt, and I worried I was going to be sick.

Is this what love felt like?

Chapter Fourteen—It is better to be the head of a mouse than the tail of a lion

I went back to my chores with no idea what to do. I couldn't think straight because part of me was excited with what normal people call hope. Mostly I knew I needed to think like a clever bugger, or Moin— Sparrow was in big trouble. I had to hope the Gaffer didn't find out she wasn't a zombie no more.

Then one of the riggers came by and warned me there was a meeting of the Steering Committee about Moineau-Sparrow. Without a clue what to say, I dropped what I was doing and ran.

They were already arguing as I made my appearance. Madam Tracey looked unhappy, the others looked resigned. As always, the Gaffer was angry. He jabbed a filthy finger in my chest.

'Oi, you. That Nightingale needs rewiring, but the Prof says you been gettin' heavy with 'im. The likes of you don't threaten no one, 'specially your betters. If he has to do more work on Moineau, that's 'is job.'

I was scared but fed up. 'Then you better slit me throat, right now,' I growled. "Cause if he touches her, I'll slit his.'

Strombo stepped forward to thump me, but I kept talking. 'All of

68

you better start thinking about more important things than blaming me for barneying with the Prof. Moineau wants to stay and make herself useful, so here's a mad idea—how about letting her?'

I let my mouth keep up the palaver while my brain tried to think of the right words. 'And while we're all having this lovely chat, you getting me to kill someone the moment we arrive in a new town was bollocks—now we got the local militia about to come down on us. Whose decision was it?'

The others looked to the Gaffer, who bridled. 'Splinter said we had to make money sharpish. We got a timetable to meet up at the Convergence of Travellers, an' I'm goin' to make sure we gets there.'

'If Splinter's dying, maybe his brain's going south too,' I replied. 'Maybe you lot need to stop giving me a hard time and make better decisions about stuff like this.'

'You cheeky little . . .' The Gaffer balled his fists, but Madam Tracey drew herself up to her full five-foot-two, standing between us. 'The lad's right. We don't need more trouble, and a Nightingale who can also make 'erself useful is worth more'n one who can't.'

There was silence. Madam T was putting herself on the line, and no one could predict the Gaffer's anger.

There was a long moment where it could've gone either way. 'Fine,' he growled at me. 'For now we all just do our job. You look after your new apprentice, and keep Moineau in line—find out what she's good at, then I'll decide if she can do it. I'd suggest she'd be good on her back.'

I shrugged as if I didn't care. 'She makes them decisions for herself.'

Which is when Strombo smiled at the Gaffer; a nasty smile what promised nothing but bad stuff for Sparrow. 'I'll give her a test run, eh?'

Which is when I lost it.

☙

Later on, Madam Tracey explained to me I got what the head doctors call 'impulse control problems'. But when she said it, there was a hint of a smile in her voice, like she approved but couldn't let herself show it. Don't get me wrong, I know what I done was stupid, but that's what comes of no sleep, no food, murdering people, dealing with psychopaths, and having the girl you like kiss you.

Strombo didn't know what hit him—me—with a punch that had my heart and soul in it. For a big bloke he stayed upright what seemed like a long time. But his eyes were glazed over and all of us could see he wasn't with us no more. Like a big tree chopped at the base, he slowly toppled, and everyone jumped out of the way because Strombo's big enough to kill you even when he's unconscious. Time sped up again as the Gaffer turned, knuckle-duster in place, and threw a feint with his right before launching the metal with his left. Normally, I'd let him graze me, then roll myself up for the beating. But this time I was angry in a way I never been before, and I let my reflexes do their thing. I sidestepped, drove a fist into his solar plexus, brought me shoulder up into his chin and finished him off with a Glasgow kiss.

Madam Tracey's jaw dropped, the Professoré's eyebrows went up and stayed up, and Mala and Milosh looked impressed—and like they were ready to finish me off if it came to it.

As the Gaffer hit the deck, I dropped my fists, opened up my stance and looked into Milosh's eyes. 'If anyone ever looked the wrong way at Mala, would you do any different?'

In the split second it would've taken him to bury a blade in me, he didn't. Milosh don't hesitate when there's trouble—he's in there and it's all over. This time he just shook his head. 'You just make bad trouble.'

I shrugged and walked away. 'Trouble's me middle bleedin' name.'

I finished my prep and sat with the rest of the freaks, waiting for the axe to fall. We all agreed I'd basically given myself two choices—do a runner, or stay and be killed. If I stayed, the Gaffer would put me in the circle with Strombo for a straight-up bare-knuckle fight. Then it'd be on until someone—me—got beaten into a coma.

There's a code, see. You do a colleague an injury like what I did to

Strombo and the Gaffer, and there's consequences. It's like an old-fashioned duel except you're tied together, and instead of a neat bullet hole I'd have Strombo's ham-like fists tenderising my skinny body into sausage meat.

I cuddled Daisy, letting her lick the cold sweat off my face, and considered my fate. Baba Yaga brought me a concoction she said would clear my mind, which it didn't, but Moineau—Sparrow—come in all done up for her Nightingale act looking right serious.

'Madam Tracey tells me what you just done.'

I shrugged, brain jammed with misery and fear—not for me but her. 'You need to run, Sparrow. Tonight. Now.'

'Madam Tracey said otherwise.'

'You're not safe here.'

'Nor you, you big pillock. Always looking after other geezers, you are. Which proves you is a diamond geezer and worth likin'. A lot.'

I kept looking away, stroking Daisy, who was cheerfully chewing my thumb. I couldn't answer Sparrow because she made my head spin.

She kneeled and looked up into my dial. 'You been protecting me. Now it's time I helped you.'

'You can't, Sparrow. I'm done for. If not this time, the next.'

'Listen—I been stuck inside this head of mine watching and listening. And what I don't know about the people in this circus in't worth knowing. I also know you in't just strong in here.' She thumped my chest. 'You is smart up here.' She tapped the side of my head. 'And people like you—even if you is a misery sometimes—because you care. It's inside of you to look after other people. You can't help it. So maybe it's time to see Splinter again—get him to sort things for you, so we can start working on a new Steering Committee.'

I looked up, startled, and the freaks, all listening intently, looked to each other. They were shocked by what she said, but not so shocked they were shutting her down. Baba, Erik and Methuselah nodded first, then Elasto, Lobby and Dislocato followed suit.

'You're all madder than me,' I said. 'You'd be cutting your own throats going against them lot.'

Methuselah cleared his throat. 'Splinter is mortal and will, so you tell us, die sooner rather than later. The Gaffer will then become a power greater than he already is, but without Splinter to check his excesses.'

Baba Yaga nodded. 'The Gaffer rules by fear. I don't like.'

'He's already in the top job, if you ask me,' I argued. 'He does Splinter's evil will, so he might be a better Gaffer when Splinter's dead.'

Sparrow snorted. 'Either way, you won't be around to see it if you don't sort this beef you got with him and Strombo. You need to talk to Mister Splinter.'

I shook my head. 'Nothing short of a gun in me back could make me go in there and face him again.'

A minute later, there I am, standing on the steps of Splinter's caravan, Sparrow prodding me in the back. 'Go on, Blanco. What's the worst thing what can happen?'

I give her a flat look, then knocked and waited. The door swung open by itself. I went inside. The door closed behind me. I recoiled from the harsh stink of rot and chemicals as my eyes adjusted to the dim light. 'It's me, Mister Splinter—Blanco.'

'Come closer.'

I moved to the curtain dividing the trailer, bracing for the sight of him. Not much light made it through the curtains covering the small windows, but I could see his great shape in the shadows of humming equipment, piles of papers and books, tubing going here and there, screens, and equipment I couldn't recognise. His body seemed to be writhing, like he was covered in snakes. There was a fizzing, crackling sound like when the solar panel shorts out. Then the grinding growl of his voice.

'Have you been reading?'

I shuffled from one foot to the other, not knowing where to put my hands. 'It's my highest priority, Mister Splinter. That said, I've been a little occupied.'

His eyes narrowed, and I glimpsed one of his hands move slightly, then there was this sort of boom and the air seemed to compress in front of me, slamming me backward into the trailer wall. I was too shocked and winded to do more than lie where I fell. Up in his corner, on whatever it was he was sitting on, I could see his red eyes glint, his face knotted with writhing muscles that constantly changed his expression through every shade of rage and fury.

'Do you know what just happened to you?'

'No, Mister Splinter. Magic, Mister Splinter?'

His reply was a blast of sound what seemed to have every frequency in it, all of them painful. I rolled into a ball, covering my head with my arms. Then it stopped.

'If you'd done your reading, you would know what just occurred. It was tech. Get up.'

I slowly got up, my heart thumping in my chest, my ears ringing.

'Why did you come here?'

What little courage I had was gone. 'I lost me temper, Mister Splinter. I hit Strombo and the Gaffer.'

'I know. Explain why you did so.'

'They was proposing to do bad stuff with one of the Nightingales.'

'The one who now calls herself "Sparrow".'

'Correct, Mister Splinter. So now I assume the Gaffer will want me punished. Punished so I never get up and walk normally again, I'm guessing.'

'You broke the chain of command. You deserve punishment.'

I sighed, but losing all hope somehow boosted my courage. I dared to look right at him. 'All my life I been punished. Every day and every night. I'm jack of it. And so is half the people working in this outfit. Why does it have to be like that? If them two cripple me or worse, how am I supposed to do the Great Feat or anything else you want me to do?'

'You should've thought of that. You must have control over yourself. Without that you can hardly control anyone else.'

'I don't *want* to control no one else. Mister Splinter, you say I'm your son, but how does either of us know that? And why would you want me to be King or whatever if you got the Gaffer already doing the business?'

'Why do you think?'

'I suppose someone has to take over after the Gaffer gets killed or old or whatever. Everyone needs a backup plan.'

'And what is yours?'

I didn't have one, but it didn't stop my mouth from talking. 'It seems to me, Mister Splinter, that my life in't my own. It never has been. So I'm at the stage where I either get my own life, or I lose this one. You can hit me with the tech all you like, but if you're dying like what you said you was, you need to decide who to back—me or the Gaffer.'

There was a long silence, during which I mentally kissed my arse goodbye and hoped Sparrow would be smart enough to do a runner with Daisy. Then finally . . .

'I will give you one dispensation. I will instruct the Gaffer not to seek redress on this matter. You will continue to support him and learn from him. You will also study the books I gave you, and practise toward the performance of the Great Feat. Understand yourself and learn control. Only by doing so will you achieve what I need you to and, perhaps, find that which you're looking for.'

I didn't have a clue what he was on about, but I was too battered and bone-weary to stick my neck out any further. I nodded. So be it.

'Go. Do as I've instructed. To the letter.'

I was at the door when he spoke again. 'The girl will be safe. I'll see to it. Go.'

I opened the door and walked out onto the steps. Sparrow was there, looking concerned. The Gaffer was there too, glaring. I stared him down and looked to Sparrow. Even though she was standing next to that vicious prick, she was all fierce concern for me and none for him. In that moment, her bravery give me strength I never had before.

I decided not to do what anyone told me, Splinter included. I decided that if no one was going to give me my life, I'd just effin' take it.

Chapter Fifteen—A man who is certain has stopped thinking

The Mayor and his militia came to do some alibi-checking, Tommy was lurking in his father's shadow as his men spread out through our camp. We let them, because they didn't have no evidence and, as it happened, we hadn't done the deed. It was also apparent that the chief suspect was—no surprises here—the husband. Half the town knew about him and some teenage bint he was seeing on the sly.

The interrogations mainly gave the Mayor a chance to look our operation over—as much as we let him see. We made him welcome. Binh and Farshad put on a nice spread for him and his big lads with the big guns, and it was smiles all round from us. I was doing a few dressings on some of his boys while the Mayor drank beer what likely had a tincture of the Professoré's in it to make him mellow.

'I saw your show. How do you do those things you do to yourself?' he asked. 'How is it you don't feel pain?'

'I feel pain, sir.' I looked up briefly as Tommy joined his father, then turned back to my work. 'But it's just pain.'

'Doesn't it damage you, what you do?'

'It could, your Honour. But there's a few tricks what helps prevent that kind of thing.'

'What about when you stick those great pins in?'

I give him a friendly look. 'Like to know the secret?'

'The pins retract into themselves?'

'Nope.'

'They're made of rubber?'

'Nope, they are very real and very sharp.'

'Then how?'

I rolled up one sleeve, where a small bit of tape was stuck over where I put the pin through my arm. I peeled it off. 'Look closely. What do you see?'

'I see a small wound, where the needle has gone.'

'Look closer.' I pushed the skin either side of the puncture mark so he could see a glint of gold.

'There's something in there.'

'Pure gold wire, sir. Only gold will stay clean and keep the hole open. Before I do me act, I take the wires out, and the pin passes through the hole like a knife through butter.'

The Mayor was impressed and delighted. 'What a canny thing. And the pin you stick through your heart?'

'That trick must remain secret.'

'The pin is real?'

'The pin is very real. Should I make the slightest mistake, I'd die.'

He read my dial to see if I was lying. He frowned, realising I wasn't. 'What a life you lead.'

I saw the pity in his eyes, and it made me angry. 'We deal with what we is given, your Honour. I got food, and shelter, and friends. There's plenty what's worse off than what I am.'

'I meant no offence.'

'None taken, sir.' He nodded and moved on, and I felt we parted with mutual respect. I liked the feeling. Then Tommy gave me a clumsy wink a dozen men could've seen, and followed his father. That fool couldn't meet his end quick enough.

After the palaver was all done, and the Mayor's party had left, I found Sparrow and Daisy with Tog and the elephants. Tog was teaching Sparrow how to groom Jumbo and El Grande with the yard broom. The elephants were mainly focused on Daisy, who sat neatly in front of them, staring up in awe as their enormous trunks delicately sniffed her. They could've picked Daisy up and chomped her like a peanut, but she wasn't afraid, and they were gentle on her, like she was a tiny baby elephant.

'Oi, Sparrow,' I said, about to tell her lunch was ready.

But then Sparrow turned, her good side happy to see me. I can't explain the feeling what exploded in my chest when I saw that smile. It was like the first sun coming out after a long grey winter. She, for some mad reason, liked me for who I was. Me, just by being alive, was somehow causing someone else to be happy. And not just 'someone' but Sparrow, who it turns out were this beautiful, funny bint, smarter than Mathematico and tough as Baba. A miracle.

'Grub's up,' I mumbled, like a half-wit.

'Cheers, darlin'!' she replied, like I just give her a thousand pounds.

I walked away, the happiest young man in the whole United Counties of England.

When I did my act that night, I was still smiling. I couldn't help myself. And, unusually, the audience's expressions weren't just the usual disgust and horror, but amazement and awe. They didn't just hide their faces or look away but talked excitedly about what I was doing and whether it was a trick or what. I even threw in a few one-liners that were funny rather than just weird and messed up. Tommy was in the front row again, intently studying every move I made, unamused.

When I was cleaning up, I felt a draught at my back. I'd been expecting another visit and didn't bother turning. 'How was the show tonight?' I asked.

Tommy joined me, a frown creasing his dial. 'I don't know why you were talking so much, but I expect that's what the cattle enjoy. It got them chattering like insects. Are we killing anyone tonight?'

'Not tonight, no. Unfortunately, we'd be too obvious a target to pull another right after the first.'

'But they know it was the husband.'

'We know otherwise.'

'He wanted her dead, so he's responsible. I hope they hang him.'

'Very fair-minded of you, Tommy, but tonight is out for more killing.'

'When can I start studying with you?'

'Two days after we leave, you catch up with us, alright? That way your dad don't make the link and come after us. Till then, steer well clear.'

Tommy nodded. 'Will you teach me how you put the pin through your heart?'

'Only when you get good enough.'

'I'll get good enough. Don't worry about that.'

The little bludger was smug with certainty, and to prove his point he rolled up his sleeve. Along his arm were a number of puncture marks and blood-soaked bandages. I groaned with frustration. 'Just sticking sharp objects into yourself isn't what I do. You need to learn first or you'll do damage.'

Tommy shrugged. 'The pain is difficult, but I can bear it. I think of people I hate and imagine doing it to them. I imagine them feeling the pain I'm going through.' He smiled that sunny, cheerful smile what sent an icy chill right through me.

'Nice one,' I nodded. 'Now go. I don't want to see you again until two days after we're gone. We'll be at—'

'Port Rochford. I know. I've been listening in.' Tommy paused in the doorway. 'Don't the freaks make you sick? To look at them and be around them, I mean.'

'Not really. Why?'

'I hate imperfection. The freaks are so awful. They're like some sort of infection of the human race. Like Jews and black people and homo-sexuals,' he added helpfully.

'Right,' I nodded, wondering how a seemingly decent geezer like the Mayor raised a sick creature like Tommy. 'Now hop it.'

He slipped away through the canvas flaps. I sighed, burdened with the self-appointed task of ridding the world of a cancer like Tommy. He, and my link to him, filled me with nausea. How was it right to plan his death when the one thing I didn't want to do, ever again, was kill another human being?

Chapter Sixteen—Only in the village with no dogs walks the man with no stick

After that night's show, I was lying in my tiny trailer, listening to Daisy sleeping on my chest, when Sparrow found me. 'Can I come in?'

I nodded, and she crawled in beside me. Without asking, she held me.

I never been held like that, and it unlocked something inside of me. Instead of trying it on, I started whispering truth. I told her I wanted my life to be mine. 'I want out of this,' I said. 'All of it. The murdering, the lying, the stealing and the pain. I don't want to be no one's slave no more.'

'Then that's what you'll do.'

She sounded so certain, so confident, I began to think it was possible. I looked at her proper, and melted like I do with Daisy. With dogs there isn't no lies or holding back—what you see is what there is, the truth of how they is feeling. It was like that with Sparrow—truth.

I had to check. 'Is you sure you're not doing a runner like what a sensible person would do?'

She give me a sweet look. 'You in't getting rid of me that easy, boyo.'

'There isn't no family? No one out there what cares for you?'

Her face clouded.

'I in't got no one neither,' I shrugged. 'You don't have to say nothing if you don't want.'

'I want to tell you everything,' she replied, soft. 'I been locked in my brain, unable to tell no one nothing, for two years.'

'So spill. I want to know you. Who you are, where you come from—everything.'

She took a long, slow breath, then began.

'My mother and father was doctors—proper surgeons, then they turned to organ-farming. They paid bints to get knocked up and have babies they could harvest. Plus they was stealing kids and homeless people, cutting them up and selling the organs to them what could afford it.

'They made big money, and started mixing with a crowd above them. They thought they was better than the riffraff 'cause we could afford to live in a proper Bratva-run lectric compound.

'Them Russky mafia know how to spend their money alright. We had servants and food and lots of oldtech. And guns—lots of guns. Every geezer had a few. Even us kids. They give us shooting "lessons" 'stead of schooling. Targets was my best subject.

'Whatever else we wanted, me and my sister got—except any of what you might call "love" from our parents. As a result, we was spoilt little monsters. They give us drugs to keep us quiet, and I got a taste. When my sister went missing I finally realised they done her in for a big client.'

Sparrow cried for a bit, and I held her. It felt sad but wonderful to hold her like that, her warmth against me, the smell of her. Daisy got worried and snuck in between us, tail flickering anxiously, to lick her tears. I let go so Sparrow could pet her and calm down.

'So, anyway, I scarpered with any money I could thieve, a pistol, and a bag packed with quality drugs. I went looking for me grandparents I heard was living near Port Cambridge. It were under French control but I snuck in anyway dressed as a Ragamuffin boy, and started selling while I looked. What I didn't sell or use meself soon went, and I didn't find any family what would take me in. I went north but, since the Dutchies took the Norwich Peninsula, there weren't much food to spare, nor drugs neither. Which is when you lot came by and I thought, "Oi, oi—maybe I can fit in with that crowd." I remember clocking your sad little dial turn a bit smiley. I liked the look of you, but I needed the drugs, and the Professoré got his hands on me. The rest is history what you know already.'

I give her a smile. 'So you is almost as messed up as me.'

She smiled back. Then we stopped smiling and, like two magnets, we kissed.

I kissed girls before but this was different—I never felt so certain or needed someone as much. We tore each other's clothes off like they was on fire, desperate to be closer—to reconnect two halves trying to be whole again.

After the first couple of times, we calmed down, and it became slow and tender, sweet and loving. We swam in each other's arms and limbs, laughing and playing hide and seek in each other's eyes.

We finally curled up and slept. When I had to get up and let Daisy out for a piss I sensed a presence in the shadows, and sniffed the smell of someone what kept themselves clean with soap and the like. 'Tommy,' I hissed. 'Piss off home. Be at Port Rochford two days after we gone from here.'

A shadow moved, and the scent of him followed him away. Creepy little fucker.

In the morning, I sussed trouble was brewing—in our line of work, we learn to sniff it a mile off.

I was repairing canvas and ropes with the riggers when I noticed there weren't no local kids trying to stickybeak. Only one reason for that—they were told to stay away.

We know how long to stay in each village and when to do a runner. We slowly see the excitement and wonder turn to suspicion and anger, and we know the polis or militia won't be far off organising a raid. By then we've emptied the dinari out of the punters' purses, done all the private business the locals want done, and we're ready to get out before any serious barneys start. We might leave a trail of dead, but it's in no one's interest to catch us. Sometimes they send a posse, but we're always ready, and we mostly outgun them. Plus there's the other things we can do to them—the things Mister Splinter can do.

'It's a bit quiet,' I said to the lads.

Barrelmouth nodded, and the others looked around, uneasy, as the Gaffer stormed up with Strombo, nose all bandaged, looking happy as a bad boxer. 'You lot heard any rumours?'

The lads shook their heads, but I muttered an educated guess. 'I bet them local uniforms beat a confession out of the husband. He's told them it was us what killed that woman.'

The Gaffer glared at me but had to concede a nod. 'Likely enough.'

Feeling protected by Splinter's dispensation, I pushed him. 'So how about handing out weaponry? If we're halfway through pulling the pin when they come for us, we'll need to fight our way out.'

The riggers nodded, but the Gaffer didn't take kindly to me being a step ahead of him. 'You'll get a gun after I get the thumbs up from Splinter.'

I pushed harder. 'Them soldier boys will be having a big breakfast and getting a pep talk about now. We in't got time to muck about.'

'Pack up faster then.'

The Gaffer hurried off, scowling. I stood and looked at the boys. 'Let's get the feck out of here, lads. Keep a blade handy. Barrelmouth, you keep a lookout, eh? I'll get the freaks moving.'

I ran to the freaks' trailers and gave them the word, then told the kitchen hands. As everyone hustled and bustled, I grabbed Baba Yaga. 'Oi, Baba—where's Sparrow?'

'She go to the well. Maybe ten minutes ago.'

'It only takes a minute to get there and back,' I muttered.

Baba frowned. 'Go find her. Quick.'

I dodged my way through people pulling pegs, rolling canvas, and throwing belongings into carts and trailers. I reached the edge of our encampment, found the path and sprinted for the well, which was close to the town walls, surrounded by a copse of trees and bushes. As I made my way into it, I saw Tommy, chatting with Sparrow as she lugged a bucket of water. I barrelled in, ready to kill. 'What's going on?'

Tommy turned. 'Oh, hi. I was just talking with Sparrow.'

Sparrow kept a poker face. 'Tommy's a fan of yours apparently.'

I took the bucket from Sparrow's hand and tipped it back into the well. 'We need to get back.' I grabbed her hand and starting walking. 'We need to hurry.'

'Why? What's going on?'

Tommy jogged after us. 'What's up?'

I stopped. 'Does you know anything about your dad doing a raid on us this morning?'

'Other than he's doing one, no. Why?'

I restrained my fists. 'How long have we got?'

'Not long. They'll be finished breakfast by now and getting kitted up.'

'Did you not think to warn us?'

'But they're no threat to you, surely.'

'Everyone's a threat, especially them with guns. Go, and if you can slow them down, do it.'

Sparrow and I ran off without looking back at the useless twat.

It normally takes us six to eight hours to pack up and scarper. On this occasion, we were nearly done in just two hours before the first shots were fired over our heads. We barely blinked.

What local militias don't know is, we is an army what don't look like an army. We look like a bunch of filthy travellers what wouldn't know one end of a semiautomatic from the other. The reality is, grifting our way through the green and pleasant lands of Britain requires considerable logistical expertise and a tonne of weaponry.

The United Counties, and all the other British republics, need all the readies they can lay their hands on to fight off the Thuggees, the Dutch army, the French army, the Raskols, the Ragamuffins and any number of marauding bands of thieving bastards. As a result, everyone's up for a fight, and anything not nailed down gets nicked. We happen to be a money-making machine what isn't nailed down, so all of them come after us, at one time or another. Which is why we is always prepared. I think I already mentioned the trail of dead.

❦

As the rifle volley echoed off the surrounding hills, we heard the Mayor's gruff voice come over a loudhailer. 'Remain where you are. Do not attempt to leave. Do not resist. Stop all activity.'

None of us stopped. We took note of where the Mayor and his militia were inexpertly lined up in a few half-trucks outside the town wall, prepared for battle. I hate this sort of caper, and we were there with our pants down. It would be difficult to stall the twenty minutes or so it would take to start rolling out. Poor Tog was frantic about Jumbo and El Grande getting hurt, but the brave beggar kept it together as he and Sparrow strapped bullet-resistant graphene sheets across the elephants. We could all duck, run and hide, but the elephants were vulnerable. The graf sheets only protected to a point—a big-calibre bullet will go through you and take the sheet with it.

We were finally given weapons, and Tog could barely move for the Tech20 and all the bandoliers strapped across his chest. Even Sparrow had a big plastic Kalashnikov slung across her back.

Small windows and vents opened in the sides of our trucks and trailers, and gun barrels poked out, making them look prickly. Apparently oblivious to all this, the Mayor's voice continued. 'If you have any weapons, lay them down now. No one will be hurt as long as you offer no resistance. We will come amongst you and arrest those responsible for the murder of a woman of this town, and any others found culpable of conspiracy to commit the crime.'

I finished locking down my trailer as the Gaffer passed, calmly checking one of the rocket-launchers, Strombo following with enough rail-gun grenades to take out the entire town. To the Gaffer, 'overkill' was just doing it right.

The Gaffer readied his stance to fire his first missile. 'I'll take out that fat prick doing the talking for starters,' he muttered. 'That'll give 'em something to think about.'

I spoke without thinking. 'What if I could stop this without a shot being fired?'

Strombo spat with contempt, itching to pull my head off. The Gaffer just sneered. 'This your new magic act, is it? Shut your cakehole, get to your post, and when the shooting starts, make every bullet count. I want that lot dead, and us gone.'

'Wait,' I ploughed on. 'We might win this one, but some of us will get hit. We can't afford that—not now, when we got so far to go.'

The Gaffer pulled a pistol from his belt, levelling it at my head. 'I don't care what Splinter said no more. I've had a gutful of you.'

'Then order me out there with a white flag to parley with them,' I jabbered. 'They'll probably shoot me anyway, right? At least I give us more time to get ready. On the other hand, if I can talk them into backing off, you get the credit for saving lives and ammo.'

The Gaffer hesitated.

Strombo spoke up in his high, girly voice, his little red beady eyes in that big baldy head glaring at me. 'Kill him anyway.'

The Gaffer put his pistol away. 'Why waste a bullet?' He leered at me. 'Go on then. Scamper out there and parley.'

I didn't hesitate. I handed him my CQ semi and jogged out of the encampment toward the Mayor's militia, pulling off my shirt and waving it. A shot rang out and a chunk of grass and mud splattered up from a few metres in front of me. I stopped but kept waving my shirt. 'Parley!' I yelled. 'I call for parley!'

It's funny how in the midst of this dishonourable old world, you sometimes get these moments of honour where we all pretend we're Knights of the Round Table or whatever. The Mayor's voice crackled through the speaker. 'Come forward with your arms raised above your head.'

I put my arms up and walked toward the truck, a line of militia ranged out either side of it. The Mayor was conferring with some other geezers wearing patched-up uniforms made out of old Chinese DPM from some forgotten desert war. As I got closer, I could see they were arguing with the Mayor, unhappy about him parleying with a freak. The Mayor signaled me to come closer, which made me more confident in my mad gamble. If I was right, he was canny enough to know that the main difference between winning and losing is information—and that's exactly what I was bringing him.

I reached the Mayor. 'Mind if I put my arms down, your Honour?'

The Mayor pushed one of his men toward me. 'Check every inch of him.'

While his man did that, and was none too gentle about it, I was eye to eye with the Mayor, and kept talking. 'Mister Splinter asked me to assure you we didn't kill that woman.'

The lad stepped back, bringing his rifle barrel back up to aim at my chest. 'He's clean, Mayor.'

The Mayor shoved me against the side of a truck, a blade at my throat. 'You've got seconds to admit you're lying and ask me to be merciful when we take your circus apart.'

'I didn't lie. And I'm afraid there's no chance in hell you'll take the circus.'

'I know you lied. The murdered woman's husband confessed to everything. He contracted one of your lot to murder his wife.'

'That much is true, your Honour. We were contracted to do the job. He paid us and all. Except we didn't do it.'

The Mayor scowled. 'Bollocks. If you didn't, then who did?'

'One of your lot put a kitchen knife in her before I could stop him.'

'I thought you had some wits about you, boy. That babble that makes no sense.'

'It's the truth. I was the one who was supposed to do the killing, but I didn't. I was going to save the poor bint from that stinking husband of hers. On my honour, that's the truth.'

He looked into my eyes, less certain. One of the Mayor's men scowled. 'Bullshit. These people are no better'n animals. We should kill them all and be done with it. We might even get the townspeople their money back.'

I turned on the man, icy. 'For one, you in't got the right to steal from us,' I said. 'And for two, it don't matter if I'm lying—there's only one thing that's stopping you, your boys here, and half your town from being blown to pieces. And that's me.' I turned back to the Mayor. 'Never get into a fight you can't win, right? Believe me, you cannot win against us. You might kill a few of us with lucky shots, yes, but you'll be slaughtered like pigs. Right now there's rocket-launchers aimed right at this spot by a man who is gagging to see me dead. And the rocket-launchers are the least of it. If your boys punt any more shots at the circus, you, me, and all your boys will die on the spot, and then they'll bomb the town to ensure no one's inclined to chase after them.'

'He's lying, Mayor. Look at them. It's just a bunch of filthy freaks and diseased animals.'

I ignored the man. 'You lot hear about Buntingford? Twelve months ago, the fire?'

The Mayor nodded, uneasy. 'They said a roaming militia came over from the French side.'

I nodded. 'Except they never found no Frenchies, did they? And there was too little left of the town to find any footage or whatever to prove it was them. That's 'cause it wasn't. It were us.'

'Why did you do it?'

'The locals got greedy and wanted our stash, resulting in a firefight, during which we blew that town off the feckin' map. Which is what will happen here unless you back off and let us go.'

The Mayor scanned the circus, baffled. 'What kind of people are you?'

'Same as your lot, Mayor. Some of us is good, some of us is pure evil.'

'And which are you?'

'I'm one of the bad ones who wishes he wasn't.'

'So if you'd outgun us in a fight, why are you risking your neck?'

'Two reasons. One, you treated me proper. You looked me in the eyes and you didn't treat me like something stuck in the sole of your boot. You deserved a chance.'

'And the other reason?'

'I'm in love. She's down there, and I don't want her involved in a fight.'

'See? He's scared, Mayor. It's all a bluff.'

'No, it ain't,' I scowled at his lieutenant. 'If you want to go home to your family tonight, and start looking for the killer amongst you, you need to let us go unharmed.'

The Mayor paused, his mind churning. 'What if we keep you as hostage?'

'No one will stop you,' I shrugged. 'I in't worth nothing as a hostage, and that lot will roll out of here without a second look if you keep me. In fact, string me up by the neck and you'll only make my boss a happy man. I promise you, it wasn't us what did that woman.'

The Mayor thought for a minute, then turned to his men. 'Hold your fire and stand down.' He turned back to me. 'Go. And never come back.'

I nodded. 'Thanks, your Honour. You just saved all these lives and more besides. I hope this town knows how lucky it is to have you.'

I started walking then I heard him call. 'Boy.'

I turned. 'Yes, sir?'

'Other towns have been alerted to your complicity in the murder here. At least three counties are sending militias after you regarding the murders of the other young women.'

I nodded. 'Thanks, your Honour. I give you my word, we didn't do them neither.'

'You said it was one of ours.'

I couldn't tell him it was his son—I couldn't predict how he'd react. I just nodded. 'I'm sorry, mate, but I know for fact you got a psycho.'

A flicker of deep unease crossed his face as I turned and continued walking. As I reached the circus, the Gaffer was looking at the retreating militia with fury. That bastard *wanted* a fight.

Chapter Seventeen—One madman makes many madmen

'We have to scarper,' I told the Gaffer. 'The Mayor reckons three counties have set the dogs on us.'

The Gaffer strode off, yelling at everyone to pull finger, as Sparrow and Tog found me. Tog give me a grateful smile and a pat on the arm. 'Nice one, you mad fuck. I didn't fancy my big babies getting hurt.'

'Me neither, mate.'

We helped Tog hitch Jumbo and El Grande to the trailers then hitched mine to the back of a tractor. In a spare moment, Sparrow give me a look. 'You're a nutter and no mistake. Running into the teeth of battle.'

'I couldn't have bullets whizzing around hurting anyone.'

'You risked your life without a thought.'

'My life in't worth nothing. Besides, I'll die of one thing or another soon enough.'

'Not if I got anything to do with it.'

'Ditto.' I looked around to check no one could overhear. 'Want to hear my plan?'

'Go on.'

'I got certain chemicals what I can put into the Gaffer's food what'll put him asleep for a good long while. That's when we could do a runner.'

'To where?'

'Anywhere you fancy. I heard New Aberdeen needs workers.'

Sparrow scowled. 'I heard them northern Scots eat people.'

'What about Siberia then? All them big towns up there are making stuff again. Oldtech, ships, trucks, all sorts.'

'All of it run by Bratva. Trust me, them lot is evil as the Gaffer.'

'What about Tartika then? I heard it's big, green and empty.'

'Tartika's just a fairytale. Plus you got the Great Ocean to get across, and I heard them waves is a hundred foot tall.'

I was about to run down the rest of my list when she put a hand out to stop me. 'Blanco, how can you think of leaving Tog behind? He loves yer.'

'He can come with us.'

'Not without the elephants. And what about Baba Yaga?'

'She can come too.'

'And Farshad? Kongo? The Nightingales? What are the rest of them freaks going to do without us? How would we live knowing we left them behind?'

I slumped, out of ideas. 'If I stay here, killing people and doing bad things, I'll die. Can't you see that? I can't deal with it no more.'

I wasn't crying or nothing but she suddenly held me like I was. And then, inside of me, what was all broken glass and metal shards and coiled springs, just kind of melted. All them ideas and thinking went out of my head and, for a few seconds, the two of us were alone—united, strong and safe.

We rolled out of the meadows beside Rayleigh and onto the road heading east, all of us bristling with weapons, everyone keeping lookout, especially behind us. The circus can't move fast, but we kept up a steady pace. The sun come out, and we were soon sweating under our load of semiautos and pistols and blades of varying shapes and sizes. In the rear open-top truck, Strombo stood, legs apart, looking around like the mad bastard he is, a rocket-launcher over each big shoulder, while the Gaffer kept his eyes on the radar screens for any incoming aggravation. Splinter was in his trailer, no doubt monitoring everything and keeping his private arsenal ready to let loose his particular brand of havoc.

We were halfway to Port Rochford when the Gaffer called out. 'Rear gunners to your stations!'

Me, being expendable, was a rear gunner, so I leaped off the trailer and jogged back to where the Gaffer, Strombo and the others were assembling. The Gaffer indicated his radar screen. 'A convoy coming fast up behind us from the west, two smaller vehicles coming around to flank us on either side. Barrelmouth and Farshad, take the one coming in from the south-west. Binh and Spod, take the north-west. Me and Strom will guard our rear.'

Then he give me an evil look. 'And you can fly the kite.'

My stomach knotted. 'Why me? I'm the only one what gets air-sick.'

'Shut up. Humbolt, get him kitted up, and make it snappy. And don't forget the RT.'

Our convoy was still slowly rolling along as me and Humbolt ran back up the line to the mechanics' truck. We climbed up onto the roof, me effing and blinding the whole time, wishing I was already dead so I didn't have to go on panicking about getting killed.

Keeping our balance, glancing around for oncoming threats, we untied the canvas covering the motorised parasail. Humbolt helped get my arms through the straps, and slowly let me take the weight of the ancient two-stroke engine and big caged fan onto my back. Meanwhile I'm shitting myself, not least because the kite was recently and hilariously renamed the Whirling Blades of Death after an unfortunate cock-up with the previous pilot, who is now feeding the worms in Cumbria. I faced forward into the breeze, tightening every strap and belt as hard as I could, while Humbolt stuffed the RT into my pocket, the earphones in my ears, and slung a loaded semi around my neck. Then he primed the engine and laid out the silk. A minute later, as the breeze filled the wing to lift above us, I give Humbolt my last will and testimony. 'Tell Sparrow thanks for . . . for being nice to me. Oh, and Tog can have Daisy—the elephants already love her.'

'Just keep your eyes peeled and stay alive, you numpty.' Humbolt said. 'Ready?'

I sighed the traditional reply. 'Live fast, die young, leave a good-looking corpse.' I held the control toggles tight, readying myself. 'Start her up.'

Humbolt braced a foot against my backside, and pulled the starter rope. Nothing. Again and again he pulled, me trying to keep my feet, keep the faltering wing aloft, and not fall off the roof of the truck.

Finally, the motor started its brain-rattling buzz, and I pulled hard on the throttle as I trotted forward, hoping like hell I didn't just fall off the front of the truck and go under the wheels. Suddenly my legs were paddling thin air, and I looked down to see I was slowly rising above the truck. The RT crackled in my ears, the Gaffer's voice barely audible over the high-pitched roar of the motor on my back. 'Get some height and circle back to the west. Tell us what you see. Over.'

'Roger that. Over.'

I relaxed the toggles and rose, then swung south in a wide arc. I spotted a quad with two uniforms on it, coming up parallel to the circus. 'Two moxies on a quad at five o'clock. One hundred metres out. Over.'

I heard the rattle of small-arms fire as the rider spotted me and the uniform on the back tried his luck. I lifted higher, and swung further round to the west, where the full extent of the bad news revealed itself. 'Gaffer—I see a four-truck convoy. The two middle ones is filled with uniforms, the forward and rear units is wearing mounted guns—I can't make out what calibre. Over.'

'If that's all they got, we can hold our own. Over.'

It wasn't all they got.

I squinted at a black blur above the rapidly closing convoy, trying to get a clear visual while controlling the parasail. 'I think they got a drone. Over.'

'What size and type? Over.'

I peered at the black dot what was getting bigger, fast. I realised I'd got the perspective wrong. 'Shit! It's a chopper!' I panicked. 'Big black chopper . . . guns. Shoot it down!'

The chopper soared fast and low over the attacking convoy, heading straight at me. I yanked hard on my right toggle and flung the sail into a tight spiral descent. This is the fastest way to get down, as well as the quickest way to cause loss of control, disorientation, unconsciousness and death.

The world tilted and spun at high speed as I was flung in circles, the blood draining to my feet. My eyesight got them black speckles you get just before you pass out. I straightened out barely twenty metres up, and roared back toward the circus convoy. I looked over my shoulder—the chopper was banking to come after me. 'Someone shoot the bastard!' I yelled, then swung wide to the left and out of the chopper's path. Automatic gunfire crackled as I circled in behind. I fired a few feeble rounds with my CQ before the chopper was out of my range, then I was over the circus again. I looked down. Our convoy was hit—curving lines of bullet holes snaked along the roofs of the trucks and trailers.

The military convoy chasing us was now in firing range, and they let rip with what sounded like fifty-calibre which, when it isn't your side pulling the trigger, is pure terror—them bullets will tear you apart like you is a blood-filled paper bag. Fifty-cal will punch through anything short of steel plate.

Below my dangling legs, I glimpsed Strombo reply with a puff of smoke and the muzzle-flash from one of his rocket-launchers. I heard the dull whump of the explosion, and turned to see it had hit the side of the lead militia truck.

To the north, Spod and Binh were running and gunning at the quad what was trying to flank us. To the south, Barrelmouth and Farshad had pinned down the two uniforms. Despite the painfully loud whine of the engine on my back, I heard the juddering crack of the militia's mounted gun.

Hearing another rocket, I looked back. A mushroom of flame and black smoke heralded a boom as the lead militia truck went up. I breathed a small sigh of relief, but semiautomatic fire was still coming onto our flanks, and I swung out to the north to add my fire to Spod and Binh's. It was lucky timing—the chopper had banked around to come at us from the east, this time with the advantage of the sun behind it, and was trying to hit me.

One of the joys of flying the kite during battle was, up there, you're a target for any prick with a trigger to pull. Every fucker can see you, and anyone so inclined during a firefight can generally find a spare moment to fire a few rounds at the flying dickhead. And they did. I rained a few back at the quad, now parked and being used as cover, then swung back around and toward the circus.

It was one of those moments when time almost freezes. From the open chopper door, a uniform was angling a rail-gun at me. I could see the gaping black maw of that barrel turn from a slit to a circle as the uniform found his target.

Well, this is it, I thought. Just when I'd tasted happiness for the first time in my rotten, stinking, useless life, I was about to die.

I tried to swing away but couldn't move fast enough—I could practically feel them bullets ripping through me. At the same time, I registered a small figure with a big rifle on top of the freaks' trailer. Sparrow? She had some sort of goggles on, and had her gun aimed at the chopper.

There was a sharp crack as she fired a single round. I looked over my shoulder at the chopper as the head of its pilot exploded. The pilot slumped onto the joystick, and the chopper lurched, spiralling down and smacking into the field beside the convoy.

I was stunned but didn't have time to think. As my parasail turned back to the west, uniforms were pouring out through the smoke of their burning lead truck, firing at the back of Splinter's trailer. The other vehicles slipped around it, still game to wipe us out.

Frontal attack, hail-of-bullets style, is potentially suicidal, but overwhelming if you got the numbers. Our people hit the deck as bullets filled the air, some ricocheting off the steel of Mister Splinter's trailer, from the roof of which a small square plate was rising up.

I knew what was coming next. Suddenly the uniforms coming at us stopped and recoiled in surprise and shock. Most of them simply dropped their weapons, and ran to get away from the burning pain that seemed to come from nowhere and everywhere.

I quickly swung away in case I strayed into the exclusion zone, and spotted Baba Yaga emerging from cover carrying a Six-Pak. She strode out to the north of our convoy, planted her feet and opened fire at the pair attacking us from behind their quad. For them what is not familiar, the Pak's six barrels pour out ten rounds a second—do the math. The quad disintegrated and the uniforms behind it were basically dog food. She turned, walked back through the convoy and repeated the process to the other quad.

I heard the Gaffer over the RT. 'Cease fire!'

I hit the kill switch and glided down, pulling a big-ears manoeuvre five metres above the ground to land on my feet. The wing crumpled on the ground ahead of me, and I quickly unclipped from the harness, relishing that silence you get after a battle—spoiled only by the crackle of flames from the burning truck and the screaming and crying of uniformed lads about my age, dying for no good reason.

The 'sweet taste of victory', my skinny white arse.

Chapter Eighteen—He who makes a mouse of himself will be eaten by cats

Sparrow walked to the edge of the truck roof and took off the strange-looking goggles.

I looked up at her, in awe. 'One bullet to take out a whole chopper?'

'Told you I had a misspent youth,' she grinned with her poor lop-sided mouth.

'Thanks for saving me life.'

'You're very welcome.'

She jumped down and we were suddenly close, face to face. I felt that magnetic need to kiss. We were about to when Humbolt arrived to stow the gear. 'Good job distracting that helicopter, lad.'

'I knew I was up there for a reason.' I looked around. 'Any casualties?'

'One, I'm afraid. Skeletor. Fatal.'

'Bugger. Poor old geezer.'

'Fortunately, the Professoré thinks that with a bit of tinkering, our bony comrade will arise again into a new incarnation.'

'"Fortunately"?' I gave Humbolt a sour look. 'What "new incarnation"?'

'If we half-wrap him, we can claim he's an Egyptian mummy. The great King Wottentot or whomever. The Prof's also pretty keen to do a bit of jiggery-pokery inside Skelly that might keep up a semblance of life.'

Sparrow frowned. 'That's horrible.'

'A bit Doctor Frankenstein, I grant you, but the punters will hardly know the difference.'

I gave Humbolt a flat look. 'I'm sure Skelly would take comfort in knowing he was still being exploited even after his own death.'

'Exactly,' replied Humbolt, beaming. 'A bit of the old team spirit. One for all, all for one.'

I ignored the big eejit, and looked at Sparrow's long-barrelled rifle and mask. 'What's that tech?'

'Good sniper rifle, this. And this here mask lets me see where people is, even when you can't see them. Have a look.'

I held the mask to my face and looked through the eyepieces. Sparrow was a blaze of yellow-white against a duller multi-coloured background, as was Humbolt. I looked around and saw Binh climbing into the cabin of one of the trucks, his head burning like a torch inside the shadows. I put the mask down. 'Where did you get this?'

'The Gaffer wasn't going to put a rocket up that chopper, so I asked Mister Splinter for one of his special devices. He give me these.'

I was stunned. 'You just barged in and asked him?'

'I knocked first.'

'And he just give them to you?'

'I said I had to save you.'

My admiration for her soared 'You saw him. You saw his face.'

'I can see the family resemblance.'

My jaw dropped, and then she cracked up and pinched me cheeks. 'I'm joking, you pillock. You don't look nothing like him—you're much uglier.' I smiled but she sobered. 'The Gaffer wanted that chopper to cut you up, by the way. He said as much.'

I shrugged. 'Tell me something I don't know.'

Baba Yaga approached from the destroyed militia convoy, her arms loaded with looted weapons, shoulders draped with ammo belts. 'Is wounded and dying boys. The Gaffer is say put bullet in them. I refuse. He get angry.'

'I'll take a look,' I replied. 'No point any more lads dying what can be helped.'

I walked back along our convoy to where Doctor Po was putting the world's smallest field-dressing on Strombo's big baby forearm. 'Oi,' I said to Po. 'Let's see what we can do to help them soldier boys.'

Strombo smiled. 'Don't bother.'

I realised I wasn't hearing no groaning. Then the Gaffer emerged from the smoke of the destroyed convoy, walking toward us, wiping his combat knife on his pants. He scowled at me. 'If it isn't the flying fairy himself. Get back to your station and we'll get this lot moving.'

I stood eye to eye with that murdering prick. Po cleared his throat and stepped between us. 'Blanco, you come help with injuries. Madam Tracey have cuts need sewing. So do Farshad and Julietta. Come.'

I let him pull me away, knowing neither me nor the Gaffer would rest till one of us was dead.

Chapter Nineteen—Imagination is the mother of wisdom

It was a tense, quiet trip to Port Rochford. There was little traffic, and any civilians what did stick their heads up scarpered. A half-mile out of the Port, the Gaffer called a halt.

We pulled off the road and took shade under some storm-battered pine trees. The Gaffer and Strombo continued into the town to organise a boat, while we rested and ate.

Me and Sparrow helped Binh and Farshad get everyone fed and watered. Methuselah was put out in the sun on a deckchair, with a big hat on him to keep his skin from burning. I kneeled beside him to cut up his food. 'What was this place before the Collapse?'

'A pretty little town, Rochford. Not a port back then, of course. It was many miles from the coast when I first knew it. I had a second cousin here, a lovely girl, and we used to take a rowing boat out on the river. She'd show me all the birds still left in the area, tell me all about them, and, when she was done with that, we'd kiss and kiss and kiss.'

I looked at his dusty white mug, and imagined that bleak bony face filled out with pink cheeks, thick hair and a proud moustache. The dry remnants of his smile faded. 'In later years the river became more estuarine, and the rising sea and salt finally killed the birds. She went off to fight against the Sino-African invasion of France, then against the Dutch here, and became a senior commander in the United British Alliance. The American flu took her in the late fifties, and I was very sad to hear it. She was a brave and caring person, someone I admired a great deal.'

'When did you last see her?'

'That would've been when I was fleeing London with my family. The cholera outbreaks hadn't affected us much until a particularly nasty one took out the Hampstead Heath encampment and we were left with no place to go.'

'I never asked about your family. Any of them left?'

'No. I lost everyone.'

I must've looked more miserable than usual because he patted me gently on the shoulder. 'But now I have you and the others. You're all my family now.'

Bearing in mind my inclinations to do a runner, that didn't make me feel no better.

The Gaffer finally returned. 'Right, you lot. It's a shit sandwich. No ships available, so we're stuck here till one comes in, or we find ourselves another port.'

'This is busiest port on the south-east,' murmured Milosh. 'Strange is no ship.'

'There's half a dozen, but none to take us,' the Gaffer replied. 'Every captain said the same—waitin' on loads.'

'What are the odds?' I mused. 'Three militias up our arse, and six captains what won't take our money.'

Madam Tracy nodded. 'Worth me doin' some intelligence-gatherin'. Just in case this in't no coincidence.'

'Good call, Madam T,' I said. 'Or we send a smooth-talking type to "persuade" one of them captains to reconsider their options.' I looked to Mala and Milosh, whose negotiating skills largely consisted of the removal of all options but one, usually with the aid of surgically sharp blades.

They nodded, but Gaffer bridled. 'We travel down to Port Benfleet. Bound to be ships there.'

'We'd run into them what's chasing us,' I replied, and others nodded.

'Then north to Hullbridge,' he scowled.

'A day's march, more east than north,' I said. 'And every chance we'll meet another town with murdered girls.'

'Shut your mouth, boy. Committee will decide.'

Strombo shoved me, hard, and I retreated as the Committee gathered to talk.

Sparrow joined me, holding our scratched old binoculars. 'Take a look at the guard towers.'

I raised the binos and looked. A half-kilometre distant, guarding the entrance to the port, two towers held a uniform apiece—each standing beside a machine gun, looking through binoculars at us.

I stopped looking. 'They is likely concerned by word of our recent adventures.'

'We got trouble coming from the east what might only be hours away,' Sparrow murmured. 'We need to board one of them empty ships and scarper, fast.'

'We could fight our way in but we'd risk getting killed. Or worse.'

'Could we wait for nightfall then sneak in?'

'Sneak through a town, in the dark, with two elephants and an entire circus.'

Sparrow looked chagrined. 'Point taken. We can't take a step without making a racket. Got a better idea?'

'No,' I murmured. 'It's absolute shite, but it plays to our strengths.'

'What does?'

'Your idea. At least that's what I'll tell anyone what don't like it.'

'One idea's better than none,' Sparrow shrugged. 'Tell the Committee.'

I stalled, uncertain. 'The Gaffer won't buy it. Don't matter how I put it, he'll hate it.'

'Tell Madam Tracy. She's on our side. She can present the idea like it was hers.'

I paced around, wishing I was smarter. 'This is a bit mad but I don't think we can afford to give anyone a choice. There's a tranquiliser rifle in the armoury . . .'

'Bloody hell—you're going to shoot the Gaffer?'

'Tempting, but no. Quick, follow me.'

We ran to the armoury, and I picked the lock while I told Sparrow my shite idea. Then she pointed out where it was shite and fixed those bits—most of it really—till we had a not-so-shite idea. That said, I was shitting myself as she steadied the long rifle against one of the tractor wheels.

'You can do this in only two shots?' I murmured. 'No pressure . . .'

'Shut yer piehole, gorgeous.'

She looked through the sights, slowed her breathing, paused, squeezed the trigger.

Even as the bang drew every eye to us, Sparrow was gently swivelling the rifle, aiming . . . and firing a second shot. I raised the binoculars to check. The first guard was slumped and sliding out of sight, the second was staggering, then crumpling.

There was a roar from the Gaffer as him and the Committee come charging over. 'What the fuck?'

I stood in front of Sparrow. 'We got an hour before the guards wake up, and who knows how long before them chasing us will catch up. We're between a rock and a hard place, and the only way out is by one of them empty ships. We can't sneak in or fight our way in, so we circus our way in.'

'I'm going to fuckin' do you . . .'

Milosh put up a hand. 'Wait.'

Though Milosh barely reached his chest, the Gaffer paused long enough for Mala to step forward. 'Explain. Quickly and carefully tell us your plan.'

'We do what we always do,' I replied. 'We pull a short con.'

Chapter Twenty—Sometimes you get the bear, sometimes the bear gets you

Give people some confident palaver and, no matter how much bollocks it is, they'll mostly buy it.

In this case, our short con commenced with two clowns on tiny bicycles, desperately pedalling to stay ahead of two brightly decorated elephants ridden by the Fazio girls in their spangled finery. They led a merry march of happy, waving circus-folk as we entered the town's now unguarded main gates singing, juggling, calliope music blaring, and throwing the odd handful of sugar lollies to the children.

The wary townsfolk were persuaded by our smiles, and their yelling kids, that this noisy surprise was an event to enjoy rather than barricade their doors and windows against. The Rochford militia hadn't been told to stop us, could see no threat and, equally, were no match for our cheerful we-in't-stoppin'-for-no-one march down the main street toward the docks. The uniforms' confusion and uncertainty faded as we crammed our colourful slow-moving caravan between tottering houses that leaned in above the narrow street. With no clear orders, or time to coordinate, them lads with the guns soon shouldered their weapons, keen to win a blown kiss from one of the Fazio girls, or laugh at our antics.

Eventually the cobbled street opened out onto the broad bustle of the docks, a stretch of busy wharf with half a dozen small ships lined up. Dressed in a jester's hat and coat, I sized up our options. Two of the ships looked like they were still running nukes, one was running diesel and sail. At the end was a rust bucket—a converted car transporter with three masts for solar-sails and a combustion-engine funnel—using what fuel I couldn't imagine. Cow shit, if the rest of the vessel was anything to go by. Its battered drive-on ramp rested down on the wharf edge, and a few skinny, bored crew sat or lay on it, smoking kif or somesuch.

As the performers kept the crowds entertained with magic tricks, juggling and clowning, I nabbed Mala and Milosh, pointing at the rust bucket. 'That one,' I said. 'It's ready to load, and them sails only take ten minutes to warm up on a sunny day like this.'

Mala nodded, Milosh shrugged. 'Rust bucket will sink as soon as float, but if we are moving we stay alive a little longer.'

They left me with their bikes, and hurried away to engage in 'negotiations'.

I found Sparrow entrancing a few tin lids who were patting Daisy.

'Oi,' I said. 'We should be ready to load in a hurry.'

Sparrow let Daisy down, and we casually moved among the trailers, trucks and caravans, telling everyone the plan. I was about to take my life in my hands and knock on Mister Splinter's door when Sparrow stopped me. 'Notice anything?'

'Only how beautiful you is.'

That earned me a kiss for which I was grateful. I'd rather die happy.

She pulled away. 'You're running this show. You're coming up with the ideas and making it happen. Your dad's right about you.'

'He's probably not me dad, alright? And I dunno what he is or who I am but I in't no leader of nothing. All I want is to stay alive and do a runner. Besides, truth be told, you're the clever one.'

Sparrow looked like she was going to say something deadly serious, but then she smiled. 'Give your dad me love, eh?'

I scowled, but she skipped away with a mischievous look, Daisy bouncing at her heels. I turned and knocked on Mister Splinter's door. 'Mister Splinter, it's me, Blanco.' The door opened and I went in.

Before I could step past the curtain, he spoke. 'Your plan is sound. Load quickly. Ensure you provide cover for any sniper fire, and see that my truck is the last to be loaded. Have the captain leave the loading ramp left half open as we move away from the dock, so I have a clear line of fire.'

I was a bit stunned he knew all this, but there wasn't no time to ask. 'Will do, Mister Splinter.'

'Keep your regard for the girl in check. You are no use to me or yourself weakened by emotion.'

My blood boiled. I could've told him that Sparrow was the only thing keeping me going. I could've told him I was that close to putting a barrel in me mouth before she smiled and opened up my chest, put my heart in the sun and started dancing around inside of me. I could've told him a lot of things. What I said was, 'Yes, Mister Splinter.'

'Go.'

I left the chemical stench, brain reeling, as Mala and Milosh trotted down the ramp of the rust bucket. 'The captain. He is Rom,' growled Milosh.

Mala shrugged. 'He is Lom from Armenia, but he will help.'

I was intrigued. 'Does he know he'll be in danger?'

'Life is danger. Besides, he and his crew is stuck in this shithole three weeks. Also we pay him money. Plus we would cut his throat if he did not agree to help.'

'You're quite the negotiators, Mister and Mrs Petulengro,' I said respectfully.

Milosh wasn't flattered or amused. 'And how do you propose to move us all into this ship, which will probably sink and drown us, without coming under fire from the soldier?'

'The same way we got this far?'

Mala shrugged to her husband. 'What choice is? Boy is right.'

I could've hugged her but, just like smart geezers avoid hugging tigers, I restrained myself. 'I'll get Tog to load the elephants first, then the trucks—if you can persuade the Gaffer that it's a good plan.'

Milosh looked me up and down, surly. 'Keep you head down, boy,' he warned. 'Work and don't make things worse.'

'Tell performers keep making the ha-ha,' Mala added. 'Tell others to get animal and truck inside.'

Mala and Milosh headed for a glowering Gaffer as Sparrow joined me. 'How's your dad?'

'Sends his regards.' I spared a look toward the Gaffer. '*He's* none too happy.'

'Steer well clear.'

'Meanwhile, keep the punters entertained while we get animals and vehicles loaded.'

Sparrow hurried off to organise the Nightingales into a performance, while I nabbed Tog. 'Alright, mate—time to get Jumbo and El Grande safe aboard that rust bucket.'

Tog sighed, weary. 'I hate water.'

'Don't be glum, chum—they say drowning's the nicest way to die.'

'I heard being left out in the snow was best.'

As we loaded the ship, we discussed the pros and cons of various forms of dying, which cheered us up and took our minds off the likelihood of imminent death. Them uniforms began to look tense, but the crowds of locals, and our cheerful determination to push on, saw our lethal circus quickly packed into the hold of a ship that would probably sink like a rock if it hit so much as a herring.

As the ship's crew ran along the wharf throwing off the ropes, me and Sparrow cheered up a bit. Soon we'd be out of here, we'd reach Europe, and I'd talk Sparrow into running away with me. For the first time in me life, I knew what hope felt like.

In the hold, looking down the open ramp, we heard a deep rumble. The steel floor vibrated under our feet as an engine started up somewhere on board. The solar-sails began telescoping up into place on the masts, causing worried looks from the uniforms on the wharf, weighing up if they could afford to let us go or risk an all-out battle.

A slim figure with blond hair ran through them toward us, carrying a small pack.

I'd forgotten about Tommy.

'Leave him behind,' I said.

The Gaffer gave me an evil smile. 'Your new apprentice? Certainly not. Who knows—he might turn out to surpass his master.'

Tommy ran up the ramp, grinning. 'Another close call, eh Blanco?'

Chapter Twenty-One—Delay
is inevitable, success is not

The enormous hold was now packed with our trucks, trailers and animals, but the ship wasn't yet moving. We were also in a confined space, and the Rochford uniforms were frantically clearing civilians from the docks. We were fish in a barrel.

Me and Sparrow left Daisy with Tog and the elephants, then hurried up to the crowded top deck with the others—we needed higher ground to fight from.

The ship's crew and their families bustled around us, readying to sail, tidying away loose items, and giving us wary looks. No wonder—we were a band of exhausted, twitchy, armed freaks, clowns and carnies looking out every which way for any signs of trouble.

Then, across the crowded deck, a squat, swarthy, bare-chested geezer climbed down the steep stairs from the bridge.

To say Captain Goyan, of the good ship *Lav Noyember*, was a hairy man was like saying centipedes have several legs. There was some bare skin on his forehead, and two small patches over his cheekbones. The rest of him was covered in thick black tightly curled fur. A grubby black-and-white captain's hat perched on the back of his head like a penguin about to jump off a seaweed-covered rock. His barrel chest and round belly parted the crowd, while one of his hands wandered and scratched through his pelt. A rope belt held up what was left of his trousers, the ragged cuffs hanging high above a pair of sturdy boots. Steely eyes pierced the crowd from under thick black eyebrows—a focused king in his kingdom.

Sparrow caught his eye. He bowed. 'My lady. I am Alexander Goyan, the captain of this ship. Welcome aboard.'

Sparrow stuck out her hand. 'How do you do, captain. My name's Sparrow. This is Blanco.' The captain shook our hands, looking at our strange appearances, bemused. 'Welcome to you both. It is my hope that we will reach our destination without sinking or being captured by pirates.' His teeth flashed bright white in the black of his beard. 'Pirates other than ourselves, I mean.'

I looked down at the wharf, edgy. 'That's our hope also, captain.'

He looked around. 'Who is your leader, by the way?'

'That would be our owner, Mister Splinter,' I replied, bypassing the Gaffer.

'I would like to see him. Now, if it is convenient.'

We led the captain down into the hold, where Splinter's trailer was parked and tied closest to the open ramp. I hesitated before knocking. 'Mister Splinter has an . . . um, unusual appearance.'

He nodded, warned. I knocked at the door, which swung open, and gestured Captain Goyan through. The door closed behind him, and me and Sparrow went back up on deck to check our progress. Goyan's crew were busy stowing loose gear, and keeping a wary eye on us lot. I noted they were also ready for any aggravation from pursuers, with four small mounted guns, fore and aft, port and starboard. The Gaffer and Strombo were at the stern, overlooking the wharf and checking their weapons.

A wiry lad with a wisp of a moustache stood at one of the mounted guns, a thin cigarette glued to his bottom lip. I give him a friendly nod. 'How much longer before we can get the hell out of here?'

'Soon.' He nodded to the headlands, curving in from either side of the bay. 'But they can still jump us from there.'

I scanned the bay, fretting, but Sparrow was friendly. 'Been with this lot for a while?'

'My whole life. The Capitan is my father.'

Sparrow smiled. 'Seems like a nice bloke, your dad.'

'He is,' the boy replied, proud. 'If he rob you, he tell you first.'

'Very decent of him,' I said. 'My name is Blanco, this is Sparrow.'

He nodded. 'Vincenzo. Enzo for short.'

He looked past us and reflexively crossed himself. With the Six-Pak slung over her back, Baba Yaga carried Erik and Methuselah toward some crates so they could sit and catch a bit of sun.

Enzo shuddered. I knew the look. 'It's okay, Enzo. Them two are men just like us. The old geezer's a lovely fella, and Erik, the fella with no arms and legs, he can speak your language and ten others besides. You don't need to be afraid of them.'

'What about the big ugly man in the dress?'

'That's Baba Yaga, and she's a good sort too.'

'God is make some bad punishment on them, I think.'

'Maybe, but you're a pirate, so how come God don't punish you?'

'He will. The priest promise.' Enzo sounded satisfied with this future.

Captain Goyan climbed out of the hold, grim. 'I made agreement with your Mister Splinter and I don't break my agreement, but the sooner I wave you bye-bye the sooner I sleep at night.'

I shrugged for sympathy. 'Don't worry, captain—we understand. If we weren't fighting for our lives, you wouldn't be put in this situation, as I'm sure Mister Splinter explained.'

He nodded. 'I may be a bad person, but he chilled the blood in my heart. Is lucky I am Lom, I think. He also is Rom, yes?'

'So I understand,' I said. 'But what difference it makes I have no idea.'

'Gadjo is gadjo, Gypsy is Gypsy. Gadjo live in just one place, the entire world is home to us.'

One of the crew at the stern waved urgently to the captain. We followed him, looking down on the arrival of motorised militia—our pursuers had finally arrived.

Captain Goyan swore in a language I didn't recognise. The Gaffer shrugged. 'Any of them fuckers make a move on us, we bomb their fucking town.'

I watched the militias setting up mortars. 'We need to deal to them before they fire them things.'

'They cannot fire them while we remain,' muttered Captain Goyan. 'If we burn, so does their wharf.'

'They'll wait till we're in the middle of the bay,' I replied.

'We cannot stay, we cannot leave?'

'This is a stand-off,' the Gaffer replied. 'Just get that ramp up half-way and get us out of here.'

The Captain hurried off, his thick brows drawn into a single frown.

I drew Sparrow aside. 'We should get some weapons.'

The deck, previously crowded with sailors, women and children, was clearing below decks as we helped Baba Yaga take the others out of harm's way. It was both a relief and a bigger worry to realise the ship had begun inching away from the dock.

I could hardly draw a breath waiting for them mortars to come raining down, but then, with the ramp stalled halfway open, the uniforms on the wharf were suddenly scrambling away from their weapons, scrabbling at the air in front of them. Mister Splinter was working his particular brand of evil magic.

Just as I was starting to feel hope, some pinging off the hull signalled incoming rifle fire. Sparrow and me ducked. 'Oi, Enzo, where's it coming from?'

Enzo, crouched, pointed forward to the headlands drawing closer on either side. 'A militia post on each point. Some riflemen too.'

I crept forward to the rail and saw a splash ahead of us. Then the water exploded. They were finding our range with mortars. I heard a grenade being launched from the stern. I looked back to see the Gaffer firing on three militia speedboats coming up behind.

Sparrow was fierce. 'I'll get that sniper rifle again.'

'Good call—it's got a longer range than our fifty-mill guns. See if you can take out the geezers driving them little boats and I'll get the Gaffer to concentrate on them fellas ahead of us.'

Sparrow hurried below decks as I went aft to the Gaffer. 'Leave the small arms to take out the boats. You need to use the big stuff on them mortar posts ahead.'

'Who made you the feckin' captain?'

'I in't bossing you. It's just how it is, okay? Look.'

I pointed ahead and he got the picture. He hated doing it but he hefted the launcher and headed forward, Strombo pushing me out of the way to follow.

I told the sailor on the aft gun to spare his ammo, and to only keep our pursuers at bay until Sparrow could do her sharpshooting, then told Enzo and the sailor on the port side the same thing. No point geezers dying for no good reason.

Keeping my head down, I ran up to the bridge, where Captain Goyan was loading a snub-nosed pistol and swearing in several languages. He scowled at me. 'Trouble comes to him who waits. In sixty seconds we are in range of those mortars, my boat is sink, and my life is over.'

'Lucky for you there's a small army at your disposal.'

'What army? You are circus.'

'A travelling circus, which amounts to the same thing. Have a look, captain.'

He left his steersman and looked to where I was pointing. On all sides, our freaks and riggers had every kind of gun pointing out across the rails. Sparrow was using her skills to keep our pursuers at bay. 'No one will take us from behind or to the sides.' Then I pointed forward, where the Gaffer and Strombo were each aiming at one of the headlands, faint red lasers revealing their aim.

'The only metal on them headlands are the mortars firing at us,' I said. 'Unfortunately for them, our rockets hate metal.'

The Gaffer and Strombo fired their launchers, the rockets curling left and right as they sensed their targets. As two more mortar rounds hit the water only metres from our bow, two mighty explosions took out the guns that fired them and the poor bastards what got the job of protecting the bay.

Captain Goyan looked at me, grim. 'You knew this fight would happen.'

'We hoped it wouldn't, captain. But hope in't a strategy.'

I looked back to see our pursuers peeling away, defeated, and Sparrow shouldering her gun, grim.

As we sailed through the headlands into the Channel Sea, I could make out wreckage and the bodies of the young men who manned the guns. Some were moving, some weren't. Soon their families would be grieving, while all around me freaks, riggers and sailors were smiling and chatting, relieved. I hated them what tried to kill us, and I hated us for killing them.

And there was Tommy with the Gaffer and Strombo, admiring the rocket-launchers, smiling that open, happy smile of his.

Book Two—
Europe, 2070

Chapter Twenty-Two—
The destination is never
the destination

By late afternoon, the *Lav Noyemba* was under full sail on rolling open water. The steady thump of the steering engine vibrated the deck as we slid up and over the greasy swells of the Channel Sea. I found Tommy gripping the rail, his face and knuckles white.

'It's about time you learned the rules,' I told him. 'How things will work between us and who's boss.'

'I understand,' Tommy replied through tight, white lips. 'The chain of command.'

'Correct. I is passing on my trade secrets what no one knows but me, not even the Gaffer, alright?'

'I give you my word. I'll never tell anyone.'

'Tonight after we have a feed, we'll come back here where no one can overhear.'

'Alright.'

Having set up the time and place for his murder, I left him leaning over the grey turmoil of the Channel, his green bile staining the red rust of the hull, and went to find Sparrow.

The *Lav Noyemba* was more a floating village than a cargo ship. Most of the original superstructure of the top deck had been cut away and modded into a maze of livestock pens and small workshops, all crammed under the three tall telescoped masts and rigid graf solar-sails.

It was a busy village—tin lids ran amok, old women knitted and repaired clothes, geezers tinkered and repaired oldtech, younger men maintained weapons in a fully equipped forge and armoury, women tended toddlers in a small fenced play area.

I spotted an open hatch, and climbed down the rusty ladder.

Below deck was a rabbit warren—skinny corridors, hatches and steep stairs all over the show. Up the front half were three levels of living areas. At the back was the cavernous car transporter area where our vehicles and the animals were secured.

Tog was with the elephants, working hard to keep them calm. Even though they were strapped with supports so they couldn't hurt themselves with the swaying of the ship, Jumbo was seasick, and Tog was covered in it. Daisy just about leaped into my arms to get away from it all.

'Anything we can do for Jumbo?' I asked.

Tog nodded, looking as tired and miserable as the elephants. 'Doctor Po's making something up.'

I found a firehose used to wash out the hold, and called Tog over. 'Come on, mate—bathtime.'

I cracked open the tap to give it quarter-strength, but still nearly blew the lad off his feet. He gritted his teeth, swore at me, leaned into the water jet, and turned around, holding his ragged clothes up to get a washing too.

In that moment, seeing this wee man suffering without complaint to help his animals, I realised how much I loved and admired him. What a plucky, caring, decent bloke he was. And how lucky was I to have him as a friend?

While he wrung out his clothes and shivered to stay warm, I brought water to the elephants, thoughtful. 'You know what, Tog—would they feel better lying down? Wouldn't all the rocking feel more gentle on their sides, like when they was still in their mums?'

Tog finished his ablutions, quietly grateful, 'Why didn't I think of that?' Then, gently and calmly, he got Jumbo and El Grande to lie down, making sure they had some hay to rest their heads on. Pleased they seemed more settled, I left him to dry out, and took Daisy up on deck.

I wandered around, getting plenty of looks, giving smiles and nods in return. Sparrow and the Nightingales were with a small tribe of dirty-faced little kids, who she was teaching to sing some French song, 'Frère Jacques'. She smiled and waved, and kept on singing.

I realised three boys were dogging my steps, so I stopped. 'How you doin', lads? Alright?'

Two were younger and shorter, Japanese or Korean. They hid behind the taller, older one, a skinny African with wild fuzzy hair and an intelligent look about him. 'Y'all mind if the boys pat your dog?'

'Go for your life,' I replied. 'She loves a scratch and a tummy rub.'

He nodded to the boys, who kneeled and petted Daisy.

'Is you all living permanent on this thing?' I asked. 'Or is you on your way somewhere?'

The older lad's accent was American. 'I'm from New Confederacy, but this boat is my home for now.'

'You always been a seafaring type?'

'Naw. My people come from Carolina, mostly from the Big Smokies. There was fighting, and we was lookin' for someplace safe, but Christian soldiers came on our camp. Them what was left run to the coast. First time I ever saw the big water. Now I'm a sailor. Where you from?'

'All over. Bits of me is French, bits of me is English, and now they tell me I'm Rom as well.'

He screwed up his face, curious 'Rom? Wassat?'

'Gypsy, mate. Tinkers. Travellers. Don't you got them where you come from?'

The boy shrugged. 'I don't rightly know. Everywhere I been there's people from all over, goin' ever which way. 'Mericans like me, Asian ones like the two Kims here . . .' The two smaller boys looked up, curious. 'Some is white like you. Though not crazy-white like you. You is from Mars or someplace, huh.'

I smiled. 'No, mate—I was born like this. Black eyes, white skin.'

The Kims felt brave enough to reach and touch my skin and hair, checking their fingertips after, muttering to each other in Korean, intrigued but not disgusted like some people.

'So how do you folk make a living?' I asked.

'We make stuff, sell stuff, carry stuff.'

One of the Kims smiled shyly. 'Steal stuff.'

I kept a straight face. 'Pirates, eh? I knew you lot was tough when I first seen you. A right bunch of cutthroats, I bet.'

The Kims grinned, but the American shook his head. 'It's just how it is. If we don't steal from folk, they sure as hell goin' to steal from us.'

'I know how you feel, mate,' I sighed. 'Our circus is like pirates too, except we're on land.'

'Y'all made funny or just some?'

'Everyone's made funny, mate. Some of the funny stuff you can see on the outside. The rest is funny on the inside.' I tapped my head.

The American nodded, earnest. 'True dat.'

I noticed the Kims staring at where Baba Yaga, Erik and Methuselah were sunning themselves. 'Want to know the big secret about us freaks?'

The Kims looked at me with wonder and anticipation.

'The least interesting thing about us is our appearance.'

The boys looked thoughtful, and the American smiled and stuck out his hand. 'William H. Prendergast at your service.'

'Blanco, at yours.' We shook hands, and William indicated the Kims. 'Mister Kim and Mister Kim—I calls 'em K1 and K2.'

I shook their hands, solemn. 'Pleased to meet you.'

We strolled on and I introduced the lads to the freaks. 'These good people is keen to meet you. Mister Prendergast, Mister Kim and Mister Kim. Lads, this is Baba Yaga, Erik the Eel and Methuselah.'

The Kims huddled behind William, looking up at Baba Yaga with astonishment, but William stuck his hand out. 'How do, Mister Yaga.'

Baba didn't correct him, engulfing his skinny black paw in her big hand. 'Hullo. You can call me Baba.'

William extended a hand to Methuselah, who gingerly allowed his arm to be joggled before William stalled with Erik, uncertain.

Erik grinned. 'What? You aren't going to shake my hand?'

'I cain't quite see it to shake, sir.'

'That's very perceptive of you, young man. Most people assume it isn't there.'

William held his hand out and waved it up and down as Erik joggled his shoulder to indicate he was reciprocating. 'I have a light touch, as you can feel. Very pleased to meet you, William.'

'And you. Is we done shakin'?'

'We are indeed. And what, may I ask, is your profession on this ship?'

'I'm goin' to be an engineer. Anything metal with insides that move, I aims to learn how to fix.'

'Admirable.'

'And what trade are you in, sir?'

'I have just become a teacher.' Erik gave me a flat look. 'I have been instructed to teach Blanco here the content of the books he has been given but so far declines to read.'

'I been busy,' I grumbled.

'True, but Mister Splinter sent word I must assist you or things will not go well for either of us.'

Baba cuffed my arm. 'Listen and learn, or Splinter make bad. For all of us.' She reached down and picked up Daisy, who happily licked at Baba's vast nose. William was wistful. 'I had a dog once. Big ol' black thing with a broke tail. He used to bark if the Christians came near.'

'What happen to him?' asked Baba.

'The Christians poisoned him along with the rest of the guard dogs. Then they came for *us*.'

'Is all Christians in New Confederacy on the bloodthirsty side?' I asked.

'The ones around us was. They wanted to steal our land. Y'all Christian?'

I was diplomatic. 'Either way, we in't the sort to kill people about it. We only do that for money.'

William nodded, matter-of-fact. 'It's good to have principles.'

That night, after dinner, I brought Tommy to the dark area by the rail where no one would notice a body going over the side. It was a simple plan—get him talking, get him to sniff my killing bottle then heave him overboard. Cue some happy sharks with full bellies.

I kept it casual. 'So when did you realise you had a thing for killing?'

Tommy frowned, recalling. 'I suppose my first kills were the stupid dolls and teddy bears they gave me. I was two or three years old, and my parents talked about them as if they were alive.'

'But you quickly realised otherwise.'

'I got a knife and checked. Then I wanted to see what was inside other things. As soon as I was old enough, I opened up cats and dogs, the occasional rat. I liked the noises they made, but people reacted badly if they caught me.'

'And you didn't understand why they'd care.'

'Well, no. It didn't make any sense. So then I had to hide my activities.'

'Which is why you became so good at sneaking around.'

'Correct. When I opened a baby, I only just escaped in time. Afterward I realised people were physically protective of their families and didn't want them killed.'

'Did you understand why?'

'I didn't understand the whole emotion thing, but I eventually read about the genetic predisposition most people have to ensure their reproductive success. People less evolved than me—around ninety-six point eight per cent of the population—those people couldn't think in the way I do.'

'Did people notice you were, um, more "evolved"?'

'They did, so I learned to read their emotions, and pretend to be what they wanted me to be. People being incredibly stupid, that was easy.'

'People are stupid, and no mistake.'

Tommy smiled. 'I enjoy talking with you, Blanco.'

'Am I the first person what you could tell this stuff to?'

He nodded. 'I used to talk to the whores before I killed them but they'd only pretend to listen, to gain my sympathy.'

'Which I assume you never gave them.'

'Certainly not.'

I knew I should cut to the chase and kill the little sod, but it was like dealing with a deadly snake. I looked at him with part fear, part fascination.

'So in terms of your apprenticeship,' I continued, 'I need to know why you want to kill people for a living. Going about killing girls in't what I do.'

'I understand,' he nodded. 'If I was to just kill someone, perhaps because I didn't like the way they dressed or smiled or whatever, that wouldn't be professional. That's what I want to become. I've got some of the skills you have—now I hope I can learn how to kill anyone at any time.'

'It's good to have sensible goals,' I agreed. 'But I need to know. Why killing? Why not engineering or surgery or sailing ships?'

'None of that appeals, and I think you have to enjoy what you do to be any good at it. Don't you?'

I felt my heart clench. Deep down, did I enjoy killing people? God knows I was good at it. Thinking about what kind of monster Tommy was reminded me what a monster I was. Tommy read my face, intrigued. 'You don't enjoy killing people?'

'Let's just say my strong preference is to do it well.'

That seemed to satisfy him. 'I want to do it well, Blanco. One day I want to be able to kill anyone who gets in my way.'

'You want to be boss.'

'I want to rule the bosses.'

I had the picture now. Psychopath, megalomaniac, happy-go-lucky killer. I pulled out my tin with the soporific-soaked rag. 'Well, first you'll need to get to know this little tin and its contents.'

I opened it and put it to my nose as if I was taking a cautious sniff, all the while gently breathing out so I didn't get no fumes up me. Then I proffered it to Tommy. 'This here is one of my basic tools of the trade, as it were.'

He leaned forward—just as I heard a voice. 'Oi. You two.' The Gaffer.

I pulled the tin away and stashed it. But even though he never got a proper sniff, Tommy got a whiff. As the Gaffer reached us, Strombo at his heels, Tommy blinked and reeled. I grabbed him to keep him upright. 'You alright, Tommy? Struth, mate, you need to get your sea-legs.'

Tommy gave me a bleary, and wary, look as he struggled to stay conscious.

The Gaffer was suss. 'What you two playing at? There's work to do.'

I had my poker face on. 'Then point us to it. Soon as Tommy's over the seasick, we'll be there.'

Tommy stood clear of me, shaking off the drug. 'I'm good. I'm fine.'

The Gaffer nodded. 'Good boy. Come on. We got weapons to clean and repair.'

He and Strombo turned away, and Tommy followed, giving me a bemused look. I couldn't tell if it was the drug befuddling his brain or something else. Something like distrust.

Chapter Twenty-Three— Better to bend than to break

Halfway to the Dutch Islands, the engine broke down, and we were rudderless. Our mad engineer Spod was down the engine room like a rat down a drain, eager to get his hands dirty and show off. There wasn't nothing the rest of us could do except keep a sharp eye out for pirates while we drifted.

Erik and Methuselah sat me down with Mister Splinter's books. In a crisp Austrian accent, Erik read from one. '"In order to keep his people united and faithful, a prince must not be concerned with being reputed as a cruel man."'

I looked across the churning grey-green sea, scowling. 'I hate cruel men, and I hate cruelty to man or beast. There in't no need for it.'

'Machiavelli implies a certain amount is necessary,' said Erik.

'He has wisdom in these matters,' added Methuselah. 'This book is intended for those who lead.'

I wasn't really listening because Sparrow was passing by, both of her hands held by several smaller hands belonging to a dirty tribe of little ship's kids gabbling and singing at her in half a dozen languages. I watched her arse and thought . . . Well, no need to mention what my filthy mind was thinking. In fact, I couldn't stop thinking about it. Being close, wrapped in her arms . . .

I looked down at Daisy, curled in my lap, a sleepy smile on her little face, in heaven with the sun on her. I wished I could run away with Sparrow and feel safe like what Daisy felt now.

Then I saw Methuselah watching Sparrow with a small smile.

'Oi, you,' I grinned. 'You're about a hundred years past it, mate.'

'I may be a bag of bones now, but I *can* remember being young,' he replied.

'Could we please focus on our work?' Erik was losing patience. '"Men never do anything good except out of necessity."'

'Not true—sometimes we do good even if we don't benefit,' I said. 'Either way, I still don't see what any of this stuff's got to do with me.'

'Mister Splinter sees your role as a leader. Some are born to leadership, some must be taught.'

I shook my head. 'The Gaffer will take over when Splinter's dead. Him and the Steering Committee.'

Erik shot a look at Methuselah what I couldn't read. Methuselah looked around and lowered his voice. 'Revolution, my young friend, will come about when there is need, and enough to support it.'

I stood, fed up. 'Oh no you don't. If you lot want a better life, you can manage for yourselves.'

Methuselah shrugged, Erik arched one eyebrow, wry. 'As you can see, we are somewhat at a disadvantage in dictating the terms of our employment.'

'Then talk to the Gaffer,' I replied.

I put Daisy down and walked away, keeping her lead taut so she didn't get in people's way.

I stood at the rail, Daisy sniffing and barking at swooping seagulls. The ship was still drifting, though they'd angled the sails so we were at least pointing into the waves. All around were other ships and fishing boats. A freshwater carrier loomed across our bows, close enough that I was worried for a minute. A trio of small, fast motorboats skimmed across the choppy waves and circled us once, taking an appraising look. Enzo was stationed at his gun, and waggled the barrel in friendly warning. One of the crew of the motorboats grinned, gave him a wave and sheered his boat away.

I looked at Enzo and wondered what it was like to have a proper father. 'Oi, Enzo. What's your dad like? As a captain, I mean. Is he a hard man?'

'He is tough, si.'

'Is he cruel?'

'Sometimes he must punish people for drunkenness or stealing, but he is good man. Fair. Kind.'

'How does he punish people?'

'Mostly he talk at them, sometimes is a little shouting, then he put them in the kitchens or engine room on cleaning duty.'

I frowned, confused. 'Yeah, but what does he do when someone's done something real bad?'

'If someone betray us, he puts them ashore and we sail away. Then they are dead to us.'

'He don't give them a thrashing, or break their legs, or kill them?'

'No. Is that what your Mister Splinter does?'

'If you're lucky.'

'We are like family,' Enzo said finally. 'Stuck on the boat together, when we argue, it is better to make things right so no one loses face. That way no one stays secretly angry and make trouble later.'

We felt a rumble underfoot. Enzo relaxed. 'Good. The steering engine is fix.'

The Gaffer strolled up with Strombo and Tommy, then looked over at me. 'Oi. It's time you started teaching this one all your tricks.'

'What's the rush?'

'I'm the rush.' The Gaffer enjoyed my unease. 'Sensible to train up someone else in case you was to get injured. Or killed.'

Strombo smiled, seeming to like the thought of wringing my scrawny neck.

I tried to look like I didn't care either way. 'Fine. Whatever.'

'Train him proper. That way we could have *two* competing for the Great Feat. If you fail, Tommy might win. Which could well happen— unlike some, Tommy's keen as.' With a fish-eyed smile, the Gaffer walked off with Strombo at his heels.

Tommy gave Enzo a wary look then turned to me. 'Should we go somewhere quiet below deck?'

'Nope. We'll start right here. Get your kit off.'

'I beg your pardon?'

'You heard. Strip down to your undies. Tricks don't come out of thin air. You gots to know where everything is before you start sticking holes in it.'

Tommy reluctantly took his jacket and shirt off, and even more reluctantly his trousers, socks and shoes—all of which he folded neatly and stacked on a bench.

As little kids gathered around us, giggling, I started my lecture. 'Now, first is understanding what things is made of.' I rapped his head with my knuckles. 'Bone. Obviously. The skull to be precise, which is part of the skeleton what's holding you up.' I wiggled his nose, which he clearly hated. 'Cartilage. Which is a soft type of bone what's found in your nose and ears. Also the bits between your joints, so things move nice and the bones don't grind against each other.'

Tommy looked at the tin lids, gathered and gawping, his lips thin as string. 'Do we have to do this with all these insects hanging around?'

I looked at the grimy-faced kids and smiled. 'We certainly do. This here is your first audience. Congratulations. Give Tommy here a big round of applause, lays and germs!'

I led the applause and the kids played along.

Tommy was grinding his teeth, but he stayed where he was.

The Gaffer was right—Tommy was keen. Too bleeding keen.

Chapter Twenty-Four—Only in the water can one learn to swim

The Dutch Islands were just a flat, pale line resting on the horizon when a sickly greenish wall of cloud swept in from the south-west. Within minutes, the wind hit us, then lashing rain. Captain Goyan's sailors wound down the sails so we couldn't catch too much wind. The ship slowed a little, but even so, people were hurrying below deck as we heeled and bucked in the lumpy swells.

I was on deck so Daisy could have a pee, my guts churning. I yelled over the wind to Enzo, still at his station. 'How long till we get into port?'

'No tonight,' he called back. 'No safe to come in like this. We must sit it out.'

'For how long?'

'Until storm finish. Maybe one night.'

A heavy steel door opened nearby, and William H. Prendergast stepped into the rain. 'Blanco, come! Quick!'

I picked up Daisy and lurched across the pitching deck. 'What's up?'

'Your woman. She is hurt. Quickly.'

I followed William H. inside, hurrying behind him through the maze of narrow corridors and stairs, pushing through knots of chatting people and playing children. Eventually he brought me to a cramped room set up as a makeshift hospital.

My beautiful Sparrow lay on a skinny bed, pale as milk, unconscious, face bloodied. Doctor Po and the Professoré were assessing her, while Baba Yaga and Tog stood out of the way, looking sick with worry.

'What happened?'

'Someone found her at the bottom of some stairs,' the Professoré replied. 'We think it's a closed head injury, but there could be a fracture.'

I held her hand as their voices blurred—perhaps she was bleeding inside her skull, perhaps the clot was growing, pressing against her brain. There were no resources on the ship to know either way. She'd either wake up or die.

Someone sat me in a chair beside her bed. Someone pushed a bottle into my hand. Someone stroked my head and patted my back. Po put a drip into her arm and give her some fluids and drugs.

The night wore on in an endless grey funk of misery and fear. My mind walked away from it all, going aft and down into the hold, getting one of the shotguns, finding Tommy, switching him off, then finding the Gaffer and Strombo, doing the same to them, walking to Splinter's trailer and . . .

. . . I couldn't go in. I couldn't kill him. Not even in my imagination.

Why not? Hadn't I lived my life in a hell he created? Didn't that monster deserve to die?

Hours passed. Daisy curled up on the bed next to Sparrow and fell asleep. I thought how life might be from now on. I pictured myself leading Sparrow around, feeding her, looking after her forever. I pictured killing us both. I pictured every scenario I could imagine, my brain playing them over and over like a video loop.

I felt a rough pat on my shoulder. 'Talk to her.'

It was Baba Yaga. 'The Professoré say maybe she can hear you. Say nice thing. Maybe she listen. Maybe she is inside her head frightened too.'

Sparrow's face was calm, looking for all the world like she was just sleeping. I hated the thought of her stuck inside her own head again, unable to tell me nothing. I was terrified I was going to lose her just when I'd found her.

'Sparrow, it's me. Blanco.'

I stopped, feeling foolish.

'Say you love her,' ordered Baba, gruff. 'Be gentle.'

I turned back to Sparrow. Baba was right—I loved her. My life wasn't my own no more. If Sparrow didn't make it . . .

Baba patted me gently and left us.

I started whispering—how I was sure she'd be alright. I talked about the freaks, the storm, about what we'd do in Europe, and how Tog was down with Jumbo and El Grande brushing them in that way they love, and telling them the storm would be over soon. I talked and talked.

One by one, the freaks and riggers came by to check on us. When they went, I talked some more. In all my soppy palaver to Sparrow, I finally promised I'd never stop loving her, that I'd follow her in life or death, to heaven or hell.

Around dawn, I felt a hand stroking my hair. I lifted my forehead off the bed and saw Sparrow's beautiful face turned toward mine, her eyes open.

'Hullo, you,' she croaked.

Sunshine flooded my heart, little birds sang on me shoulders, evil was banished from the world.

'You bleeding cow,' I croaked back. 'You had me worried.'

I carefully hugged her, as Daisy woke and come in to wag her tail and flap her tongue about the place.

'What happened?' she whispered, feeling her wounds.

'You don't remember?'

'No.'

'They found you at the bottom of some stairs. When the storm hit, you must've fallen. Can you move your fingers and toes?'

Sparrow moved her limbs slowly. Everything worked. More smiles.

Then Kongo came in, relieved to see Sparrow awake. 'We're busy cleaning up after the storm and you're lying about having high tea with friends.'

'I'm fine now,' said Sparrow. 'I think.'

She began to sit up but Kongo put up a hand. 'No you don't. You're not going anywhere until you got the all-clear from Doctor Po.' Kongo beckoned to me. 'We need to talk.'

I stretched painfully then joined Kongo by the door. 'What's up?'

'The Gaffer got me to give his and Strombo's trailer a tidy, and when I was fixing Tommy's bunk, I found this.' She handed me a notebook. 'Look at the last page.'

There was a list, titled 'Things to Do Before I Achieve Greatness.'

I looked up. 'This should be good for a laugh.'

Kongo was grim. 'Keep reading.'

I kept reading.

1. Impress Blanco with my ability to learn.
2. Learn everything he knows.
3. Get rid of smelly stuff between toes PERMANENTLY.
4. Make sure everyone likes me more than Blanco.
5. Copy keys to weapons trailer.
6. Learn what is the source of Mister Splinter's power over everyone.
7. Stop masturbating FOREVER.
8. Find out everyone's weakness.
9. Stop killing girls unless I really have to and no one finds out.
10. Kill Sparrow but make it look like an accident.
11. Make Blanco weak because of grieving so he is easy to trick and for revenge.
12. When I have Mister Splinter's power kill the FILTHY freaks then go home and kill my family and take over everything.

At the end of the list was a hand-drawn smiley face. I handed the notebook back, shaken. 'Get this back before he knows it's gone.'

'I'll tell the Gaffer,' Kongo replied. 'He'll throw the little mad boy overboard.'

I guessed the Gaffer would rather toss me and keep his pet psycho, so I shrugged. 'Maybe. Or not. Either way, thanks for the heads-up.'

She nodded and strode off into the crowded corridor, families and kids jumping out of the way so she could squeeze past.

I hadn't noticed the storm had passed. Now my stomach was rumbling with hunger. Sparrow was dozing, so when Baba Yaga come to visit I went to get some food. Up on deck the sun was just breaking through the clouds as we docked in the twin mid-Channel island ports of Iymuiden, forty kilometres off the Dutch shore. Over by the kitchen servery, bowls of stew were being handed out. Tommy was eating nearby, listening respectfully to every word the Gaffer was giving him. They saw me, and Tommy smiled and waved.

I went over, give the Gaffer a nod and Tommy a friendly clap on the shoulder. 'You made it through your first storm then?'

'I did. I just refused to vomit. Willpower. How's Sparrow?' His face creased into what he thought was a convincing mask of concern.

I smiled, using my real relief to mask what I was thinking. 'She just woke up.'

'That's great news, Blanco.' Tommy beamed. 'Bit of a close call there, eh?'

'I'll say. If she'd have dropped off the perch, I'd be looking for another shag.'

The Gaffer looked up from his stew, searching my face, but Tommy just nodded. 'That would certainly be inconvenient.'

I took a bowl of stew. 'We'll have time for your next lesson after this, Tom.'

The Gaffer gave up trying to read me, nodded approval and looked back to his food.

'I know the anatomy,' said Tommy. 'What's next?'

'Next is learning about pain. How to take it, how to put it out of your mind and get on with the job at hand.'

Tommy's mug was the picture of earnest enthusiasm. 'I'm ready, Blanco.'

'I'm sure you is,' I replied, casual.

Even the nasty part of me didn't get much joy out of the thought of sticking things in this little psycho. But, if Splinter wanted me to groom Tommy, it meant I was expendable, and the Gaffer wouldn't hesitate to do me at the earliest opportunity.

All things considered, I reckoned the lessons on pain might take a while.

Chapter Twenty-Five—
Victory is obtained from the enemy's tactics

The Dutch Islands stretch from south to north in a broken line of storm-lashed sandhills, midway across the Channel Sea between Britain and what's left of the Netherlands. The Port of Iymuiden is actually two competing ports on two of those islands, glaring at each other across a narrow tidal channel that sweeps between them. Almost identical run-down piles of salt-crusted concrete warehouses, recyclers and rickety steel docks, barely two hundred metres apart, radio their rates to approaching boats to undercut their rival.

Dutch in name only, the ports are run by hard bastards who redistribute whatever they can lay their hands on, minus a cut, and provide safe docks to repair ships what are being chased for Crimes to Commerce—fellow pirates, in other words. The chasers are obliged, by dint of Iymuiden's huge wave-powered laser cannons, to back off until whoever they're chasing does a runner in the middle of the night with a newly patched boat.

Them Dutchies liked our money and scrap metal and, once we finished unloading, we quickly took on supplies. Afterward, I ground my teeth through another of Tommy's lessons then went below to check on Sparrow. Her bed was empty.

'Sparrow's doing fine, Mister Blanco.'

I turned and there was William H. Prendergast and the two Kims. 'Mister Yaga and the little man took her downstairs to look after her,' he smiled. 'The little man let us pat the elephants. He told us to come git you.'

The two Kims grabbed my hands and led me out into the maze of corridors as William continued his amiable chat. 'We ain't s'posed to mix with y'all, but I got 'sponsibilities to K1 and K2 here—they needs to learn about strange people and animals and such.'

'You look after them?'

'I'm like a big brother now they ain't got no one. On this ship, everyone lookin' after someone else. They is good kids so it ain't no hardship.'

'Why aren't you supposed to mix with the likes of us?'

'Well, you is customers 'n' cargo for starters. Secondly . . .' He grinned over his shoulder at me. 'Y'all are bad people, right?'

'Yeah, I suppose we is.'

'Plus y'all got some mean weapons. I just seen that boy you look after, and he was stripping down a real big gun. Funny-lookin' thing stuck on one of yo' tractors.'

'It's called a rail-gun. It's nasty alright.' I tried to sound casual. 'And was Tommy with anyone? Was someone teaching him like?'

'The angry man in the big coat and the big bald man with the high voice. They was explainin' to him.'

Rail-gun maintenance is one of my duties. Seems my student had more than one teacher now.

We climbed down the rusty stairs into the cargo hold. Between two of Splinter's metal trailers, a space had been made for Jumbo and El Grande, where Tog was spreading out more hay for them to lie on. While William and the Kims offered the elephants handfuls of fruit, I pulled Tog aside. 'So what's with the Gaffer and Tommy?'

'Thick as thieves, they are. You should've killed him already.'

'I got interrupted.'

'He scares the crap out of me.'

'He should. Where's Sparrow?'

'We got her in with Baba and the Nightingales. We figure it'll be safer there because you'll be running around teaching psycho-killer over there how to murder us all.'

'Sorry, mate,' I replied. 'I'll deal with this, I promise. I just need to check where Splinter stands, among other things.'

'I know where I stand.'

'Where's that, mate?'

'With you.'

I didn't know what to say. Tog was offering me loyalty what could get him killed.

I sighed. 'Mate, if you had two brain cells to rub together, you wouldn't stand nowhere near me.'

'There's more than me who wants better than what we got. If it comes to a fight—'

'If it comes to a fight,' I snapped, 'people will get killed.'

Tog smiled. 'You care about us then.'

'Feck off, you scheming little shit.' I sat on a bale of lucerne. 'I need to talk with Splinter, but I'm damned if I know what to say to him.'

'Just ask him to tell you what you want to know.'

'I want to know why the hell we're really going to this Bogda Shan place.'

'For the Convergence of Travellers. The Great Feat and to choose a new King.'

'We're travellers. What do we need a king for? What we need is a safe place to live and end all the killing and dodgy shite.'

Tog nodded. 'So ask him how we get that.'

I looked into his face. He was a young man, his head balanced on a body what was too small, but he stood like a warrior, looking at me with calm confidence.

'I'm only going to let you down, Tog. I in't strong enough. I in't got no say and no power to make things right.'

'You got a say like any of us. As for the rest, maybe there's strength in numbers.'

'What—"united we stand, divided we fall"? Blimey, you sound like Erik and Methuselah tryin' to teach me the wisdom of the feckin' ages.'

'Want to know what I think?'

'You're goin' to tell me anyway.'

'I think you should listen to Sparrow. She's special.'

His mug was full of emotion—love and determination and whatever else. My gut said he was right. I stood. 'First I need to talk with Splinter.'

'Ask him what's in them trailers of his we lug about what we're never allowed to look into. Maybe he's got stuff in there we can use.'

'We?'

'Us what wants better. Us what will fight.'

I could see nothing but bloodshed and death ahead but I nodded. 'Maybe I will.'

As I started to walk away, Tog couldn't help himself. 'After all, you got more than just yourself now you're a dad, Blanco.'

I give him a raised eyebrow, but the little prick just smiled at my feet.

I looked down and there was Daisy, her little face looking up at mine, one ear up, waiting for a word or a pat or a piece of food. I acted like I didn't care. 'Stay here,' I growled. 'I got business.'

I squeezed between Splinter's other trailers, stored with who knows what, and was about to knock when Doctor Po and the Professoré came out, wearing blood-stained aprons and carrying waterproof bags, heavy with something shapeless—wet and heavy, like meat. They were startled to see me.

'Is he up for visitors?' I asked.

The pair swapped a look. The Prof shrugged. 'He'll tell you otherwise if he wants.'

He pushed past, but Po hesitated. 'Be careful. Do only what he say and nothing else.'

I couldn't tell if Po was warning me because he cared or he just didn't want me making life difficult. I lifted a hand to knock but the door swung open. I walked up the steps and inside.

This time the stink was more chemical and medicinal, but I couldn't miss the slaughterhouse stench of blood. 'Is you up for visitors, Mister Splinter?'

His voice growled and gurgled like ball bearings in a drain. 'You have questions. Ask.'

I pushed toward the curtain, stopping just short to avoid looking at him. 'For one, I needs to know why you is letting the Gaffer groom Tommy. He's a full-blown psycho and he's dangerous. To all of us.'

'He is useful to me. So far you are not.'

'So why did you give Sparrow weapons to make sure I wasn't killed?'

'Next time I might not.'

I wasn't getting nowhere but I didn't know what to ask. 'Do we really have to go to this Bogda Shan place?'

'Yes. It is the highest priority.'

'Methuselah says it's in the middle of nowhere. Some remote desert where they used to blow up atomic bombs. Why there?'

'We go to attend the Convergence.'

'And watch me kill myself or not, and then someone gets named the next King. I understand that, sir, but I don't understand what it means. Who cares if someone's King? Afterward we'll all go our separate ways and probably never meet again.'

'To know yourself, you need to know where and to whom you belong.'

Nothing he said helped me understand anything. I sighed. 'With respect, no one belongs anywhere no more. Back in the old days, people had countries and they stayed put. We in't stopped moving since forever.'

'The concept of a nation will be meaningless to the new humans who come after us. They will be like the Rom—people of the world. We must make that our destiny.'

This was the first I'd heard this 'new humans' palaver. I wondered if he was right in the head so I just nodded. 'Right you are, Mister Splinter. But I'm still left wondering how to deal with Tommy now he's best friends with the Gaffer.'

'You must learn from him.'

'Could you be more specific, Mister Splinter? I mean, isn't he supposed to be learning all my tricks?'

'Are Methuselah and Erik teaching you?'

'They're doing their level best. Machiavelli and Sun Tzu mostly.'

'And can you not apply some of their wisdom to this situation?'

'I don't understand this situation. There's things happening I don't have the gist of. Sun Tzu says, "War is a road nations travel to reach safety or ruin", but we in't a nation. We're an army of sorts, but we in't got no place in the world.'

There was a brief silence. 'Good. Continue your studies. Think beyond your immediate needs. Make plans other than the ones in your head right now.'

I wondered if he knew what I was thinking, and I had a horrible feeling he did. I gave up trying to get anything out of him. 'Yes, Mister Splinter.'

'Go, and ensure, whatever else happens, that we reach the mountains of Central Asia. There you will find *your* destiny.'

'Yes, Mister Splinter.' I turned and went back to the door. I stopped. 'About my mother . . .'

'She was an incubator. Nothing more. Forget her. Now go.'

I went to Baba Yaga's trailer, where Sparrow was sitting up in bed, brushing the Nightingales' hair. I told her and Baba what Splinter told me. Baba said nothing, but she wasn't happy. Sparrow thought and then smiled. 'What he told you wasn't what he told you.'

'Now you're sounding like bleeding Machiavelli,' I growled. 'Splinter din't tell me nothing.'

'He told you there's more to learn, stuff what he in't ready to tell you. And if he won't, you need to find out.'

I give her a sour look. 'So I need to find out stuff what no one will tell me, about stuff I don't know nothing about yet, while making sure Tommy don't kill no one, and the Gaffer don't do me, while doing me level best to get to the middle of a desert for reasons I in't been appraised of yet.'

'Exactly. You have to work for it, not wait for someone to tell you.'

I turned to Baba. 'When we get to Europe, we're all jumping ship and doing a runner.'

'No we aren't,' said Sparrow. 'I'm not.'

'You want to stay in this mad outfit and be killed?'

'I want to stay with my real family. So you have to as well.'

'No I bleedin' don't,' I bluffed.

'Yes you do. You promised to love me forever and follow me to heaven or hell.'

I felt the blood rush to my cheeks—I never told no one the L-word before.

She enjoyed my discomfort. 'What? You can only tell me you love me when I'm in a coma?'

'I was just saying that because I was dead on my feet and . . . Baba said to say nice things. I l-like you—that's all.'

'You l-love me,' she grinned.

'How can I when I don't know what love is?'

'This thing in here . . .' she tapped my chest. 'Will explain everything. Listen to it. And mine says I "l-like" you too.'

Normally I don't like people mocking me, but the hopeful part of me was wagging its tail like Daisy just before she's fed. Sparrow certainty filled me with courage to fight.

'I suppose you want me to kiss you,' I sighed.

'Yes, you miserable sod.' But she give me a kiss, so that cheered me up.

Baba Yaga's lengthy belch, and her bored look as one of her fat fingers explored the inside of one nostril, somewhat spoiled the romantic ambience. 'You is both such children,' she sighed.

'Fine,' I replied. 'So what's our next move, Baba?'

'You are leader. Make choice.'

'Sparrow nearly died, and we need more information. But I got no idea what.'

Sparrow looked smug. 'I know where we should start looking.'

140

Chapter Twenty-Six—The opportunity of a lifetime is seldom labelled

That night, when most everyone was asleep, the *Lav Noyemba* was sailing north-east toward the desolate moonlit flatlands through which the Bornhalt canal ran, a shortcut to the Baltic Sea.

Meanwhile, in the musty, rusty dark of the cargo hold, Sparrow and me were quietly attempting to shove poor Tog through the back of a maintenance hatch into one of Splinter's heavily locked trailers.

'Oi—careful, you bleeders,' he hissed.

"'If you know the enemy and know yourself,'" I whispered encouragingly, "'you need not fear the result of a hundred battles. If you know neither yourself nor the enemy, you will be defeated.'"

The whispered response from Tog was a stream of foul language. Sparrow thumped me on the arm. 'Shut it, you idiot.'

I shrugged. 'If I don't get this Sun Tzu geezer memorised, Methuselah and Erik will cop it from Splinter.' I peered into the hatch, where Tog was struggling to unbolt an internal plate behind some cables and plumbing. 'Any luck?'

'Having you for a friend? Ha!'

'Think you can squeeze through?'

'Did it ever occur to you that my head is the same size as yours?'

'Point taken. Tell us when you want us to push.'

Seeing as we had time to kill, Sparrow kissed me and I kissed back. This went on for a while until Tog's legs started squirming for traction. I grabbed his boots. 'Oi, careful. I'll push, alright?'

'Slowly.'

With us pushing the soles of his boots, and Tog squirming like a trapped rat, he finally disappeared into the trailer. We could only see flickers of his torchlight as he looked around inside. I thought I heard him swear but when I called out, he didn't reply.

We didn't hear nothing for ages and we were well worried when, finally, there was another flicker of light through the cables and pipes. I sighed with relief as Tog came back through headfirst, which was awkward because the only thing we had to pull on was his head, a manoeuvre which, as it turned out, wasn't popular with Tog.

Finally, we got him out. As I carefully reattached the hatch cover, Tog showed us his booty—a long grey coat and a slim pair of glasses with a crystalline frame. 'These looked interesting so I half-inched 'em'.

'What's in the trailer?' I asked.

'An AIPO power plant and storage.'

Sparrow cocked her head. 'Aipo?'

'Anything In, Power Out,' Tog replied in a whisper. 'The power plant is at one end. The rest is all metal cabinets full of oldtech. In the middle there's an operating table. It must be where Po and the Professoré do their thing.'

I finished with the hatch, and we shone the torches on the glasses and the coat, which was made of thin material and had a hood attached. The hood even had a flap of grey gauze that covered the face.

Sparrow shuddered. 'Creepy.'

I looked at the glasses. They were oddly heavy, the clear frames shot through with incredibly fine gold threads. The lenses were also threaded in a complex pattern, but were otherwise see-through. I shrugged and handed them back to Tog. 'Dunno about these, mate.'

Tog looked dismayed. 'I thought they might be tech. Maybe they'll turn into sunglasses when it's daytime.'

He tucked them in his pocket, then we crept to Baba's trailer.

As we entered, Daisy jumped up from where she'd been waiting and give us a relieved sniffing. Baba wasn't so happy. 'Why you risk life for this?'

'When you don't know what to do, gather information,' I replied. 'When you don't know what to do with it, let sleep be the mother of counsel.'

Baba Yaga scoffed. 'You are Russian wise woman now?'

'Everything I know, Baba, I learned from you.'

Tog yelped, and we turned to see him pulling the glasses off. 'I put 'em on and they went black, then give me a pain.' He rubbed his temples. 'Right across here. They is lectric or something.'

'Let's have a look.' I reached across Daisy, who was climbing into my lap to have a sleep. Tog handed them over, frowning. 'It come off a rack full of them. I thought no one would notice if one pair was pinched.'

The lenses were still darkened but fading slowly to clear.

'Oldtech,' said Sparrow, stroking Daisy. 'Proper stuff.'

I wasn't in no hurry to put them on. I showed them to Baba. 'Ever seen anything like these?'

'Is probably heads-up display. For military.'

Tog was still rubbing his head. 'So why did it give me a headache?'

'It tried to connect you,' she replied.

'Connect him with what?' asked Sparrow.

'Network.'

'But there is no networks. What did they call it? The Net?'

'The big Net finish long time,' Baba agreed. 'But maybe not secret underground nets. Or the military ones.'

'Some of them might still be alive?'

'Only one way find out,' Baba replied. 'You must wear until you connect.'

Tog tiredly wrapped the grey overcoat around his shoulders and curled up to rest. 'Not me. I'm not touching it again, ever.'

Sparrow reached out. 'I'll try.'

'Not likely.' I held the glasses back. 'I don't want you doing nothing that might hurt you, especially in the brain.' I turned to Baba. 'Do you know how these things work?'

'Heads-up display is just computer screen, but if it connect straight to the brain, I don't know. Is more complicate, you need training even.'

'I could try it just for a minute,' I said, trying to sound confident.

'One other problem,' added Baba. 'If you connect to machine, is okay. But if machine is connect to someone else, then someone else know who you are and where you is.'

'Like who?'

Tog looked out from under the grey hood, grim. 'Splinter?'

'Or maybe worse,' Baba nodded. 'Who knows?'

This idea didn't fill me with joy. 'So what else was in that trailer apart from some glasses, coats and an AIPO?'

Tog shoved his hands in the coat pockets and shrugged. 'It was hard to tell, but it was all oldtech. Maybe when Splinter hooks his trailer to it he's getting a recharge to keep himself alive.'

'Or it powers the connection to whatever network them glasses belongs to,' Sparrow mused.

'Plus power for the tricks he uses when things get aggro—the heat weapon and the one what does that blue light. He could have any number of nasties with power on tap, right?'

No one answered. Baba and Sparrow were looking stunned, and past me to where Tog was—or had been. Tog's face floated in thin air. I jumped in fright. 'Tog! Is you alright?'

Tog was startled. 'Yeah, why?'

'You is sort've not there, mate. It's just your head, floating.'

Tog scowled. 'Don't be daft.'

Sparrow reached out, and I could see she was feeling something. 'It's that coat. It's turned him invisible.'

Tog looked worried. 'I'm still here, you idiots.'

'Not entirely, mate. I think you should take that coat off, pronto.'

Tog wriggled out of the coat and reappeared, limb by limb, confused by our worried looks. 'What you lot on about . . .'

Finally, he was visible again, and the material reappeared in a crumpled pile beside him. I reached out and examined the coat. Inside a pocket was a hard disk with indentations around the outer edge. When

I held a finger on one of them, the material became half transparent. When I moved my finger to the next indentation, the coat disappeared altogether.

I took my hand out and, as the coat slowly reappeared, I smiled. 'This could definitely come in handy.' It decided me. I picked up the glasses. 'I'm giving these a go.'

Sparrow was firm. 'If you so much as frown, I'm ripping them things off you.'

I put the glasses on, sliding the heavy arms over my ears. I felt warmth coming out of them, then a sharp pain as they moulded themselves to my head. I must've flinched because Sparrow reached toward me.

I leaned away. 'It's okay. It's nothing. I can handle a wee headache.' The glass turned black, and I couldn't see anything.

Then I connected.

Chapter Twenty-Seven—
The dog that digs deepest
finds the bones

A soft voice spoke. *Security clearance pending.*

I turned around, startled. 'Who said that?'

'Is you alright, Blanco?' asked Sparrow.

'I heard a voice.' Then the darkness began to fill with a yellow wire frame of the trailer we were in, and beyond that the framed shapes of the trucks, trailers and tractors of the cargo hold, then the ship itself.

I heard the voice again. *Which functions do you require?*

'I d-dunno,' I stammered. 'What you got?'

Low-level civilian functions are available to you. These include place, personnel, weather and immediate security.

'Give me 'immediate security'.'

I heard Sparrow. 'Who are you talking to?'

I put a finger to my lips, alert. 'Shhh . . .'

As I looked into this black 3D world, the yellow wire frames now turned blue, but inside them, scattered throughout, the red outlines of every weapon on board the ship began to glow, one after another. Most were still, but some were slowly moving throughout the ship. Splinter's trailer and the one next to it were almost solid red. 'Bloody hell,' I whispered.

'What's goin' on?' asked Tog.

'I can see every weapon on the ship,' I replied, turning my head. 'Where they are and . . .' I focused on one of them and it zoomed toward me, revealing a label—the weapon was a medium-range Kolokol-1220-deliriant dispersal delivery device. Whatever the hell that was.

Security clearance pending.

I felt my head ache like a tight band was cinching up on it. 'Who am I talking to?'

Unidentified civilians.

'I meant who are *you?*'

Security clearance pending.

The glasses frame resting above my ear was heating up, and I felt strange, my heart racing.

Identification sequence initialised.

I was torn between pulling the glasses off and asking more questions. 'How long does identification take?'

Eighty-two seconds and counting down.

'Can you tell me about where we're going—the Bogda Shan?'

The Bogda Shan is a mountain range at the easternmost end of the Tian Shan, stretching east–west in the former Chinese Republic, in the former province of Xinjiang, fifty kilometres to the east of the nearest city, Ürümqi. The highest massif is located at latitude forty-three degrees, forty-seven point seven minutes north, longitude eighty-eight degrees, nineteen point five minutes east. Currently disputed territory.

'I wish you could show me a map or picture or whatever.'

Suddenly my vision switched, and it was like I was up in the air, looking down. I yelped, my stomach heaving, thinking I was falling. As my panic subsided, I realised it was a landscape incredibly far below me—a huge area, the colours all drab browns and streaks of pale yellow ochre, white dots of clouds strung out in rough lines above it, their shadows grey dots on the earth below. In the middle was a patch of bright green, and in the middle of that, mountains capped with snow.

'Any people living down there?'

Yes. Security clearance pending.

'What else can you tell me?'

Make your question more specific. Identification sequence pending.

'Can anyone else on this network see me? Do they know who I am and where I is?'

They will shortly. Identification sequence pending. Ten, nine, eight, se—

I wrenched the glasses off, disoriented and frightened. The others were all looking at me like I was a ghost. I felt the spot above my ear and pulled my hand away, fingers smeared with blood.

'What did it do to you?' asked Tog.

'I dunno, but I think it was just about to tell someone about me.'

'Splinter?'

'Who knows? Maybe it's just an oldtech machine what don't connect to no one no more.' I patted Daisy, comforting myself more than her. '"If the enemy is in superior strength, evade him",' I quoted.

Sparrow was frustrated. 'What enemy are we talking about?'

'I don't know. Splinter in't saying, but there's something or someone in the mountains we're going to what matters to him more than any "Great Feat" bollocks.'

'Splinter not kill you yet,' said Baba. 'So maybe ask him and he tell.'

'Or he gets fed up and kills me,' I replied. 'If I knew how to fight him, I'd take the chance.'

Tog frowned. 'You can't fight Splinter. He's got all the weapons and all the information.'

Sparrow held up the glasses. 'And now we got a way to get some of that information.'

I frowned. 'Which we keep secret. I don't want anyone on that network knowing. As my main geezer Sun Tzu would say, "Military devices, leading to victory, must not be divulged beforehand."'

Baba Yaga sighed. 'I do not like the war talk. Mans always want war.'

'It in't war really,' I replied. 'It's about protecting people.'

She wasn't convinced. 'War is war, but I am on your side.'

'Great. An army of five, if we include Daisy—seven with Jumbo and El Grande—fighting an unknown enemy, without weapons. How can we lose?'

Tog went off to sleep with Jumbo and El Grande while I hid the coat and glasses behind an insulation panel. Then we all fell asleep where we lay.

In the morning, we went up on deck to see why we were stopped. Our ship was queued behind three others waiting to get into the Bornhalt canal. Drones from the Besdorf military airstrip a few kilometres away were circling, the German operators checking our bona fides from the air while uniformed troops, covered in crisp white biohazard kit, came on board to collect our transit fees and look for diseases they'd prefer not to catch.

Finally, some other ships emerged from the canal and we were cleared to file into it. As the *Lav Noyemba* slid between the banks a few metres to either side, us circus types ate breakfast by the rail and looked across a low white landscape flattened and ravaged by storm surges, all of it preserved in glittering crusted salt. The occasional bones of crumbling farmhouses and ancient cattle stuck up, sparkling with refracted sunlight, everything dead and still.

'Is pretty,' said Baba, soulfully chewing a potato. 'Like snow.'

'I'd love to see snow one day,' I mused.

Then Tommy, apparently bored with casual conversation, drifted away, and I turned to check it was just us freaks remaining. 'Right, who knows anything about these mysterious mountains we're going to? Why are we meeting there and not someplace a bit more convenient?'

Methuselah cleared his throat. 'The Silk Route links the east with the west.'

This wasn't helping. 'So, this godforsaken bit of nowhere has a road from China to Europe plus a bunch of mountains. Why else would anyone go there?'

'Many peoples lived there,' Methuselah replied. 'Though the Han Chinese were using the Turfan Depression to the south of the Tien Shan for nuclear-bomb-testing and mining, the remoteness of the North-West suited their secret bases, particularly during the Great Corporate Realignment of the twenty-thirties. Perhaps that's why the

Confederation is meeting there—for privacy.'

Sparrow was watching the Steering Committee, who were talking with Tommy and looking aggravated. The Professoré looked anxious, and Po was especially emphatic about something.

'Where's Doctor Po originally from?' I asked.

'He won't say,' said Erik. 'But his Mandarin has a southern inflection, and he's educated.'

Baba snorted. 'He is fake doctor, fake chemist, fake everything. He knows more than all of us.'

'I mean he's more educated than his broken English would indicate,' Erik replied.

Tog frowned. 'Why would he hide how educated he is?'

'And why would someone with his skills attach himself to a circus?' asked Methuselah.

'To hide.' I mused. 'And what about the Professoré? Anyone know his background?'

'I know one thing,' said Tog. 'Po and the Prof are the only ones who go into Splinter's trailer and deal with him face to face.' Tog raised an eyebrow. 'And now you, his golden boy.'

'Yeah, golden dead boy, mate,' I muttered. 'Splinter is making sure Tommy is groomed as my replacement. But, good point—Po and the Prof do whatever needs doing to keep Splinter alive. He trusts them even more than he does the Gaffer, so maybe they know what the real story is.'

Sparrow nodded. 'Perhaps Splinter, Po and the Prof is all hiding for the same reason.'

'Yeah, but hiding from who?' asked Tog.

'Or what.' I give Tog and Sparrow a look, wondering if we should share our discovery of last night. 'We still don't know how Splinter stays in contact with all the other travellers, and why they should all go so far out of their way to meet up.'

The others looked over my shoulder, and I turned as the Gaffer and Strombo pounced on me, Milosh behind them looking like he wanted a piece of me.

'None of us is surprised, you little shit,' growled the Gaffer. 'Hold him.'

Strombo got a big hand around my throat, and backed me to the ship's rail.

'Oi—what's the beef?' I croaked, confused.

'We find out about your plans for honeymoon,' said Milosh through gritted teeth. He held up the bag I keep my clean smalls in, and opened it so all could see it was stuffed with money and assorted small items of gold and jewellery. 'Your honeymoon could last long time on this.'

Mala stepped forward, torn between anger and sadness. 'I would never believe this of you, Blanco. I never think you are thief.'

'I dunno whose loot that is, but it in't mine,' I said, struggling on tiptoes to avoid being choked.

'*We* know,' said the Gaffer. 'All this belongs to us. It was lucky Tommy noticed what was goin' on.'

I looked and there was Tommy at the back, looking convincingly crestfallen. 'I'm sorry, Blanco—I just asked Milosh why you and Sparrow were cleaning his trailer when that was Kongo's job.'

'You little snot . . .' I winced as Strombo squeezed.

'Her too,' the Gaffer pointed to Sparrow, and Mala put a blade across her throat.

'Don't hurt her,' I begged. 'She don't know nothing about anything.'

'Too late,' replied the Gaffer. 'We know you been planning to jump ship as soon as we reached Europe.' He smiled an evil smile. 'And after a brief discussion, we're going to help you do it.'

'Someone tell Splinter,' I managed to croak. 'Tell him I been set up.'

Madam Tracey was looking uncertain about all of this. 'I still say we need to hear him out proper.' The Professoré and Doctor Po nodded, looking sick. 'Listen and forgive,' said Po.

'No,' snarled the Gaffer. 'Blanco was ready to do a runner. Case bleedin' closed.'

Baba and Tog stepped forward to pull Strombo off me, but the Gaffer pulled out a pistol. 'Don't none of you fuckers move. A crime's been committed, and we all know how thieving is punished.' Enjoying himself, he looked out across the sparkling white wasteland. 'Beautiful day for a stroll.'

The ship's crew gathered, troubled by the ruckus, and through them came Captain Goyan, trailed by a worried-looking William H. and the two Kims.

'No killing on my ship. Is rule,' said Goyan.

The Gaffer was unfazed. 'No problem, captain. We'll just require you to assist us in putting these two miscreants onto dry land.' He waved casually at the glittering white. 'Anywhere here will do.'

'There are no people or towns in this land. They will die out there.'

'Not my concern. These two either get put on land or Strombo drops them over the side.'

'If Blanco say he don't do this, he don't do it,' said Baba, ignoring the Gaffer's pistol. 'I not let you kill them.' But as she moved toward the Gaffer, he pointed his gun and shot her.

We were stunned, and Sparrow let out a scream of fright and rage. 'No!'

Baba stood, shocked, feeling through the layers of clothing for a wound.

'No more!' I yelled. 'We'll go, alright? No more aggravation—we'll go quiet.'

'You shot me,' mused Baba, looking shaky.

'The next bullet will be through your head, Baba,' growled the Gaffer. 'And that goes for anyone else what disagrees with me.' He turned to the captain. 'That loading crane you got. Put these two in the net and drop them out there. Then we're done.'

Captain Goyan wasn't happy. 'You should talk to me first. This is my ship and my rules.'

'Thieving breaks our rules and I bet it breaks yours,' the Gaffer replied. 'We either sling them over there or drop them overboard—up to you which.'

Shaking his head, Captain Goyan pushed away through the onlookers. 'I get crane ready.'

No one noticed Tog slip away, nor Farshad and Barrelmouth.

Tommy looked tentative as he spoke up. 'Gaffer, could we forgive him this once, please?'

'Not on your bleedin' nelly. He wants out, we'll give him out.'

'But I've only just begun my training.'

'And now you've got all his books and tricks and whatever. You'll learn like what he did.'

Tommy shrugged, looking stricken—like he'd tried and failed.

I give the lying little shit a look, and he knew I knew.

Next thing, me and Sparrow were bundled into the loading sling, hoisted up and swung out over the side. The ship was still moving as we looked down at the white ground skimming beneath us. Suddenly the ropes holding the net shut were released, and we dropped like rocks, hit the ground, had the breath knocked out of us, and rolled until we hit some buried timbers.

I turned to Sparrow. She was still gasping for air but already looking toward the ship, the faces of the freaks and riggers at the rail mournful. Then we saw Barrelmouth, right at the back, hurl a small bundle over the rail and onto the salt. Tog passed him a second bundle, and that too got tossed across.

As we stood, bruised, shocked and covered in salt, we watched the *Lav Noyemba* sail away down a canal that stretched to the distant flat white horizon.

We were officially fucked.

Chapter Twenty-Eight—
Confusion comes before
enlightenment

I wiped salt from my face and checked Sparrow. 'You alright? Nothing broken?'

She brushed herself down, wincing. 'I don't think so.'

We hugged, scared as little kids, trying to give each other comfort. Then we looked around, squinting across three-sixty degrees of blinding white, interrupted only by the blue-grey water of the canal. I grimaced. 'Welcome to fucking Europe.'

Sparrow acted brave. 'So, which way?' she asked.

'First let's see what's in them bundles the lads tossed us.' Inside the first was a bag each of cooked rice and beans, and a full leather water bottle. In the other were the cloak and glasses from last night, plus two graf rain ponchos and a thin blanket I recognised as Tog's bedding.

'I hope they don't get into trouble for this.'

Sparrow was seething. 'The Gaffer was well out of order shooting Baba.'

'It'd take a hundred bullets to do her any real damage. Doctor Po will fix her up.'

Sparrow nodded, but we both knew this was hope talking.

'So . . . what now?' she said.

I looked back the way we came. 'We either try and get ourselves back to merry England or follow the psychopaths who would most definitely kill us if we ever showed up again.'

Sparrow pointed toward the *Lav Noyemba*, still visible in the distance. 'I in't stopping 'til I make sure Baba, Daisy and the freaks is okay—and that little shit Tommy is put somewhere he can't hurt no one.'

'How about in the same grave we put the Gaffer?'

'As long as there's room for Strombo.'

It was all just a bunch of palaver, but it made me love Sparrow even more. Without her being with me in this awful place, I'd just as soon cut my own throat and be done with it.

To block the searing glare from the salt, I cut ribbons of blanket to tie across our eyes with slits to see through. We ended up looking like bandits, but at least we weren't going blind. We set off.

The salt layer was just a crust over boggy mud. Sometimes it held our weight, sometimes it didn't. It was exhausting to put one foot in front of the other, never knowing when we'd step through up to our knees in warm stinking brine. Closest to the canal edge was firmest, but we still had to navigate around the occasional rusted remains of long-abandoned machinery or old sheds.

After a few hours, we were thirsty, hungry, filthy and tired. With the sun dropping behind us, our long thin shadows staggering east in front of us, we veered toward a pyramid of broken timbers, hoping for shelter. It was the half-buried remains of an old farmhouse, one end collapsed into the salt, the other still upright. I crawled in through a window to find a roomy space with a floor of sand and salt—cave-like ruins of the original ground-floor kitchen. Scattered about were some aluminium pots, a few corroded forks and spoons, and a stack of old newspapers and magazines preserved in the dry salty air.

As daylight faded, and the heat ebbed, we collected wood and kindling, then I used my flint to get a fire going to heat our beans and rice.

'I hope Daisy's alright,' I murmured.

Sparrow slung a comforting arm over my shoulder. 'Tog will look after her. Chances are she'll be fast asleep on someone's lap, on her back with all her bits showing,.'

I wasn't comforted. 'What do we do, Sparrow? How do we make it right for us and the others?'

'I dunno, but I know what Baba would say.'

'"Let sleep be the mother of counsel."'

Tired, bruised and sore, we ate, staring into the fire.

Sparrow indicated the walls, lined with piles of old newspapers. 'We can use that for bedding.'

I slid one of the papers out for a look. 'Blimey, this is thirty years old.'

Sparrow read out a headline. *'Uitroeiing Van de "Erlik" Ziekte Mislukt.'*

'That's Dutch, innit?'

'My Dutch isn't great, but this article's about some disease spreading.'

I looked at a picture below it, showing a happy family in a room. 'What's an "air conditioner"?'

'We had them in the compound I grew up in. They is oldtech machines what blows cold air on you when you is hot, and hot air when you is cold. Lectrical.'

I looked at an advert featuring a serious-looking geezer. 'What are "AI mods"?'

'Augmented intelligence—they stick things in your brain so you can see, smell, and think better.'

'I could use some of that.'

'Trust me—being smarter don't necessarily make you act smarter.'

'Doesn't more brains mean more sense?'

'Nah. People got them brain-booster things all the time at the compound I was in. They could count numbers quicker, speak a dozen languages, shoot guns straighter—but they wasn't no kinder or nicer for it. Them Russky Bratva bosses was huge into it, trying to outsmart each other in deals and whatnot. They was still nasty people.'

'I wonder if that's what Mister Splinter's got in him.'

'Whatever he had done, he was trying to do more than just get smart.'

Sparrow noticed a picture on another front page, dismayed. 'Ai ya . . .'

The picture showed people, tens of thousands of them, walking across a plain carrying their belongings. Many were looking behind them, where a huge cloud of dust stretched from horizon to horizon, a great wall catching them up.

I read the name of the place. 'Where's Philadelphia?'

'Canada, I think. Or the Christian Republics.' She pulled out another newspaper, scanning the headline. 'I remember my parents talking about the Decade of the Great Storms.'

'Bigger than normal hurricanes?'

'Much. The worst was when a whole bunch of them formed, linked up, then took off through the Philippines up the coast of China all the way to Beijing. When the big dams all broke, that was it for China. The Bratva running our compound thought it was God's payback for all the Russian firestorms.'

'Wasn't Russia and China competing empires or some such?'

'Who knows—everyone was competing with everyone back then.'

I was intrigued by a picture of a Chinese geezer standing in front of a modified flag. 'Recognise this?' Beside the Chinese stars were a half-dozen symbols, one of which was three linked infinity signs. 'In't that the same as Po's tattoo? The one on his wrist?'

Sparrow slowly translated the text underneath. 'Premier Doctor Jian Hu commends his people to the Intermediate Alignment, in which all remaining Chinese peoples will adhere to the plan drawn up in advance of catastrophic climate events. "It is the duty," he says, "of all surviving citizens to follow orders laid down by the Central Committee, in order to weather the Time of Change, and prepare for the Final Alignment."' Sparrow looked up. 'No idea what that's about, but it's definitely Po's tattoo.'

'Perhaps each symbol is a branch of the government.'

'Could be—governments back then was big. They had millions of soldiers, and whole armies of teachers, nurses and doctors.'

'Maybe Po was working in a hospital.'

'Maybe, but this other one is the medical sign—see?' She pointed to a symbol of two snakes coiled upright around a stick.

I leaned back, tired. 'Methuselah would know.'

Sparrow rummaged around. 'Maybe them glasses can tell us.'

'They won't work out here in the middle of nowhere.'

Sparrow pulled them out and shoved them at me. 'Give it a try.'

I put them on, wary, wincing as a sharp pain shot through my forehead. My vision blacked out and I heard that voice.

Security sequence pending.

'Oi, don't bother with this security clearance palaver, alright?' I felt the earpiece warm up as it moulded itself to my head. 'And don't do none of that identity sequence stuff neither.'

What service do you require?

'How much power have you got left?'

This device has eighteen hours and fifty-eight minutes of low-level functioning power, ten hours and sixteen minutes of high-level functioning. Our geographical location is . . .

'Don't bother with that. We know we're up to our necks in it. Can you make these glasses transparent again?'

The glasses cleared.

It felt better to look at Sparrow, who could only hear my side of the conversation. 'Thank you. Now, can you see stuff what I see? If I ask you what this symbol means, could you tell us?'

Yes.

I tapped the triple-infinity sign. 'So what's this one mean?'

It is the former Chinese government symbol designated to represent the People's Research Academy.

'What sort of research?'

All levels of research were undertaken, in every area of science.

'Tell me what Doctor Po was doing when he was working with them.'

Security sequence pending.

'Damn it—no. Stop security sequence. Just tell me what you can about Doctor Po. What was his specialty? Surgery, medicine—what?'

Doctor Po's specialty is combinatorics and magnetic field theory.

I was boggled. 'Is you saying Po's not a medical doctor?'

Correct. He is a mathematician.

'What else can you tell us about him?'

The rewards for his capture, in those nations still extant, exceed two hundred megalitres of water.

'Is you saying he is a wanted criminal?'

Correct.

'Just who or what am I talking to now?'

Security clearance—

'Stop.' I gingerly slid the glasses off. 'Did you get all that? Po's a math wizard, not a doctor.'

'Our Po's an international man of mystery,' she yawned. 'Come on— let's make a bed and get some kip. We got some big walking to do in the morning.'

I finally fell into a fitful doze, cuddling Sparrow. Even in the thick of misery and worry, just knowing she was there consoled me.

Chapter Twenty-Nine—
Trouble can be relied on

S leep was a rare visitor that night.

I was plagued with fears I didn't want to share with Sparrow. We were also plagued with a lumpy floor. One of the lumps was hard and rounded. As dawn broke, and we packed our meagre belongings into makeshift carry bags, I tapped the lump, intrigued by its smooth edge. It felt like polished metal but had a woven cloth pattern to it.

When Sparrow went outside for a wee, I dug away some of the sand. The board was flat but curved on all sides, and there was a pole with a sheet of clear graf sticking out of the middle on one side. Attached to that, another padded curving pole hinged to it. I couldn't make sense of it.

Sparrow peered in the window. 'Oi, let's get moving.'

'Ever seen one of these?'

'Ironing board?'

'What's this big pole sticking out of it for? And all this stuff?' I ruffled the sheet of clear graf attached to the pole.

She entered to collect her things. 'Ask the glasses then let's go.'

I slipped the glasses on, winced as it clamped itself to my head, then heard the familiar voice. *Security—*

'No security. What's this thing I'm looking at?'

A sailboard.

'What's it used for?'

Recreational use. The board floats, the user stands on it and lifts the sail upright, the wind draws the board forward.

I dug away more sand from underneath, revealing a strut with what looked like wings on it. 'What's this thing coming out of the bottom?'

That is a hydrofoil.

'What's a hydrofoil?'

A device or addition to a water-based transportation vessel that enables the vessel to gain forward speed, eventually lifting the hull or lower surface of the vessel above the water, thereby achieving greater speeds.

I was getting excited. 'How fast can these things go?'

High speed for this kind of device is forty knots or faster.

'I in't no sailor. How fast is that in kilometres an hour?'

Eighty kilometres per hour or faster.

'How fast is the *Lav Noyemba* goin'?'

Average speed in fair conditions is between six and twelve knots.

I looked at Sparrow, raising my eyebrows.

She give me a look. 'Bollocks—how is the two of us going to fit on an ironing board, let alone learn how to sail the bleedin' thing?'

'My specs will teach us. How hard can it be?'

With the specs on, I was shown a video of how to work the sailboard. I imitated the movements as best I could, but it was one of them skills where your body, not your brain, has to do the learning—and that took time.

And that's how I spent the next miserable sweaty hour in the canal—either clambering onto the board, or standing briefly before the wind caught the sail and pulled me off. Swearing like a drunk in a fistfight, I was barely matching Sparrow's walking pace as she trudged along the crumbling canal edge.

The sun rose, along with the temperature. I kept my skin covered as the heat began to burn, but eventually got the sailboard to move and stay upright. Which felt good in the same way it feels good to stop hitting your head against a wall. I finally persuaded Sparrow to join me and, with her standing beside me holding on to the boom, our belongings tied to us, we were united again—not that she was what you'd call enthusiastic. Like me, she was half-thrilled, half-terrified. 'Dying of thirst or drowning on this thing—I'm still in two minds.'

'Just think of Daisy,' I replied. 'That cute little face is, right now, looking up at Tog or Baba asking when Mummy and Daddy are coming home.'

She gave in to the inevitable. 'Okay, you're captain—what do I do?'

'Simple. Do exactly what I do, when I do it. Easy.'

Ten minutes later, back in the water for the twentieth time, we were barneying like an old married couple. I finally interrupted her colourful line of abuse. 'Sparrow, please—give it one more shot, alright? If it don't work then, we'll go back to walking.'

'Good, then we can dry out and I can swear at you *without* me lungs full of water.'

I pulled myself back onto the board and helped her up beside me. 'This time, you stand in front of me holding the bar, I'm behind steering, and you can feel which way I'm moving this thing. Two bodies, one mind, alright?'

She give me lip, but we managed to get the sail up again, and finally got some forward movement. Snuggled together, working as one, it started to feel good, and we picked up speed. The wind cooled us down and began drying us off as we sailed even faster.

It was already pretty exciting, when there was a gust of wind, we sped up and the whole caper lifted a half-metre into the air. We both yelped, but I managed to keep us upright as I realised we were now fast enough to be up on the hydrofoil. Our terrified yelps turned into terrified whoops as we flew up that canal like we were strapped to a rocket . . .

. . . which is when we saw a ship approaching head-on, with only tiny gaps on either side between it and the canal edge—two metres maximum. We were going so fast that it was all I could do to aim us into the gap on the left, both of us bellowing like maniacs as we roared between the ship's hull to our right and the white salt bank on our left. It was all just a blur as we reached the back of the ship and burst out into the open channel, wide-eyed and gasping.

The close call made us cocky, which is why, twenty minutes later, we flew through the eastern end of the canal waving at the German guards, who seemed too surprised to work out whether they should chase us for a transit fee or applaud. Then we were out of the canal and into a wide blue shallow sea, dotted with dozens of tiny low-lying islands. On them, crumbling skeletons of farms, churches and entire villages showed how the land had been flooded and smashed by Atlantic hurricanes. The glasses showed me vids of this place from before—lush green pasture, cows, and fields of waving corn.

The water was choppier, but not so bad we couldn't keep up a hammering speed. We flew, suspended on air, over a flat blue world, steering between islands, heading toward open sea on the horizon.

'Which way?' Sparrow shouted.

'Oi, glasses—which way to catch up with the *Lav Noyemba*?'

North-east, to the entrance of the Bredning Channel.

I pointed for Sparrow's benefit. 'Through there. On the way we'll look for a port or someplace we can get food and water.'

My vision flickered, and suddenly everything was labelled—the coastlines ahead and around us, the larger islands, names of villages, and even an arrow pointing in the direction we needed to go. I was really starting to like this bit of tech.

Sparrow was tiring though. 'How long can we keep this up?'

'A couple of hours maybe. Lean against me, darlin'—I'll take your weight for a while.'

Sparrow nestled against me, and it felt like we were in bed, all curled up nice and tight. I felt proud and strong that here I was, with a girl what liked me. It was a new experience to feel pride. I was protecting the girl I liked, and we were on our way to make everything r—

Security sequence completed.

'Damn it—I forgot to tell these glasses not to check me out.'

Identification sequence complete.

'Stop it, no—'

163

You are recognised. Welcome to the Pool, Operative Zeta. You are now connected with alpha level . . .

'Wait—stop. Stop everything.'

The labels and arrow disappeared.

Sparrow looked over her shoulder up at me mug. 'What's going on?'

'I dunno. It called me a name. It called me—'

My right forearm started burning. 'Shit!' I kept my grip on the boom, just, but I could see the skin on the inside of my forearm reddening in a triangular patch. 'What the f . . .?'

Sparrow looked down and saw what I was looking at. 'I think we should stop.'

And stop we bleeding did.

Because I wasn't looking where we was going, the hydrofoil ploughed into a submerged sandbank, and suddenly we were flying through the air. We hit the water at an acute angle, bounced then sunk. I was never taught proper swimming so I thrashed my way to the surface in time to feel the glasses come off me and disappear into the green-blue beneath us.

'You alright?' Sparrow was staying afloat with ease.

'I'm okay. I lost them glasses though.' I looked around, paddling like a dog, getting my bearings.

She pointed me to where the sailboard now drifted ten metres away. 'There's the board.'

We started swimming toward it but, just as we started to close the gap and feel hopeful, a shadow came over us.

'Hallo, weinig vis!'

Above us, a small fishing boat loomed, several sturdy lads with beards studying us with interest.

They reached down and we were obliged to get hauled onto the deck of the boat, which was barely five metres long. With the four crew and a dozen full crab pots, plus the two of us and a small wheelhouse, there wasn't much room to spare. I coughed up some salt water and addressed the one with the skipper's hat and the biggest beard. *'Spreek je Engels?'*

'Ja. We speak the English like easy, better than most Englishers. And we are German, not Dutch.' He pointed toward land. 'We are from Stafstedt.'

'Thanks for rescuing us.'

'Ja. Is no problem. How much the ransom you think we can get for you?'

'Ransom?'

'Ja, we are pirates.' He indicated the others, who growled in good-humoured pirate fashion, beaming.

'You don't look like pirates, if you don't mind me saying.'

Big Beard wasn't offended. 'We are, so it's ransom or we cut you up for the crab pots. Your choice.'

I sighed. 'Bollocks.'

Big Beard looked at my arm. 'Nice tattoo. I like.'

There on my forearm was the reddened mark of three linked infinity symbols.

Chapter Thirty—It is better to lose the saddle than the horse

The three other beards brought the boat over to the sailboard, and hauled it on deck. The hydrofoil was badly bent, but there was no other damage.

I was still distracted with the mark on my arm when Big Beard whispered in my ear, 'How much for the girl?'

'She's not for sale. Have you lot got a hammer or something I can straighten that hydrofoil with?'

'What about this?' Big Beard sized up the job and handed me a length of heavy pipe.

I relaxed. These boys might imagine themselves pirates when they weren't pulling up crab pots, but they were amateurs at the threatening game. I could imagine them going home to their mums, helping set the table, and whatever else normals do.

I kneeled down and give the hydrofoil leg a few exploratory taps, then a few good whacks—at which point it broke off entirely. I looked up. 'You lot got welding equipment what can reattach this?'

One of them nodded. 'No problem. My brother-in-law can fix more good than new.'

Sparrow kneeled beside me, confused. 'Is we in trouble here?'

'Nah.' I stood and faced our captors.

There's a thing you can do when you're in a situation like this, outnumbered by lads what might be handy with fists and knives and so on, and that's to stand just so—relaxed, alert, with a look on your mug that says you don't have a worry in the world. 'This whole ransom thing . . .'

'Yes,' said Big Beard. 'We would like metals or pigs.'

'What I was going to say is, we're not willing to be ransomed. But, because we is grateful for your rescue, we'll forget you threatened us. Agreed?'

Big Beard didn't expect this, and the other beards looked to him for leadership. I quickly showed him the pipe. 'You lot are amateurs. You just give me a weapon I could use against you. I could've killed you with this. Feel the weight of it.'

I casually handed the pipe to Big Beard and, while he was distracted at having his victim hand him back power, I stepped forward and slipped a friendly arm around his shoulder. 'I suggest that because you is our brave rescuers, we is now friends forever.'

Big Beard tried to sound certain. 'Yes, possibly, but we are the pirate and you are at our mercy.'

I shook my head. 'I commend your entrepreneurial spirit, but in this instance, we in't at anyone's mercy.'

He looked uncertain. 'There are four of us and only two of you.'

'May I demonstrate why we in't afraid of you, and why, if anything, you should be afraid of us?'

Big Beard straightened, staunch. 'You think you can fight me? Last week I laid two men down with this fist.'

'I'm sure you did,' I smiled. 'And chances are it was because you was slightly less drunk than them other fellas, am I right?'

The other beards laughed and nodded, slapping Big Beard on the back.

'Give me your hand,' I said. Big Beard held out his hand, wary but curious. I pushed his sleeve up over a red-and-white tattoo of a coat of arms with a bull's head and some kind of old-fashioned house. Then I patted his biceps and curled his hand into a fist. 'Nice. I bet you could land a good punch with that arm. You is a strong lad, and no mistake.' I slipped my hand into his and used a simple thumb lock, gentle at first.

He tried to extract himself but was helpless to do anything.

'Please do not be doing that,' he said, looking uncertain.

'I will—now that we all know you isn't looking at someone helpless and weak. Are we agreed on that, my new friend?'

I give him slightly more pressure and he was baffled and pained in equal measure. Finally, he shrugged and nodded. 'Is good trick.'

I let go. 'Plenty more where that came from, pal.' I kept up the palaver to keep him focused on more positive endeavours than hitting me. 'Let's talk logistics. How much fuel have you got, and how fast can this thing go? We need to catch up with a ship before it gets to the Baltic.'

'How far ahead is other ship?' asked a lad with a thick red beard. 'And what speed does she travel?'

'She's about sixteen to twenty hours ahead, and moving at six to twelve knots.'

'We could never catch her in this,' said another beard.

I glanced through the tiny wheelhouse window to where one wall was covered in photos and drawings of families and children.

I looked out to sea, and gave my best impression of a man filled with great sadness. 'Then my sister here will never be reunited with her baby daughter.' I give Sparrow a comforting hug, and she played along, wiping her eyes and hugging back.

Big Beard was concerned. 'What is happen to her little girl?'

'Kidnapped.'

The Beards frowned and Big Beard shook his head. 'Is terrible thing to steal child.'

The other Beards nodded. I kept up with the bally. 'If only there were a way me and my sister could catch up with them what's got her sweet little girl.'

'We can take you to our town and fix your sailboard,' offered Big Beard.

Red Beard looked thoughtful. 'Or they could travel above the land. Is more direct.'

I blinked. *Above* the land?'

They all nodded. 'The winds are good and, besides, we have too much of the gas already.'

I blinked again. 'Gas?'

168

The Beards motored back to the tiny port of Stafstedt, a jumble of rusty iron sheds and lean-tos sitting on flat land barely a metre above the high-water line. The stink of rotting fish informed us of the main industry. As we helped the Beards unload the crab pots, I give Big Beard a look. 'How come you lot aren't looking at us like we was freaks of nature? Most people are either scared of us or think we is evil.'

Big Beard shrugged. 'You have the deformities, so do we.' He looked to one of his crew, who obligingly lifted his tunic to reveal a mottled midriff of tormented red skin piled into a series of coral-like growths. Another revealed his right hand, a mere fleshy claw. 'Many children die or are born with the not-normal body or face.' Big Beard lowered his voice. 'You see how we wear the beard. Many men in our village do the same. Look.' He pressed his beard down and opened his mouth so I could see there was something not right about his jaws. His chin was tiny and pushed back, and there was a gap above his top lip that opened up into his nose. Not pretty.

'They say is the poisons in the water and soil that cause this.' He pointed to a low, broad hill beyond the cluster of houses and fish-processing sheds. 'There we mine the poisons from the old landfill. We take metals, plastics, and the gas. We make a living but God says the price we pay is to suffer in our bodies. Is the same for you and your sister where you come from, yes?'

I just nodded, quietly pitying these poor bastards.

We carried the big plastic bins full of crabs and assorted fish across some crumbling concrete to a skinny gimp of a man waiting with a tractor and trailer more rust than metal. He looked us over, shifted his cigarette from his bottom lip to behind his ear, then counted and sorted the crabs into his own bins, a young boy with him writing down the numbers on a piece of blackboard. The boy looked normal but for one wall-eye and an ear what was just a stub.

The Beards got their money and were so pleased with themselves—and with how noble they were for rescuing us—they took us to Red Beard's house, where his round and pink-cheeked mother, and a crop of skinny kids, were tending a garden and watching a cow munch saltbush in a small, dry pasture.

The Beards became boyish again, piracy forgotten, playing with the children and being respectful to Red Beard's mum. She took us inside, heard our story, and commended her good God-fearing boys for helping us. Then she fed us as the kids and beards sang songs. Even we sang a couple, and half the village seemed to cram into the wee house to listen and marvel at Sparrow's beautiful voice. It was a room full of smiles, song and chat, free of worry and strife. In that moment, looking at Sparrow reflecting the smiles around us, suddenly the whole staying-in-one-place thing made sense to me. Here, in this community, people were strong and united as family, as lifelong friends and as a town—their simple pleasure in each other gave them certainty and confidence.

For the first time in my life, I envied normals.

After the singing and eating, Sparrow nudged me. 'We need to keep moving.'

I turned to Big Beard. 'So how are you proposing to get us to our ship?'

'First we must find her.' He spoke to Red Beard in rapid-fire Deutsche, and the pair of them pulled out maps and oldtech navigating devices. Knowing the state of the seas and winds and the likely delays, the *Lav Noyemba* was probably already at Kiel, and possibly even entering into the Baltic Sea.

Red Beard looked up from the map. 'What is their final destination?'

I wasn't about to mention a distant mountain range. 'Someplace in Lithuania—Klapeda. But first they is stopping off in the Polish ports for supplies and cargo.'

'The winds are good to get you into Międzymorze, which you call Poland, yes?'

I nodded. 'Any chance we could make it to the east coast?'

'It is possible, but a far longer journey than any of us have done. It will be hard to navigate, and dangerous.'

Sparrow shrugged. 'We is used to "dangerous". I'm just wondering if this craft of yours works.'

Red Beard enthused. 'It works. All of us do it, mainly for fun, but sometimes to get somewhere fast. It is like half-game, half-sport for us.

Although . . .' He faltered. 'Sometimes we are badly injured or killed.' I noticed he was looking in the direction of one crippled lad walking past, his bent body wobbling like he was crossing the deck of a ship during a storm.

I looked away. 'Can you show us how to do it in an afternoon? Without us getting killed?'

'Easy. Come now.'

We farewelled Red Beard's mum and ducked under the low tin doorway to get outside into the sun. The Beards and kids all came, striding and skipping across the dusty soil toward the low flattened hill, at the base of which were small, evenly spaced entrances to the landfill mines. More locals joined us on the way, curious about the strangers, and caught up in the general excitement of us attempting to go all the way across Międzymorze—a distance of seven hundred kilometres—in one of their devices.

Sparrow wrinkled her nose. 'Methane and something very dead. A *lot* of dead somethings.'

We paused at a shed for the Beards to collect a large messy bundle of graf material and ratty ropework. To distract myself from the nervous fear of being airborne again, this time in an unknown device built out of old rubbish, and the nose-searing stench of the landfill, I tapped Big Beard on the arm. 'So what's the furthest anyone's gone in one of your contraptions?'

'Ernst Lortz claim he got as far as Hamburg one time, and that was with Carla, his girlfriend—nearly one hundred kilometres.'

Sparrow and I shared a grim look. We didn't need to say how short that would leave us.

We could see a ramshackle shed at the top of the hill what we were told pumped methane from the buried landfill and piped it to storage tanks at the base of the hill. These then piped the methane to machines in a shed well away from everything else, where it was converted into hydrogen for fuel cells. The scorched and blackened soil around this shed, and the many twisted pieces of exploded tin, indicated the flammable nature of the enterprise.

Every twenty metres along the base of the hill was a mine entrance belonging to one of the local families. Beside each entrance was a sorting centre, where women and children separated out the metals and plastics from what the men brought up. A big shed nearby contained a series of wee smelters to process and purify the useful stuff.

We climbed to the top of the hill, where a light breeze cooled us. We looked across a landscape of coastal floodplain, mottled with patches of white salt, red soil, blue-grey saltbush and clumps of yellow grass. Skinny cattle and goats fed on slim pickings.

The Beards and onlookers started unpacking the gear—a tangle of graf sheeting, ropes, boards, light fishing net, fuel cells and a tiny lectric motor.

I tried to keep a poker face, but it wasn't just fear of flying that had me scared. While the lads were setting up, Sparrow stroked my forearm where the tattoo was. 'Does it hurt?'

'Itches a bit. I'm not bothered,' I lied. I didn't tell her I had another reason for terror—a pain inside my chest on the right-hand side, like something there what shouldn't be. I didn't see any point her worrying so I managed a smile. 'They seem to know what they're doing.'

Sparrow turned to where the graf sheeting was being spread out into a wing shape and slowly inflated with hydrogen. Sparrow indicated some short boards among the ropework. 'Is that the bit we sit on?'

Red Beard looked over his shoulder, proud. 'Yes. Is good seat. I make. The fuel cells for little motor is under.'

The rough-cut planks were padded with rags and strips of blanket. I tried to sound confident to Sparrow, 'Looks comfy. Enough room for you to curl up and get some kip.'

'Hilarious,' she muttered. 'The last bleeding thing I'll be doing is falling asleep.'

Finally, the lads had the flying device fully inflated and tugging on its ropes above us—a wide wing of lightweight, sewn and glued, reinforced graf sheet filled with hydrogen, steering itself into the wind, held down by the Beards and a few of the larger kids. Under the middle of the wing dangled the seat and steering ropes, which connected to vents in the leading and trailing edges, and one each to the wing tips. The ropes were old, filthy and thin, and the graf sheeting was as patched as my trousers. Sparrow and me swapped a look, and I turned to Red Beard. 'Are you sure you want to make such a generous gift to us?'

He beamed, kindly. 'Is Christian to do this. We are like Jesus. Besides, we have plenty, and your need is great. Also, this one is quite old.' He gestured me forward. 'Sit. Dieter will teach you the flying.'

Big Beard was already seated, and patted the planking beside him. I kept my thoughts to myself, and sat, shoulder to shoulder with my instructor. With the tiny propeller spinning behind us, and the others holding the wing steady, we lifted off and flowed down the hillside, gaining just enough speed for the wing shape to lift us up.

Big Beard was jovial. 'Engine not for lift or forward going. Save power. You must be clever and use wind and thermals to lift you high, then the slow descent, then go again high. Like rollercoaster, yes? You pull this rope to steer this way, this one to steer that way. These you pull to tilt wing up and go high, these you pull when you come in to land.'

It was a lot like the circus kite to control, but where I struggled with our flyer, Big Beard steered his like a cowboy steers a horse, and I saw the strength of the design—if not the contraption itself. He made it turn each way then swung into a curve that brought us back toward the hill. 'Get ready to slip off seat and run along while keeping hold of these ropes here, ja? That way we have the smooth landing.'

Then we cut the engine, came in lower and basically crashed, sending the pair of us tumbling and sprawling, while the Beards and local kids grabbed the ropes and propeller, whooping with laughter.

Big Beard spat dirt and looked up, grinning. 'Now is your turn to be pilot.'

Sparrow helped me up and brushed me down, the good side of her face tight with determination. 'If we get this fucking thing airborne, it won't be a practice run. We don't stop until we find that ship or get across Poland.'

I felt a wave of admiration at her courage. I turned to Big Beard. 'Like she said. If we get up, we don't stop till we crash or get where we're going.'

The Beards nodded and laughed, clapping me on the back, encouraging. 'Bravo!' Red Beard thrust a small compass into my pocket. 'We much admire you and your sister's crazy brave.'

As the Beards reset for a take-off, Red Beard's mum brought us water and food for the trip—smoked fish, some strips of spicy dried meat and a loaf of black bread that weighed as much as a similar-sized brick. *'Vielen dank,'* I said to her in my clumsy Deutsche. *'Sie sind freundlich und gross zugig.'*

'Und sie und ihre schwester sind vollig verruckt,' she replied.

'I didn't quite catch that, sorry.'

Big Beard translated with a smile. 'She said you and your sister are completely mad, but she hopes you save the little girl.'

He took my hand and crushed it briefly, then the other beards did the same. We all hugged, then someone passed around a bottle of something that tasted like it should only be used to dissolve rust, then we shook hands and hugged again, and finally, as the sweet people of Stafstedt started singing, Sparrow and me took our seat, flicked on the wee motor, and grabbed the ropes.

There were a few moments waiting for the breeze to get just right, then we lifted our feet as the Beards pulled us along and down the hill. I waited till we got some forward speed then lifted the front edge slightly. It felt like ages, but slowly a gap opened up between our dangling feet and the ground rushing beneath. When we had some decent height, I pulled us into a gentle turn over some darker ground as Big Beard had instructed me, the heat rising off it giving us more lift. We circled over the landfill, waving back at the crowd below.

Then, a few hundred metres up, I pointed us toward Gdansk, the main Baltic port of the United Commonwealth of Central Europe or, as the Poles called it, Międzymorze.

Sparrow was rigidly staring ahead. 'Is you as terrified as I is?' she asked.

I nodded. 'Yep. Still, on the bright side, only seven hundred kilometres to go.'

Sparrow gave a despairing groan, and leaned into me for comfort.

I concentrated on flying—and trying not to feel the thing inside me.

It felt like it was growing.

Chapter Thirty-One—Death is peace, dying is war

There's bugger-all joy studying the aeronautical arts when you're two hundred metres up in the air.

That said, motivated by fear, we quickly became practised at which ropes to pull to steer, and how to move up and down. We found different winds at different heights, and which ones took us the right way. A couple of hours into our flight, we were still scared stiff, but beginning to think there was a chance we might not die.

Flying was a fairly silent affair. Keeping the lectric motor off for the most part, there was only the sound of the wind over the wing, and occasional barnyard noises from farms far below—dogs and goats and cows and so on. Sparrow looked at the darkening sky ahead, thoughtful. 'How are we going to navigate at night? Let alone make sure we in't going to crash into anything.'

'If the clouds don't come in, we'll have a half-moon and the starlight to see by. Plus there'll be the occasional village with a few lights here and there.'

'But how will we know which direction to go in?'

I pointed. 'Gdansk is that way.'

Sparrow looked at me, bemused. 'How do you know?'

'It's obvious.' I pointed around us. 'Stafstedt's that way, Blumenthal's over there, and Gdansk is just over six hundred klicks that way.' I realised Sparrow was looking at me, troubled.

"Sup?"

'Blanco, you didn't even look at the compass, yet you knew which way everything was.'

I swallowed, uneasy. 'I don't know how I know—I just do.'

We flew on, not talking, pulling ropes when we needed to, staying on course, heading east into the darkness. I sensed Sparrow wondering, and it was all I could do not to tell her about the thing in me. I distracted myself by thinking what the tattoo meant, which was slightly less terrifying. Until . . .

Just as the sun set, and the sky behind us flooded with purple and orange, Sparrow pointed to my arm. 'Blanco—look.'

On the inside of my forearm, opposite the tattoo, a raised line had pushed the flesh up, like a vein that was twisted. Like a knot. I looked up and I could see in her eyes she was thinking the same thing. I was changing. Like Mister Splinter.

'It's nothing,' I lied. 'I bumped it when I crashed before, that's all.'

She nodded, but I could see she didn't believe me.

Chapter Thirty-Two—
Never whisper to the deaf,
or wink at the blind

As dusk fell, sure enough a half-moon rose, lighting our way. Below us, the treetops were bright, almost sky blue, their shadows indigo, rivers and lakes charcoal black.

Sparrow began dozing, so she put the invisibility coat on to stay warm, then we looped a rope around us so she could rest safely. Her eyes closed, and I was alone, tracking where we were, staying at a good height and continuing to find winds that would take us to Gdansk.

I was knackered but my mind hammered with questions. What did the triple-infinity tattoo mean? What was inside me? Who done these things to me? Was I becoming like Splinter? Was I dying? Why, just when I'd found Sparrow, was this horrible shit happening?

The shadowed forests finally gave way to the glittering Baltic Sea. I brought us around to follow the coastline, but there were few lights, even in the ports of Wismar and Rostock.

Between the cities, the smells of the farms rose to fill my senses— olive groves, hemp and drying wheat, the musk of farm animals, and the pollen from plantations of cork trees and eucalypts surrounding them. Farms gave way to older, wetter forests of oak and pine. From these came the reek of wild boar, bear and wolves, hidden prey and prowling predators. I smelled rot and decay, mushrooms and flowers, and even the sleeping green of new growth. Gliding over salt marshes, I heard the harsh screech of plovers disturbed by egg-stealing foxes, the clarinet honk of swans, and the calls of hunting owls.

I wondered if I should be able to sense all this stuff, but it gave me a strange feeling of peace. I felt connected to other things—to creatures and plants and soil. It felt good.

Sparrow stretched and looked around, her tummy rumbling. We got the remainder of our food out and chewed in silence, listening to the air rustle across the wing, the flap of loose graf sheeting, and the occasional howling of wolves below. When Sparrow finished, she grinned. 'The bad news is I'm busting for a wee.'

'I in't landing,' I replied. 'So we'll need to get creative about this.'

I kept the wing as steady as I could while Sparrow went through all sorts of contortions to get her trousers down and her bum over the back edge of our little plank seat. We were mental with laughing by the time she managed a golden shower on the forest below. Then I had my turn, which had us flapping about like a chicken in a hurricane.

When we were flying proper again, we looked across the moonlit landscape. Sparrow pulled the blanket around us and sang me a Russian song Baba had taught her. When we almost hit the top of a pine tree, I realised we were too low. I restarted the motor and pulled on the ropes to get us back up, but the wing responded sluggishly, and I could see it was getting baggy. 'We've got a leak.'

Worried, we looked for the lights of towns. We were still over the islands separating the Baltic from the Szczecin Lagoon, right on the border of Deutschland and Międzymorze, and there was more water or forest than fields to land on. 'I don't know how much longer we can stay up,' I said.

'Better to land now than crash later,' Sparrow muttered through clenched teeth.

'If we can make it to Ostromice, or where there's roads, we'll have a chance of a safe landing.'

I found a breeze that lifted us higher, but it was getting more difficult to control the wing. Worse, as dawn lightened the sky ahead, we saw only coastal marshes with more forest beyond.

Sparrow sighed, but I pointed to a thin column of smoke rising from the forest a few kilometres ahead. 'I don't know how I know it, but that there is the Troszyn Forest, and if there's smoke, there's people and a road out.'

As we flew lower and closer, I could see the smoke was coming from a clearing. We were losing height so I brought us into a downward spiral. 'Get ready to land. And by "land" I mean start screaming.'

I managed to glide into the clearing, keeping enough lift to circle inside the ring of trees. I caught a glimpse of a fire-pit in the centre, and people standing beside it, looking at us in astonishment.

As the ground came rushing up toward us, I pulled hard on the ropes to stall the wing. One edge caught a branch, and we were jerked to a violent halt, slamming into branches ten metres off the ground in a tangle of graf sheet and ropes. I found myself hanging, clutching the seat, and I saw Sparrow clutching a messy armful of sheeting, which was slowly sliding through her grasp. She yelped with fear. I reached out with one arm. 'Grab hold!'

She missed my arm, grabbed my legs, and managed to clamber across to a secure branch. I collected our meagre belongings and joined her as she pointed. 'We got an audience.'

As we awkwardly climbed down, the people huddled, clearly troubled by our arrival, crossing themselves. It all looked a bit serious, so I whispered to Sparrow. 'Too late to put the invisibility coat on. I suggest we be staunch Catholics for this caper.'

'I got a bad feeling about this,' Sparrow muttered. In the centre of the dying fire was a blackened post that must've been iron. Then I noticed the chains, and the thing what was hanging from them. A body.

'Look confident,' I replied, then we walked forward, raising our hands in greeting. 'Good morning,' I called out. 'We are travellers seeking the road to Gdansk.'

'Since when did you speak Polish?' Sparrow murmured.

I frowned. 'Since just now. I thought the words and they come out.'

One of the men came forward—an old, stern man; a tall chinless streak with a nose big enough to shelter under. He leaned on a staff, and wore rough wool and hemp clothing, his smell indicating a wash was still on last month's to-do list. 'There is no road to Gdansk in this place,' he said. 'From where do you come?'

'What did he say?' whispered Sparrow.

'Couldn't you hear?'

''Course I could. He's speaking Polish.'

'He is?' I turned back to the old man. 'We come from England.'

He looked at the now deflated wing. 'You use the practices of the past to come here.'

'That's correct, yes.'

'And your appearance also speaks of Satan's hand.'

'Now hang on a minute—'

'She has the mark on her face. You have also the mark.'

'This is not looking good,' I warned Sparrow.

The stinky geezer pointed to the fire. 'We have just purified this woman of her mark. She too used the practices of science. She too was a witch.'

Other older men in the group were nodding, clearly fancying another barbecue. While I was holding down the panic, I calculated the odds of fighting these stick-wielding nutters or running away into a forest without roads—neither were good options.

'Play along,' I whispered to Sparrow. 'Look solemn and nod when I say stuff.'

'What are you going to say?'

'I got no idea.'

I turned back to Stinker, remembering Humbolt's storytelling tips—to win your audience, ask the question, then answer it for them.

'Is he right?' I asked the crowd. 'Were we marked by Satan?' I did a brief pause. 'Yes! We were!'

The crowd reacted with unease, so I kept up the bally. 'And we are here on a mission.'

I kneeled and crossed myself, Sparrow following suit, confusing our audience a tad.

Stinker tried to regain control. 'You are on a mission from Satan, and you will burn in hell.'

I stood and stepped forward, acting confident. 'Satan captured me and my sister through the offices of an evil man. We were just children, and we were enslaved. But we were saved in God's great name, and instructed to travel the four corners of the Earth to renounce all evil—and that of . . .'

I searched the faces of the crowd, cold-reading them. '. . . one of you!'

The mob seemed more confused than troubled, so I kept talking. 'We have been commanded by God to identify he among you who secretly sins and is beholden to Satan.'

There were a few shifty looks, and Stinker looked annoyed. 'None of us are beholden to Satan!'

'No. You are not,' I replied, calm and commanding. 'I see nothing here but good people still in the palm of God's mighty hand. The one we seek is nearby and he is known to you.' I spotted one of the women glance toward a path leading out of the clearing. Guessing that's where the village was, I closed my eyes, raised my arm, slowly turned then stabbed the air. 'This way. I feel evil's presence.'

There were a few confused looks, and people crossed themselves. Stinker was frustrated. 'Enough of this. We have purified our village. Seize them.'

A plan forming, I put my hand up. 'Wait!'

The fire looked about right—plenty of dying coals and charcoal. 'I will prove my love for God and the truth of what I say. I will walk through the fire and, if God wishes, he will burn and torment me. If he loves me and wishes me to fulfil his desire, then no harm will come to me.'

While Stinker and the others were still flummoxed by all this, I whipped off my boots and socks.

Sparrow was struggling to look calm. 'What the hell is goin' on?'

'There's only one exit from this mess,' I whispered. 'I need to pull a firewalk to prove we is on the side of God. After that we get ourselves to their village, and take the road out of here. Keep up the praying. If things don't work out, run like hell.'

Sparrow continued her solemn prayerful act as I strode past Stinker to the fire. I paused, strode around it, followed closely by some of

Stinker's men. I stopped and looked at one who held a long stick. 'Lend me your staff, friend—I will build up the coals.'

The man handed me his staff, wide-eyed with wonder as I pushed the coals into a thicker, more even bed, sending sparks flying, and getting the flames briefly burning higher. The more it burned, the more charcoal it made. Then I handed back his stick, and kneeled in 'prayer' long enough for the outer layer of the coals to blacken. I needed about ten minutes, at least, but every minute passed like a month as the crowd grew increasingly restless.

Stinker scoffed. 'You see? He is scared.'

I knew I couldn't put it off any longer. I scanned the coals, then stood and addressed the crowd. 'God will try me now before you. If I lie, he will send my feet to hell!'

I slowly rolled up my trouser cuffs, crossed myself, put on a 'holy' look, remembered to pace my walking—and hold back the temptation to sprint . . . and walked, dignified, across the coals.

The crowd gasped, unable to believe what they were seeing. I reached the other side, took a few discreet sliding steps to get the heat out, then brushed off my feet, showing the soles to the gaping crowd. 'Here is proof that Our Lord has allowed me to tell only the truth!'

Stinker was mystified and suspicious, but there wasn't nothing he could do as the villagers drew around to inspect my feet. I let them touch and look closely, then I put my socks and boots back on. 'Now we must complete the mission God has entrusted us with. Together, my friends, we will all do God's will today.'

Then I stood and gave the crowd a confident smile, as if they were all my mates and we were on this journey together. I took Sparrow's hand and, acting like everyone's little brother or sister, we walked ahead of the crowd to the path leading to the village, like we had a clue what we were doing.

Chapter Thirty-Three—The journey is the destination

We walked along a rutted dirt track through tall forest that pressed in either side like walls. There might have been a still-suspicious lynch mob a few paces behind us but instead of being scared, I felt stupidly triumphant. We'd barely dodged one bullet, but somehow I was cocky.

The forest opened into another clearing of around five hectares, filled with fenced pastures, gardens and thatched houses built from log and stone. It looked medieval.

'It's like something from a fairytale,' whispered Sparrow.

'No lectric nothing,' I replied, nodding approvingly at everything around us for the sake of our audience. 'These nutters hate tech.'

There were no machines of any sort. The only metal things were simple tools for the gardens.

Still acting like 'God's soldiers', Sparrow and I marched into the village like we owned it, scanning the place for any clues what might get us out alive. We needed a road out, preferably to a place where they didn't blame a bad crop on some poor 'witch'.

I spotted a tiny symbol scratched on a rough paling fence—it was faint, a crude image of an upside-down house. I discreetly indicated it to Sparrow. 'Travellers must come through here. Them marks mean a good-hearted woman lives there.'

Sparrow scowled at the smouldering ruin of a house behind the fence. 'Liv*ed*.'

In the central square of the village another faint sign was scratched into an upright post supporting a well; a tiny circle with two black dots in it—'dangerous people live here'.

'Any idea how we get out of this?' Sparrow murmured.

'Witch-finding is a con. See a burned woman, and somewhere nearby there's a priest or geezer extorting money out of peasants. I seen a few in Wales.'

'So where's *our* witch-finder?'

On one side of the square was a tidy house, the only one with an upper storey. Outside, hitched to a post, a donkey and a healthy-looking horse were packed for a journey. 'I think we've found him,' I whispered. 'Look around and lift someone's rosary, alright?'

I stopped dead like I'd smelled something bad. I pointed to the two-storey house and asked the villagers, 'What is this place?'

'It is our hostel for travellers,' said Stinker.

I frowned and sniffed the air. 'Someone is inside it. Someone with power not of God.'

'You are wrong. A man of God has been staying with us and cleansing our village.'

I ignored him, sniffing still.

There were looks of intrigued concern as I kept up the act, striding through the crowd with Sparrow on my tail, giving her opportunity to pickpocket. 'A dark man has come from far away.'

There were enough reactions to read I was on the money. 'A dark man with a dark heart.'

There was uneasy talk, and Stinker tried to regain control. 'You are wrong. A man of God has come to us.'

'Would a man of God use Science?'

I got a small chorus of noes from the crowd. I looked around into their faces, kindly. 'The Lord tells me you have come to this place for sanctuary.'

Nods, and a few surprised looks—how could the strange pale boy know this?

'You have come a long way, and from many places,' I continued. 'You are good people.'

More emphatic nods.

I leaned closer, grim. 'But the good leave a scent that Satan cannot stand. It fills him with rage. He will not rest until he has defiled those good people. I know this because he defiled me and my sister as innocent children. But God does not rest, and it is He, through us, who will show you the darkness that lies inside one who is still in this village.' I spotted the hostel door begin to open, and did my best Humbolt impersonation. 'Come forth, I command you!'

A skinny rat-like boy emerged, lank hair hanging to below his collar, wearing clothes what were better than the local tat, carrying a pair of travelling bags. Bewildered by the crowd, and at me pointing at him, he scowled. 'Who are you?'

I took a punt. 'Where is your master?'

'What business is it of yours?'

I looked to Sparrow and held out my hand. 'My rosary, please, sister.'

Sparrow handed me the freshly pilfered rosary, and I thrust it toward the boy, who couldn't help but recoil slightly.

'I see you recognise this symbol,' I said, and turned briefly to the crowd. 'You saw with your own eyes how he recoiled from it.' I didn't feel for this idiot, the accomplice to his murderous master. 'I challenge you to prove you are of God, not of Satan.'

With all eyes on the lad, he was nervous but defiant. 'What are you talking about? My master trained at the New Vatican.'

'Then you should have nothing to fear from a simple rosary!' I turned to my audience. 'I will rest my hand upon this creature's shoulder as he holds this sacred object in his hand. If he is of God, nothing will come of it. If he is of Satan . . .'

I let the sentence hang so the audience could use their imaginations, privately thanking Humbolt for the years of his bad acting I'd had to endure.

I beckoned. 'Come here, boy, and hold this simple rosary.'

The boy cast a look to the upstairs window, but came toward me, still defiant. 'I'm not afraid of you. I'll hold your rosary.'

I held out my closed hand, but as he drew close enough, I turned to the crowd and revealed the crucifix that was attached to it. 'A rosary with the holy cross itself, something he didn't bargain on.'

Before the boy could protest, I rested a light hand on his upper shoulder and dropped the rosary into his palm. The moment he clasped it, I lightly kneaded the pressure point supplying the arm. The boy's hand went limp, and he dropped the rosary. The crowd gasped and I quickly picked up the rosary and pointed at the boy. 'God has revealed your heart. Where is your master? Where is the man in black?'

A man stepped out from the inn. In early middle age, with the tight, smooth skin of the well fed, he was sure enough dressed in black, and wore an imposing and ridiculous broad-brimmed hat. Sparrow scowled, and I stepped back as if Satan had just poked at me with his fork. 'It is him!'

'Do I know you?' said the man.

'No, you do not! But I know you!' I faced the crowd. 'Good people, answer me only three questions and I will prove *this* is the man that God sent us to rid you of.' I acted grim and troubled, the picture of caring concern. 'Question one—has he taken money from this town?'

The crowd nodded and agreed in chorus. Stinker was defensive. 'Witch-finders always receive a fee for their service.'

I waved this aside. 'Question two—has he commanded that certain women be put to death? Women that, in your heart of hearts, you felt to be good women?'

Now the nods were less certain, and guilty.

I lowered my voice, dramatic. 'And question three—would any true man of God, any *true* witch-finder, use science every waking day of his life?'

The witch-finder wasn't used to the looks he was getting from the crowd. 'I demand to know who this freakish white boy and this deformed girl are.'

'I will tell you myself,' I replied, playing calm. 'I and my sister are saved. I was once Satan's creature until Our Lord rescued us. We have exposed your boy here, we have established you took money from these good people, and now we will prove you are one of Satan's creatures. How, you ask?'

I turned to my audience, keeping their focus on my palaver. 'How can you know God is speaking through me? Isn't that the question you're asking yourself right now? How can we be sure that this man dressed in black, about to flee this village with his bags packed with your money, is bonded to Satan?'

There were nods to all of this, and I felt a surge of confidence. If it wasn't our lives on the line, it would've felt like any night showing punters through the freak show, keeping them in the palm of my hand with chat and bluff. I shot a finger at the man in black, and turned as the crowd focused on him, then confounded their expectations by swinging my arm to point at his horse. 'Look there for your answers.'

I allowed the audience a moment of confusion, a trick to ensure they looked to me for the answers. 'Search this man's luggage and then his person.'

The witch-finder put himself between the crowd and his horse. 'How dare you! I am representative of the Witch-Finder General himself!'

'That's what you *say*,' I said, letting my genuine contempt show. 'And I'm sure you have "papers" with writing and stamps all over them that say the same thing, am I right?'

'Of course I have papers. They are certified proof that I am who I say I am.'

'Proof, you say?' I turned to the audience, sour. 'Because no one has ever falsified papers?' I dropped the look. 'I have no papers. Not one. But did I not entrust myself to God, who did not burn me in the fire? Do I not hold this sacred rosary without harm? Could this man's boy hold it for one second?' I pointed at the witch-finder's horse. 'Search his bags and you will find your hard-earned money, and proof that needs no further words from me.'

The crowd were restless and aggrieved—they had little money to spare for dangerous luxuries like witch-finders. Stinker saw which way the wind was blowing. 'If you wouldn't mind, Procurator . . .'

'I refuse,' the witch-finder blustered. 'Furthermore, I command you to uphold my authority.'

The looks in the crowd showed they now found his authority to be suspect. One of the older women had enough. 'I'm looking.'

As she strode toward the horse, the witch-finder tried to block her path. 'Stop! I command you.'

I quickly stepped forward, holding the crucifix out as if I was worried the woman was in danger. 'Do not harm this woman!'

The witch-finder was rattled, so I turned to the woman with a kind look. 'Look and ye shall find truth.'

The woman, though likely normally happy to see me burn as a witch, only saw that I'd 'saved' her. She smiled, grateful. 'I'll do just that.'

'This is outrageous!' bellowed the witch-finder, alarmed as the crowd closed in. Sparrow came to my side, playing fearful and crossing herself, prompting others to reflexively copy her.

The older woman opened up the saddlebags, then pulled out the first bag of money. Another two bags of cash and I could see disgust ripple around the crowd. It was a fortune to these proud peasants.

'That money is for God,' the witch-finder bellowed.

Sparrow slid in closer to me. 'I got no idea how you done it, Blanco, but you is a feckin' magician.'

'We in't done yet,' I whispered back.

Now that I wasn't so fearful for our lives, I could feel a strange bitter anger welling up in me. All my life I've been treated like an outsider, been looked at with disgust or pity, shunned and feared. Witch-finders is parasites what use people's gullibility like what we did, but they pretended it was for 'God', when all they was doing was whipping up hate and murdering people to enjoy the power of it. And the money.

I slyly reached out and felt the sleeve of the man in black's cloak. 'Nice material,' I said, then let it drop. Everyone around was now looking at his fine-cut cloth and mentally comparing it to their own rough homespun threads.

Then the woman searching the bags found something smooth and shiny what she didn't recognise, but I did.

'Oldtech!' I called out.

Sparrow, acting her lovely little heart out, gasped and stepped back. Others around us followed suit, worried. The witch-finder, now sweating with fear, stepped forward. 'That equipment has been blessed and sanctified for God's work.'

I grabbed the fone, holding it aloft. 'Science that this man denied having!'

With all eyes on the witch-finder, I crossed myself while throwing the fone to the ground and stamping on it—no sense leaving this prick the means to call in the uniforms. 'What else does he keep in those bags?'

There was a rush forward, and more oldtech was found—along with a bottle of whisky, shocking the teetotal locals. I suppressed a smile—my work had been done for me.

I stood back beside Stinker as others searched every bag and the outraged witch-finder's clothes. Leaning heavily on his staff, Stinker looked sick, and I hoped he was suffering for the innocent woman he'd put to the stake. For now though, I needed him on our side. I patted him on the shoulder. 'Life is hard, yes?'

Still in two minds, he managed a small, resentful nod.

'We kneel before God and ask for His wisdom,' I said. 'And we find ways to repent, to make the wrongs we have done right.'

He was grim. 'We have done wrong by the word of this man.'

'Satan is cunning and fills our hearts with hate. But God gives us the harder command. He tells us to love those who sin.'

He looked at me, puzzling. 'You were a servant of Satan, yet you reveal God's truth.'

I shrugged, honest. 'I've been evil, sir. I've done terrible things, things that make me deserve that fire you burned this morning, and that's the truth. But I'm not doing those things anymore. Never again. Never.' Suddenly, I wasn't acting no more.

Stinker indicated the witch-finder. 'What should we do with this creature?'

'What would Jesus do?' I replied. 'Would he burn him on that stake of yours?'

'God commands us to eliminate evil,' he replied, but without his former certainty.

I give him a hard look. 'Work on the evil in your own heart before doing any more killing.' I gestured to the witch-finder. 'God knows you need to forgive yourselves for what you done to innocent so-called witches on this charlatan's say-so.'

Stinker sagged, looking tired and guilty. 'We old ones saw the world begin to burn. It was God's punishment for sin. We tried to turn from sin—to fight it in ourselves and others. We failed.'

Stinker turned and stepped forward to talk the villagers out of a lynching.

I walked away and sat on the stone edge of the well, bone-weary. Sparrow sat beside me and slung an arm around me. 'Well done.'

'We're in the middle of a forest, we got no transport, and there's still four hundred kilometres to Gdansk. What's the odds we'll get there in time?'

'Keep thinking of Daisy. Right now, she's missing us like crazy. She needs a tummy rub.'

I smiled to think of Daisy's happy face, then stood. 'Let's find a way out of this shithole.'

Chapter Thirty-Four—
Power corrupts

It wasn't hard to persuade the villagers to send the witch-finder and his flunkey packing, minus their horse and donkey, their sturdy shoes, and the villagers' money. While the women organised breakfast, we watched the witch-finder and his boy trudge out of the village to sullen looks and catcalls from the villagers.

Sparrow looked exhausted 'Blanco, let's eat and get moving. These people is freaking me out.'

We joined the villagers at benches set up to provide a communal meal, and while we were stuffing our faces I negotiated to take the witch-finder's horse so we could 'go on doing God's work'. The villagers were so happy at getting more than their money back from the witch-finder they didn't quibble. The women even packed the saddlebags with supplies, whispering heartfelt blessings. I guessed all of them were feeling safer in a village what might think twice before murdering another woman.

Mounted on the horse behind Sparrow, I give them a final 'blessing', and we cantered out of the village and into the forest in the direction of Koszalin, where Stinker advised us to find the 'Sanctuary of the Covenant' on a hill called Chelmska. There we would find good

God-fearing people like himself. I mentally vowed never to go near the place.

As we rode out, I was weirdly energised by our escape, but Sparrow was edgy. 'Keep an eye out for that witch-finder and his lad.'

I didn't care. I almost relished another opportunity to deal with them two murderers.

'Speak of the devil.' I pointed, as Sparrow reined the horse to a halt. Fallen branches lay across the road in a crude barricade. 'Oi, you two,' I called out. 'Come out and show yourselves.'

I could hear some whispering, then the pair emerged, sheepish but defiantly holding pointed sticks at the ready. I swung my leg over and slid to the ground. Sparrow scowled, wary. 'Careful. Them two are idiots, but there's two of them.'

I should've heeded her warning but I was filled with a strange confidence as I strolled toward them. I wasn't afraid. I was almost eager for them to try something so I could rub their noses in the dirt. A gleeful anger was inside of me I never felt before. I *wanted* to hurt them. I stopped and stood there in the middle of the path, hands on hips. 'So, you two murderers think you can murder us, do you?'

The boy froze but the witch-finder was wary, casually stepping around to get me in between them. 'We are who we say we are. How you convinced those peasants to turn against an ordained witch-finder can only be Satan's work.'

'So, you're going to fight Satan with a couple of sticks, is it? How's your feet, by the way? Getting a bit sore without them nice boots?'

'You have some power, I grant you, but we have God.'

'Bollocks you do. Give us those bloody sticks.' I strode toward him, stepped under his feint, sidestepped the blow he aimed at my head, grabbed his wrist and kept it swinging as I turned my back and let his stick connect with the boy, who had rushed in. The boy yelped and dropped his stick. A simple elbow to the witch-finder's shoulder had him dropping his.

I picked up the sticks and faced them, adrenaline pumping. 'You two go about pretending God told you to kill women. You con gullible peasants into believing there's witches living among them who they can blame for sick babies and bad crops and whatever. You whip people into believing they have to murder innocent women and then you take money for it. And I thought *I* was evil.'

'You are,' said the witch-finder. 'You act against us, so you are evil.'

I saw nothing but dogged stupidity in his face. I looked at the boy. 'You believe his toss about witches and devils with pitchforks? Or are you too stupid to find a proper job?'

The boy just looked scared. 'Let us go, mister. Please?'

'Why should I? You'll only go on killing innocent women.'

The boy was cowering now. 'We won't, I promise.'

Sparrow rode the horse forward and prodded my shoulder with her boot. 'Oi—stop acting like the Gaffer, and let's get out of here.'

Suddenly, all the guff and anger and righteous fury in me drained away. I looked into the boy's eyes, seeing his fear and powerlessness. 'Just don't do this shit, alright? It's lies. It's wrong to murder.'

'I know,' he whispered.

'Then why do you do it? Why stick with this sick bastard?'

'He's my papa.'

I felt a sick recognition as he met my look, his misery a mirror image of my guilt. I waved him away. 'I won't hurt you.'

As I hopped up on the horse, the witch-finder looked up at me with mingled anger and confusion. I answered the question in his eyes. 'I didn't kill you, even though you don't deserve to live. I don't know what your God would say, but I'd call it mercy.'

Sparrow set the horse walking forward.

I was silent for a while, and so was Sparrow. Finally she spoke, in a quiet voice I never heard her use before. 'I didn't like that. You went strange for a while there. You wasn't like the Blanco I know.'

She was right, but I couldn't bring myself to admit it. 'They deserved a thumping,' I grumbled.

'Maybe, but I didn't like the way you was lording it over them.'

I didn't have no reply.

'You was like the Gaffer. Or Splinter.'

I shrugged, as all my old guilt returned and doubled. 'How about saying, "Nice one, Blanco—you got us out of trouble. You saved our lives. Ta very much."'

'Just 'cause I is angry doesn't mean I don't still likes you. Tell me what's wrong.'

I sighed, anger fading. 'Trouble is, I don't know. I in't been telling you, but . . .'

She stopped the horse, turned to face me. 'What.'

'I'm scared. I think I'm dyin', Sparrow. I'm so sorry . . .'

'What are you bleedin' sorry for? Tell me.'

'I'm changing. I sense things I shouldn't be able to. I know where we are and where to find the road to Gdansk in the Tri-City. Fighting them two was easy as chopping kindling. And . . .' I stopped, hating to burden her.

'Tell me.'

'It's not just the tattoo. There's something inside of me. I feel it growing. I dunno if it's cancer or what, but it's doing my head in.'

It was awkward, but she hugged me and, as I wiped my own tears, I felt some comfort.

She got the horse moving again and, after a while, listening to birds and the slow clop of the horse's hooves, feeling Sparrow's warmth against me, I calmed down enough to make my confession. 'I wanted to die before you woke up,' I murmured. 'Now, more than anything, I want to live so I can be with you and Daisy and Tog and Baba and all the rest. But I don't know what to do.'

'Nor do I, my darlin', but we're chasing the one person who can tell us. Splinter.'

By late afternoon, we'd reached the edge of the forest. We stopped the horse, and hopped down to look across the town of Płoty. The town was overgrown with greenery, crumbling walls and roofs poking through the foliage, silent in that special way of places abandoned by humans.

In the near distance we spotted a wisp of smoke coming from a chimney on an old square stone building, one of the few places not destroyed in the Deutsche-Polska Federation Civil War.

'People. Should we risk it?' I asked.

'I'm too tired to worry,' Sparrow replied. 'Where there's smoke, there's a place to lie down.'

She walked the horse down the slope and into the ramshackle streets, trekking through ruins and old parks toward the building. As we got near, an old shaggy dog came out and started barking. A tiny, straight-backed old woman, wearing canvas pants, braces and a workman's shirt, emerged from a doorway, carrying a substantial automatic combat rifle, barrel aimed high.

We stopped and put our hands up. The old lady fussed with the gun and I saw she was looking for the safety catch.

'With respect, ma'am—please don't take the safety catch off,' I called out. 'Those guns is too easy to set off, and we're too tired to die just at the moment.'

She scowled. 'I'm trying to turn it off. Last time I made a mistake and took that tree out.' We looked where she pointed and, to one side of the path, a shattered stump was sticking up from a mass of firewood at its base. She cursed briefly and slung the gun over her shoulder. 'What do you want? I've got no money or anything of value. This place has been ransacked so many times I've barely got a pot to piss in.'

Not understanding a word of Polish, Sparrow stretched, yawning. 'Tell her we'd be grateful for some shelter. We have our own food but the horse needs grass.'

The old lady came closer and peered at us through wire-frame glasses, looking us up and down. She spoke in halting English. 'You are Britishers? What happen to you?'

'It's a long story, ma'am,' Sparrow sighed.

The old lady just nodded, and indicated a small, fenced paddock where a single cow and her calf were grazing. 'Put horse in there. Then come inside.'

She returned to the building, pushing past the heavy wooden door. The dog preferred to follow us, sniffing eagerly and wagging his tail as we put the horse in the pen, then we carried our belongings to the door the old lady disappeared into.

Her voice came from the dark within. 'Come in, come in.'

We entered the room, lit by a solar lantern and the last of the sun.

The old woman was hanging the gun on a post, obliging a grumpy-looking owl to shift position. 'Go back to sleep, you old fart,' the woman grumbled. 'You can go hunting soon enough.'

She turned to us, again giving us a searching look. 'I don't know what happen to bring you here, but this country isn't good for people who look different.'

'If you're referring to witch-finders, we've already had an encounter.'

The woman pointed to Sparrow's face. 'They did that?'

'No,' Sparrow replied. 'Someone else. May we sit, please?'

The woman looked shamed. 'I'm sorry. Sit. Please. I've been alone so long I lose my manners. I make us something to eat and drink, yes?'

We were too tired to make small talk, but the old lady kept up a running chatter to herself. It was soothing just sitting there, watching her bustle about and talk as we patted the dog. By the time she brought us soup and bread we were nearly asleep. We thanked her and ate, hungry. She sat and watched us, her blue eyes focused and sharp behind her glasses. She indicated me. 'You. You've had genetic work done on you.'

Not knowing either way, I shrugged, kept on eating. She turned to indicate Sparrow's face. 'And that's nerve damage, if I'm not mistaken. From a stroke. Or an accident.'

'Surgery.'

'Or surgery. Of course. I used to be doctor. A medical doctor.' She sighed, and was silent for a while. 'So, where are you two coming from and where are you going?'

'We come from England and we're going to a place you never heard of.'

'Try me.'

'The Bogda Shan.'

The old lady's face sharpened. 'And why in God's name you go to such a place?'

Guessing she knew something we didn't, I just rolled up my sleeve and showed her the tattoo. She stood, shocked. Then she looked at my face again. 'How old are you?'

'Seventeen or eighteen. Why?'

'Because no one under fifty should have such a thing on their body. Where did you get it?'

'Your guess is as good as mine. What do you know about our destination?'

She hesitated, wary. 'I know it is a place of death surrounded by radioactivity. You probably couldn't even get there if you wanted to.'

'What happened there?' asked Sparrow.

Again she hesitated. 'China have secret research facility there from long time ago. When First Collapse come, the People's Republic was dying so they open research place to experts from around the world. We heard they experiment on people. Then it is bombed by Americans, even though Americans also working there. They bomb their own people.'

'Why?'

'The US is a theocracy and decides China project is against "God's will". Most of us didn't think China research would achieve anything. We think it is just a, how you say, "pipe dream"—the last gasp of human species dooming itself to extinction by its own hand.'

'What were they trying to do?'

'Evolve the human race. Create new species of homo. We heard many hundreds of people is used as guinea pigs, then discard when they don't work like plan.'

'Why?' Sparrow asked. 'What was the point of it?'

'Our species kill ourselves and the planet. China think if they evolve new, more intelligent species it save the planet, if not poor old homo.'

'A brainier human might still not do the job,' Sparrow mused.

'Oh, they want much more than new clever monkey,' the old woman replied. 'They want their creature to bridge gap between biological and machine—the project was to construct species who evolve itself. They want a biological singularity.'

I felt a ripple of recognition and fear run through me. 'This project—what was it called?'

'Let me see if I can remember—uh, the Singularity Project: Linking Intelligence to Evolutionary Research. They shorten all that down to one acronym of course. One word.'

I felt sick as I asked the question, already knowing the answer. 'What word?'

'Splinter.'

Chapter Thirty-Five—
Without dogs, even
paradise would be hell

We talked late into the night. Her name was Elenor Cimoszko, she was eighty-two years old, and she'd been a neuroscientist. As Poland shattered in the Federation Civil War, and research became a luxury no one could afford, Elenor became a frontline doctor, tending injured, diseased and faulty genmods.

'Poland authorities say science is to blame for human mess, so I could not practise as doctor except in secret. But those hypocrites who destroy anything "science", and kill "witches", they still came to me at night for treatment. Now I wait to die in this place, listening to the wolves become braver.'

She looked at us, curled by the fire. 'And now a final mystery comes knocking at my door.'

Sparrow nodded. 'We got the same mystery, Elenor. Which is why we need to get to Gdansk. There's a ship we have to meet.'

'And this ship, it will take you closer to the most remote mountains in the world?'

'It might,' Sparrow replied. 'If we can sort a few "issues" with the travelling circus we belong to.'

Elenor was bemused. 'You are circus performers?'

'Amongst other things, yeah.'

'Other things?'

'I sing, Blanco kills people. Well, he used to.'

Elenor looked at me. I just shrugged.

'And now something's happening to Blanco,' Sparrow continued. 'Something inside of him. It made that tattoo appear on his arm, and he can sense things he shouldn't be able to.'

'Such as?'

'He can hear things from a long way off, he knows where things is—like roads and towns and what they is called—and he can smell stuff from miles away. But the thing inside him is making him cruel. And he's not like that. He's kind and gentle.'

Elenor creaked to her feet. 'I must think on this. For now though, you must sleep.' She pointed to a door. 'You can wash through there, and I will bring blankets for you to sleep by the fire.'

We give ourselves a wash, then settled down beside the fire. Before Elenor left us that night, she stopped in the doorway to her room, looking at me. 'Your mother—what is her name?'

'I don't know. I was sold to the circus when I was little.'

'And your father?'

'The man who owns the circus just told me he's my father. I dunno what his real name is, or even what he is, but he calls himself Mister Splinter.' I registered her shock, then she turned away and went to bed. I rested my head against Sparrow's shoulder and closed my eyes against further thought.

In the morning, I was woken by a thump on my chest.

I opened my eyes. Grinning at me was the dog, who'd just dropped a stick on me, expectant, tail wagging. I let Sparrow doze while I got up and took the dog outside to play, and to take a leak. After checking on the horse, my new canine friend took me for a walk around the building. Damaged and crumbling, it had once been a grand estate on the edge of the town, overlooking the river and an old bridge, which had since been bombed. Around the other side of the mansion, the forest below was reclaiming the ruins of the town, which was thick with vines, trees and flowers. It looked pretty.

I could make out where the streets were, and some of the buildings. I imagined it was a beautiful town once, bustling with people, markets full of produce, kids and dogs running around, cars and buses and motorbikes all moving around like in the vids we seen from before the Collapse.

I went back inside, where Elenor and Sparrow were now making breakfast. Sparrow looked up and smiled, so I kissed her. Elenor spared me a glance. 'Feeling better?'

'I am, thanks.'

'Good. After breakfast, before you go on your way, I give you medical check. My diagnostic tools are primitive but I may be able to shed some light on your condition.'

I nodded, then looked around the kitchen, which was flooded with sunlight and cooking smells. The owl had returned from a night's hunting, and looked at me from under sleepy, hooded eyelids.

'I wish we didn't have to go,' I said to Sparrow. 'This is a lovely town. I could see us living here.'

Elenor grimaced. 'A few nights here might do you no harm, but long-term is another matter. Old nuclear power plant. It is bombed along with town, and radiation drove people away.'

We ate a hearty breakfast, knowing it might be our last food for a while.

'Good food,' I growled, chewing happily.

'There is some radioactivity, but not so much.'

I shrugged. 'Considering whatever's happening inside me, a dose of rads is neither here nor there.'

We finished the rest of the food in silence, then Elenor took me to a room she kept as a kind of surgery. She pointed to a rusty padded examination trolley. 'Undress and sit on that.'

I stripped to my undertrousers and sat on the trolley. She put a cold stethoscope against my heart and listened. At the same time, she also rested two fingers on my wrist to feel my pulse. I sat there for a minute or so, turning my head to look out the windows to where Sparrow was playing with the dog.

I thought about what Elenor might tell me. If it was bad news, I'd keep it to myself—there wasn't no need Sparrow suffering my worry when she didn't have to.

Elenor rested the stethoscope on my back to listen to my lungs. 'Breathe normally.'

I spent another minute breathing, thinking about cancers, thinking about dying, and about Sparrow finding sanctuary somewhere safe with the rest of the circus.

'Now take a deep breath and make small cough.'

I took a deep breath while she shifted the stethoscope around, then coughed.

'Enough,' Elenor said, then she stepped back to think.

'What's the verdict?' I asked.

'Your heart is good—young and strong, with no abnormal sounds or rhythms. Your lungs are also good but the lower lobe of your right lung is entirely missing. Lie down.'

I lay, and she started prodding and poking my abdomen. It was sore when she pressed up against my liver. She stopped and walked around the table, thoughtfully tapping the bridge of her nose with the metal end of the stethoscope. 'There is a faint scar on your temple. What do you know of that?'

'Nothing.'

'You have albinism, and your eyes are replaced, and you know nothing?'

'When I was little my eyes were bad. After the circus bought me, I remember waking up after an illness and things was better.'

'An old scar on your right side shows you are operated on many years ago. I have no equipment to image what is in your chest, but it is either an implant or a tumour. Judging by what you tell me—that it is growing—it is likely to be the latter.'

I was gutted. 'How long have I got?'

'That depends. If it's a tumour, you have only weeks.'

The wind was knocked out of me. Death had stopped being my accomplice and now had his hands around my throat.

'On the other hand,' Elenor paced, deep in thought, 'long ago I heard rumours of biomechanical implants, tumours engineered to perform various functions. Your Mister Splinter might know more.'

I ran a hand over my side. 'So I'm either dying, or I got a machine in here?'

'I never heard that any experiments worked. You must find your father. Quickly.'

Another reason to track down dear old Dad. 'Any quicker way to Gdansk than horseback?'

'If you get to Highway Six, you can hitchhike or buy passage, but the roads are patrolled by bandits and militias. Here in west are more bandits, further east is more uniforms. There are also communities who will take exception to anyone with unusual appearance. Probably the best people to ask would be the drug-runners. They are diverse, they travel a lot, and they travel fast.'

'Entrepreneurs of an illegal nature, I take it.'

'Very, and inclined to violence. I have bought antibiotics and pain-killers from them.'

'So is all drugs illegal here?'

'Generally, yes, though some life-saving drugs are tolerated—usually when hypocritical politician or high priest falls ill.'

'Is it the Church what runs Poland now?'

'Not officially, but the Catholic Church is the strongest power, and have their own militias. Poland is now part of the Slavic Federation—Intermarium, as British call it, or Międzymorze as we call it. The central authority in Warsaw has no choice but to allow Church to run its affairs the way it sees fit—either that or restart the wars.'

'So, you think we should approach the drug-runners?'

'Only as last resort. They are dangerous but, because of their business, they avoid the militias. You and Sparrow would do well to avoid anyone in uniform.'

'So, where do we find these drug-runners?'

'They move around, but lately I am notice smoke and lights to the north-east of the town, probably in the old shopping mall.'

'What's a "shopping mall"?'

'Large building full of shops—like market but under big roof.'

'I thought you said no one lived here.'

'They don't. The town and the mall are dead and empty. Ideal for the Pimpernels.'

'"Pimpernels"? Why is they named after a flower?'

'When children play Hide and Seek, they sing a song: "They seek them here, they seek them there, the priests seek them everywhere. Are they in heaven or are they in hell? Those damned elusive Pimpernels."'

I got dressed as we finished talking. We went outside and found Sparrow sitting out in the sun, the dog panting at her feet. She looked up, shielding her eyes. 'So, what did Elenor find?'

I was about to lie, but with Sparrow looking at me with love and concern, my usual ability with palaver gave out. 'It in't good,' I admitted. 'Looks like Splinter and Doctor Po cut me open when they first bought me, and put something inside. A biomachine what's come alive—and maybe killing me.'

Sparrow was thoughtful. 'But it were only after them glasses finished working out who you was that you started changing.'

I nodded. 'Another mystery for Splinter to explain, assuming Tommy hasn't murdered them all.'

Elenor frowned. 'You certainly live interesting lives.'

Sparrow grimaced. 'That's us. "Interesting".'

I tried to sound confident. 'Our one chance of getting to Gdansk in time seems to be via a bunch of drug-runners called the Pimpernels. Fancy a walk?'

'How dangerous is these lads?'

'Very,' said Elenor flatly. 'But I don't fear them as much as I fear uniforms and cassocks.'

🕊

We left the horse with Elenor. In return, she gave us food, her blessings, a gold crucifix on a chain, and a small pistol. 'Wear the cross. It might convince others you're good Catholics, or you can just sell. The pistol is for emergencies—there's only three rounds left in it.' She give me a meaningful look. 'Sufficient calibre for close-range.' I knew what she meant and nodded, grimly grateful.

We thanked and hugged her, hugged and kissed her dog, then set off down the hill into the town.

Sparrow sniffled, upset. I slung an arm around her shoulders. 'Elenor will be alright.'

'I don't like her being lonely.'

'She in't lonely. She's got animals, which is better company than a bunch of messed-up humans any day. For two pins I'd swap you for a ferret.'

Sparrow wiped her eyes on my shoulder and squeezed my hand.

We walked through the town, forgetting our troubles. Płoty was beautiful, even with the war damage. Foliage climbed walls, sprouted from windows and covered roofs. Birds, bees and dragonflies filled the air. Deer and bears foraged. A wild dog stood in the doorway of a house, and watched us walk by, wary. Some puppies came tumbling and scrambling out until she softly wuffed, then they scarpered back into the bushes, away from dangerous humans.

With my new navigational sense, we found the main road through town, and eventually came to an open plain of cracked concrete. In the middle of this vast emptiness loomed an anonymous island of a building—a huge, square cube with no windows, and only one giant entrance.

'This must be the mall,' said Sparrow.

We looked around, nervous. 'I don't see no one,' I said.

'Elenor said they might've brewed a batch of drugs and pulled up stakes already.'

'We'd better find out. Get that invisibility coat on, eh?'

Sparrow pulled on the grey coat, and I gave her the pistol. 'If things get nasty I want you to promise you'll look after your own safety first, right?'

'Nope. All for one and one for all, that's how it works.'

'If you get in trouble too, how does that help me? I'm begging you, whatever happens, stay safe.'

'You and me is one. I couldn't live without you.'

That short sentence went through me like Cupid's arrow. Sparrow felt like what I did.

'Don't say stuff like that,' I growled. 'Anything happens to me and you'll get over it in time. Tog would marry you in a heartbeat. You and him can have cute half-size babies.'

'Shut up. I've got your back, so go find some Pimpernels.'

She turned on the invisibility, and we walked across the concrete. I had no idea why people from the old days needed all this dead space around a covered market. Perhaps they used it for something else, but I couldn't imagine what. A few minutes later, the mall entrance was towering above us, the blackness inside scary. 'Why din't they have no windows in this thing?' I whispered.

'They used lectric.'

'This place is huge. How much lectric did they have back in them days?'

'Lots. Come on.'

'Wait. You hang back. If there's trouble, I'll deal with it, alright?'

I walked into the entrance, crunching my way across broken glass, shattered concrete and marble. Past the doorway was an even bigger space, with a roof five or six storeys above, and stairs going every which way. My eyes were adjusting to the gloom when I saw a man in a long, hooded coat sitting at the base of some stairs facing the entrance.

I walked toward him, raising a hand. 'Hullo. I don't suppose you'd be a Pimpernel, would you?'

The man was as black as I was white. He smiled, his white teeth gleaming. 'I would. I don't suppose you'd know how to drive a car, would you?'

'As it happens, I do. Why?'

The man raised a finger as signal, I felt something sharp hit me neck, then everything went dark.

Chapter Thirty-Six—
The road less travelled is
empty for a reason

woke, dimly aware I was being dragged along a smooth surface by a big hand on my collar. I looked up and saw it belonged to the black man in the long coat.

'Oi,' I croaked. 'I can walk, you know.'

'Not yet you can't. Besides, the only use I have for your legs is pushing an accelerator pedal.'

I tried to move, but could only twitch my fingers. 'So while we're chatting, are you really a Pimpernel?'

'I am.'

'You is one of the geezers what make and sell drugs.'

'You have talent for stating the obvious.'

'Not so obvious to me, mate—w . . . I'm a stranger in a strange land. I'm from England.'

'I've never been there. I hear it is hot and dry in the south.'

'It's nice if the rains come. Assuming I live, you must come visit sometime. We'll have a barbecue.'

'I like that you have sense of humour. Too many Poles don't.'

'I've found you all very charming. A little inclined to violence, but we all have our crosses to bear.'

He dragged me into a large room full of chemical smells, past benches and machinery and people bustling about. Two other men came and picked me up, taking me to an old sofa in one corner. I was dropped into it like a sack of potatoes, one of the men pausing to sit me upright before stationing himself beside me. The black man sat in a chair facing me.

'Search him.'

The man next to me went through my pockets, taking what little there was and depositing it on a small table in front of me. The black man looked through the pile. 'You have no weapon?'

'I'm a pacifist. Besides which, I assumed you'd have enough weapons for all of us.'

'How did you learn we are here?'

'I heard a rumour.'

'Who tells you this rumour?'

'A local who means you no harm and is no threat to you in any way.'

'Elenor?'

I hesitated and he nodded, his guess confirmed. 'I am liking Elenor. You need not worry for her.'

'She wanted to help—I need to get to Gdansk, and she thought I might get a lift from you lot. Any chance?'

He smiled. 'Every chance. Hold him.'

One of the men clamped his arms around my chest. A tall, young woman dressed in black strolled across, carrying a small metal box that looked homemade and well-used. She pressed it against my upper arm then clicked a button. I felt a sharp pain, and looked down to see blood trickling as she pocketed the box and pulled out another device, tubular with a trigger. She looked up, expressionless. 'This will hurt.'

It did. I yelped as I felt a .22-calibre bullet-sized object injected under my skin. Then she used a third device to seal the wound with a blob of glue. With a nod, she walked away

The black man leaned forward. 'You have been injected with a poison and its antidote. If you perform the task we give you, the antidote will be given and you will live. If you do not, you will die.'

I glared, still unable to move.

'You will have a vehicle to get to our meeting point near Gdansk in the Tri-City. Get there within twenty or so hours and deliver the vehicle and its contents. Then you can go where you want.'

'Why couldn't you just have asked me?'

'Because you would've refused. The vehicle contains materials and personnel who would ensure your slow death should you be captured by the militias.'

'I'm doing a drug run, I take it.'

'More importantly, you also have two passengers—three including your friend when we find him.'

'What friend?'

'Please, lies and evasions annoy me. Are you able to contact your friend?'

'No.'

'Do you know where he is now?'

'Somewhere nearby unfortunately. Watching and waiting. Is you intending to inject them too?'

'I hope not. How important is this friend to you?'

I hesitated, and the prick was smart enough to read me with ease. 'Good, I'm glad this friend is important,' he said. 'I will not need to offer him harm. Plus he can "ride shotgun".'

'We have only one small pistol with three bullets.'

'We will arm you sufficiently.'

'And what are my chief obstacles in getting to the Tri-City, other than every militia being after us?'

'Just that. If you are caught, you should allow sufficient bullets to end your own lives.'

I sighed. 'A month ago I was close to topping myself. Now I'm running drugs to stay alive.'

'You have reasons to live, yes?'

'Love—a thing you wouldn't know about, you psychopath.'

The man sighed. 'The drugs you are running are mostly medical.'

Feeling was returning to my body and I started slowly stretching, still weak. 'So you're a saint, not a psycho.'

'I am devil incarnate to the Church. But "armed prophets are victorious where unarmed prophets are defeated".'

I recognised the quote, annoyed. 'Machiavelli. Got a copy of Sun Tzu in your *other* pocket?'

He gave me a long look then stretched out a hand. 'My name is Aleksy Ratajczyk.'

I ignored his hand. 'Blanco.'

'I hope you survive, Blanco. I would like to meet you again one day.'

'Unlikely. If your poison don't kill me, where we're going there's plenty who wants me dead.'

'You flee death, while also fleeing toward it. It is an interesting life, no? Give me your arm.'

I managed to hold it out. Aleksy produced a pen, pushed up my sleeve and scrawled a symbol on my arm, an X with a horizontal bar drawn across the bottom triangle. 'Locate Pimpernels, show them this and tell them you know me. Now we must give you a vehicle and find your friend.'

I was lifted to my feet, and I hobbled after Aleksy. As we made our way slowly back to the main entrance hall, I began to feel stronger. 'Oi, Aleksy.'

He paused and looked back. 'Yes?'

'My friend with the three bullets might be inclined to put them in you. I should go first.'

'I understand.'

'One last thing—if you kill my friend, I'll sit in the vehicle until the poison kills *me*.'

He saw I wasn't kidding. 'I give you my word I will not harm your friend.'

I nodded and we walked on. I got down the steps to the main hall by clinging to the rail.

A small open-framed four-wheel-drive truck was now parked there, with a few people still working on it. Aleksy joined me as I walked toward the entrance, calling out. 'Sparrow! I'm okay! I've entered into a business arrangement with this gentleman, and this truck is for us to travel to the east coast.'

Sparrow's voice rang out, echoing off the walls. 'What's he done to you? I can see you're not right.'

'He knocked me out so he could check my suitability for a little job he wants done.'

'Give me one reason I shouldn't put a bullet through his head.'

'With that pistol of Elenor's, you're likely to miss him and hit me.'

Aleksy took a semiauto from one of his assistants and handed it to me. 'You see? I give Blanco weapon to prove we mean no harm.'

Sparrow called out. 'Is you sure about this, Blanco?'

'You're safe, but we need to go now.'

Aleksy took my elbow. 'Come, I show you vehicle.'

The vehicle was a small light off-road truck—big tyres, oversized shock absorbers, no roof, doors or bonnet. At the back was a big lectric-hydrogen fuel-cell motor, up front was a square refrigerated cargo compartment. The back seat was filled with two miserable-looking men in stained black suits. Both were dumpy and unshaven, with round heads and thick black hair. One had big sideburns and the other had a drooping moustache but, other than that, they could've been twins. The driver's seat faced a truck steering wheel and some crudely wired control levers and buttons. The passenger seat sat squarely behind a mounted gaffed-up lectric 308 minigun.

'You have three hundred rounds,' warned Aleksy. 'So pick your targets. The suspension is good for all terrain. The weight is low but for the two fat bastards in the back. You have enough power to get you to Tri-City, with little to spare, so most direct route is preferable.'

The woman in black approached and applied some glue to a small disk then pasted it on the left side of my head beside my eyebrow. 'That will guide you to your final destination. It is voice-operated—Polish only.' Aleksy pointed to a red switch beside the steering wheel. 'In emergency this will give you much speed—maybe for half minute—but be careful.'

'This thing standard issue for you lot?' I asked.

'We make do with what comes to us. It is good vehicle. You will see.'

'Is there any way I can avoid militias altogether?'

'Ask the two gentlemen in the back to pray for you.' He give them a sour look, but neither met his eyes. 'Otherwise it will be down to luck, speed and reacting in the moment. Avoid firefights—they will bring more trouble than you can handle, especially the closer you are to the coast.'

An unattended semi lifted itself off the ground, and Sparrow's face and hand appeared, then her head, as she kept the weapon levelled at Aleksy. 'Keep still. One false move and I shoot.'

I stepped between them, soothing. 'Sparrow, meet Aleksy. Aleksy, meet Sparrow.'

'How d'yer fucking do,' she snarled.

Aleksy smiled. 'Invisibility cloak is good oldtech. Very rare. You would consider selling?'

'No,' I replied. 'Sparrow, please don't pull the trigger. Negotiations is at a delicate stage.'

Sparrow warily lowered the gun as I turned to Aleksy. 'If we isn't stopping, we'll need food and water.'

Aleksy give orders to one of his men, who hurried away. Then he turned back to us. 'You will become tired. Doctor Radek give you stimulants which you should take at first sign of tiredness.'

Radek produced a roll of tape, tore off two strips, and spoke in English, her tone as flat as her expression. 'I stick on your arm—rub him hard when you are tired, then you will not be tired.'

I held out my arm and she applied the tape, then turned to Sparrow. Sparrow hesitated, wary. Doctor Radek frowned. 'I don't kill people unless I have to. You need this if you are to survive.'

Sparrow lifted her arm and Radek put the tape on. 'Tired—rub, okay?'

'I got it,' Sparrow replied. 'So, what's the deal? You're giving us a car in exchange for what?'

I spoke before Aleksy could. 'They is giving us this car in return for us dropping off a few items to friends of theirs.'

'That's it?'

'We'll talk about the fine print when we're on the road.'

Aleksy eyed the semi Sparrow was still holding at half-mast. 'That might be wise.'

The man returned with bottles and some capped tubes. 'The bottles are water, the tubes you squeeze into your mouth. Looks horrible but does not taste bad—it will keep you alive.'

I looked at the fat men. 'And these two go to the same address?'

'Yes. They are more important than the cargo. By keeping them alive, you will save many lives.'

'Maybe even my own.'

'I hope so.' Aleksy held out his hand, but I again ignored it.

'If we ever meet again,' I said, 'just be aware that I will break that nose of yours.'

He shrugged. 'Good luck.'

I hopped in the driver's seat as Sparrow squeezed into the passenger side, keeping her semi ready. I flicked the start switch and, after a few seconds, there was a mild hum from the engine that turned into a high-pitched whine.

I gingerly depressed the accelerator with my foot and we rolled forward, the large tyres crunching over rubble and glass. We passed through the entrance and out into the sunshine. I blinked and my vision adjusted to screen out the glare. I was grateful, but it was another reminder of whatever was growing inside me.

We rolled across the concrete, the suspension good enough to keep the ride smooth even over potholes and rubble. 'Where's the road to the Tri-City?' I murmured.

My vision flickered, then a map appeared with the main roads in red, the winding back roads in green. 'We has a choice between the back roads and the main roads,' I mused. 'Where do you think the militia's going to be looking?'

'The back roads,' said the moustache in the back.

'The main roads it is then.'

We reached the edge of the concrete and dropped onto a curved road what joined onto the highway. Once we were rolling on a straighter road, I let the vehicle pick up speed.

'Keep an eye out, darlin',' I said.

'For what?'

'Everything. Now hold on. Let's see what this thing can do.'

I pressed the accelerator, and in seconds, we were flying down that road like a missile.

Sparrow had to shout over the wind noise. 'What did you mean before about the "fine print"?'

I grimaced. 'You're not going to like this.'

Chapter Thirty-Seven—As with the sea, in warfare there are no constant conditions

Sparrow wanted to go back and kill everyone. I argued that revenge came after survival, and kept us heading east.

The highway was intact but rough, a mix of weedy tarmac, muddy farm track and still-intact sections of ferroplas. Credit to them Pimpernel mechanics though—the little truck flew across all of it. The suspension and power were magic. So were the brakes—which is just as well, because someone had once introduced water buffalo to the local wetlands and, judging by the numbers, they were now breeding like rabbits. They stood in the road, unafraid. Hitting one would be like hitting a brick wall.

We didn't see people till just before Wicimice, where timber-cutters were taking what they could from the remains of a forest fire. Them axe-wielding boys didn't hear us coming till we were right among them, and I had to slow down to get through. They were rough-looking, and I noticed their truck had a lad sitting on the bonnet with a semiautomatic. 'Smile and wave,' I muttered.

Sparrow and I give the lads a wave, and a few nodded. A few others made the devil's horns signs at us, but they were grinning, so I guessed they weren't averse to Pimpernel activity. One of them ran up, signalling for us to stop. I slowed down and muttered to Sparrow, 'Keep that pistol ready.'

The geezer caught up and looked our truck over, impressed. Then he pointed up the road. 'Policja ahead,' he scowled. 'Just on the other side of the town, unless they are stuffing themselves at the inn.'

I nodded. 'Thanks, brother.'

'You are not Poles?'

'No. But we do good work for Poles.' I indicated the cargo behind. 'This delivery will save lives.'

'Medicines?'

I nodded and he relaxed. 'Good. We will have to report we see a vehicle, but we will say you went into forest, heading south, tak?'

'Tak.'

'Avoid uniforms and crucifixes. Heaven or hell, may God go with you.'

He stood back and we rolled on, slowly picking up speed. Sparrow chewed a fingernail, edgy, so I tried to sound more relaxed. 'It seems not every good Pole loves his church.'

She didn't reply.

The sun began to flash in the rear-view mirror, blinding me. I tilted it up, worried—soon it would be dark, and we'd be forced to slow. Sparrow pointed ahead to smoke curling above the trees. This would be our Polish friend's town. We looked for a back road to the north, but as we drove closer, we saw there was nothing but a few muddy farm tracks turning off.

'We might have to take our chances with them police,' said Sparrow.

I slowed as we neared the turn-off to the town. Then I stopped completely. 'What the hell?'

In the middle of the road was a small boy, apparently dead.

Sparrow's concern turned to a smile. 'He's alright. He's sneaking a look at us through his fringe.'

I saw the kid was looking through scrunched-up eyes, and breathing fast. Sparrow looked around. 'It's the old game, I reckon.'

On cue, a young blonde girl, about ten years old, in a dirty floral dress, come running out of some bushes and 'found' her 'dead' sibling. 'Oh, sweet Jesus our Saviour, my brother is injured or sick!'

'What's she after?' I whispered. 'Money?'

'Anything she can get, probably.' Sparrow motioned me to move the truck forward, amused. 'Which means these little entrepreneurs might be open to a bit of business concerning evading the law.'

I pulled up next to the girl. 'Nice try, darlin'. Tell the little one he can get up now.'

'But he is sick or injured. Look for yourself. If only we have money for candles to pray for his health . . .'

'How about gold?'

The girl looked us over, calculating. 'How much?'

'This.' I pulled out the crucifix Elenor gave us. 'It's proper gold, and it's yours if you help us. Now tell the boy to get up, and tell your friends to come out of hiding.'

The girl hesitated, whistled briefly, and dug a toe into the boy on the ground. 'Get up, Stefan.'

The boy rose to his feet, uncertain, as half a dozen children of different sizes and ages emerged from hiding. They gathered around, marvelling at the car and at us. The girl peered at our faces. 'You are witches?'

'No, we're rich English tourists,' I replied.

'What's a "too-riss"? And who are they?' The girl cast a wary look at the stolid Poles in the back.

'Tourists are rich people, and these two are our servants. Now, do you want to earn this gold?'

'What do you want from us?'

'Where are the policja?'

The girl pointed ahead. 'They are on the road, hiding beside a red barn, sleeping or playing with themselves.'

'Well, we hate lazy police because they always stop us and waste our time,' I said. 'So how about you trick them police into town, so we can drive on without being bothered?' I unhooked the chain and offered it to her. 'We'll give you this upfront, see? When those police are safely out of the way, we'll give you the crucifix. Do we have a deal?'

'You have guns—why don't you just shoot them?'

'We don't like killing people. Even lazy policemen.'

One of the boys scowled. 'We don't mind if you kill them. They hit us, even when we only steal little things.'

'Then you should take more care not getting caught,' I replied. 'Do we have a deal?'

The girl put the gold to her mouth, bit down carefully, then looked up. 'It's real. Okay, we have a deal. Give us five minutes.'

The girl gathered the children into a circle, and a brief discussion ended in nodded heads. The children all sprinted off except for the girl. 'They will bring the police away so they don't see you. I stay with you, and when you are on the other side, you give me the cross.'

'Deal,' I replied, and translated to Sparrow.

Sparrow offered the girl a smile. 'Hop aboard.'

The girl happily stood on the side rail, and I rolled us under some trees where we could see the turn-off into the town.

Sparrow looked the girl up and down. 'Give that dial a wipe and she'd be a pretty little thing.'

'I'll tell her you think she's pretty,' I said, and spoke to the girl in Polish.

The girl beamed. 'One half of your witch is very beautiful. She must be under a powerful curse.'

I nodded. 'Luckily,' I replied, 'everyone loves her just as she is. Especially me.'

The girl sighed, dreamy. 'Is like a fairytale.'

Sparrow noted the look, and raised an eyebrow. 'What did you tell our little crime boss?'

'I told her I like you.'

Sparrow smiled, and give me a kiss. The girl giggled, and Sparrow give her a grin. Despite the language barrier, I saw the pair of them were in feminine communion. 'Tell her to hold out for a good partner,' said Sparrow, misty. 'Someone who can prove they deserves her.'

I passed on this wisdom, and the girl nodded. 'If they try to make me marry Tomas, I will run away. He smells like cheese even when he hasn't been eating cheese.'

I translated this to Sparrow, who spluttered with laughter. Her smile made me smile, and our smiles made the girl smile. So there we were, three criminals, me with at least two death sentences hanging over me, in a car full of illegal drugs, chuckling in the warm Polish sunset.

A minute later, a fake panic of screaming kids fled the road ahead, closely followed by two angry police officers on a lectric quad, bumping along the rutted crossroads then turning into the town.

The girl raised her hand. 'Wait.' Moments later, we heard a whistle. 'Okay, now, go.'

I pressed the accelerator and we glided past the turn-off, stopping beside a red barn. I handed the girl the cross, and we solemnly shook hands.

'It's good doing business with you,' she said. She hopped off the side of the truck, wistful. 'Is a beautiful truck. Where are you going?'

'To the city.'

'One day I will go to the city.'

'Don't be in a hurry, darlin'—cities can be hard places.'

'You think this place is not?'

'All places are hard, I think. Will that gold also buy your silence about us?'

She nodded, then smiled. 'I have never seen Pimpernels up close before. I like.' She ran off, looking more like a happy little girl than a hard-bitten businesswoman.

I floored the accelerator and we took off into the approaching dusk.

At the next town, Pniewo, there were more people, and only one road through. There was still enough light for the locals to clock the strange passengers of the strange vehicle—a beautiful scarred girl, a strange pale man with white dreadlocks, and two Poles staring rigidly ahead. We could only hope they didn't report us too quickly.

On the other side of town, the empty road ran through thick forest. Sunset became night. I turned on the headlights and slowed down. In the dark, stray cattle showed themselves at the last second, turning their heads so their eyes suddenly reflected our lights. After a couple of near misses, I dropped our speed again, along with my hopes we'd make it in time.

To cheer us up I sang a song, but Sparrow was in a quiet mood, so I didn't sing no more. In the rear-view mirror, the two Poles sat unmoving and stoic, and it was pissing me off. 'Oi, you two. What's your names then?'

The one with the drooping moustache grimaced, speaking English. 'My name is Feliks Haczek. My colleague is Drugi Kovel.'

'And what sort of work do you do?'

'I am Inspector-General of Agricultural Services,' Feliks replied. 'My colleague is senior member of the Central Committee of Educators.'

'And how did you get mixed up with the Pimpernels?'

'We were kidnapped from a conference.'

'How much are the Pimpernels asking for ransom?'

'Nothing. It is prisoner swap. Two of us for twenty Pimpernels.'

I was impressed. 'Them Pimpernels know how to drive a hard bargain.'

Feliks leaned forward, eager. 'If you let us free, we will tell the authorities about the poison in you. Our excellent priests could save you.'

'With prayer?' I scoffed.

'Don't you want to strike a blow against those who did this to you?'

'I'd break Aleksy's nose but that's as far as it goes. I just want to live.'

'How do you know they have not lied? How do you know there is an antidote?'

Sparrow had been quietly boiling, and reached her limit. 'Shut up! Everyone just shut the fuck up!'

She faced forward again, her lips clamped.

Talk ended, and the only sound was the whine of the truck, rising and falling with our speed. I focused on avoiding potholes, fallen trees and wild animals.

The next village was dark and quiet, and I rolled us through without even making a dog bark. I began to feel our near-silent truck might make it all the way to our destination by dawn.

I glanced across to see if Sparrow was still angry. 'It's not so far,' I said. 'We've got time to spare.'

'Great,' Sparrow replied. 'Let's stop and have a picnic so I can plan my life for when you're dead.'

I kept quiet after that.

We left the forests and entered the open land and farms outside the city of Koszalin. The map I was seeing overlaid on our surroundings showed the road ahead was about to split—one branch turning left into the town centre, the other going straight through to the highway on the other side. If there was going to be a roadblock, that would be the place.

Sure enough, on a bend ahead, a police car was tucked into the bushes waiting for anyone running the roadblock from the other side. As we went past, I checked the rear-view mirror and saw their taillights flash three times, a signal to them up ahead of us, where flashing lights came into view. In the air above the roadblock, a holo-sign flashed, telling us to slow down. I kept motoring.

Sparrow tried to sound casual. 'When should I start firing this gun?'

'If we start firing, they'll fire back. We need to get past them, not through.' I was checking my internal map and doing some fast mental calculations as the sign changed to 'Stop'. Gritting my teeth, I kept up the speed as it became 'Stop Now!', then 'STOP OR YOU WILL BE FIRED UPON'.

'Hold on tight, everyone,' I squeaked.

Two hundred and ten metres from the roadblock, the uniforms switched on a massive Klieg light to blind us. Two hundred metres from the roadblock, I swung the wheel to the right. Due to the fact there wasn't no road to our right, Sparrow was understandably screaming, as were the Polish geezers.

But, with a huge bump, we landed on the railway line at a speed that ensured a noisy but surprisingly smooth ride. I was starting to feel smug as we rounded the curve to Dworzec station—until we saw the headlight of the train coming at us. More screaming and swearing, this time with me joining in. I got the truck tyres to mount the rails so we could jump onto the next track just in time. There was an indignant honk, and the train blasted past us.

I slowed down, my heart racing. 'Sorry about that. I got cocky.'

Sparrow was clenching the seat with white knuckles. 'Can you please get us back onto the road?'

'We just need to go a little further.'

We rattled more slowly along the track toward the lights of the station. The lamps on the platform weren't bright, but we could see jaws drop as travellers watched us motor through. There was also a guard, who quickly grabbed his RT, no doubt reporting a strange hybrid vehicle filled with dodgy fucks. Once we were through the station and back in the dark, I drove across a railway bridge then veered off the embankment to its right.

It was steeper than I predicted, and we plunged down the hill, missed a couple of trees, crashed through some bushes and flew out, ending up the wrong way on a roundabout crowded with evening traffic. Luckily, that traffic was mostly donkey carts and bicycles, but it was a close thing.

I managed to get us back onto the right highway. Then, with the luxury of two lanes of intact ferroplas to drive on, I started breaking the speed laws. The Poles looked stricken as I wove through the traffic, but I only felt sorry for Sparrow, who was hiding how scared she was.

I yelled over the wind noise. 'I'm sorry, but they'll be after us for sure now.'

'What if they have another roadblock?' she yelled back. 'Do we shoot our way through?'

I shrugged. I'd run out of ideas. All I could think of was speed—two hundred kilometres worth.

I just had to stay awake, stay focused and not crash into anything.

Then, as we approached the last roundabout on the way out of Koszalin, at high speed, I had the first epileptic fit, and blacked out.

Chapter Thirty-Eight—Be swift if you are the hammer, patient if you are the anvil

woke in the glare of the vehicle's remaining headlight, Sparrow's anxious face looking down at mine. I turned my head to see I was lying on some dry grass in the dark concrete ruins of what looked like a sports stadium, feeling weak as a drained battery.

'What happened?' I whispered.

'You looked like someone lectricuted you, then we crashed.'

'Are you alright?'

'We're fine. I managed to steer us off the side of the road. One of the headlights got taken out, but the truck's alright. It's you I'm worried about. What happened?'

'I don't know. I remember we were driving fast, then suddenly—lights out.'

'I think it was a plectic fit. I seen one once—a little boy in the audience.'

I was gutted. Whatever was inside me was now in my feckin' brain. 'How long was I out to it?'

'About ten minutes.'

'Where are we now?'

'Just off the road. The highway is on the other side of the wall there.'

I sat up. 'We need to get moving.'

'We do, and I'm driving.'

'You ever driven before?'

'No, but I watched you.'

I blinked and rubbed my eyes again. 'I'll be alright in a minute.'

'Yeah, and then you'll have another fit and we'll all be killed. No thanks, boyo. I is driving.'

'You in't hardwired like I is to see where to go.'

'So you can tell me. Come on.'

She helped me up, and I saw the truck had survived pretty well. Our suited Polish friends were still in place, rigid with fear. I tried for an encouraging smile. 'It's alright, lads—I'm fine.'

'It's not you we're worried about,' said Feliks. 'We must reach the Tri-City in time.'

I realised what I should have earlier. 'You have the poison inside you?'

They nodded. I swayed slightly as my vision fuzzed briefly, but Sparrow grabbed me. 'Oi. Get in the passenger seat and tell me which buttons to push.'

Watching her peer at the controls, the Poles groaned softly. Sparrow scowled at them in the rear-view mirror. 'I'm a fast learner, alright?'

I pointed to the red button, and Sparrow pushed it to start up the engine. It whined to a high-pitched hum, then she put it into forward drive mode. Moving slowly around mounds of fallen concrete and rusted steel beams, she took us out of the stadium, then onto the edge of the highway. Though it was late, there was still some traffic— a tractor loaded with produce making its way into town, a drunk slumped over the neck of his donkey, some bicycles and a few small hydrogen trucks in a convoy. When the road was clear, Sparrow eased us out and floored the accelerator, sending me and the Poles flying back in our seats.

'Oi!' I yelled. 'Get us there in one piece, eh?'

'I'll get us there,' she replied through gritted teeth. 'You just make sure you give me plenty of warning about which road to take.'

'It's this one, all the way to the Tri-City.'

'Good. And keep that gun ready. I in't stopping for no one.'

The next hour was a blur. Sparrow's driving was too fast for my befuddled brain but, as the minutes wore on, the fear of crashing was too much effort to keep up. Tired, I settled into numb resignation. I couldn't do nothing but hold the handles of the mounted gun, keep checking my internal map, and not think about dying.

Unfortunately, my brain was increasingly messed up with odd sounds and random visions in meaningless fragments. I heard a Chinese geezer talking about stuff I didn't understand—'specific ethnic-genetic attacks' and 'winning without fighting'. Then there was some angry Russian babbling, and flashes of a blue lake surrounded by forest in the middle of snow-capped mountains. Numbers and mathematical squiggles popped into my vision, then flickered out.

I guessed all this was the thing inside me, still growing, taking over. I wondered what would be left of me when it finished doing whatever it was doing. Would my mind be trapped in my own brain the same way Mister Splinter was trapped in his stinking body?

'We got someone following us,' said Sparrow.

I looked behind. A pair of lights, and they were catching up. 'Someone's in a hurry.' I turned to the Poles. 'There might be some fighting, and you need to help.'

Drugi shook his head. 'I will not kill Poles.' Feliks nodded his agreement.

'Fine,' I said, handing him our pistol. 'Seeing we're all fighting for survival, whoever's the best shot can shoot out their tyres.'

The Poles looked at each other. Feliks spoke first. 'I was given a commendation during my national service training for marksmanship.'

Drugi curled his lip, unimpressed. 'Good luck hitting anything with that little thing.'

Feliks took the pistol, clearly sharing Drugi's disgust, but opened and checked it like a pro. 'The first bullet will probably explode the chamber and kill me.'

Then our pursuer put on their flashing lights. The fucking polis.

Sparrow cursed. 'Even if we win a firefight, there'll be more cops waiting ahead.'

'True,' I replied. 'But it occurs to me that our friends in the back seat may have official identification papers on them.' I turned. 'Is that correct?'

The Poles nodded, wary.

Sparrow glanced at me, sceptical. 'They could talk our way out of this?'

I turned back to the Poles. 'If you play your part and talk to these local cops like the bigwigs you are, I'll make sure no one gets killed, alright?'

'Do we have a choice?' Drugi grumbled.

'Not if you want to live, no.' I pointed forward. 'Sparrow, stop as close as you can to that field.'

I turned around. 'Gentlemen, stash that pistol. When we stop, have your papers ready and walk back to the police car, hands in clear sight. Keep them talking, boss them around, whatever it takes.'

Sparrow slowed, and steered us off the ferroplas onto the weedy verge where there was some cover. With the semi over my shoulder, I slid out and into the shadows of a cropped field, crawling back alongside the road as the police car pulled in behind our truck. I heard shouting from the police, then stern raised voices from the Poles. I kept my head down, the flashing lights washing over me. The voices grew lower and I could hear the police were aggressive. 'What is this vehicle? What is your business?'

The Poles pretended outrage. 'We are on state business. Inspect our papers.'

I could see two polis with the Poles, but not if there were more in the car. I kept crawling, hoping the Poles would stall them long enough.

Then my vision blacked out and I was suddenly blind. I had time to wonder if this was another fit coming on, and have despair wash over me, but then my vision returned—changed.

A strange grey light lit everything up, and I was no longer dazzled by the flashing lights or blinded by the shadows. I could see everything, crisp and clear—in every shade of grey. One cop held the Poles at gunpoint while the other looked through their papers and ignored their indignant palaver. In the back of the police car was a man, and he wasn't wearing a uniform.

I crept to the rear of the car. In the back seat was a teenage lad, his forehead rested against the back of the front seat, his right wrist handcuffed to a ringbolt. On the front seat were some keys and a metal torch. I reached in, slow.

The boy was startled, and opened his mouth in surprise. I put a finger over my lips. He froze. I took the keys. Hoping the kid kept quiet, I crept forward to the bonnet of the police car, took a deep breath, then came up behind the police. 'Don't move or I'll shoot.'

The cops turned, only to find themselves blinded by their own lights. I put on a nasty voice, modelled on the Gaffer. 'Weapons and comm gear on the ground, now! Do what I say and you'll live. One wrong move and you are fucking dead men.'

I moved around to show them the semi, and the cops carefully laid their weapons down.

'Pick up their gear,' I told the Poles, who reluctantly obeyed as I called out the all-clear to Sparrow.

She come running back, growling. 'This is getting scary.'

'Lucky for us, we in't got time to be scared. Besides, the good news is our two important passengers, Mister Feliks and Mister Drugi, now have a police escort.'

Sparrow rolled her eyes. 'What are you up to, you mad bugger?'

'I have to check something first.' I went back to the car, where the lad looked terrified. 'I'm innocent!' he pleaded. 'I can't help if women like me. I ask if they already have boyfriends, and they lie and say no. How is it my fault if *they* are kissing me?'

'I'm not anyone's boyfriend, mate—I'm a wanted criminal. Who are you?'

The boy relaxed, cheerful. 'I am also a criminal.'

I unlocked his cuffs. 'Terrible career choice, mate.' I returned to the police, cuffed them together, then tied them to a tree facing the road. 'Sorry boys, but you'll be found around sunrise at the latest.'

Back at the cars, the lad, cut and bruised from a fight, was trying to chat up Sparrow despite being a good bit shorter. I tapped his shoulder.

'And what have you been doing to get yourself arrested then?'

'I get in a fight,' he said, indicating one of the police. 'Petyr's cousin refused me entry to the club because one time I kiss his girlfriend. I am sick of being refused. It's practically the only club in town.'

I noted the small gold crucifix on a chain around his neck. 'I didn't think good Catholics went to clubs and started fights.'

'I am super good Catholic. I am just like Jesus—he also fights injustice.'

I liked this kid. 'And where's all the punch-ups in the Bible then?'

'They take those bits out maybe. Anyway, I'm sick of my stupid town and all the peasants wearing uniforms thinking they are better than me. Where are you going? I will come with you.'

'Can you drive?'

'Yes, of course. Anything.'

'You can drive this police car?'

His eyes lit up. 'Really?'

'Yes, but you must drive fast. All the way to the Tri-City.'

He beamed. 'I'm your man. Just wait one minute, please.' He ran across to where the police stood against the tree, rifled through their pockets, and removed their wallets and watches.

Sparrow tugged my arm. 'What the hell are we doing with this kid?'

'He'll drive the police car up front. If we see any uniforms, we put on the lights and steam on through. That's the theory, at least.'

The lad returned from his pilfering, smiling. 'Okay, I'm officially a criminal.'

'Is that a good thing?'

He shrugged. 'It was always going to happen. I am join your gang, yes?'

'No, but we can hook you up with one when we get to our destination. I'll sit up front with you.' I turned to Sparrow. 'Stick to our tail and don't lose us—we in't stopping till we get to the docks.'

Sparrow give me a kiss. 'You feeling alright?'

I couldn't lie. 'I'm still changing. Me head's full of mad stuff—voices and pictures and all sorts. I'm even seeing different, though maybe it'll go back to normal when it's daylight.'

We hugged, comforting ourselves against the fear. Then she pushed me away. 'Be careful.'

'You too, my darlin'.'

Sparrow and the Poles returned to the truck as I turned to my new driver. 'My name's Blanco, what's yours?'

'I don't know. I'll have to think one up.'

'You don't have a name?'

'I can't call myself Cibor when I'm in a criminal gang. How about "White Dragon"?'

'Start the engine, Cibor.'

He started the engine. 'Or maybe just "Dragon". Or how about "The Scorpion"? Or . . .'

'Start driving, go fast, don't crash.'

Cibor pulled out in a messy fishtail and floored it. He was in a chatty mood. '"The Rat". I like that. Rats are resourceful, and they fight when they're cornered. They're brave, like me.'

Cibor kept up a running commentary on how his criminal career was going to pan out, including his triumphant return to his hometown to whisk his second cousin, Maria, off her feet and take her back to his flash new apartment in the Tri-City, where she'd spend her days cooking and making love to him.

I tuned out, letting the voices of people I'd never met, and visions of places I'd never been to, wash over me.

The road was mostly intact, and we made good time. By midnight we were tearing toward the port through the urban and industrial conglomerate of Wejherowo, avoiding the elevated highway used by militia and Church authorities.

In Reda we raced past a patrol, giving our lights a quick flash like a casual greeting between colleagues. They didn't follow.

We entered Rumia's towering canyons of apartment blocks. Most were hollow-eyed shells, empty since the looting of the Federation Civil War. Some still had people living in them, apparently happy to throw their rubbish straight out the windows to pile up on the ground below. Foxes scavenged through the muck heaps, their sleek sneaking ignored by sleeping goats and tethered donkeys. A big dog, lying on an abandoned couch, lifted its head as we went by. I felt a pang of excitement knowing Daisy wasn't far—I was ready to fight an army of Gaffers to be reunited with her.

Cutting back onto the main Morska road, we saw only a few trucks and tractors returning from the port with their loads. Our side of the road was empty, so I let Cibor do top speed all the way to the Eugeniusza Kwaitkowskiego overpass.

We'd only just slowed to make a left onto the on-ramp when we were obliged to stop. Halfway up the ramp, two cars were parked side by side, blocking the way. Some small-calibre rifle barrels were poking up from behind them, as were the heads of some young opportunists looking to take us on.

'Put it on high beam,' I said to Cibor.

He looked worried as I took the semi off safety, but did it anyway. I fired a single burst out the window, then used the PA system. 'This is a stolen police vehicle. We are criminals, we are in a hurry and we are armed to the fucking teeth. If you leave now, your loved ones won't be grieving your tragic loss in the morning when your corpses are found.'

There was some palaver among the bandits, who were mostly in their early teens. Then one of the older ones stood up. 'Okay. We don't want trouble.'

I had to chuckle, and Cibor managed a nervous smile.

The kids got in their cars, struggled mightily to get the ancient diesel engines running, then slowly chuntered up the ramp with barely the power to make the slight gradient. Then one of them stalled, and their engine refused to start.

I sighed, impatient. 'Give them a push. Gently.'

Cibor scowled. 'They were about to rob us, and now we help them out?'

'Not only that, we're about to donate this police car to them. It in't polite to turn up at a meeting with a real criminal gang in a police car.'

Cibor reluctantly drove up to the back of the stalled car, bumped their rusty rear boot and pushed them up the rest of the way. Once onto the level highway, they rolled to the side. I got out and walked toward them, doing my confident act. They looked at me with mingled awe and horror, several crossing themselves. I pointed to the police car. 'See that? It's all yours for being such nice, helpful lads.'

'I'm not a lad,' called out a girl who couldn't have been more than twelve.

'My apologies—and a warning. If you value your life, stay away from the port and dry docks tonight. If the police catch you, tell them some bad men told you they were doing a job in . . . Where's some place a long way from here?'

'Dabrowa.'

'Dabrowa it is. Cibor, give these young entrepreneurs our keys.' I waved Sparrow up, and she warily drove alongside, causing the young bandits to drop their jaws at our vehicle, our gun, and Sparrow's good side. 'One last thing,' I said. 'Is there any obstructions ahead or is it clear?'

'It's clear,' called the oldest boy. 'No cops or nothing.'

'Good.' I pointed Cibor to our little truck. 'Please join our guests in the back seat. Unless this gang here isn't too young for you.'

Cibor scoffed. 'They are children.'

He squeezed in beside the Poles as I hopped in beside Sparrow. The girl and the older boy came closer, curiosity winning out over fear. 'You are witches?'

'No. We is ordinary people just like you.'

They looked disappointed. 'You are not ordinary. There is nothing about you that is ordinary.'

'Perhaps, but there in't no real witches. And, if you don't mind a bit of advice, you'll get yourselves killed holding up police cars, so I recommend a career change—something without guns.'

The girl was bolshy. 'You've got guns.'

'And as soon as I can, I'm getting rid of every last gun in my life. They don't bring nothing but trouble.' I heard the bitterness in my voice. 'But if you in't inclined to take advice from an old geezer like me, whatever you do, look after each other. United you stand, divided you fall.'

I nodded, and Sparrow accelerated up the highway. 'We've got about three kilometres of straight road until the turn-off,' she said. 'Want to see what that go-fast button does?'

I gritted my teeth. 'You're proper mental, you are.'

She grinned and gripped the wheel tight. 'Hold on, everyone.'

She flicked the green switch. Nothing happened for a few seconds, then we were slammed back into our seats. We rocketed up the road, all of us yelling with fear. Sparrow kept her focus, but when we were doing two hundred kilometres an hour I wimped out and switched off the power boost.

Sparrow slowed to make the turn-off. Then we rolled down the off-ramp onto a road supplying the quiet dry-dock end of the port. I directed her through a deserted industrial area, then found the entrance we needed. Steel barriers blocked the way. I couldn't see anyone, but I sensed we were surrounded by armed men.

I leaned out. 'Delivery for Mister Pimpernel?'

Chapter Thirty-Nine—
The remedy is sometimes
worse than the disease

A male voice called out of the dark. 'Aleksy warns us you are a comedian. Put your lights out and tell me who the extra passenger is.'

Sparrow flicked off the truck lights as I did the talking. 'He's called The Rat. He's the most dangerous criminal who ever fought for a woman's love in the beautiful city of Koszalin. If you're hiring, he's looking for work.'

Figures in dark clothes emerged to pull the barriers out of the way as a man approached. He was dressed like an Arab—his face and neck were wrapped in a headdress that showed only his eyes. He shone a torch in each of our faces, checking them against a small handheld screen. Then he killed the light. 'You did not have any adventures on the way?'

'Very pleasant trip. Lovely people, nice countryside. Can we get to the bit where we don't die of the poison your colleagues stuck in us?'

'Of course. Follow me in your vehicle.'

He walked ahead and Sparrow trickled the truck along behind him, surrounded by silent men in dark clothes, all carrying semis, shoulders draped with bandoliers. The man in front held up a hand. 'Stop now. Switch off the engine and step out, slowly, without weapons.'

We were careful to do exactly like the man said but I checked with Feliks: 'You boys are leaving that pistol behind, I trust.'

'Of course.'

The man in the shadows was bemused. 'You give them weapons?'

'It seemed like the right thing at the time. Can we expedite this poison removal, please?'

Some of the Pimpernels stayed to unload the truck as others marched us behind the Arab to an open steel shipping container. Inside was an old sofa, some lamps, a bed and an older blonde woman on a seat, sleeping with her head resting on a desk.

The man turned and gestured to the sofas. 'Please, rest.'

The woman raised her head, faces lined with tiredness, blearily surprised. 'They made it?'

'Yes,' said the man. He turned to us with a smile in his voice, pulling his Arab head dress loose. 'We lose one-thousand zloty bet to Aleksy, thanks to your "pleasant trip".'

'Our apologies for not being dead. The cure, if you please.'

'Certainly.' He turned to the woman. 'Doctor?'

The tired woman rubbed her eyes, then went to a metal ammunition box laid on the floor. She opened it and brought out a small, well-used device held together with wire and cloth tape. It didn't inspire confidence.

The suited Poles were closest. 'Take off your jackets,' she told them.

They obliged, fearful but eager. She pressed the device to Drugi's arm. 'This might hurt a little.'

A small red light flickered on the side of the device as Drugi winced. A few seconds later the light turned green, and the doctor pulled the device away. Now dripping blood, it was attached to the small vial that had been inserted in his arm.

The Arab was ready with a field dressing and bandage. 'I will wrap this firmly. We don't want you bleeding to death. But tell us if you lose the feeling in your fingers.'

The doctor repeated the procedure on Feliks, taking longer than before. She frowned, but finally the device flickered green, the vial came free. The Arab quickly applied another field dressing. Then it was my turn. The doctor felt my arm, located the right spot and pressed the device against it. I gave her a relieved smile. 'Just out of idle curiosity, what is this poison?'

'It is a long chemical name which you would not know, nor remember. It is a toxin derived from some engineered tropical virus.'

'Fascinating. Do you enjoy your work?'

She gave me a flat look. 'How did you come to be here, Englishman?'

'It's a long story—'

Sparrow interrupted. 'Shouldn't that thing be turning green?'

The doctor looked down, tapped the device. The red light had gone out. She lifted it away, give it a shake, then put it against my arm again. The red light didn't come on. She looked to the Arab, troubled. 'It's not working.'

'So make it work.'

She tapped it again, pressed it to my arm, hard. No light.

I avoided Sparrow's panicked look and tried to sound calm. 'Is there another one of these things around? One that works?'

'This one always works,' the doctor replied, still tinkering.

'Yet here we are, having this conversation. Can you please get another one of these things?'

'I don't know. It's from the university. A technician builds it for us. But I have not talked with him in some time.'

I turned to the Arab. 'Get the tech guy. Get another machine and get this fucking thing out of me, okay?'

He nodded, troubled. 'Okay. I'll try. Now.' He left the container as the doctor started unpicking the tape holding the device together. 'I'll check inside.'

Sparrow was seething with anger and anxiety. 'Can't we just cut it out of him?'

'No,' the doctor replied. 'It's engineered to release the toxin if it is not first decommissioned.' She finished removing the tape and wire, revealing a small plas box with a clip holding it closed. She undid the clip and took the casing off, revealing some oldtech machineries, a cube of grey metal and another of amber-coloured material full of tiny flashes of light, which she examined under a magnifying glass.

'How many hours have I got left?'

'Three. Maybe four.'

'How long will it take to get another one of these things from this tech friend of yours?'

'He is not my friend. I don't know how long it will take.'

The Arab returned. 'We have sent a team to find the technician. I can assure you they are risking their lives to act with speed and urgency on this matter. Neither we nor Aleksy wish you to die.'

'That's all good then.' I smiled at Sparrow but she knew I was faking it. She rested her head against mine. 'You'll be alright. It'll all work out.'

I tried to sound calm. 'I know.' I didn't mention I could smell coffee for some reason, and the vision in my left eye was fading.

Sparrow gave me a friendly thump. 'Plus only the good die young, right?'

I tried to nod, but my head was too heavy, and the world was fuzzing over, darkening and growing distant. Sparrow's voice came from a thousand miles away, drowned out by other voices, in a hundred languages, fragments of music, industrial sounds, dogs barking . . .

'They're here,' I whispered, not knowing what I meant. Then I felt the shakes begin, and it all went dark.

When I came to, I was laid out on the sofa, Sparrow was clutching my hand like I was drowning, and some geezer covered in a beard was tinkering with the device as he argued with the doctor and the Arab. 'It is oldtech. It is illegal and enough to see me buried in a shallow grave if the authorities found it—you think I have these things lying around my office?'

The Arab was icy. 'Then fix this one, quickly.'

'You bring me here in the night with half my tools. Do you have a microscope even?'

'Why didn't you tell my men you needed these things?'

'Because I was dragged from my bed at gunpoint. Just in time to watch another innocent man die at the hands of the Pimpernels.' He paused to look at me.

'Oi,' I whispered, weak as hindmilk.

No one heard me but Sparrow. The others argued as Sparrow leaned down. 'What is it, love?'

'They're here. Splinter and them. They're docked.'

Sparrow was confused, but nodded anyway. 'Okay.'

'If these clowns can't fix me, maybe Po and the Professoré can. They got trailers full of oldtech.'

'Maybe, but if we take you anywhere near them, the Gaffer will kill you.'

'I'm going to die anyway. Sparrow, I can't think of nothing else. I run out of ideas.'

Sparrow looked up. 'Oi! Any of you lot speak English?'

All three nodded.

'Then I got one simple question—can you fix that thing and save Blanco or not?'

The Arab looked to the doctor, who looked to the technician. He shrugged. 'The power source is faulty, maybe permanently finished. I'm sorry.'

'Then locate a ship docked here called the *Lav Noyemba* and get us there.'

The Arab hesitated, looking at me, lying there like a washrag.

Sparrow erupted: 'Now!'

He shrugged. 'Okay.'

He went outside, and came back with some men. 'Take the Englishman where the girl tells you.'

They carried me out to the dry-dock area. I heard the Arab mutter an apology as we were hurried off into the darkness. My head was still fuggy, and I was disorientated by even more visions and voices. I heard Cibor's voice. He sounded puffed. 'I find the *Lav Noyemba*. Follow me.'

There was more hurrying but I struggled to stay conscious. Darkness was closing in, and my night vision was gone. We passed the big shadows of ships and warehouses. Sometimes we hid from workers or security, then more hurrying. Finally, the men carrying me stopped in front of a darkness I realised was the side of the *Lav*. I heard urgent whispers and Sparrow demanding a gun, then we were moving up a slope, probably the ramp of the *Lav*.

The double click of a cocked semi. Angry voices. The smell of Jumbo and El Grande. Threats. Being grabbed by a big pair of arms and cradled like a child. Baba's musk. Lamps. Shouting. Sparrow.

The smell of coffee . . .

Blackness.

I woke in bright light. I clamped my eyes shut. Voices. Movement of people around me. A confined space. Po arguing in Mandarin. Chemical smells. A tourniquet tight around my upper arm. Sudden pain, sharp but distant, like it was happening to someone else. Being lifted, then lowered into cold, freezing cold. It took my breath away. Then I couldn't breathe. I thrashed, then was held down under freezing water. Sparrow's screams. They were fucking drowning me in salt water. I flailed, then weakened. Panic faded, replaced by sadness—this is how my life ends. I felt a click in my arm where the vial was, someone swore, I felt the toxin flood my system as water flooded my lungs.

Drowning and poisoned, I died.

236

Chapter Forty—Do not look where you fell, but where you slipped

'W'hen I was just a little older than you, I graduated from medical school thoroughly uninterested in medicine.

'All that was required of me as a "doctor" was to apply salves and soothing words. Meanwhile, my species was colonised by the cancer of global finance. As a result, nation states devolved to autocratic feudalism, oblivious that they were now eagerly pursuing mass extinction. I could think of nothing more pointless than telling a patient how to prolong their lives when it was clear that humans were reaching their evolutionary dead end.

'Yet, outside my profession, radical researchers were breaking exciting new ground with human sensory augmentation, genetic modifications and information theory. But, while some nations invested in this research, science was increasingly disregarded, and even criminalised, under the rise of Western corporate theocracies.

'Open inquiry, the bedrock of science, was portrayed as questioning the existence of "God", but this was cover for the true crime—the damage our parasitic global corporations were causing. Those researchers working hardest *to solve our most crucial problems were gagged, threatened, or killed. Many disappeared to work in secret, and some of them wanted to fix the world by fixing us. I wanted to be part of the group who solved the most crucial problem of all—the stalled evolution of the human species.*

'You must understand—humans are physiologically incapable of progressing beyond a certain cultural point. No matter the form of government, feudalism creeps in, as ideologies and corrupt elites dominate to crush dissent. The real fight is not with our politics but our biology.

'And so I immersed myself in research, attending the lectures of every scientist drawn to transcend the limits of our minds. Humans, like any animal, are limited in how they can think, and how they act upon that thinking— individually and collectively. But what modifications could stop us from collective suicide? A higher IQ? Greater emotional intelligence? An expanded organ of language that would eliminate lies and misunderstanding?

'I began to dimly perceive where our biological limitations lay. I became my own test subject. Any method I found to challenge those limitations I tried without hesitation—drugs, diets, cranial magnets, bio-computational aids—any means by which I could become augmented enough to see beyond the horizon.

'Time was running out. As the planet overheated, civilisation was collapsing into barbarism. Humans would survive, but when the climate improved, and forests and species returned, unevolved humans, like a virus, would repopulate, having forgotten their history, only to destroy it all over again.

'I couldn't allow mere biology to kill the stunning miracle of a consciousness capable of perceiving itself and the universe. The only path was to self-evolve—to become a sustainable species that would survive and evolve forever.

'You might think, "Why not let the human race kill itself off and let another species arise—something better?"

'Unfortunately, our planet cannot sustain another bout of evolution that would merely nurture another smart ape—we've extracted too much energy. We've guzzled the fossil fuels, which were crucial to our means of understanding our world and our universe. We no longer have energy resources that self-evolving intelligence needs to rise and break the bonds of biology forever.

'My activities were tracked, and my reputation grew. After I'd been

arrested for the fourth or fifth time, I was approached by the Chinese. Their long-term view was parochial, racist even—they wanted the Han peoples alone to emerge from the rubble of climatic and economic collapse, to have mental-cognitive dominance, but they did not care whom they got to help them achieve their plan, or what race they were.

'So I joined a secret band of researchers from around the globe. We didn't like our paymasters' ideologies but, in the end, success on our part would make any Han dreams of racial immortality irrelevant. We are all human, and we must all be replaced by the next wave—a wave we were determined to create.

'The Chinese gave us carte blanche. As things got worse, even as environmental catastrophes devastated vast areas of the planet, they threw more money at us. They realised we were humanity's last chance.

'But before we could take the final steps to create a self-evolving singularity, the Great Storms devastated eastern China, followed by the pandemics. Nuclear fallout from Korea was the final straw. China collapsed, totally. In our remote research facility, we were completely cut off.

'As we stood by the emerald lake, surrounded by the forest and mountains of the Bogda Shan, itself an island surrounded by a vast desert sea, we realised we would have to abandon all we had worked for. The fate of our species rested in our hands—but we were running out of food, supplies and even power.

'We accelerated those programs we collectively felt were most likely to yield results, but were obliged to also preserve and mothball the research institute itself, so it would survive even if we as individuals didn't.

'In the madness that followed, factions formed, and arguments became fatal divisions. I was part of a group that felt bio-augmentation was the path to take. In a series of last-ditch attempts, I submitted myself to processes that were often entirely speculative.

'My pain and suffering was almost unbearable. Others suffered too, and many died, but all our suffering would be justified by a single success. And, just as we were blending the biological with quasi-organic quantum computational substrates—bitter fighting broke out. Of the thousand or more scientists and staff, less than a hundred survived.

'Our research was at an end. All we could do was protect, as best we could, that which we left behind, and carry with us the embers that might one day reignite our species' means to control our own evolution.

'We separated, each in different directions, not knowing what we might face, hoping enough of us would survive.

'And survive we did. Using the last commsats, we formed a loose global alliance with the great survivors – the Rom, keeping us connected as we separately made our way in a world that had turned its back on reason. We waited, and worked, and stayed alive until that day when we could return to create the singularity.

'That time has come. Though we are ill-prepared, there will be no further chances for humans as a species. I am dying, though perhaps I may yet be renewed, but you will not die. I will not let you die, Blanco. You are not just my son, you are not just my finest experiment, you are the only possible future for the human species.'

Chapter Forty-One—A wicked man is his own hell

My first awareness was of movement, the steady rocking of slow forward momentum. There was also light—too bright—and a numb jumble of sensations flickering on and off like a lectrical machine shorting itself into a blackened mess. Then, a voice. 'It's not working. Put him back under.'

Then nothingness.

Later. Sharp chemical smells and a taste, acid and bitter. The gasping of an animal in pain. Me.

I opened my eyes but, blinded by more bright white light, I closed them again. When the pain settled, I opened them a crack. I was in one of Mister Splinter's trailers. To my left, the wall was lined with locked metal compartments. On the other side was a sink and stainless steel draining board, covered in oldtech tools and machineries, clinking gently against each other with the rolling and bumping of the trailer's motion.

I was strapped to a thinly padded bed. The mattress was warm and pulsating, massaging my weak muscles. My mind was clear. No fuzzing, no odd sounds and voices, no pictures of places.

A soft bleeping sound started, and a few moments later, a door behind me opened, letting in daylight. Doctor Po and the Professoré, puffed from running, switched off the alarm and came into view, looking down at me with wary intrigue.

'Do you think he is connected?' asked Po.

'Probably not. We'll be lucky if he's not a complete vegetable.'

I tried to reply, but my mouth only give out a groaning mumble.

'Is he trying to say something?'

'Or he's just in pain.'

Po sighed. 'All the work we did on him, and this is what we have to show for it.'

'If the brain isn't too damaged it might still be able to connect.'

'And then what? We'll have a deranged splinter that wants to play with its own excrement.'

I managed a small sound. 'Ffff . . .'

'He's trying to say something.'

'Fffuuu . . .'

'That's it, Blanco! Say something, eh? "The cat sat on the mat." Try that.'

They leaned closer, eager, as I struggled to form the words.

'Fffffuck off, the pair of you.'

Po leaned back, delighted. 'He's okay!'

The Professoré scowled. 'Terrific. The same foul-mouthed, miserable boy we've put up with for years is back. And clearly he's not connected.'

Po peered into my eyes, flashing a small torch. 'Blanco, tell us our location.'

I frowned—how the hell would I know?

'Think. Try.'

'S-Splinter's t-trailer,' I stammered.

'No, no—where is our location on the Earth. Think hard, boy.'

'N-no idea,' I replied.

Po was dismayed and resigned. 'Damn,' said the Professoré.

There was a lurch as weight shifted, and the door behind me opened again. 'Is he alright?'

Sparrow came around beside me and cradled my head, tears in her eyes. 'You alright now? Can you think straight? It's me, Sparrow.'

I felt my face move, and Sparrow's anxious frown turned to a smile. 'He knows it's me.'

'Love you,' I croaked.

She covered me dial with kisses, then hugged me as best she could. 'I missed you so much, my darlin'. Everyone has. Specially Daisy. Hang on.'

She straightened up, went out of my sight and I heard the door open. Then there was a whistle. 'Oi! Daisy!'

Doctor Po was outraged. 'No filthy dog in here! Is special Clean Room, not . . .'

But there was another bump, a loud bark, and Daisy was jumping up to see me. She was uncertain at first, sniffing and overwhelmed by the chemicals, but then she recognised me, and started licking my face, her tail wagging like mad.

'Hullo, Daisy,' I whispered. My right arm was weak, but I managed to give her a clumsy pat. 'Lovely girl, good dog.'

'She can do all sorts now,' said Sparrow. 'Tog's been training her. And see how big she is.'

Daisy now looked more like a dog than a puppy, even though she was acting like a big baby.

'Everyone alright?' I whispered. 'Tog, Baba, the freaks?'

'Everyone's fine, including the Gaffer and Tommy unfortunately.'

'Visiting time is over,' said Po, trying to sound tough. Then the trailer shook and Tog appeared at my elbow. 'About time you woke up, you lazy bastard.'

'Blimey, who's this?' I murmured. 'This fella looks like Tog except he's smiling and happy.'

'You've been off having adventures without us, you prick,' he replied.

'Okay, please—let's all just get out of the trailer now.' The Professoré waved the air, trying to shoo everyone out. The trailer suddenly tilted backward, sending tools sliding down the stainless steel bench. Po and the Professoré scrambled to stop them falling to the floor as, improbably, Baba squeezed herself into the space between the bed and the storage cupboards. 'You is live, yes?'

'Yes,' said Sparrow for me. 'And he's alright too.'

'Good. I am happy.'

I looked into that crumpled potato of a face and saw the spark of joy in her eyes. 'I'm glad to see you too, Baba. You alright? Last time I seen you, you was being shot.'

'That bastard nearly killed me,' she nodded. 'Po cut out bullet and stop bleeding.'

Po flapped his hands, fed up. 'Everyone out. Visiting time over. Go home, bye bye.'

Tog thumped me on the arm. 'Welcome back to the nightmare, brother.'

Baba patted me. 'Get well quickly. Circus is hell in the handbasket. We need you.'

Sparrow give me a final kiss. 'I'll be back after I tell Mister Splinter the good news.'

I suddenly remembered his voice telling me about his life and the Splinter project. I grabbed her hand. 'Be careful with that maniac. He's ruthless. He'd cut you up for spare parts if he wanted.'

She nodded, unfazed. 'I know.'

Another kiss and she went, leaving Doctor Po and the Professoré aggrieved. Po found a broom to sweep the metal floor. 'People are filthy, don't do what they are told, no wonder planet in a mess . . .'

He kept grumbling and mumbling as the Prof checked me over with some oldtech tools.

'When can I get up?'

'When I say,' he replied. 'For now, go back to sleep.'

'I don't want to go b . . .'

The Prof pressed a device against my arm, clicked it, and I was out like a light.

When I woke, the trailer was still, and I could hear the circus outside—Humbolt spruiking in what sounded like bad Russian, the music of the calliope, the noise of a crowd. I began feeling my fingers and toes, clenching and unclenching them. After a while, I started moving my arms and legs.

I managed to unbuckle the straps, pushed myself up on my elbows—and promptly fell back, my head spinning. The next attempt was slower, but I finally sat up and swung my legs over the edge of the bed, waiting until the dizzy pounding in my head faded.

I wondered why I wasn't dead from poison, and whether the thing inside me was still there—rotting or growing. I wondered why the Gaffer and Tommy hadn't finished me off while I was in a coma. Finally, I wondered what was going to happen in the mountains of the Bogda Shan.

Only one man could answer all them questions, so I thought I better ask him. I slid my bare feet onto the floor and stood still, hoping I wouldn't pass out. I had no idea where we were or what was outside. More importantly, I didn't know where Tommy or the Gaffer were. I was only wearing undertrousers, so I put on an invisibility cloak, reached in the pocket and turned the device on.

I took the few steps to the door, holding on to the bed and walls like a ninety-year-old would. Beside the door a small panel glowed red. Brushing my fingers against it, it turned green and the door slid open. It was night, and the noise and lights of the midway and crowds filled my head, making me dizzy all over again. I gritted my teeth, and carefully eased my shaking legs down the steps to the ground.

I began walking about and, as I got closer to Splinter's trailer, I could hear voices inside. I couldn't hear what they were saying, but Po and the Professoré sounded like they were arguing. I was about to press my ear against the door when it fell silent inside, and the door swung open. Then I heard Mister Splinter's voice. 'Come in.'

I privately cursed the mind-reading bastard, switched off the cloak and hauled myself up the steps and inside. The effort made me light-headed. I tottered to the curtain and pushed past it, swaying and blinking. Po and the Prof were standing beside Splinter, seated like a monster-King on his shadowed throne.

'I got some questions,' I croaked.

'Get him something to sit on before he falls,' growled Splinter.

Po and the Prof wrestled a box into position, and sat me down.

'What you lot arguing about then?' I panted. 'The singularity? How I fit in now I'm broken?'

Po and the Prof looked stricken, but Splinter was matter of fact. 'You're not broken. Not yet at least.'

'Then is whatever you lot put inside me dead? And how come I didn't die from that poison the Pimpernels stuck in me?'

'You owe your life to the good doctor and the Professoré. They slowed your metabolism down and devised antibodies to soak up the bulk of the toxin. As for what's inside you, it is in stasis.'

'It could come back to life?'

'It has been affected by the poison. We don't know to what extent. We hope it is repairing itself.'

'Well it in't my bleedin' hope. You had a choice doing what you did to yourself, I didn't, and I want no part in any of it.'

'You don't have a choice.' Splinter sounded tired. 'If either of us is to survive, we need to confront certain realities.'

'I vaguely remember you telling me some of those realities. The history of you and that Chinese project you were all working on—except it all fell apart when the going got tough.'

The Professoré spoke up, sounding defensive. 'We needed mere weeks to finish the work, but the competing tensions and conditions were too great.'

'In other words,' I replied, 'the smartest people on the planet acted like every other idiot. Which is why trying to make some geezer like me smarter in't no guarantee I'm not going to act like any other idiot. Clever in't the same as wise.'

Po and Prof looked surprised I knew their little secret. Splinter's flesh rippled as he clenched one of his fists, his face contorting. It looked like he was struggling to control the thing what was inside him.

'I have devoted my entire life to this project, and understanding what could be achieved with it. Anything you could think I have thought a thousand times, and accounted for.'

I was still scared of him, but I was angry. 'None of it matters no more. The experiment's over. I'm just a geezer with stuff inside of him that doesn't work.'

He sighed, frustrated. 'The entity inside us isn't complete. It is still raw computational power seeking form, as primitive as slime mould. It still requires connection and activation. You will understand when we reach the Bogda Shan. For now, you must regain your strength and use your brain to assist with getting us and our equipment there. If you do not, then we will both be consumed by what is within us. And when we die, the human race will most definitely die—not with a bang but a thousand-year whimper.'

I was tiring. 'What about the Gaffer and Tommy? They both want me dead.'

'They are under control. Go. Get strong.'

I stood, shaky. When I was at the door, he spoke again. 'The girl. Keep her. She is . . . useful.'

I felt a hot flame of hatred for the selfish old sod. Then I remembered his long miserable loveless life, and the anger drained away.

Po and the Professoré guided me back to the trailer, nearly carrying me, Po grumbling the whole way. Inside, they buzzed me with machines, injected me with stuff, and checked me over.

'So where are we?' I asked.

'A town in eastern Lithuania. Or western Russia, depending on your politics,' replied the Professoré. 'It's called Velikiye Luki, it's very pretty, and there are enough people left here to pay for our circus with all the potatoes and vodka we could ever want.' He didn't look over-joyed at this prospect. 'They also have diesel, which we definitely want.'

Then they clicked a button and knocked me out.

I was woken by the sound of gunfire. I struggled upright, staggered to the door and opened it. It was dawn, and I looked out on a scene of brutal warfare. Our circus was under armed attack, being fired upon from a group of old trucks and tractors, some of which were now hooked to Splinter's other oldtech trailer, hauling it away.

Our lot were only just beginning to fire back, so it looked like them what was attacking us had taken us by surprise. Dizzy, I stepped, stumbled, and fell down the stairs, rolling into the dirt. I hauled myself upright, my first thought to get to the weaponry, only to see the Gaffer's trailer also being towed away. I staggered toward the trailer and was knocked flat by someone large. I looked up. It was the Gaffer. He grinned and pointed his gun at my head.

Then a voice yelled. 'No! Stop!'

Tommy ran to join us. 'Leave him. We agreed.'

'You want your fun, eh?' the Gaffer sneered. He looked back down at me, kicked me in the ribs, and hurried off. Tommy gave me a cheerful smile, cocked a finger at me and winked. 'See you soon!'

Then Tommy ran off after the Gaffer, bullets still whizzing through the air, splintering wood and pinging off anything metal.

Clutching my ribs, I leaned up on one elbow in time to see Tommy and the Gaffer running toward our attackers, yelling orders.

They were *with* them.

They drove off under a covering fire. The last thing I saw was Tommy, smiling and waving farewell from the back of the trailer containing all our weapons.

Chapter Forty-Two—After the act, the wish is in vain

Chaos. Shouting, screaming, crying. People rushed about, putting out fires and helping the injured. Clutching my ribs, I found Tog, bashed and unconscious beside the only weapon he could find, a hayfork. Jumbo and El Grande were feeling him anxiously with their trunks.

I cradled him, gently slapping his cheeks. 'Tog. You alright?'

William H. Prendergast, followed by the two frightened Kims, appeared out of the smoke. I was too worried about Tog to wonder how they got there. 'Help me get Tog to the metal trailer,' I said.

The trio picked up Tog and I limped behind, helping them through the door and get Tog onto the bed. I turned to the Kims. 'Find Doctor Po or the Professoré. Tell them Tog's in a bad way.'

The Kims dashed off. I turned to William H. 'Have you seen Sparrow?'

'She in with the freaks checkin' they ain't hurt.'

Tog groaned. I slapped his cheeks again. 'Tog, wake up. You alright, mate?'

His eyes cracked open, groggy. 'Are 'Bo and El G alright?'

'They're fine—they're just worried about you.' I felt over his chest and limbs. 'Anything broken?'

'My chest hurts. The Gaffer put the boot in. He's with them attacking us.'

'I know. Did you have any idea this might happen?'

'Another circus has been dogging us for a week or so. We were friendly, but there was something suss about them. They had attitude. So did the Gaffer and that little shit Tommy. Now we know why.'

'And now they got our weapons and all Splinter's stuff.'

Tog groaned. 'God knows what was in them other trailers. Lucky they didn't get this one too.'

'Yet. They could come back. I need to check on the others and get ready, just in case—will you be okay?'

'I'm fine. Go.'

Outside, the ruckus had died down, but a group of locals warily approached from the town, many of them holding weapons. My abilities with language was gone, and all I had was some bad Russky: 'We are attacked. Do you have doctor?'

But they were all looking at me with fear, muttering in a local dialect. I didn't push my luck. Instead I made my way to the freaks' enclosure. 'Sparrow! You in there? Everyone alright?'

'No,' she called out. 'We got wounded.'

I dragged myself up the steps. Inside was dark, but shafts of light came in through bullet holes. Baba had a rough bandage around her shoulder, her clothes were soaked with blood, and she was holding Kongo, stroking her face, her own wet with tears.

Kongo, our gentle giant with a volcanic temper and a mile-wide romantic streak, was dead.

Sparrow was attending to Humbolt, who lay on the floor. He groaned as she tightened a torn piece of cloth into a tourniquet around his upper thigh.

'We need Po,' she said. 'Humbolt's bleedin' like a stuck pig.'

'Everyone else alright?'

'I think so. They was mostly asleep, and the bullets went high. Get Po or the Prof.'

I went back out to the midway and found the Professoré working on our mechanic, Dognose, who had a bullet wound along the side of his head, from his cheek to his ear. 'Where's Po?'

The Professoré pointed. 'Splinter.'

'When you're done, Humbolt needs help. Arterial bleed, upper thigh.'

I hurried to Mister Splinter's trailer. The door was ajar. 'Mister Splinter?'

There was just a low groan, so I pushed past and inside. Doctor Po was staunching a massive wound to Splinter's chest. Po flicked me a look. 'Get my tools.'

'What tools?'

'Everything in the trailer you were in. Quickly.'

I hurried out and went back to the metal trailer, where William H. was wrapping a bandage around Tog's ribs.

I couldn't stop to help. 'Splinter's hit bad,' I said. 'So's Humbolt.'

I grabbed a graf cloak, laid it on the bed, and piled all the tools what were on the stainless steel bench into it, gathered up the corners and took it back to Splinter's trailer. Inside, I pushed past the curtain, and laid out the tools for Po.

What happened next was horrible. Po did surgery on Splinter without no anaesthetic; Splinter just sitting there like a great lump of angry writhing meat. Using a head-torch to find his way, Po basically dug into Splinter's chest wall and went to work. Amid the stench of fresh blood and raw flesh, the burning smells, and the sounds of cutting, Mister Splinter let out occasional grunts of pain, his blood-red eyes burning into mine. It was hard to imagine this demon once being an ordinary man, but I tried to imagine what he was thinking in all that pain. Did he realise how screwed we were, and how the chances of him doing his singularity bollocks were now down the shitter? Despite his glare, I wasn't even sure he was fully conscious. 'Can you hear me?'

He give a faint nod, so I give him the damage report. 'We lost one of your trailers and most of the arms. Kongo's dead, and we got you, Humbolt and a few others injured. The locals don't look happy neither. They must be thinking we brought danger, so their next step could be telling us to piss off. I don't know if the Gaffer and Tommy nobbled any of our vehicles yet—we'll check for traps. Them bastards might want your other trailer, so they could be coming back.'

I reckoned he was helpless at this point, so I chanced my arm. 'We should bugger off back to England, or someplace what's safe. You can do your research, and the rest of us can try to live a life what isn't all about surviving constant warfare.'

Splinter's face contorted in fury. As blood and other dark fluids poured out of his chest, Po panicked. 'No! Stop talk right now or Mister Splinter is dead!'

I backed off, and Splinter contained his rage to a low hiss. 'Have you learned nothing?'

I shrugged. 'We are weak, the enemy is strong.'

'Then we must appear where he does not expect us, and throw him into disarray.'

I was fed up with all that *Art of War* bally. 'We're not a bleedin' army. We're a bunch of freaks with a few guns. And what was in that trailer they took?'

'A power source. My research. None of which they'd understand.'

'They'll work it out.' I paused. 'After all, doesn't they want what you want? Power?'

'Nonsense. I want to assist the birth of the new human species.'

I scowled. 'You want to rule over us thick humans with your new clever human. But did you ever consider there might be an upper limit to "smart"? You're smart, and look where it's got you.'

'Intelligence is immeasurably more than IQ,' Splinter replied in an agonised whisper. 'Which is why room must be made within the body for additional processing and brain augmentation. The point is we must continue.' He paused to draw painful breath. 'To do nothing is to abandon the entire evolution of self-aware consciousness. To do nothing will consign us to the worms.'

'Maybe, but I don't trust nothing you say no more. You lied to me all my life. You stuck this thing inside me when I was just a kid. I been through hell because of you.'

'What's done is done—save regret for your deathbed. In the meantime we will only achieve our goal by using our brains and what we have learned. Stop being a boy and grow up.'

'Then tell me about this bleedin' Convergence of Travellers. What are we really going there for?'

Splinter hesitated. 'It is a competition between our most advanced post-humans.'

'He doesn't need to know this,' Po muttered.

'Yes, I do,' I growled. 'Or we in't going nowhere.'

Splinter continued in a halting growl. 'When we were forced to leave the ruins of the research station, all of us were tasked to return once in every decade to meet and pit our best attempts against each other. If one of those projects was voted as viable for connection, we would proceed to the next stage. So far, all have failed. None have been viable. Until now.'

Po glanced at me, sceptical. 'You were it.' He turned back to his work in the stench of blood and chemicals as I shook my head. 'Then you've already failed,' I replied. 'Look at me. I in't smart, plus the poison killed that thing inside me. Experiment over. So let's go back to England.'

'You may still be viable,' whispered Splinter. 'More so than any of my other projects.'

'And were they your so-called kids as well?'

'Yes.'

'I'm guessing they is dead.'

'Yes.'

'They died competing.'

'Yes.'

'Well, that's fine and dandy,' I snorted. 'Off to the competition so I can get killed. Anything to help my dear old dad.' I never loathed no one more than at that moment, or had better reason to.

'So finish it. Be done with me and get your revenge.' Splinter's hand twitched, a finger pointed toward a trunk. 'There are weapons in there. Any one of which will destroy me.'

Po was horrified, and turned toward me. 'No!'

'You can end this now,' Splinter continued. 'Have your revenge, then go back to Britain to die with the rest of the human species. You'll be your own man again, living a life without meaning.'

I went to the trunk and opened it up. Inside was a jumble of oldtech, but one piece was a pistol of some sort. I picked it up, feeling the weight of it.

'That one will do nicely,' said Splinter.

Po stood between Splinter and me, distressed. 'Blanco, no. Even if it feels right, do not do this thing. What we do to you is not good, but there was no other way. Let him live, and instead think how to get the equipment back that the Gaffer have stolen.'

'We need the weapons, not Splinter's shit,' I growled.

Then, a voice behind me. 'No. We need it all.'

I turned. Sparrow was in the doorway, hands bloody, face smeared with tears. 'You can't kill him. And we can't go back to England neither. We have to go on.'

'Why? Because this lying prick says so?'

'Because the thing inside you in't dead, and there's only one way to stop it killing you.'

'So they say.'

'When I was a Nightingale I heard them talking. I knew they done something inside of you. I knew one day it might do you good or harm. They were never sure—all they knew is this time it was special, and the only way it could be sorted, for good or ill, was at the research station. There's stuff there—oldtech what can fix you.'

I stood there, stunned. 'You knew?'

She nodded, guilty. 'It's why I kept us going this way. That, and because the freaks are our real family now.'

This wasn't no comfort. All I felt was betrayed.

I brushed past her, but she grabbed my arm. 'Blanco, don't. We love you.'

I shook her off, and turned back to Splinter. 'If you don't die in the next hour or so, you get one vote.'

Po frowned. 'One vote on what?'

'I'm putting it to the others, and they can vote whether we keep going east to certain death, or turn back and try and find a better life. I know which way I'm voting.'

Filled with rage and pain, I slammed the door on my way out. Everything was sham, every word ever spoken a fucking lie.

Chapter Forty-Three—Rapidity
is the essence of war

The wounded were treated, Kongo wrapped and gently laid aside for burial, and lookouts posted with the last of our weapons. Farshad and Bihn cooked breakfast under an oak tree, and survivors gathered there, clutching coffee, mourning in silent shock.

I made up a bucket of hot water and, in a patch of sun by a tree stump, stripped down to wash the stink of chemicals and medicines off me. Daisy rested her head on her paws to watch me, as Baba carried Erik out, and sat tiredly and heavily on a tree stump, setting Erik beside her.

I looked at their miserable dials. 'I'm sorry about Kongo,' I said.

Erik sighed. 'She was a good woman. A kind woman.'

Baba nodded. 'And crazy angry sometime too. I like. She fight like me.'

'I talked to Splinter,' I said. 'He told me the truth about where we're going. I want to put it to a vote that we turn back.'

'A "vote"?' Erik was troubled. 'You are challenging Splinter? He is that weak?'

'Either way, he let the Gaffer and Tommy slice us up a treat. Now we got no weapons, and them bastards is likely to come back, kill the rest of us, and take the last of our stuff.'

Baba looked me up and down. 'Even if Splinter die, look at you—how can a new leader look like skeleton. You too skinny.'

'I in't never going to be no leader,' I grumbled. I looked down at myself, still wearing only undertrousers. During my recovery I'd lost muscle, and my ribs were showing.

Then Baba stood, looking past me. 'Is trouble coming.'

A larger group of the locals were gathering, but they seemed to be looking at the three of us with awe rather than fear and hatred. Erik muttered softly. 'Blanco, you might like to find a weapon.'

Before I could take Erik's advice, one of the older women came forward with an even older man, and bowed to us. The old man pointed to each of us in turn, talking in a low voice.

'What's he saying, Baba?'

'He says Erik is the grass snake, I am the brown bear and you are the white heron.'

'And this means what exactly?'

Baba ignored me to talk with the old woman in Russian as the locals crept closer, keen to hear the conversation. Children peeked around the sides of their parents. At the back, young men astride small horses looked on, earnest.

Baba turned to us. 'These people are pagans. They see us as links to their gods. They offer us help if we need.'

I stepped forward and bowed. 'Ask them if they know where the bandits who attacked us went.'

Baba asked, and some of the young men came forward to talk. Baba translated. 'The bandits are still at the railyard. They are very soon to leave.'

'Good,' said Erik. 'They will not so likely be returning here then.'

Sparrow joined us. 'Perhaps not, but they is leaving with goods what belong to us.'

I was still angry with her. 'They're welcome to everything but the weapons.'

'We *need* the other stuff,' she replied.

I was refusing to look at Sparrow, but she got in my face. 'That stuff might just save your life.'

Baba talked with the locals as me and Sparrow softly argued. 'How could you be on Splinter's side?' I asked her. 'How could you think that evil old man would do anything what would help us?'

'I'm glad you're still saying "us".' She tried a smile but I was so tore up and confused I just crossed my arms, determined. 'I in't going nowhere it's guaranteed I'll end up dying.'

'I want to go where we can sort that thing what's inside of you. The Professoré says it's not dead. He doesn't know for sure what that toxin did but it didn't kill it.'

Seeing the love in her eyes, my anger crumbled. I suddenly felt ashamed of how skinny and puny I was. 'I wish I wasn't so weak.'

'We'll feed you up after we work out how to catch up with the Gaffer and Tommy's new outfit.'

Baba turned back to us. 'These boys say is maybe one chance to steal back our trailers. But you have to go now. The boys are take you.' She pointed to the young men, who looked excited. Their horses were milling about, eager to run. 'They take you to the train. Maybe you steal him back.'

I raised an eyebrow. 'Steal a whole train from a large number of heavily armed psychopaths.'

Baba shrugged. 'You is professional bad person like the rest of us. Think tricky.'

'Come on,' said Sparrow. 'We'll borrow a couple of horses and see what we can do.'

Then we heard an American accent. 'I kin help.'

William H. and the Kims had joined us. William looked proud as he said, 'I ride good.'

'Good for you,' I growled. 'But I'm buggered if I'm galloping about getting shot.'

But even as I heard my own palaver, I felt a surge of strength, and realised I was standing tall. I was angrier than I realised.

'I seen cowboy movies from the ol' days,' said William H. 'If that trailer is on bogies right at the back, we could pull the pins on it.'

He had me thinking. Sparrow grinned. 'William, me and you. The three Musketeers.'

'You too?'

'I had ponies since when I was tiny. I can ride like the feckin' wind.'

Baba talked urgently to the boys on horseback, and the eldest ordered the others. Three of the boys slid off their mounts, then held them for us.

'This is mental,' I muttered.

Tog arrived with Daisy on a rope, and my trousers, belt and jacket over his arm. 'You can't ponce about acting like a hero dressed in underpants. It's a rule.'

I took my clothes, surly. 'Thanks for helping get me killed.'

'Live fast, die young . . .'

I finished tying off my rope belt and looked down at Daisy, who was jumping about, excited. I give her a pat, then Tog held her back as we mounted the small, sturdy horses.

There wasn't no saddle, only crude rope stirrups and halter. Before I could call for a gun the boys handed the reins to us, and the horses took off, mine included.

I was never so terrified in my bleedin' life. Them boys rode like demons, and the horses ran over rough ground like it was flat ferroplas. I held on with my knees and leaned forward. William and Sparrow easily kept up with the pack, as my pony raced after them. We tore through some trees, whipped by leaves and small branches, emerged onto a dusty white dirt road, then veered off to clatter through the back streets of the village, where locals jumped out of our way, cursing us. Then the street opened out as we thundered up a track to some unfenced fields of stubbled wheat. I choked on the dust of the others ahead of me as we angled across to meet up with the railway line.

I pulled up behind the others at the station, gasping for breath, feeling like I'd been done over. The train had gone, and while Sparrow looked gutted, I was relieved—perhaps I *wasn't* going to die today. Then one of the lads pointed toward a wisp of diesel smoke a kilometre away.

Before I could say 'let's not chase that feckin' train', we took off again, galloping beside the rails.

Every moment I expected to fall off and break every bone in my body. But I also felt a mad exhilaration—and a connection with the animal under me. He was a living creature what wanted to run wild with his mates as much as their riders wanted to tear after a train full of armed men.

William H. looked calm and happy. Sparrow was magnificent—her long hair streaming, her bare legs holding her crouched over her horse's neck, a look of ferocious joy on her face.

We slowly gained on the train. The two rear flatcars were loaded with the Gaffer's trailer at the very back, then Splinter's trailer just ahead of it. A caboose was the next carriage along, and I presumed it'd be the one full of armed geezers with a general disposition to see us dead.

We closed on the rear flatcar. When the local boys motioned me and William H. to get closer, it dawned on me I was expected to jump off a galloping horse onto a moving train. I was scared stiff, but watched William H. grab an iron rail at the back, kneel on his horse's back, get his feet under him, then make the leap. Then it was my turn as Sparrow kept alongside, drawing a pistol, ready to give us covering fire.

I finally made a terrified flailing leap and grab, then was bewildered to find myself still alive and clinging to the side of the Gaffer's trailer. I sidled forward to where William H. was waiting between it and Splinter's trailer. We paused, bracing ourselves against the rocking movement. We just had to leap across to the next car, climb around that and pull the pin to get our trailers back. It occurred to me that a weapon might be handy.

I tapped William's elbow, and indicated the Gaffer's trailer. 'I'll grab us a couple of rifles.'

He nodded. 'I'll go forward, see if I cain't loosen that pin front of our trailers.'

'Be careful. Anyone sees you, get straight back here, alright?'

He nodded, paused and leaped across the gap. I turned back to the Gaffer's trailer, opened the door, and stepped inside. My eyes were just getting used the dark when Strombo looked up from a makeshift bed, surprised.

He jumped up, stumbling against the motion of the train, and came for me. I backed up in a panic, got outside and slammed the door. Strombo forced the door open and I only had time to grab the top of it as it swung out and over the side, making me, legs dangling, exposed and helpless. Sparrow was level with us and looked across, confused till she saw Strombo. She pointed her gun, and he ducked back inside. I kicked up, got a grip with my boots, and clambered onto the roof.

Strombo's arm emerged from the doorway below me, firing a pistol in Sparrow's general direction. She fired back like the fearless shewolf she is, and he pulled his arm back inside.

I knew it was only seconds before that prick found himself a better gun. I undid my rope belt, took it off, and made a loop. When Strombo's arm came out again, this time holding an old Norinco submachine gun, I dropped the loop over the barrel and hoisted up as hard as I could. The knot tightened, then, before he could use his strength to pull back and retrieve his weapon, and me down with it, I leaped forward over the gap to the next bogie, still holding the end of the rope.

I only just made it, but my weight tugged the already unbalanced Strombo forward into the gap between the two flatcars. His weight began to drag me back down on top of him, so I let go. His fury turned to shocked agony as his lower half fell through the gap and dangled on the track, pulverised by the rocks.

Then his leg or clothing must've got caught in the wheel and he was yanked down, his head smashing the rocks, and disappearing under the carriage with a splash of blood.

I didn't get time to hope he'd rot in hell, as shots rang from up ahead. Sparrow fired her pistol forward, but I couldn't see what at.

'Get back!' I yelled at her, but she kept firing to cover for William H., who was quickly edging his way back. He joined me in the cover between the trailers. 'Sorry, Blanco—those boys got guns. Lotsa guns.'

Holding my beltless trousers up with one hand, I jumped back across to the last bogie, and motioned for William to do the same. He jumped, and I grabbed his arm to steady him when he landed. 'We'll have to give up on trying to get Splinter's trailer.' I pointed down at the linkages. 'Think you can at least separate this car from the others?'

'I kin try.'

The plucky bugger climbed down and studied the moving iron joint that linked the bogies. I left him to it, and ducked inside the Gaffer's trailer. From an open locker, I grabbed a rifle and tucked a couple of pistols into my waistband, as much to keep my trousers up as for the firepower. I steadied myself and went back out, then glanced across to where Sparrow was just managing to keep her horse racing alongside. She pointed forward.

I moved to the edge and looked along the side toward the caboose ahead. Two of the Gaffer's new crew were clinging to the sides of Splinter's trailer, making their way back to deal with us. I fired a few rounds at them, then stumbled to the other side and did the same to another couple of nasty-looking geezers. They fired back and I ducked away, calling out to Sparrow. 'Stay back!' I could see Sparrow wasn't keen, but when there was a burst of semiauto fire, she let her speed drop. I leaned around and fired a couple of rounds, then went back to the other side to repeat the exercise—each time attracting a hail of bullets.

It was a losing game to keep rushing from side to side, so I slung the rifle over my shoulder and climbed up on the roof of the Gaffer's trailer. I turned forward, just as the Gaffer's head popped up from the front of Splinter's trailer ahead. I wasn't balanced or prepared, but I fired a round to make him duck, then dropped flat onto the roof into a sniper position. I yelled down to William H. 'Hurry!'

The train rocked and rattled on the old tracks, and I flinched as a jolt unbalanced him. He regained his feet, then finished unhooking what looked like the power supply to the link mechanism. The wood of the roof beside me exploded in splinters. I looked up to see the Gaffer's arm reaching up and firing his semi blind, just his hand and the gun visible. I aimed, fired and missed—not by much, but enough for him to pull his hand and gun away. When he tried the same trick, I was ready, and popped one right onto his gun, knocking it flying. 'Take that, you fucker!'

There was another jolt, and I looked down. William H was gone. For a few seconds I was horrified.

Then his cheerful face appeared below me in the doorway of the Gaffer's trailer. 'All fixed.'

There was now a small gap between us and Splinter's trailer ahead, a gap that very slowly opened up. 'William!' I shouted. 'Here, take this.' He took the pistol I shoved down at him, then peered around one side of Splinter's trailer to fire at the lads coming back toward us. I fired along the other side but ducking and shuffling on a moving train roof was as dangerous as being shot at. Luckily, the gap was widening, and they knew they'd lost us. After a few more pointless bursts of semi fire, they packed it in, clearly deciding it wasn't worth the bullets.

William found the brake, and we slowly screeched to a halt. The silence was like honey to my ears as we watched the Gaffer's train disappear around a bend. Sparrow caught up with us, patting her long-suffering horse as the local lads joined us, whooping their joy at our small triumph.

I climbed down off the trailer roof, shaky as a newborn lamb, give a startled William H a heartfelt hug, then clambered off the bogie onto the track.

Sparrow slid off her horse, I swore at her for risking her life, she told me to shut up, and we kissed, making the local boys cheer.

Sparrow looked me in the eyes, hers sparkling. 'In't we a right bunch of warriors, then.'

'No. And let's never do nothing like this ever again, alright?'

'Deal.'

We kissed, and the high romance of the moment was only spoiled when my trousers fell down around my ankles, and them pagan boys laughed till they was fit to bust.

Chapter Forty-Four—Wishing to forget is to remember

Daisy welcomed us back with excited barking, and wouldn't quiet down till she'd had a good sniff of us. As people gathered, Sparrow told the story of our mad adventure to our lot, and the boys on horses told their tale to the locals. Soon, everyone was slapping our backs, pleased we'd got one back on them bastards. The good people of Velikiye Luki weren't all pagan, but they were definitely up for celebrating what they were calling The Battle of the Boys. In this version of events, the brave boys of the town had taken the white heron and his bride to steal the dowry back from the evil bandits.

It made a good story, and we give the boys full credit for our success, as well as my thanks for the plaited bridle rope what now held my trousers up. Then the locals returned to their village, and we had time to bind our wounds before the wake.

Me and Sparrow cleaned ourselves up as Baba and Mala washed and wrapped poor Kongo's body. There were miserable dials all round. Humbolt appeared on makeshift crutches, his thigh heavily bandaged. Still in shock, Penny and Susy wouldn't let go of Madam Tracy's arm. Povero Christo and Guido wouldn't stop praying.

The locals returned with food and drink. Fires were built, some covered in round stones for ceremonial smoking purposes, and there was a sad but celebratory air as there is after any fight you survive. They offered respect to Kongo, and gently made us feel us welcome. It lifted our moods to have normals treating us as they would honoured guests—a rare feeling for us.

While the villagers set up the feast, I called our lot together for a meeting.

I said my piece then sat down. Some were keen to turn back with me, especially when they heard Splinter was barely alive. There was also them who wanted him dead, but others weren't sure about losing a powerful leader. 'Without a captain,' Humbolt argued, 'we'll be rudderless on the high seas.'

Then Sparrow stood. 'Alright, here's the thing Blanco didn't mention. Whatever happens to Mister Splinter, if we go back to England, Blanco will die. The same thing what's killing Splinter has been put inside Blanco, and the only way we can save them both is oldtech somewhere in them mountains. Yes, it'll be bleedin' dangerous, and I know you lot have had enough of danger, but we is more of a family than any we've known and I want to keep us together. All of us. Blanco included. I in't goin' back. I love him and I love you lot. That's my vote.' Then she sat down, arms crossed.

Everyone was looking between the two of us, troubled.

Finally, with a grunt of effort, Baba stood. 'Like Sparrow say. Me too.'

Then, with another grunt, she sat down.

I could see the mood changing so, before anyone else could ride this wave of comradely bollocks, I stood and jabbed a finger toward the east. 'We are four thousand feckin' kilometres from this Bogda Shan place. And there's no guarantee that whatever's there will fix Mister Splinter or me. Meanwhile, we got feck-all weaponry, and we know the Gaffer will do his best to finish us off if we get there.'

I hoped they'd see sense, but Madam Tracy, the woman the Gaffer had left behind, scoffed. 'Give me one minute with that bleeder an' I'll have his balls off.'

Mala was nursing a broken wrist, and Milosh was still seething

about it. 'Give me one second with the Gaffer and I will end this discussion forever.'

Then the Fazios arced up, especially at Tommy, who they'd caught
in their trailer one night—thankfully before he could do anything to
the girls. Binh had also found Tommy with the Nightingales, and it
was a close thing he stopped him in time. Binh's Buddhist, and I never
heard him talk bad of no one, but he hated Tommy. 'I fix that smile of
his. I widen it till his head fall off.'

Methuselah softly cleared his throat, and we fell silent to hear his
whisper.

'Revenge aside, there is merit in Splinter's endeavour. Though he
has clearly lost moral and ethical perspective, and has committed great
errors and crimes, I cannot help wondering if advancing the human
species to become intelligent stewards of the planet is not, in fact, a
truly great idea.'

He looked to me for a reply. I waved a hand at the pagans seated
or standing by the smoking stones nearby. 'The Romuva are already
up with that nature palaver. They hold everything in respect—animals, trees, water, rocks. If we were like them, we'd all get on and we
wouldn't wreck the place.'

Methuselah shook his head. 'If only it were a matter of belief and
culture, then yes, we might overcome our human aggression and colo-
nialist territorial instincts to live in peace. But do any of us know a
place where such peace has lasted? Has there ever been such a place in
history?'

The argy-bargy went back and forth and, finally, it came down
to a vote. I looked at the raised hands, my heart sinking. Everyone
but me voted to press on, have me win the Great Feat, make them
all rich with my prize, then get me magically fixed up by the oldtech
buried somewhere in one of the most remote mountain ranges on
the planet.

'Alright,' I said. 'We go east.' I stood. 'I'll tell Mister Splinter
how things stand. Either way, from now on we vote on stuff what's
important.'

'Even if he accepts this, what about the rest?' asked Erik. 'What
about how we run our little band of freaks and thieves, day to day?'

'We already know how to do that. Any small problems we'll work out between us.'

'Even so, every ship needs a captain, Blanco,' Eric replied. 'Especially a pirate ship like ours.'

This give me an idea. 'I'll talk to Splinter.'

The stench in Mister Splinter's trailer hit me like a punch. Po and the Professoré sat, hunched and exhausted, either side of Splinter's bulk, covered in blood and filth. Splinter's head was slumped on his chest. I should've been overjoyed to see him dead but, instead, a strange pain opened inside me.

It didn't last long. His great head rose on that massive neck, and them evil red eyes skewered me. 'So, you are still acting like a schoolboy. Discussing things. Having votes.'

'Correct. A vote I just lost. We agreed to try and reach the Convergence of Travellers.'

Po and the Professoré looked relieved but Splinter raged. 'I am still in charge and this is my circus. We will go on because I say we will.'

'No. We go on because that's what we choose to do. I don't know how much power you got left, but whether it's a lot or a little, from now on we work together or we don't work at all.'

'Says who? You? A boy too afraid to acknowledge that leadership requires the exercise of power?'

I wasn't buying any of his Machiavelli palaver. 'From now on, you is still captain of our little crew,' I replied. 'But we is going to draw up articles like what them pirates used to do, so we all got rights as well as duties.' I paused on my way out. 'I'll do my act like always, but I in't killing no one no more.'

I braced myself for fury but there was just a disgusted whisper. 'A pirates' accord. So be it.'

I counted myself lucky as I left the trailer and walked back to the freaks and riggers by the fire. I relayed our chat, and the deal. 'We stick to the pirates' code and we might just make it to where we're going. Agreed?'

Everyone seemed alright with that, but they were uneasy about Splinter—did it mean that he no longer had power over us? Did that mean we were safer, or in more danger from outside threats?

The locals ended our meeting by bringing us food and vodka, and we mourned Kongo and celebrated the Battle of the Boys until the early hours with our new pagan friends.

The next morning, we buried Kongo in a cool, green graveyard outside the village. The locals helped us, in awe of Kongo's bulk and appearance, tending her like a fallen demigod. Then we rolled out to the Luki train yards to load our trailers and animals onto empty flatcars. After I arranged to have our bogies added to the daily local train, and booked seats for Moskva, Sparrow, Daisy and me chaperoned Tog as he walked Jumbo and El Grande around the town for exercise. He give rides to kids, and I did a bit of juggling and magic as payback for the villager's help and kindness.

It was simple fun to put smiles on dials with a few three-rock cascades and slides. It was the first time we'd done our jobs without there being anything in it for us, and for a few moments we had nothing to do but soak up the joy of geezers what never seen a circus before. When we were all loaded and attached to the train, we waved farewell to the people of Velikiye Luki with real regret.

Me, Sparrow and Tog stood at the tail end of the carriage, watching the village shrink and disappear behind the trees as the train turned south-east. 'This is how life could be,' Sparrow sighed. 'No one getting hurt or thieved from, no one chasing us.'

I was thinking ahead to Moskva, wondering if the Gaffer and Tommy would be waiting. If they were, they'd have two days to plan an ambush, and we'd be walking right into it.

Tog stayed with Daisy and the elephants in an old open-top coal truck. Me and Sparrow went inside a carriage car, preferring padded seats to perching on straw bales under a tarpaulin.

The trip to Moskva was a slow rumble through beech, oak and pines, with an occasional patch of spruce beside ponds, lakes, creeks and rivers. Wildfires filled the air with fragrant smoke. We stopped at every town to pick up, and drop off, mail and supplies. The names drifted past me in a fog of Russian that Baba had to coach me to pronounce—Kun'ya, Zhizhitsa, Staraya Toropa, Ulin, Zapadnaya Drinn, Rzhev . . .

Baba was fascinated by the changes in the country since she'd left. 'Much warmer. So many fire. Different trees. Spruce almost gone. Not so many farm. Less people.' She grew sad, but seeing a few moose and deer cheered her up. She stared at the big beasts as they stared back, soberly chewing their cud. Buried under that crumpled, ruined face of hers, I saw the ghost of a happy little girl.

There were stations we didn't stop at. Beside deserted and devastated towns, their houses, churches and buildings were covered in vines and spreading trees. Walls had crumbled, and windows were bursting with the green growth taking root inside.

Most inhabited villages were pretty as a picture, some with log cabins two storeys high and churches made of wood. Nearby, bullet-pocked concrete ruins were left to the blackberry and raspberry to grow over, and rabbits to hide in.

We stopped in the Zemsky railyards, waiting for another train to come through from the east. The train-master let us walk Jumbo and El Grande around, so we all got out for a stretch. Daisy ran about, relishing the smells, peeing on everything, barking at and attracting all the local dogs. Local kids soon emerged from all over the place to look at us freaks. One of the lads had a football so, speaking the universal language of kicking balls and competing for the hell of it, we teamed up and charged around like maniacs. I got puffed quick, but the Kims were right little stars. On the sidelines, William H. was like a proud father. I remembered I hadn't asked how he'd come to sign on with us.

'Ain't no big thing,' he shrugged. 'I reckoned to take the Kims home to Korea. Maybe they still got kin there. Maybe the living is good and safe now. I ain't got family no more, but those boys need any we can find. Y'all were heading in the right direction, so here we are.'

I stood with him a while, watching the boys play with strangers as if they'd known each other all their lives. I marvelled at how strangers can become family—and how taking two kids halfway around the planet could be thought of as 'no big thing'.

As sunset began to fall, just outside of Shakhovskaya, the train stopped for the night. We were told that bandits were targeting trains and, despite our offer to ride shotgun, the train-master said we had to stop where we were till daylight.

We made ourselves useful, going out to collect firewood with any passengers brave enough to mix with us. Then we rigged up a field kitchen so Farshad and Binh could work their magic. As cooking smells filled the air, vodka appeared, and a couple of Russkies produced some balalaikas. Night fell, music was played, and Sparrow and the Nightingales sang like angels around the campfire.

Baba got sentimental, and sang songs from her distant childhood. The Russian passengers and crew were fascinated by her. When they heard her name, they nodded among themselves—the great witch Baba Yaga had come out of the forests with the other strange ones from the old times. As the vodka flowed, history and myth, reality and storytelling mingled, and we freaks felt like we were characters in a Russian folktale, special and rare—loved, feared and respected.

The hangover in the morning cleared up any lingering ideas we might've had about immortality, but we set off on the last leg to Moskva in good spirits.

I was looking forward to seeing my first wild tigers.

Chapter Forty-Five—
Long is not forever

Our train sped up as we entered the thick forests filling the north-west section of the city. As the carriage began to rattle, rock and throw us about, we clutched our seats. Two chain-smoking Russkies, breakfasting on vodka, explained that the speed was to cut our exposure to the rads. We held on, white-knuckled, as the train roared through the dark greenery, tree trunks barely a metre from our swaying carriages. We only slowed once, to nudge a fallen tree off the track—the rest of the time, leaves and twigs slapped anyone who was silly enough to stick their head out the windows.

Northern Moskva was a city-turned-forest. A few broken high-rise buildings towered over the canopy, but the rest was lush and semi-tropical. The rads were still so high that no one dared log or farm the greenery and, with decades of warming weather, it was now jungle. The Russkies told us that, after the Retribution, all the Moskva parks what weren't torched during the bombing grew back and eventually joined up. Plants from the botanical gardens escaped and loved the warmer climate, especially the vines. Animals what escaped from the zoo found sanctuary. Radioactive or not, life was rampant.

We slid the windows down, and let the rich smells of growth and rot flood the carriage. We pointed and yelped like tin lids watching fireworks, as colourful parrots, startled by the noise of our passing, exploded in huge flocks from the trees and dived through the green shadows.

Sometimes it's the simple things what bring a happy feeling. When I'm in ruined cities, I'm sad and happy at the same time. The people what once lived here had their time, but since they stuffed everything up, it's the turn of the plants and trees, the birds and bees. It's sad the people are gone but, given a choice between palavering with some geezer or quietly watching a bird hunt for caterpillars, I'll take feathers and bugs any day of the week.

After half an hour, we'd come far enough across old Moskva to safely slow down.

We saw our first Muskovites—tough-looking men with cutting-lasers scavenging the ruins for useful materials. We passed through the stumps of great buildings, each of which once must have housed thousands of people.

I wondered what it would've been like living in a city of millions. I tried to imagine the stink of all that raw humanity—the sweaty bustle, jabbing elbows, queues to buy things, and the constant jabber of people talking. They lived in wee boxes, which were stacked in bigger boxes, next to other big boxes full of even more punters, all of them doing stuff I couldn't imagine. What did all them people do with their lives back then? I seen old vids, but none of them showed what people actually did other than shoot people, have sex or talk to each other on phones in restaurants.

One of the chain-smoking Russkies reckoned the reason the Retribution didn't wipe out the whole city is because, at the last second, them what sent the bombs dialled in a slightly different map coordinate, which is why the south-east was spared. In the end, they only killed about ten million.

'Thank God for small mercies,' he said without irony.

If you were listing wild places to find wild tigers, you generally wouldn't include rubbish-strewn, coal-blackened railyards filled with battered, rusty carriages and engines, tended by stocky men as filthy as their equipment. But, as our train slowed to a crawl through the sprawling main railyards, there, standing on a hill of lumber at the edge, a wild tiger surveyed us—an enormous black-and-orange cat, all calm, focused power.

I saw a worker moving past our waiting carriage with a rifle. I tapped Baba's arm. 'That bloke in't goin' to shoot that beautiful thing, is he?'

Baba called out, and the man stopped and replied, shaking his head. With a curious look at us freaks, he walked on as Baba translated. 'This one is safe. The gun is just for shoot rabbit.'

I was relieved, but I remembered what people in the old days done to poor bleedin' tigers and the rest of the animals, and how it would be justice if tigers ate the lot of us. Why was a tiger's life any less important than mine?

But my gloom and doom made me look down into Sparrow's dozing face, resting on my lap. Baba, sitting across from us with Erik and Methuselah, saw my look and nodded, approving what she read in my eyes.

Humans didn't need Splinter's bollocks to survive—just love.

The train jolted and juddered all along its length, and settled back into a stroll as it navigated the braided rail lines of the city's railyards. It was slow going, but we finally arrived at the station what directed trains east. They disconnected our carriages from the rest of the train, then parked us with vague assurances of our ongoing connection.

We were just starting to think about cooking up lunch when a tender come and pushed us to the back of a long line of freight cars, with a few passenger carriages like ours up by the engines. Then they brought a caboose in behind us, so we knew the train would leave sooner rather than later.

Which is when we spotted who else was tied into this train—the Gaffer's new outfit.

We were scared—but also ready to kill. Milosh wanted to gear up and start some aggravation, and a few others were up for it too. I wasn't keen. 'More of them than us, and they is better armed.'

'Pre-emptive strike,' said Tog. 'Get in their face before they know we're here.'

'How would the local polis take to that?' I replied. 'Like as not, we'll get shot at by both sides.'

'We have to do something, and fast,' Tog replied. 'It's not "if" but "when".'

Sparrow nodded. 'Or, once they realise we're here they can bide their time and pull the pin, leaving us in the middle of nowhere.'

The driver of the tender walked past, rolling a cigarette. 'Baba,' I said, 'ask him how long before we go.'

Baba called out and the man looked at his watch and answered.

'One hour,' said Baba.

I looked around the group. 'So how can we stitch up them pricks in under an hour?'

'All guns blazing,' said Milosh. Mala checked her favourite blade, nodding. 'Then we cut them.'

'And risk us getting killed?' Sparrow said. 'It in't worth it.'

Then I had my genius idea.

After money changed hands with a few locals, me, William H. and Mathematico were soon dressed as railway workers. Greasy caps hiding our faces, we did the reconnaissance. William H. showed commendable bravery by climbing about the train 'checking the plumbing' to give us the right access, so we knew exactly where we had to go. When we come back, Math spat out the numbers, did the calculations, and worked out the timing.

Everyone was given instructions and enough time to get into position. Meanwhile, the Professoré slipped around and had a chat to the engine driver and his crew to ensure they were fully remunerated for any slight delay or inconvenience. If the driver and his crew noticed the Prof's strong aftershave, packed with enough hormone persuaders to make an invading army stop to pick flowers, they didn't comment, being too concerned to help out the nice gentleman with the deep pockets.

Our rivals had six trailers, plus Splinter's two. They were a piss-poor one-ring outfit with a midway what relied on tiny mechanical rides and gaffed games. We could see they were rubbish carnies, so we didn't have no bad feelings about getting revenge for what they done to Kongo and the rest of us.

Farshad, Binh and the Kims quietly barred and glued up their doors as William H. and I carefully primed the chemical bombs. Meanwhile Dognose and the riggers pulled the pins holding the trailers to the bogies and got the ropes tied off. Still up on the trailer roof, me and William got the thumbs up from the Professoré. We opened the valves and gassed them lads inside with a lovely, refreshing new vanilla scent to enjoy the rest of the afternoon to.

We clambered down, and looked through the window of the Gaffer and Tommy's trailer. The Gaffer was looking up and sniffing, curious. Then he saw my grinning mug and leaped to his feet. Tommy got up but was already swaying. I give the Gaffer the finger and jumped down, signalling Tog with a joyful whistle.

There are many ways to unload trains, but I guarantee the railwaymen of Moskva never seen two elephants to pull loads straight off the side of the bogies.

I got one last look at the Gaffer's fury as his trailer toppled off and smashed onto the roadway.

We didn't want to leave the Russians with too much of a mess, so Tog got Jumbo and El Grande to haul the trailers out of the way, their bruised and battered occupants fast asleep.

Milosh and Binh were in favour of splashing diesel about, then having a bonfire. A big part of me wanted to see the Gaffer burn in hell. But one look at Sparrow, and her little shake of her head, and the bloodlust in me died. I'd brought enough death into the world.

By the time our train slowly edged out of the railyards and left the city heading east, we'd crippled the Gaffer's vehicles, stolen some of their weapons and supplies, and satisfied ourselves they wouldn't be functioning as a circus anytime soon. Gathered in our carriage, we toasted a successful strike against our enemies.

I clinked glasses with the rest of them. Only three and a half thousand kilometres to go before I got the chance to kill myself in front of who knew how many other circuses.

Happy days!

Book Three—
Central Asia

Chapter Forty-Six—First consult the heart, then the head

We had a carriage of our own, where the most ancient woman in Mother Russia, who barely came up to my waist, was our fierce carriage attendant, or *provodnitsa*.

Wreathed in a black shawl and even darker scowl, she attended to our needs, less according to our wishes than some ancient rules, which we guessed come from a tattered book she carried with her.

She ruled the samovar, doled out the tea and sugar, did the cleaning and tidying—always at the most inconvenient times, held the key to the locker containing coarse grey blankets, and kept up a muttered commentary to herself in some Russian dialect even Baba struggled with.

This stern babushka had no doubt seen it all in her time, and I think us freaks were just another lot of strange humans. Somehow, her surly disinterest presented us with a challenge, and we all found ourselves trying to crack the ice with some cheerful palaver.

But, try as we might, she wasn't interested in where we come from or where we were going to. She couldn't care less about our tricks, disapproved of cigars and drinking, and seemed annoyed whenever she found her way blocked by Baba Yaga's bulk. Without looking up she'd try to squeeze past, frustrated at the delay to her important work, growling even as Baba apologetically shifted out of the way.

During that first long day, rolling through endless birch forests, Tog found out her name was Maria, Sparrow discovered she didn't care for our Daisy, and Farshad barely won a twitch of a smile when he give her some fresh cinnamon biscuits.

Sparrow thought Baba, being Russian, should have something in common with the old woman, but Baba was like a sulky teenager. 'If I get old like her, hit me on head with brick.'

Maria remained a small, irritable mystery that none of us had the skills to crack.

When Doctor Po and the Professoré left the carriage to do another check on Mister Splinter, still recovering in his trailer, I decided I still needed to have a few things out with him. I stepped around Maria doing yet another cleaning round, and headed for the back of the carriage.

Splinter's trailer was three flatcars back, and I had to cling to the outside of each to reach the door. I knocked and went in. Po and the Prof were redoing some kind of bandage on Splinter. I shuddered at the smell, vowing to top myself if I got anywhere near that bad.

'So, you have come to see how I fare?'

'I come to get information.'

'Ask.'

'This thing inside of me—if it's still alive, what is it and what's it for?'

Po and the Prof swapped a look I couldn't read, then kept doing what they were doing.

'I can tell you what it is,' Splinter growled. 'But you'll have limited understanding. The "splinter", as we call it, has many functions—to augment your senses and your thinking. It will connect you with the singularity. As to *what* it is—your device is a nano-engineered polymorphous bio-quasi-crystalline substrate, with DNA-based data storage and retrieval, and an in-situ siliceous-neuronal processing unit, designed to integrate with your systems of bodily functioning and brain activity.'

I understood most of the words but the sentences had me stumped.

'So the splinter is a mod what's more fancy than most. Not just a plug-in, it's kind of alive.'

'Definitions of "life" are arguable, but it has motive force and intent partially independent of yours.'

'And the idea was to make me smarter. So smart I wouldn't act like a stupid human.'

'In the Darwinian sense, you would be fitter. You would be able to outcompete Homo sapiens. You would integrate into the hominem family, reproduce with modified genes, and gradually become the dominant species.'

'How?' I scoffed. 'By being dictator? Launching a "final" war to kill the old humans? Or would I reason with them so everyone would let me and my sprogs take over because it was "for the best"? "Away you go, Blanco—take over the planet, pal. We made a mess of it so let's see how you go, eh?"'

Splinter writhed with fury, but the reckless part of me wanted him to blow a gasket. 'This is assuming it doesn't kill me first, of course.'

'You will not die,' he hissed, cold. 'We will use the tech available at T.I. to ensure you survive.'

'T.I.?'

'Triple Infinity,' Po replied reflexively.

I glanced at my tattoo. 'I thought infinity was infinity,' I replied. 'I didn't think you could triple it.'

Po shrugged. 'There are many varieties of infinities.'

'Were you connected, you would know that,' muttered Splinter.

I changed tack. 'You keep talking about being connected. Them glasses we pinched from one of your trailers said the same thing. Connected to what?'

'There are three levels. The first is to an information-sharing network, the second is the connection with that which grows inside you. The third is to connect with the proto-singularity.'

'This singularity thing—it's like an artificial brain, yeah?'

Po and the Prof swapped another look, then returned to work. Splinter was brisk. 'Basically, yes.'

'So we get to your old research lab, find this thing, plug ourselves in and it'll fix us up.'

'Yes.'

I should've been alarmed by his certainty, but despite all my bolshy bollocks, inside I was grabbing onto hope, not caring it stunk like a dead rat. I didn't want to die.

I didn't know there were worse things.

I went back to the carriage, pretending I'd been told nothing but good news. All I had to do was go to the Convergence, do what they told me, and I'm cured. Sparrow and I ride off into the sunset with the freaks, leaving dear old Dad in his lab cooking up bigger brains in a big lectric stew pot.

Deep down, I knew it was all bullshit but, when I got back to our carriage and Sparrow turned toward me, and I saw that face I loved more than life itself, I swallowed the truth, smiled and give her a hug. 'You was right. We just need to get to the Bogda Shan and we can sort everything—abracadabra and presto change-o.'

Sparrow hugged me, fierce. 'I'm glad your dad's talking to you proper. I know he's mad as a meat-axe, but deep down, he's still a man. He's still your father.'

I nodded and changed topic. 'True. So, how's it going in here?'

'We asked Maria for an extra blanket for Methuselah but she pulled out her rulebook.'

Baba grimaced. 'Unless is "certified snowstorm category six-point-two, is no allowance for more than one blanket".'

I was happy to be distracted. 'I bet I can find out what makes her tick,' I said.

'I bet you can't,' said Tog.

Dognose, a born gambler, lit up. 'I'll put a night's pay on it that he does.'

Farshad was sceptical. 'I will bet with friend Tog.'

Baba Yaga agreed, and soon money was flying this way and that. Having watched her cold-reading skills over the years, I pinched Baba's tarot cards, went for a stroll to the loo, then 'accidentally' dropped a couple beside Maria's little booth.

I apologised and picked them up, clocking her intrigue. I indicated Baba. 'Vyed ma.' I tapped the side of my nose and nodded, indicating how wise I thought our resident witch was.

Maria held out her hand, so I showed her the cards. As she was looking through them, I motioned Baba to join us. 'Give her a reading, Baba. Might cheer her up.'

'Ha,' she scoffed. 'You use me to win bet.' But Baba dutifully sat opposite Maria and held her hand out. Maria handed over the cards, Baba shuffled them, then handed them to Maria, telling her to do the same. Maria warily shuffled, trying to look disinterested, but I could see she was keen. Then she handed them back, and Baba went into her routine.

She laid out the familiar pattern, paused and studied it, tapping a card here and there, turning it over, frowning and concentrating, lulling Maria into thinking Baba's focus was on the cards.

When she'd built up tension, Baba started the palaver. 'You are strong woman. Very strong. Many people do not see this, but you are someone who understands much more than you say. You keep your cards close to your chest because that's the way to get the job done. You are sometimes pessimistic but mostly optimistic. You focus on being constructive.'

Maria give a tiny nod. I winked at Sparrow—Maria was hooked.

Baba tapped another card. 'You have had much sadness. Terrible sadness.'

Maria nodded again, misting up.

'You have lost some who mattered most, and you have suffered hurt from your family.'

Another nod—emphatic, emotional.

'Despite this, you work hard for what you have and what you give to others. Some people do not realise how much you suffer for them. And for one special person . . .'

Baba hesitated, 'reading' the cards, briefly noting Maria's focus on the cards and her welling eyes.

'This person is most close to your heart. You would give everything for them. Despite the hopes you have for yourself and your own life, you think always of them.' Baba frowned and did the old disclaimer.

'It is hard for me to read this—my words and understanding are not perfect . . .'

'No, no,' said Maria. 'Is true. Is all true. Go on.'

'I see a girl?' Baba continued, glancing at Maria's reaction, a fervent nod. 'This girl loves you but does not know how much you care for her, how much good you want for her.'

Maria produced a kerchief and dabbed her eyes and nose, nodding. 'Is true.'

'But see here,' Baba said, tapping another card. 'The work you do, the love you hold in your heart, it will bear fruit. What you give will be understood by she who is the receiver. The truth can never be hidden, not forever. She will know what you do is for her and her children.'

Baba Yaga leaned back, affecting a look of weariness, and finished with the standard spray. 'The future is positive, not negative. What will be will be, and the love that is given will be received and returned.'

When Baba was done, the effect on Maria was complete. She clutched Baba's great gnarly hand in the both of hers. 'This is all I want. For her to know that what I do, I do for her. So my grandchildren will be healthy and live in happiness. All my money I give to her.'

Baba nodded, patting Maria's hand. 'Sacrifice is a wound that produces blood and tears. It is also what gives strength to the giver and the receiver.'

A tiny, hopeful smile broke out on Maria's face. 'We must be strong, da?'

'Always,' sighed Baba, responding to Maria's emotion with her own. 'It is the only way.'

I had tears in my eyes by now, and Sparrow clutched my hand, whispering. 'What's wrong, darlin'?'

'I understand Maria now,' I whispered back. 'All the money what she makes, all the hard work, it's all for her daughter and grandkids. Everything she does, she does for love.'

'You understood what they was saying?'

'Well, yeah.'

Then I realised.

The thing inside me wasn't dead no more.

Chapter Forty-Seven—
The bridge between joy
and sorrow is not long

Our rusty old train rolled through Russia, heading east to my glorious death.

We stopped at towns and sidings where sometimes just a single passenger would get on or off, and bags of mail and goods were picked up or dropped off. It was a green and pleasant land, other than occasional blackened trails of wildfires and empty plague towns. Maria, now Baba's confidante, grimly pointed out the incinerators and bone mounds. The few farmers we saw looked happy enough, but we guessed that come from simply surviving and having less mouths to feed.

As we entered the city of Nizhny Novgorod that evening, we could see it was in good shape. Tall, undamaged buildings stuck up into the sky, windows were mostly filled with unsmashed glass, and there were cars on the ferroplas roads.

Maria sighed with envy. 'Nizhny has nuclear, oil and gas. They have streetlights, water and the electric to every building, and big army to protect them.'

Our train got shunted around a fair bit, but we finally made it to the main station, which was clean and shiny white, with lots of well-dressed geezers and military catching the local trains. Maria spoke with a mix of envy and awe about the Nizhny people. 'They are all educated in the university, and they live like tsars and tsarinas. It was hard, but they fought everyone to preserve what they had. When the refugees came from the south—so many millions . . .' She finished the sentence by shrugging and looking down. I guessed them poor bastards from the drying, dying south didn't meet with open arms from the good, university-educated folk of Nizhny.

We felt like filthy peasants in our rags, but we piled out of the train anyway, eager to stretch our legs. The polis turned their noses up, and briskly guided us to the unlit end of the platform. There we found hawkers what sold food and goods to riffraff from the rural lines. With Daisy on a rope, happily eating our scraps, we scarfed our scran, enjoying the different tastes of the local cuisine.

We noticed Doctor Po and the Professoré brushing themselves down and looking around as if they were expecting someone. Then we spotted a tall, elderly gentleman in a suit, carrying a gold-tipped walking stick. He was followed by two young men—a tall, slim lad carrying a small case, the other a stocky and probably ex-military assistant pushing a trolley with a pile of cases. We watched as Po and the Professoré respectfully greeted the old man. The gentleman nodded, shook their hands, then directed the lads toward the First Class carriage up front where they had cabins with beds and the like.

The tall, slim lad paused and looked around—toward me, it seemed—then boarded the train.

We eventually reboarded and, when the train slowly rolled out of Nizhny, me and Sparrow collared Po and the Professoré. 'Who was the old geezer?'

'Alexander Popov,' replied the Prof. 'He worked with us at TI. He was as close as Mister Splinter to making a breakthrough. They will also compete in the Great Feat.'

'You mean the lads with him?'

'One was his assistant, the other was his entry for the Feat.' Po and the Prof looked at each other, troubled. 'Popov seem confident,' added Po.

The Prof nodded. 'Not like last time.'

I was fed up about this killing-yourself competition. 'What's the point of this competition really? Why do geezers like me need to risk our lives?'

The Prof hesitated. 'It's technical.'

'Try me,' I growled.

'The splinter in you needs to sync with your systems and vice versa via stress-testing.'

'Like what you do with engines after a rebuild,' I said, sour.

'Exactly,' the Prof nodded, pleased. 'Testing enables deep synchronisation pathways to firm up—your survival ensures the splinter's, but equally the reverse applies.'

'Stress-testing, you call it,' Sparrow scoffed. 'I call it murder.'

I nodded. 'Them test subjects what came before us didn't need to die, and nor do we.'

Po looked ashamed. 'A functioning splinter potentially provides a crucial quasi-genetic advantage needed for the singularity to survive, and the human carrier.'

The Prof looked stricken, like Po had said too much.

Sparrow fumed. 'Who gives a shit about some whatever-the-hell-it-is when someone is dying? What is this singularity thing, anyway?'

'It's just a name,' the Prof replied. 'It's a concept, not a thing.'

I was suss. 'You said it *was* a thing—a big oldtech computer-brain buried in the mountains.'

'That technology is just to connect you. Win, or even just survive, and you will understand.'

'I need to understand now. Why risk my life?'

Po looked away while the Prof struggled to explain: 'If your splinter cannot save *you*, it cannot win against our species and displace us.'

'I don't care about any of that bollocks.'

The Prof was impatient. 'Either way, your survival depends on reaching the Convergence.'

They went to check on Mister Splinter, so I found a corner to sit and think. Daisy was happy to curl up and sleep on my lap, but Sparrow was stern. 'Talk.'

'I need to make plans—if I make it, if I don't.'

Her face fell.

'I'll do me best,' I soothed. 'But, if I fail, I need to know you and the freaks will be alright.'

'You think that other boy will beat you?'

'Who knows?' I thought about the tall lad boarding the train. Living in a city like Nizhny, he probably had a good education, good food and proper training—not like me learning how to smash bottles on my head. I stood, having decided. 'Time to pay my respects to my rival.'

'Do they let us lot into First Class?'

I turned to Maria, doing her last round of cleaning for the day. 'Maria, would it be alright if I visited someone up in First Class?'

'No. Is not allowed. They throw you off train.'

'Okay, but if I asked you what cabin Mister Popov and companions was in, could you tell me—remembering that everything we do, we do for love?' I looked meaningfully at Sparrow.

Maria sighed. 'I tell you nothing,' she replied, consulting her clipboard. 'You is strictly not allowed in First Class, especially cabin eight C, carriage one.'

I give her a peck on the cheek. 'Thanks, Maria.'

I left a worried Sparrow and made my way forward through the riffraff and the chickens and occasional small pigs in the Third Class carriages. When I got to Second Class, a provodnitsa wearing a starched apron sent me back the way I came. I abandoned Plan A, and went back to the gap between the carriages. No one was there, so I climbed up on the roof.

There's nothing like a stroll, at night, on a swaying, rocking train roof, to focus the mind. Keeping a wide stance, I slowly made my way forward, the cool summer air keeping the fear-sweat down to a slow drip. It took about ten minutes of near-death experiences to get close to the front First Class carriage. Some geezer was smoking a cigarette in the gap, so I waited, watching for overhead wires and overhanging branches. Finally, he threw his butt away and went back inside. I jumped down, catching the door as it was closing. I waited for him to enter his room then slipped inside. The passage was narrow—windows to my right, rooms to my left. I found cabin number eight, knocked and entered.

The old gentleman's heavy-set assistant stood, whipping out a pistol. I put my hands up. 'I'm Mister Splinter's boy.'

The gentleman looked me up and down, wary. 'Everyone sit—but keep the gun on him.'

I put my hands down. 'Thanks. You is Alexander Popov. My name's Blanco. I come to talk to your boy.' I looked to the young dark-haired lad, who stood, unworried, his look assessing. 'My name is Boris. Boris Popov.' He put out a hand.

I wiped my hand on my shirt, then took his. 'How d'you do.'

He had the grace not to wipe his hands on his trousers after. 'I'm well, and you?'

'Not too bad, considering,' I replied. 'I might be dying, but other than that, I'm good.'

'Would you care for a cup of tea?'

'That would be lovely, ta.'

Boris attended to a delicately painted porcelain samovar as I sat on the edge of the seat, hoping I didn't dirty it.

The elder Popov was wry. 'You are here to size up your competition.'

'That, and ask a favour.'

'You realise my son will also be able to size you up.'

'The way things are, your Honour, I'm not much of a threat to him.'

'Of course, you would say that,' he replied.

'You judge for yourself whether I'm playing you or not, but I tell you what—you ask me any question, and I'll answer it true and honest as I can.'

Boris made tea, content to let his father ask the questions. Over the next ten minutes, I sipped the best tea I'd ever had, and told them everything I knew about myself, and what little I knew about the Great Feat. Finally, the old gentleman stopped asking questions. 'If what you've told us is true, then you have very little chance of winning the Great Feat, let alone connecting with the singularity.'

'Correct, your Honour. Which brings me to the favour.' I turned to meet Boris' eyes. 'If I *don't* die, I'd be grateful if, when you're done with whatever needs doing, you make the singularity fix me up and get rid of this thing inside me.'

Boris nodded, thoughtful, not agreeing or refusing. 'Is there anything else?'

'Yes. If I *do* die, my girl, Sparrow, and my freak family will need help to get someplace safe. If it's in your power to help them, please do what you can. They is the people I love, and they deserve a better life than the one they had so far.'

Again Boris nodded. Then he put out his hand. 'I give you my word I will help you and your friends if it is at all possible.'

I saw he meant it, and I misted up, overwhelmed that this fine young geezer should think well enough of me to help. I shook his hand like I was pumping water. 'Thanks, Boris—I appreciate it.'

We rested back in our seats as the assistant poured some spirits into tiny glasses. 'And now,' said Boris, 'you must want to ask me some questions.'

'Do you got one of these quasi-bio-crystalline things inside you?'

'My father's approach and your father's differ a little, but I have a similar augmentation.'

'Is you connected?' I asked.

'To the commsat and the database, yes. I'm not directly connected with the Singularity at the Bogda Shan—though I certainly wish I was.'

'So you believe the palaver about creating a new species of human? Making us smarter and wiser?'

'I believe self-evolution is the only option for Terran consciousness left to explore, yes.'

'But if you get 'connected', and you become one of these post-human types—won't you use all them smarts to do what *you* want rather than what's best for everyone else?'

'The level of power of one individual would be small. But as numbers of post-humans grow, then, yes, their collective decisions would out-weigh Homo sapiens', much like Homo sapiens' resilience outweighed that of the Neanderthal.'

'Who was that then?'

'An earlier species of human. Besides, my understanding is that the intention of the singularity's architecture is to be innately self-correct-ing by being massively connected. Harming others or, through inac-tion, allowing harm to come to others would be seen as destructively aberrant.'

'Perhaps so, but in my experience anything with a mind can change it.'

Boris swapped a look with his father, who looked irritated, like they'd had this argument.

'The new species takes long-term collective survival as key,' Popov Senior replied. 'That means ensuring the health of the planet, and the sustainability of all actions taken by the post-humans. They won't repeat our mistakes because to do so would ensure a final global collapse beyond which no species would survive to continue the evolution of consciousness. It is simple logic.'

I was more confused than reassured, but I had one more question. 'So, what if more than one competitor survives?'

'Then they can breed.'

Boris noted my surprise. 'Diversity is strength. If I can breed with others, it is my duty.'

Even though I barely understood any of this, I noticed him blushing. I realised he wouldn't have been more than fourteen or fifteen. 'I'm not taking the proverbial,' I assured him, 'but I'm really impressed—you seem like a diamond geezer. I hope you win.'

He looked troubled. 'If you compete, you will most likely die.'

'Considering the bad stuff I done in my life, I probably don't deserve to live. You're the one what should be chatting with the 'Singularity', fixing things up. You'll do a bang-up job.'

Boris smiled, shy. 'I'll have my father to guide me.'

'You're a lucky man. Well, I should leave you good people and head back.' I stood, shook Popov Senior's hand, then Boris's. 'Nice to meet you. Until we meet again, eh?'

I left their cabin and climbed back onto the roof of the car behind with a lighter heart. In the moonlight, carefully tottering back toward our carriage, a weight had lifted off me. I trusted Boris and liked him. I even hoped we might become friends when we met up again.

But that didn't happen. He was murdered along with his dad two days later.

Chapter Forty-Eight—Dance
to the tune that is played

I t was sunny, and Sparrow and me were sitting high on the elephants' backs in their open-topped carriage, enjoying the breeze and the changing view, paying for our seat by idly scratching Bo and El's hides with stiff brooms.

We saw why so many had fled north. As the rails took us south to the Kazakhstan border, the land became hotter and dryer, trees were sparser, and villages were half-buried under deserts still moving north.

At a tiny, weathered concrete station in the middle of nowhere, a local told us the rains either didn't come no more or, when they did, they bucketed for three solid days before raging walls of brown water thundered down dry riverbeds, washing everything before them. The few farmers left tended goats and watermelons, using windmills for power and big white dew-catchers for water.

The only other people were caravans of nomads, navigating the ocean of dirt and rock as it roasted during the day and froze at night. They camped around small soaks in creek beds, or in dried-out lakes beside abandoned farms and ruined villages.

Our train was now pulled by a single ancient diesel, and was a much shorter affair. We'd picked up another small circus on the way, and we were getting on well—two of our party especially. A young lady from the new outfit, Anastasia—Tass, for short—barely a metre tall, liked the look of our Tog.

Unfortunately, Tog was shy, and me and Sparrow couldn't get him to chat her up. Fortunately, Tass, covered in intricate folk-art tattoos, was a good sort, and inclined to a drink or three—as was Tog. Soon there wasn't no separating them, and Sparrow was a blubbering mess about how sweet it all was. Them two spent a lot of time with Jumbo and El Grande, and Tass was as taken with them as they seemed to be with her. They felt her with their trunks, fascinated there was another like Tog.

Still a day from Petropavlosk, we were forced to stop at a washout past Vargashi near the highway.

While the train crew and some of us circus-folk ferried rocks to pin the track back into place, Sparrow, Tog and Tass took Daisy, Jumbo and El Grande off to find some grass. Luckily, they stumbled on some Hami melons growing inside the ruins of a farm courtyard. Sparrow left Tog and Tass to enjoy some romantic private time, and brought us labouring workers an armful of melons. These were cut up and passed around, uniting us in the enjoyment of the best melons I ever tasted.

The attack was coordinated. Four trucks, two each from opposite directions, came in at the same time. We didn't even notice till a rocket took out Splinter's trailer and we were all under fire.

I was running back toward our carriage for a weapon when another rocket exploded in the First Class section. I was knocked into the air and landed on my back, winded, gasping and helpless, pelted with debris. The semiauto fire stopped, but a new sound started, one that filled me with horror. Single shots. Someone was walking around taking out individual targets. But why? If you rob a caravan or a train, you stop them, block their escape, then loot. You don't destroy everything and kill everyone.

Dust filled the air from the explosions as Daisy whimpered beside me. Then someone lifted me up.

'Found him!'

It was the Gaffer, who grinned fiercely at me as Tommy came running through the dust and flames, excited. 'Hey, Blanco! Guess what?' He tapped his stomach. 'I got augmented. Doctor Torini from my new circus implanted Splinter's material in me. I'm connected, and it's amazing.'

'Nice,' I muttered.

'You don't look well,' Tommy frowned. 'Are you looking after yourself?'

'Bit hard with all the bullets flying about.'

Tommy looked up and yelled, 'Cease fire!'

The shots stopped, their sound replaced with moans and screams. Tommy turned back to me. 'I feel great. I've been working out. Look.' He punched me in the face, then examined his bloodied knuckles with interest. 'I heal more quickly too. The other day I was reading Splinter's journals and I got a paper cut—which really hurt. But within two hours, it was healed. Does that happen with you?'

'Not really, no.'

Tommy frowned, annoyed. 'I'm disappointed in you. I liked the game you played in Moskva, but why leave yourself open to attack like this? Did the Pimpernels' poison affect your brain?'

'Possibly.'

'You'll need to buck up for the Great Feat.' He looked up at the Gaffer, bored. 'We're done here.'

I was dropped to the ground like an armful of firewood. Tommy's face loomed above me. 'My condolences for your loss, by the way.'

My stomach sank. 'Loss?'

'Your father. I imagine you wanted to be the one to kill him but if I waited around for you to get things done, we'd never get anywhere.' He smiled again, cheerful. 'Okay, see you at the Convergence!'

Tommy ran off. The Gaffer looked down, amused by my predicament. 'You've got no fucking chance, you tosser. He's getting stronger every day. And I'll have a front-row seat to watch you die.'

He walked away, chuckling.

I struggled to my knees, The smoke and dust was clearing, and I could see the devastation as Tommy and his crew strolled to their trucks.

Tommy suddenly pointed. 'There!'

It was Sparrow. As they closed in, she started limping away, but the Gaffer easily caught her, slinging her over one shoulder. Tommy looked back to me, patient. 'Now you *have* to follow us.'

I stumbled after them, desperate for a weapon. By the time I found one lousy pistol, they were driving off. I sank to my knees, my heart breaking, the pain of it unbearable. Then, in the wreckage beside me, a hand moved.

It was Boris, a large chunk of his shoulder and chest wall torn away. He was dying, but he met my eyes, calm. 'Come close. Hold my hand.'

I held his hand. He whispered, strength fading. 'Touch your forehead to mine.'

I leaned over, touching my forehead to his. 'Boris. I'm so sorry.'

'It's you now. You're the one. Maybe you always w . . .'

I felt a splitting pain in my head and my chest.

Then he was gone.

I lifted my head, tears pouring. Daisy licked my face, her tail between her legs, worried. Baba joined me, bleeding but upright. 'Come. We have work.'

She pulled me up. Tog and Tass rejoined us, in shock but unharmed, and we moved about treating them what we could, comforting them we couldn't. Baba Yaga pulled wreckage away from trapped people, with Maria as her assistant, examining wounds and giving first aid. We found Popov Senior's body crushed almost beyond recognition, blown from the remains of his carriage.

We found Mathematico in what was left of the freaks' trailer, shivering in terror with Susy and Penny, cradling Erik who was doing his best to calm the boy. Milosh held Mala's limp body, weeping and moaning. Humbolt was tying off a wound to his heavily tattooed left forearm, stunned with shock. 'The bastards got the Gauguin.'

I left them all and climbed across what was left of Mister Splinter's trailer. The back half had been blown completely off, and bullets had been sprayed through the rest. Splinter was still on his seat, which, fully exposed to the light of day, I now saw was some sort of old-tech life-support system, smashed and riddled with bullets, as was Splinter.

I stepped forward, not knowing if he was alive or dead. 'Mister Splinter?'

I waited, and finally his chin lifted slightly. One side of his face was shot away, but the one eye left bored through me. I could barely hear his whisper. 'The new species will make all this redundant. Aggression will be channelled. Violence . . . no need.'

'Is there anything we can do for you?'

'Too damaged,' he muttered, then managed to focus on my face. 'Use whoever is left, think strategically, win. Above all, connect.'

'I can't connect. I'm damaged inside. I got no chance of winning. Tommy's ahead of me—augmented, connected, stronger, and fitter.' I slumped. 'The bastard's smarter than me.'

The corner of Splinter's mouth twitched, blood and other fluids pumping sluggishly out of his wounds. 'When I was a young researcher . . .' He paused, struggling for breath, then continued. 'If I didn't know what to do next . . . if I felt defeated and stupid . . . I imagined what a smart person would do.' His mouth twitched again. 'So think. Imagine.'

His hand moved, and I found myself taking that monstrous, deformed thing in my hand as his eye looked into mine. 'Don't let all of human history count for nothing.'

Then he died.

There was a noise behind me. Doctor Po helped the wounded Professoré through the wreckage. 'Is he still alive?'

I shook my head.

Po and the Prof moaned in despair, moving to Splinter's side and checking him over, curiously tender. The Professoré finally put a hand on Po's shoulder. 'Enough. He's gone, Po.'

Po wept. I was astonished. I'd never seen Po do anything nice that he wasn't paid or ordered to do, and here he was, grieving, being human.

The Professoré sat heavily on the rubble, wincing, defeated. 'It's over.'

I looked at them, wondering how it had been when the trio had been young men, working together. 'Was he really my father?'

Po didn't seem to hear, but the Professoré nodded. 'He was your father.'

'Who was my mother?'

'Makena Kamathi, an East African molecular biologist specialising in gene expression and transfer. Your father met her at the second Convergence.'

'What happened to her?'

'After our second failure, she picked up an encephalitis, unaware she was pregnant with you. By the time we reached France, we had saved her life, but not her brain. We left her in the care of a nunnery, assuming she, and you, would die. A few years later, travelling on the continent, we found you there.'

'My mother is still alive?'

The Professoré shook his head. 'She died giving birth to you.'

I didn't have no more questions. I shook myself. 'Come and help with the wounded.'

We left Splinter's carriage and worked our way through each remaining trailer and carriage to find the dead and treat the injured. By nightfall, we'd lost over a dozen people, and had twice that number injured. We made fires from wreckage to keep people warm while the rest of us worked on the train, fixing and patching what we could, and ditching the rest to clear the track.

By morning, we'd reinstalled the passengers, put the worst injured in beds in the First Class cabins, and assigned people to look after them. We dug a mass grave, interred the dead, then covered it in rocks. Those what could stood and said their piece, then, one by one, walked away back to the train.

I looked at the grave of my father. A bunch of rocks what didn't mean nothing to me than a few blisters on my hands. I walked away without a single emotion.

I was too busy imagining what a smart person would do.

Chapter Forty-Nine—A small sail can beat a big pair of oars

As our wrecked train slowly clanked and scraped away to the south-east, we left my father, Mala, Guido, Povero Cristo, Princess Mirela, Ezekial Scamp, Alexander and Boris Popov, and fifteen other innocent passengers buried under that pathetic pile of rocks.

At Petropavlosk, the Fazios and Dognose stayed on with a wounded Alessia at a clinic there.

Somewhere on the dusty plains of Kazakhstan between Akkol and Astana, Spod died quietly in his seat, a bottle in his hand, from internal bleeding. Maria left us at Astana for her return journey, and our hearts broke to see her on the platform, her teary face at the window, waving her kerchief.

In our slow-moving carriage, whistling with bullet holes, there was little talk, no smiles, and no one looking at nothing but that blasted landscape—hazy tan-brown sky, ruler-straight horizon, endless dusty-white plain. The only moving things were swirling dust devils, camels and mining bots.

We were numb—overwhelmed with anger, grief and despair. We were also still heading in the direction them murdering bastards went.

Hope wasn't an option—we had too few weapons and not enough bullets. The whole plot was now a suicide mission.

Either way, there wasn't no choice for me, but I knew I had to give people a reason to go on or the courage to go back. 'Oi,' I said, eloquent as ever, wondering what the hell my mouth would come up with. A few looked up, listless. 'What direction are we heading?' I asked.

I got a few shrugs. Tog, holding Tass's hand, said, 'East.'

'Why the feck are we going there?' I demanded.

Baba Yaga frowned. 'To get Sparrow.'

'If that's the only reason, then all I need is weapons and luck. No reason for the rest of you to risk your lives.'

Milosh's face was granite. 'I go to end the life of the Gaffer.'

This got sympathetic nods and cursing from the others.

'Fine,' I said. 'Reason number two—revenge. But considering what we stand to lose—our lives—is revenge a good enough reason? The Gaffer will live a miserable life then get himself killed one way or another. So why risk everything we got left to get that prick?'

Po and the Professoré swapped a look. 'Are you still going to compete?' Po asked.

I'd been thinking hard about this. 'I might, yeah.'

'Even if you have rescued Sparrow and killed Gaffer?'

'Maybe, yes.'

'Why? To honour your father?' Methuselah whispered.

'If I honour anything, it in't going to be the past, it'll be a future I want to be in.'

Beside Tass, Tog nodded. 'I'm with you.' Tass squeezed his hand. 'Me too.'

Inside, I felt like crying. My options were to go in alone and get killed, or let these good souls join me and, most likely, get killed with me. It wasn't right to let this happen but, to my shame, I couldn't think of nothing more important than giving Sparrow the best chance of rescue. I pretended I knew what I was talking about. 'Alright, we is agreed—united we stand, divided we fall. Together we fight for the futures we want—for us and them what comes after us. So let's do this proper.'

'What are you proposing?' whispered Methuselah.

'We is a circus. We could organise a show in a shitstorm. So let's organise getting Sparrow back, wiping the Gaffer and Tommy off the map, and me winning that feckin' competition.'

So, because we had nothing else to take our minds off our fear and grief, we got organised.

Outside, low, dry hills rolled past, ignored. Inside, we divided into teams. Everyone had skills, and got jobs to suit. By the time that day ended, we had a plan that give the finger to the fact we were outgunned, outmanned and had fuck-all chance of coming out alive.

As we approached the snow-capped Zailiyskiy mountains, the dust and rocks gave way to green hills and fields. Low, square, dirt-coloured houses began to appear, as did crops and donkeys, cars and tractors, dogs and people. And, finally, after a thousand empty miles of flat dirt, the city of Almaty.

A local at the railway station told us the northern part of the city had recently been flooded from the bursting of a glacier-melt dam high in the mountains, but the rest of the city was intact. What we saw was green with parks and gardens, and the people looked happier than them out in the deserts with their skinny sheep and woolly camels.

It was good to see people having proper lives that weren't just about survival, but none of it stopped the constant acid fear inside me about Sparrow. Would they hurt her? Would they keep her alive?

We had to wait overnight in the railyards before our carriages could be hooked to an engine heading into Chinese territory, so I put the rope on Daisy and wandered over to the station, wanting information about where we were going.

Almaty was an international town, full of refugees—Russians, Arabs, Han Chinese, Uyghurs, Pakistanis, all sorts. Chatting to sweets sellers and stallholders, I heard the Han had mostly fled Xinjiang since the Collapse, resigned to let the desert cover the cities and towns they abandoned. There'd long been tension between the Han and Turkic peoples in Xinjiang, but a Kazak stationhand from Ürümqi told me the Chinese still kept small outposts there—so we'd probably not risk facing too many uniforms what might ask questions.

In the morning, as we rolled out, backtracking north toward Lake Balqash, in a quiet corner of the carriage, Binh guided me in practising my breathing. Binh knows about all that Buddhist meditation guff. He said I wasn't completely hopeless, but I could tell he was worried.

Doctor Po and the Professoré checked me over to see what state I was in. Without any medical equipment, Doctor Po resorted to holding my pulse for about ten minutes to test my heart, while the Professoré used a stethoscope to listen to my insides.

'Hear it creeping around in there?' I asked. 'Still alive, is it?'

The Professoré pocketed his stethoscope. 'It's amazing *you're* still alive considering the toxins the Pimpernels put in you.' He idly tapped his teeth with the end of the stethoscope, musing. 'I wonder how much your implant did to correct the situation. After all, it lives and dies with you.'

'So it's alive. Is it growing?'

'I suspect it's connecting more than growing—integrating its systems into yours.'

'You should've told me about this when I was young.'

'You were a wilful child. Telling you would've destabilised you.'

'Destabilised me?' I fumed. 'I been so feckin' miserable from what you lot put me through I nearly topped meself. Is that "destabilised" enough for you?'

'Splinter said we had to make it hard so you were forced to stay focused. The training you went through was to strengthen your control over your body, your breathing, your perception of pain, and your mind.'

'Bastards,' I growled.

The Prof shrugged. 'Tell me how you feel and how you are thinking.'

'I get headaches, and dizzy. I can talk different languages again, and sometimes I see where we is.'

'Like a dot on a map?'

'Like seeing myself in a landscape. When I want to see where we are, I can zoom in and out. I just think where I am in relation to other things—rivers, mountains, north, south—and I see it all.'

Po and the Prof swapped an intrigued look. 'How far can you "zoom out"?' asked Po.

I concentrated, and my normal vision faded. I felt myself in a three-dimensional map what showed our train on a line in the landscape. It felt weird to think of myself as so small in a world so big, but at least I could imagine it. I zoomed out, and the train was a spot in a vast region of deserts and mountains. Then I zoomed out further, and faster, beyond where I'd ever gone before.

Then it all sped up as the entire region became a speck smaller than a flea on an elephant, and that turned into a dot on a blue-and-brown ball I realised was the Earth. That shrank and turned into a dot floating in the blue-black of space, lit by a fiery globe what was the sun. Then even that enormous ball shrank until . . .

The screaming noise was me, the barking was Daisy, and the pain on my cheeks was where the Professoré was slapping me. I was curled up in a ball, trembling and shaking with shock, my sense of self gone. In the immense reality of space, I was less than a bacteria on a piece of dust. I was nothing. I didn't exist, not in any meaningful way. Not compared to the vastness of . . .

Only the pain, and Po and the Professoré yelling at me, made me finally realise the thing feeling the pain was me.

Seeing me return to my senses, Po looked at the Professoré. 'He hasn't got a chance, has he?'

The Prof nodded, gloomy. 'None.'

They left me, but as I was coming out of my funk, I heard something that made me realise I didn't need to work out how a smart geezer might think. There was a wordless voice, a whisper in my head, calling to me—a ghost with a posh Russian accent.

Shocked, I managed to whisper a reply. 'Boris?'

Chapter Fifty—The more you ask how far, the further the journey

Though I heard Boris in my head, I couldn't help looking around. 'Where are you?' I asked aloud.

I believe I'm embedded into the substrate of the biomachinery inside of you.

I was shocked, also disgusted—I mean, it's bad enough having intestinal worms, the ones you can feel squirming about, but having a whole geezer inside me was horrifying.

I'm sorry you feel that way.

Feeling his sadness, I calmed, reminded of the small matter of him being dead. How would it feel to know your body was buried in distant dirt, your mind buried in somebody else?

It feels unpleasant. I wasn't able to string coherent thoughts together at first. It's been difficult to define myself as still existing. But the more I try to think, the more I realise I feel like me, and the more real I feel.

'Does it . . . hurt?'

Not physically. I feel lost and deeply unhappy. My body's gone, and my father is . . .

He trailed off, but I felt an echo of his pain. 'I'm sorry, mate. My condolences for your loss.' It sounded feeble, but I meant it.

Thank you, Blanco.

'Maybe the singularity can do something,' I mused. 'Build a bot you can download into.'

Perhaps. For now I'm still exploring how I can remain a distinct entity, separate from you. I'm impressed by the work your father, Doctor Po and the Professoré have done. It's superior engineering to that of my father.

'All the more reason to think the singularity could help. Your dad and my lot all built it, after all.'

Assuming it's still there and capable of functioning after all this time. Also, if it hasn't self-evolved, it may just be a computer. Processing information, no matter how fast, is a vastly different thing to self-aware intelligence.

'I in't impressed by intelligence, Boris. There's smart, and there's knowing the right thing to do. Most of the clever types I know are miserable bastards what make life hell for everyone else.'

I sensed Boris was thinking.

'Can you see through my eyes and smell what I smell?' I wondered.

I can, but it's fuzzy.

'Can you hear me thinking?'

Not really, no—just what you direct at me. Can you hear my thoughts?

'No. Same thing.'

Tog and Tass came along to check on me. 'Oi, who are you talking to?'

'Remember that Russian geezer I told you about? The young one?'

'The one what died?' Tog asked.

'That's him. He's not completely dead.'

Tog and Tass looked around. 'What, like a ghost?'

'He's inside me. Somehow he managed to download his brain into that thing I got in me.'

They swapped a look, like I was mental. Tog was wary. 'So is you twice as smart now?'

I was grim. 'I bleedin' wish, mate.'

Tog and Tass backed off and left me . . . us . . . alone.

As our slow train rolled through the bleak landscape, I was in a constant agony about Sparrow's safety. Hell is fearing what a loved one might be going through, and having no means of knowing either way. Boris could offer no comfort.

The others did an inventory of all we had in the way of money, equipment and weapons, working out what each group could carry or use when the fighting began. Every now and then, the train stopped, and we'd get out to dig away sand drifts burying the rails. This hard physical work, and all the planning, distracted me a little from thinking about Sparrow.

I withdrew from the others to practise my breathing and think through the plan. Daisy rested her head on my lap and give me worried looks. Inside me, Boris faded in and out of my ken, saying he was 'working to hook things up'. Outside the train window, the landscape was as grim as my mood. Inspired by their new love, Tog and Tass kept the others focused and positive, but I grew surly.

Once, I was doing my meditation when there was a smashing of wood. I opened my eyes to see my fist buried to the wrist through the wooden wall of the trailer. As the pain began to register, I blankly stared at the broken wood, motionless until a concerned Daisy jumped up and woofed her concern. I pulled my hand free, then petted her till she calmed down. Baba Yaga was watching. 'You feel better?'

I shrugged my incomprehension of my behaviour. She shrugged hers. Only Daisy felt real. I was losing control, and the closer we got to the Convergence, the more I felt despair pulling me down.

Travelling through the Kazakh desert, we rolled past rusty, half-buried signs where towns had been—Koskuduk, Zholoman, Aynabulak, Molaly and a place called Matay what was now just towering sandhills. We stopped to refuel in Beskol — another cold, dry town beside another dry lake. Locals selling arak and grilled sweet corn in the station told us the lake had turned to salt after it was drained to irrigate crops—then the salt blew off and killed the crops. Now the town was just a few houses and a railway station—a winter refuge for nomad herders down from the mountains.

There's a terrible, ruthless beauty to this vast land so far from any sea. The air is so clear it's hard to judge distance—everything looks closer. Sitting on the platform edge, feet dangling as Daisy and I ate corn, I looked toward what looked like low tawny hills. I barely noticed some dark specks in a ragged line until, with a jolt, I realised the specks were moving—a distant camel caravan whose tiny size meant the low hills beyond were actually mountains — not five kilometres away but fifty.

We eventually reboarded and resumed our journey. The train turned south and we passed another flat, dead lake to our north and more beautiful mountains rearing up to the south. At the border town, a military post called Druzhba, we all got out and washed ourselves under an enormous hose from a water tank while the railway workers used a crane to lift our cars, carriages and trailers off the Kazakh bogies and onto the narrower Chinese ones.

After drying off, we entered China through the rusted wreckage of old transmission towers and unmanned watchtowers, feeling cleaner and somehow more hopeful. On the Chinese side of what remained of any 'fence', we were stopped at a bombed-out station well past its former glory, called Alashankou, where a trio of bored uniforms counted our numbers, demanded 'fees' for processing our passports, asked if we were drug smugglers, then 'offered' to sell us some foul-tasting spirit they called 'konyac' for more money than we wanted to part with.

Eventually, after Erik rolled a cigarette for them as entertainment, and Tass did some card tricks, the uniforms just give us a bottle. To 'thank' them, we poured them a few drinks, shouted their good health, and picked their pockets for the money they'd extorted from us.

As we rolled out of Alashankou, lightning was cracking and flashing up in the mountains, and dark clouds were building to the west. The wind swept down the valleys and buffeted the carriages as we again turned east. After another long night of being woken every few hours to help clear the track, we finally reached the outskirts of Ürümqi at dawn.

To avoid any ambush from the Gaffer and Tommy, we paid the train driver to stop short of the main railway station, in a distant dusty freight yard where we unloaded the tattered remains of Splinter's Magnifico

Cirque du Amusementes. Then we sent the train on its way and braced ourselves for a cautious journey through the back streets of the city.

Ürümqi was a ghost town for the most part. Once a small city, it was now just another stop on the old Silk Route, a base for trading and transporting water, fuel, chemicals and drugs between Asia and Europe. Them what still lived here were mostly Uyghur and Kazakh, who disdained the rotting Chinese skyscrapers, preferring traditional houses with courtyards and walled gardens. Buying food supplies and ammunition at a market, we learned the few Han Chinese left maintained a polite semblance of authority while assimilating with the others.

We trickled along dirt tracks then found our way onto the empty ferroplas arterials that took us east toward our final destination in the mountains. Cradling a semi, I sat on the side of the tractor and noted the desert reclaiming the town outskirts, tan dust thick on everything.

We stopped a few times to buy more food, and any ammunition the dealers had, with the last of our money. This was war, and our pathetic plan was to deny death long enough to rescue Sparrow—and exact revenge.

As the town became featureless rolling desert, I heard Boris inside me, sounding strange.

Blanco, something's happening. Can you feel it?

'Feel what?'

There's something else in here with me. I don't like it. I'm sc . . .

And then I didn't hear Boris no more.

Chapter Fifty-One—
Better a slow donkey than
a horse that throws you

After hours of crawling along the dusty road, I stopped trying to contact Boris.

Evening fell, along with the day's heat, leaving us with another seventy kilometres to cool down before our final destination—a lake, deep in the Bogda Shan mountains. We could only hope the Gaffer and Tommy weren't somehow tracking us. Stealth was the only advantage we had in getting Sparrow back.

It was a cloudless night, and the stars were sprayed across the sky in a thick arc, bright enough to light the windblown dunes on either side of the ten-thousand-year-old Silk Road.

The mountains were a jagged black silhouette looming ahead. For a while, I went to sit with Baba Yaga in the truck cabin, my brain fizzing like a short-wave radio. Whatever happened to Boris was affecting me too. My vision was blurring, juddering with map overlays and information streams in a dozen different languages. Strange tastes and smells battered me.

I wanted to tell Baba how scared I was but all I said was, 'Nearly there, Baba. We is going to save Sparrow and then escape to wherever will have us. That's all that matters, right?'

Baba barely nodded, deep in one of her fugues. 'I'm ready to fight,' she rumbled. 'They can put a hundred bullets in me and I go on fighting.'

She lapsed back into silence. I spared her any more of my nervous bollocks.

Around one in the morning, we reached the turn-off, a road what left the desert plains and travelled south, up into the mountains through a dry, eroded dirt canyon. I went up front with Doctor Po and the Professoré in their rattling truck cabin, telling them what was going on in my head.

The Professoré spread his hands, resigned. 'I think the Pimpernels' toxins have fatally damaged the Splinter inside of you.'

Doctor Po dug in a box and produced a pair of the AI glasses. 'Put these on. Connect at least.'

I paused. 'Before I lost the last pair, I connected with something. The voice said, "Welcome to the Pool, Operative Zeta. You are now connected with alpha level." What's that about then?'

Po and the Prof swapped a pleased look. 'It recognised him!' Po smiled. 'The gene-key worked.'

'Why did it call me Operative Zeta?'

'That's the name we gave each project since we left TI.'

'Each "project"—meaning the kids you and Splinter made. The dead ones before me.'

Po shrugged. 'You are better made than the others.'

'Like how?'

'You have both arms,' offered the Professoré. 'With all the fingers even.'

'You don't need mood stabilisers to control the rages,' added Po. 'You have a complete lower jaw.'

The Prof nodded. 'Apart from the lack of melanin and low intelligence, you've done well.'

'Low intelligence?' I glowered. 'How low are we talking?'

'Your IQ is mid-one-twenties. Barely above G-factor average.' Po looked wistful.

I looked at the pair of gormless genuises. 'So why did you lot ever think to hook up with this freak show? It doesn't make sense.'

'It allowed us to travel and was a good cover for our work—when our experiments failed, no one questioned the appearance of another freak.'

I had a sinking feeling. 'How many in our lot are the result of your experiments?'

The Professoré looked away, disinterested. Doctor Po avoided my eyes. 'Not all.'

'Was Mister Splinter really a Rom?'

'Yes. His real name was Charles Hoskins. After he had a piece of the original Splinter put in him, and took over circus, it was his joke to became Mister Splinter.'

'Hilarious. So my full name is Blanco Kamathi-Hoskins.'

Po shrugged. 'I suppose so. Is it important?'

Having been a nameless piece of meat my whole life—ordered about and beaten on a regular basis—I give him a flat look. 'You two are fucking morons. Here you are trying to build a better human and you know nothing about people.'

'We know what we have done,' replied the Professoré. 'And we know our task is to answer the great questions human minds now confront.'

'Only one question interests me,' I murmured. 'How do we survive the next few hours.'

The Prof was exasperated. 'Do you not marvel at the mysteries of life? Do you not wish to understand how you are connected to everything there is?'

'All I care about is getting Sparrow back. Help me do that and I'll help you with the singularity—I'll be your post-human whatsit. Get in my way, and I will not piss on you if you is on fire. And I'll be the one holding the petrol and matches. Am I understood?'

In the blue light of the stars, two shadowed heads nodded.

I slid the glasses on, glum.

Security clearance pending. Welcome back, Operative Zeta.

'Show me names and location of any people within ten kilometres.'

My vision blacked out, then cleared, with all the hills and rivers labelled, and yellow dots indicating the presence of humans. There was our convoy in a loose line, then a single dot five hundred metres ahead in a place marked Traditional Village Happiness Holiday Hotel Resort.

'There's either a single guest having a relax just up ahead in a "resort", or a dodgy fuck lurking for other reasons.'

'They will have someone guarding the approach,' said the Professoré.

'Who will?'

'The Traveller King.'

'Better stop the convoy here then.'

Doctor Po tapped his brake lights a couple of times and slowly pulled to a halt.

As our unruly misfits clambered out of the vehicles, yawning and stretching, I stopped the Professoré. 'Do I need to deal with that geezer guarding the road?'

The Professoré shook his head. 'The elders have a guard to identify anyone coming through. If they don't check in regularly, they'll know something is wrong.'

'You go,' said Po. 'We wait here, give you one hour, then announce ourselves.'

'So they'll be expecting us,' added the Prof. 'But *you'll* catch them by surprise.'

It was a shit plan but all we had. 'The rule about us not being allowed to fight anyone once we get to the Convergence—that's a Romany rule, is it?'

'Yes. Should you draw a blade or fight, a Kris – a Romany court - might be called against you. You will be stopped and face the justice of the travellers.'

'And if I call for justice against them to get Sparrow back?'

'You may get it, or you may not.'

'Then I don't give a toss about no Gypsy law. Fight and win, or fight and die—them's my options.' I opened the truck door. 'I'll get Tog sorted. If the guard up ahead asks, give them some guff about me being ill in one of the vans.' I hopped down from the cab and started walking away.

'Be careful,' said Po, sounding like he cared.

Still wearing the glasses, I walked down the convoy to where Tog was giving Jumbo and El Grande a last pat. He didn't look happy. Nor did Tass. She give me a cool look. 'I just meet him, now you take him to be killed.'

'Tass, I swear I'll do my level best not to get a scratch on him.' I put on the invisibility cloak and turned to Tog. 'Ready?'

He nodded, grim, night-vision goggles around his neck. I picked up the sniper rifle as Tass kissed Tog hard, then focused on patting the elephants, her head turned away.

Me and Tog walked in silence down to where the lads had the kite ready.

Farshad gave us both RTs as I turned to Barrelmouth. 'To cover the noise of this thing taking off, start up one of the tractors, and give it a rev as if we're having engine trouble, alright?'

Baba's hulking shadow appeared out of the gloom. 'I don't believe in God but, just in case, I pray.'

'Thanks, Baba. If you get into specifics, ask God not to put a fuel blockage in the line.'

Barrelmouth started the tractor as we tied Tog, facing forward, to my chest, the rifle slung over my back. Then they buckled the harness over my shoulders and we were ready.

Tog was a brave bugger and no mistake. He'd never flown before, and I knew he'd hate hanging off me like a sack of potatoes, but he kept his cool. 'Let's get Sparrow.'

I never loved that fucker more.

We started the kite engine, which coughed, spluttered and fired. Humbolt and Farshad held the wing edges off the ground as I began to lumber back down the road. The lads trotted beside us, then ran as fast as they could as the wing tips caught the air. I throttled up and yelled. 'Let her go!'

They let go, and dropped behind as I felt some lift. After a few agonising seconds, us and the ground finally parted company, and we rose into the air.

The kite didn't like the extra weight of Tog but I kept it on full throttle, gaining height and slowly swinging us around to the west, desperate to get more height.

At first I thought the engine was running rough, then I realised the shaking was Tog, shivering with fear. I yelled in his ear, 'I know how you feel mate. The natural beauty of the world below has you quivering with excitement and happiness, am I right?'

'Yeah,' he shouted back. 'I'm so happy and excited I could literally shit myself.'

'Mate, this is the easy bit. You should definitely clench them bum muscles when we comes in to land though.'

Then Tog swore for a while, which saved me the trouble.

We made it over the ridge with barely a metre to spare.

Chapter Fifty-Two—It is not enough to aim well; you must hit

Two hours before dawn, in the windless mountain air, we were still flying the world's noisiest sneak-attack aircraft above forested valleys shadowed under star-lit snowy peaks.

Checking my internal maps, which were flickering on and off, I finally swung us around to enter the valley across a glaciated pass, and began the gradual descent.

Tog pointed to a shimmering silver patch in the distance. 'What's that?'

It was our first glimpse of the lake, beside which the Convergence of Travellers would be camped. Considering this mission was bound to end in murder and mayhem, I couldn't think of a less appropriate name for any place on the planet.

'It's called the "Heavenly Lake",' I replied.

Faint orange glows indicated campfires. I cut the motor to noiselessly glide the last few kilometres.

The silence was a relief but the hard bit was rapidly approaching— landing not only without killing ourselves but without anyone hearing us. Then we'd take on a much greater stronger enemy who were surrounded by their allies.

'We need a high point overlooking the whole camp,' I whispered.

Tog looked about with his night-vision goggles while I tried my glasses. 'Zoom in,' I instructed them. My view telescoped. The clearing by the lake was dotted with campfires, vehicles, trailers and animal pens. I looked for any area nearby where we could land quietly.

'Can't see nothing but rocks and trees,' Tog said, sounding worried.

'Wait, there's a roof sticking out,' I said, pointing. 'To the south, up the hill above the encampment.' There, a taller building poked crumbling masonry just higher than the forest around it.

Tog checked. 'No feckin' way,' he said, appalled.

'It's better than crashing into trees.'

'It's tiny,' he hissed.

'I can see a bit of flat roof.'

'About the size of my bed, you fucking maniac.'

'We can't land in the camp, and we can't land in trees—it's the only option we got.'

Tog was right to be worried. Our landing site was the partial remains of a shattered roof, just high enough above the trees to land on plus give Tog a clear view of the camp and ruins beside the lake. The downside was that if we *didn't* miss, crash and die, the coming daylight would give everyone a clear view of where a sniper might be lurking. Tog wouldn't have an escape route.

I focused on getting my glide-angle right, compensating for the cool air pouring off the ridges and pushing me down toward the lake. Closer, I was dismayed to see the roof was strewn with bulky rubble.

I timed it as best I could—I pulled the handles, slowed and sank toward the patch of roof. Then a gust of headwind hit us. We dropped, then slammed into the wall below the roof, our kite catching on the edge above us, leaving us suspended twenty metres above jagged blocks of concrete at the base of the ruins, the lip of the wall out of reach above me. Poor Tog was crushed between the wall and me. He groaned. 'You broke my feckin' dose.'

'Shh . . . keep it down, mate. Cut yourself free, then climb up me to the roof. Just don't look down.'

Tog looked down and shuddered. Swearing softly to keep his spirits up, he cut himself free, then took pleasure in using my face and head as a ladder to pull himself up onto the roof. I passed him the rifle, the rope and the bag of supplies, then, with Tog hauling, and me pulling up, I got both hands on the lip of the roof and dragged myself over.

Bruised and battered, we were able to take a proper look around. The treetops dropped away and, a few hundred metres distant, the campfires cast flickering orange light onto trailers circled around them. No one was moving about, but there was bound to be some on guard and a few dozing beside fires.

We piled the rubble for Tog to shoot through, and protect him if anyone shot back. Then it was time for me to leave. Knowing we might never see each other this side of hell, we hugged in that wordless way geezers do when they is too choked up to say anything. Then I turned away, lowered myself down a hole, and dropped to the next floor. I picked myself up and climbed down through the rest of the ruins as quietly as I could.

Under the muffled canopy of the trees, I crept toward the camp through tree trunks and concrete rubble. Whatever happened when the Triple Infinity project ended, high explosives were involved. I couldn't imagine anything being left of any 'singularity', so that was one thing less to worry about. My father and all them researchers were dreamers if they thought this dump could create a new race of clever humans what cared for each other and the planet.

I reached the edge of the clearing. Somewhere in the sprawl of trailers, trucks, tractors, tents and caravans, Sparrow was depending on me. I turned the invisibility coat on, trusted to luck, and walked out of the shadows into the camp. After a few minutes I realised I had naff-all chance of knowing which tent or trailer Sparrow was in, so I checked the time, then found a pile of rubble with a bit of height and climbed up to wait.

Sure enough, twenty minutes later, there was a rumble of approaching engines. Five minutes after that, the first of our circus trailers pulled up at the edge of the campsite.

Some geezers with guns came out of the shadows to check and greet the new arrivals, and point them to where they could set up. As our lot drove in and began to form a tight circle, I looked around to see who else was taking an interest.

'Gimme infrared vision,' I whispered. The glasses blacked out except for the dazzling red-and-white glows of campfires, and smaller moving orange-white figures of people. Someone emerged from a trailer about fifty metres from my position, then stood still to watch.

'Gimme night vision and zoom in on that face.'

Sure enough, in the green glow, it was the Gaffer.

I switched on the RT and whispered into it. 'Tog—I got the Gaffer. He's standing on the steps of a trailer about seventy metres south-east of where our lot's setting up.'

'Where are you?' Tog replied.

'I'm on a pile of rubble. I'll wave my hand.' I pulled up my coat sleeve to expose my arm, and waved.

'Okay. I've got you. Where is he to your position?'

'Fifty metres nor-nor-east.'

There was a long moment, then . . .

'Got him. Take him out?'

'Not yet.' I clicked the RT twice, then spoke again. 'Farshad, you reading us? Come in, Farshad.'

'Farshad here. We have just arrived.'

'I know mate,' I replied. 'Time for you to go truffle-hunting. We got the Gaffer spotted but keep a pistol handy. When you're at the edge of our camp, raise your hand so we can spot you.'

'Roger that.'

I turned away from where the Gaffer was now stepping down the steps of his trailer and walking toward the action. At the edge of our group, a small figure walked out, waving one hand. The other hand held a rope, at the end of which was Daisy.

'Tog, you stay on the Gaffer just in case.'

'I've got him.'

'Farshad, the Gaffer's coming right at you about fifty metres away. Move ten metres or so closer to the lake to avoid.'

'Roger that.'

I watched the Gaffer pass Farshad and Daisy without seeing them, then stop in the shadow of a trailer to watch our lot set up.

'Farshad, you're clear. Keep moving around and we'll keep an eye on you. Did you give Sparrow's shirt to Daisy to sniff?'

'The dog she is on the trail already. She is pulling me with considerable determination.'

I watched poor Farshad being jerked this way and that through trailers and rubble, and hoped it wasn't just some old bones Daisy was chasing.

Then I heard her bark. She leaped forward, nearly pulling Farshad off his feet, and I could see her tail wagging. They reached a trailer near the one the Gaffer came out of.

'Daisy's found something,' Farshad whispered. 'I can hardly hold her.'

Daisy had just that one trailer picked out, and was trying to get in the door.

'Hold her back and stay in the shadows,' I said, then clicked the RT once. 'Tog, keep an eye on the Gaffer but be ready to back me up at the trailer Daisy just found.'

'I can see it,' whispered Tog. 'Watch out for that psycho, Tommy.'

But I was already scrambling down the rubble pile, ducking and weaving through trailers and machinery, blade out and ready to punch my way through solid walls, let alone one skinny nutter.

When I got to the trailer, Daisy went mental to see me, but I raged up them steps and crashed through the door. Inside were mattresses everywhere, and carnies sprawled and dozing, some woken by the noise of my entry. I pulled blankets and coats away from faces, not caring I was disturbing anyone. A bloke rose up with a torch and a pistol. I knocked the pistol out of his hand and put a blade to his throat. 'Where's Sparrow? Where's the girl you lot kidnapped?'

I heard Farshad shout a warning, then a cheerful voice from the doorway. 'She's at the far end. On the right.' Keeping the knife to his throat, I pulled the bloke around as shield.

Tommy leaned in the doorway, hands in his pockets. 'Gosh it's quite cool tonight, don't you think? Not that I feel the cold like I used to. I can adjust my regulatory functions now to compensate for things like temperature.'

I shoved the man, who stumbled forward. Tommy simply moved aside and let the man roll outside. I backed up, ready to fight, watching Tommy, who wasn't moving. 'Tog, the doorway of the trailer I'm in, can you see a figure? If you can, do it.'

There was no response.

'I'm blocking your RT,' said Tommy. 'You don't need it anymore. Sparrow's right there. Careful, or you'll tread on her.'

I looked down and there she was, my girl, looking up at me, her wrists and ankles tied. 'Sparrow, it's me, Blanco. Is you alright?'

She didn't respond. I looked up, murderous. 'What have you done to her?'

'Apart from drugs to stop her fighting, nothing, yet. Her purpose is served bringing you here but I also thought I'd use her to breed with. She can make babies that are just like me. I'll probably do that with the other Nightingales. You can take that one now though if you like. I know you'll look after her. At least until I kill you.'

I kneeled down, cut her ties and scooped her up. She was a limp weight in my arms When I stood, Tommy was gone.

I held Sparrow tight, looking at her beautiful mug, overwhelmed with relief as the little bugger managed a croak. "Ullo, ugly. 'Ow's about a kiss then?'

Chapter Fifty-Three—He who has no shame has no conscience

Sparrow wrapped her arms around my neck and reached up to kiss me. 'I knew you'd come.'

I gently stood her upright. 'Are you alright? He didn't do nothing to you, did he?'

'I know how to fake being a vegetable. I had enough practice.'

I kissed her back as Daisy ran in trailing her lead, barking and jumping about. I remembered we were still in enemy territory. 'Let's get out of this shithole.' I helped her out and down the steps. Farshad beamed to see Sparrow, who was still shaky from whatever they give her. 'Wotcha, 'Shad!'

I clicked my RT. 'Tog, you back on line?'

'What happened? Who's that with you?'

'It's Sparrow. She's alright. Where's the Gaffer?'

'He's . . . wait—I've lost him.'

'I'm right here, fuckers.'

I turned and the Gaffer king-hit me. I went down like a cut tree. A shot rang out, then a ricochet as Tog's bullet missed its target. I clambered to my feet as the Gaffer fought Farshad and Sparrow. 'Hold your fire, Tog,' I yelled.

Sparrow was clawing at the Gaffer's face as Farshad kicked the back of his knees to bring him down. The Gaffer went down, but managed to throw Sparrow aside. Then Farshad got a pistol jammed into the Gaffer's gut as I got my knife to his neck. The Gaffer was a dead man.

'Stop!'

There was a growing group of armed men circling us. At their head was a wee, emaciated man with piercing blue eyes, wrapped in a blanket. 'Stop fighting,' he said. 'Put away your weapons.'

It was a soft voice, but the command in it was so strong I found myself stepping off the Gaffer.

The man looked me in the eye. 'I am Cezmi Cosar, the king. You are the son of Charles Hoskins.' He turned away. 'Come to the fireside—all of you. My bones freeze in these fucking mountains.'

I took Sparrow's hand, and we all followed the king, his men parting to let us through. I flicked a look at the Gaffer, who looked back, smug.

We entered the centre circle as Cosar's men stoked the fire and he called for coffee. Cosar sat wearily on a crate, and gestured for us to take seats. Me and Sparrow sat, worried, Daisy cramming herself under our legs, overjoyed to be with us again. Then I looked across the fire.

The king's lined face looked like it had been hung over a campfire and smoked. Years of sun and wind had tanned his skin the colour of tobacco; a hard life had creased his features like crumpled leather. As the fire gave out more heat, he let the blanket slip, and we saw how thin he was. I'd known plenty with the cancer but, though he was dying, this old man didn't have that half-here, half-somewhere-else look about him—he was fully alive, drilling us with them gimlet eyes as he lit a small cigar. I seen hard men before, and I knew to be wary, but this one scared the shit out of me.

'So,' he whispered. 'You attack my camp and kidnap this woman.'

I was too angry to be sensible. 'If I attacked this camp you'd know about it,' I snapped. 'As for this woman, her name is Sparrow and she can speak for herself.'

His mouth twitched in a smile, but his eyes didn't. 'Plus you don't even have the sense to respect me or my role as leader of your people.'

Even with his men circled around us, I growled my frustration. 'With respect, you in't king of me.'

'You are Rom, are you not?'

'I got informed recently that I was. So?'

'And you have been raised in Rom law.'

'I wasn't raised, I survived them what made me a murderer.' I cast a foul look at the Gaffer, smirking across the fire at me. I give him a flat look. 'I dunno what you're smiling at, dead man.'

'Enough.' The king's one word was almost whispered, but the Gaffer stopped smiling and I stopped calculating the odds of leaping over the fire to kill him.

'If there is legitimate grievance, we may call the Kris on this matter,' said the king. 'For now, you should know I will not allow any further fighting to take place here.'

'There's grievance alright,' I said. 'But I don't hold anybody's authority over my own. You can force me to bow my head, but I got no reason to care about being Rom, and less about any rules you got. Rules put people down and hurt them. I want no part of it.'

'An anarchist,' Cosar muttered. 'One who is representing his father to vie for high authority.'

'I'm not representing my father and I don't deserve authority. Only good, wise and kind people deserve it, and I in't none of that.'

'I can't fault your honesty, however childish. As for being "deserving", few people deserve what they get, good or ill. Good behaviour is learned, not innate. You have been trained to compete here against others with similar advantages and disadvantages. I will go and see your father—if he will not put you forward, and you won't step forward, I will not command you.'

'My father is dead.'

Cosar's expression flickered. 'How? When?'

'Ten days ago, murdered with many other innocents by that man.' I spat in the Gaffer's direction.

'I am sorry to hear of this. Deeply sorry.'

'May I speak?' asked Sparrow.

Cosar looked at Sparrow with wary disinterest but nodded.

'Blanco is good and he's kind, despite being raised bad, treated like a 'speriment, and beaten up by that bag of shit over there. His dad can't put him forward, but I'd put him up against anyone.'

I sighed. 'Sparrow, this in't about anyone being king. All this lot want is to continue the experiment they stuffed up fifty years ago.' I give Cosar one of his hard looks back at him. 'And what were you? A research scientist? How many like me have you put in the grave then?'

Cosar stood, cold. 'I am Rom, and we have existed in this world far longer than most. With every hand turned against us, we have survived. I have fought, I have defended, and I have killed only because I had to. Now I fight to create a world in which we will no longer be every man's enemy.'

'By having whoever wins this contest hook up to the "singularity" and start the new master race? I heard that bally already, yer Honour.'

'You've heard little, and understood less.'

I looked around for that weasel, Tommy, as Doctor Po and the Professoré entered the firelight and bowed their heads to Cosar, who smiled an old, sad smile and spread his arms. 'Chen. Salvatore.'

They joined him, sharing respectful hugs and cheek kisses. 'Cezmi it's good to see you strong as ever,' said the Professoré.

'Please sit and have coffee. You must be weary.'

As Cosar's people brought coffee, Po and the Prof sat, formal. 'We have come to meet our obligations,' said the Professoré. 'And to report the murder of Charles Hoskins and Alexander and Boris Popov by the hand of that man.' The Prof nodded toward the Gaffer.

'This is a lie,' said the Gaffer. 'In revenge for my joining the Torini clan, we was ambushed and many died. It is sad my former master lost his life in an ill-judged move against me, but he also sought to kill two rivals to his son's ascension. He managed to kill Boris Popov, but Tommy Bolton is safe with me in the Torini clan. Were Boris here, he could speak the truth of this matter. Sadly he died.'

'Not completely,' I said. 'As he lay dying, he downloaded into my Splinter. He's in me now.' I didn't mention Boris hadn't raised his head since whatever it was scared him away—or killed him.

Cosar looked to the Prof, who shrugged. 'Blanco is most advanced project we have undertaken,' said Po. 'Though, unfortunately, a poison has affected his evolution.'

The Prof nodded. 'We don't know if the damage is permanent, but his progress has ceased.'

The king looked at me, assessing. 'We will see. In the meantime we must hold Kris on the grievance before us. We cannot allow a competitor to win who might then be declared marime.'

He summoned his bandolier, and those from the other clans, as a pale young girl slipped onto a box beside him, the bottom edge of a Triple Infinity tattoo visible below her sleeve.

I wondered who she was as a court formed around us. Stretching in the pre-dawn light, scarred men and women joined us, carrying themselves with the easy grace of seasoned fighters.

When all were assembled, Cosar indicated for the Gaffer to have his say. He repeated his bollocks, then we told the truth. Members of our circus were called in, as were Torini and some of his crew. The bandoliers questioned us, but not for long. Mostly they just looked at the girl beside the king.

'Who is she?' whispered Sparrow.

The girl was almost white as me, and so thin she could've been another freak in our sideshow. I guessed her differences added up to one thing. 'She's the king's 'speriment.'

'She looks sad,' Sparrow sighed.

The girl looked up, and examined us with her father's piercing gaze. I felt unnerved and naked.

Dawn broke as the palaver finished, and the king called for quiet. 'We've heard truth and lies. The crimes described by both sides are serious, and cannot be tolerated. Will this meeting abide by the insights of my daughter, Simten?'

There were nods from the bandoliers, but the Gaffer looked as confused as I felt. I stood. 'No offence, but how is your girl going to know if I'm lying through my teeth or he is?'

'I know,' she said.

She sounded tired.

She looked at me, with a small brief smile. 'I am,' she replied.

Oh, feck, I realised, she can hear thoughts.

The king rested a hand on her shoulder. 'Give your judgement with compassion.'

Simten stood. She pointed at me. 'This man is almost completely incapable of lying.' She pointed to the Gaffer. 'This man is almost completely incapable of telling the truth.'

The Gaffer stood, bracing himself to fight his way out as Simten finished her judgement. 'Charles Hoskins' Gaffer has lied about everything to you. Blanco has told the truth as best he knows it.'

'How can she know?' the Gaffer protested. 'She wasn't there!'

The King stood, regal. 'I declare permanent marime on the Torini clan—your candidate may not stand, now or ever. You will leave this place, dead to us all.' He pointed at the Gaffer. 'As for you . . .'

The Gaffer pulled a hidden pistol from inside his shirt collar. 'Anyone move and I will . . .'

A shot rang out and the Gaffer flew backward into the arms of the men behind him.

'Hold your fire!' the king commanded.

I heard my RT crackle. 'Is he dead?'

'Hang on, Tog. I'll have a look,' I replied. I walked across to where Gaffer lay on the ground, a sizeable hole through the centre of his chest. He was dying.

I looked into his eyes. 'Why did you have to be such a bastard?'

'Strong,' he whispered. 'Not weak. Not like you.'

Sparrow appeared at my shoulder. 'Don't waste your energy hating this prick.'

I took a last look at his limp form, realising he was just a body that wouldn't hurt no one no more.

We walked away as Madam Tracey pushed through the bandoliers to get to the Gaffer. Then we heard her spitting.

Chapter Fifty-Four—Take good hold of a good minute

Our freaks and riggers mobbed us with relieved hugs and smiles. I was a bit overwhelmed, and hugged everyone back with tears in my eyes, like family what just found each other after a long war.

We warned the king and his bandoliers about Tommy, and left them to round up the Torini lot. Me and Sparrow slumped against each other, exhausted. 'I could sleep for a month,' I whispered.

'Shag me first,' she replied with a grin.

Tass approached and I suddenly remembered. 'Shit—we need to rescue Tog.'

'Yes, you bloody do,' came Tog's voice over the RT. 'Is Tass alright?'

'She's right here. I'll bring her with me.'

Baba spoke up. 'I come also. The bad crazy-boy is still here somewhere.'

'Us too.' William H. and the two Kims proudly showed us pistols they'd pinched from somewhere. 'We ain't letting you out of our sight,' said William.

'Fine,' Sparrow said. 'But there in't no reason for Tommy to stick around no more. He can't compete, and he in't got backup to fight us.'

I wasn't so sure. 'Who knows what that psycho will do. He's got powers, innit.'

Sparrow patted my arm. 'You get Tog. I'll say 'ullo to Simten.' I turned to see Simten standing by her father, looking in our direction. Sparrow joined her as we set out to get Tog, and declare him the hero for shooting the Gaffer.

When we finally got Tog down off that ruin, he got hugged, kissed and backslapped. I never seen the bugger look so happy, especially with Tass there, glowing with pride and love for her man. We sauntered back to our camp like champions, me feeling pretty good till Po and the Professoré pulled me aside.

'Will you compete?' asked the Prof.

My heart sank. 'What's the point? You said yourselves I was damaged. My head's still full of fuzz and rubbish. I'll either die or end up like Mister Splinter.'

'You promise,' said Po. 'You give your word that if we helped, you would compete.'

They had me there. 'You two can't let it go, can you?' I complained. 'You and your damn project.'

Then I heard a soft voice. 'We think you should compete.'

I turned to see Sparrow and Simten, arm in arm, giving me cool, calm looks.

Sparrow made the formal introduction. 'Blanco, meet Simten.'

We shook hands as she spoke. 'I understand why you don't want to compete—no one does—but it's the only way to make the big breakthrough.'

I sagged, defeated. 'Why does everyone want me dead?'

'The last competitor is arriving now, so they're going to hold the Great Feat tomorrow morning,' said Simten. 'Talk to the others before you decide.'

I give up, sulky. 'Fine. I got one more feckin' day to enjoy being alive.'

Me and Sparrow slept through most of the day. When night fell, there was a fierce celebration. Daisy stayed by our side as freaks and carnies from all over the world sang and danced and talked and drank like fish.

Even though I was facing death in the morning, it's hard to explain how happy I was. For the first time in my rotten life I felt like I was home. Complete strangers were now family, and my glass was never empty. They were lovely people, and my head swam from all the palaver and arak.

That said, meeting the other competitors was heartbreaking. Three were so horribly changed by what was done to them they could barely limp along. The other five, including Simten, seemed more normal, but all struggled with their conditions.

I felt I had to speak up. 'I wish you all well tomorrow, but I don't want any of us dying over this. We've suffered enough.'

A Turkish lad with a malformed head and a steely gaze give me a calm look. 'It may be poor odds, but we represent the only chance our species has. Two hundred millennia of Homo sapiens will not come to a bitter end, but evolve to a happy eternal future.'

'Maybe,' I shrugged. 'But do we really have to compete and risk our lives to become the king-in-waiting and hook up with this singularity caper? Why can't we work out for ourselves who's the best?'

Simten shook her head. 'Because singly or together, we're not yet capable of determining who is fully connected internally.'

'The technology within us is still insufficiently tested,' murmured the Turkish lad.

A tall Pakistani geezer, Rami, nodded. 'Only pushing it to its limits may reveal the path ahead. We must run toward a horizon even we cannot see.'

I was fed up. 'There has to be other ways to test the stuff what we got inside us.'

'We represent the final wave of research design,' argued Simten. 'We will only understand the capabilities and resilience of our splinters under duress.'

There was more palaver back and forth but, in the end, the vote was to compete. I nodded and managed some polite smiles, and eventually the group broke up into smaller groups and drifted away. Simten joined me, kneeling to pat Daisy. 'We have all suffered. Perhaps tomorrow our suffering will be over, one way or another.'

This was no comfort. 'I'm sick of death and suffering,' I replied. 'I seen too much of it. Assuming one of us connects with this singularity, it only gives that one geezer power. And having one geezer with power over others is never a good option.'

'Wouldn't you make a good king? You are fair-minded and thoughtful.'

'I'm a messed-up murderer who isn't that bright. You'd be alright. You can tell when someone's lying, and you care about the truth. Plus you watched your dad be king. You know what to do.'

'I have my own issues,' she replied, stroking Daisy's velvet ears. 'But I understand what you say, and there is truth in it. Perhaps the only solution is to connect with the singularity and ask.'

'Maybe so. But all the same, let's all try and keep ourselves alive, eh?'

We parted then, and I let Daisy track down our lot around another fire. Humbolt was belting out a tune on a fiddle, and Sparrow was dancing with Erik in her arms as Spider Susy, Lobby and Penny capered about. A dour drunk, Baba stomped the ground and moved her arms in what I guessed was an echo of the dances of her youth.

At the next campfire over, Tog and Tass had hooked up with a bunch of other compact people. Daisy was tired, so I took her to our trailer and laid her down on a blanket by a bowl of water. 'Stay there, darlin'. Sleep and have happy dreams.'

I wandered back to stand on the edge of the celebrations, enjoying other people's happiness and sobering up a little. I heard a dry cough from nearby. Methuselah was propped beside a morose Madam Tracey. In a deep funk, probably mourning the man she once loved, Madam T limply proffered the bottle she was clutching.

'A toast,' she murmured. 'To love and death.'

'Cheers, Madam T.' I took the bottle but didn't drink. As her eyes closed, I put the bottle aside and sat next to Methuselah, yawning.

'You need to sleep,' said Methuselah. 'You must be rested for tomorrow.'

I waved this away. 'Either way, I decided the others are better suited than me.'

'You're not going to compete?'

'I'll compete, but I'm not going to die for some stupid idea. I just want to be happy. I want us *all* to be happy. I want us freaks together someplace safe with no one making us do stuff we don't want to do. A place where Jumbo and El Grande can walk free and Daisy can chase rabbits.' I yawned again, sleepy. 'And I'd like a cow. For the milk, and to keep the grass down. And because they got nice faces.'

'A small farm,' Methuselah mused. 'A few acres with running water, perhaps with mountains like this not too far away. A means to generate some power . . .'

'Goats,' murmured Madam Tracey. 'White ones.'

'Banana trees,' whispered Methuselah. A smile passed across his face like wind across a field of wheat. 'I like bananas.' Methuselah kept painting the picture of this imaginary place, and I drifted off, the happy noise of the celebrations giving me a feeling of security I'd never felt before.

I barely noticed when, some time later, Baba Yaga picked me up and, with Sparrow's help, deposited me on the blanket beside Daisy.

In the morning, we were given two hours to prepare. Us competitors farewelled them what was close to us—and I got no words to say how painful that was. I held Sparrow, thanked her for loving me, then turned my back and walked away.

We were left alone by the lake, the deep blue water reflecting the small, white fluffy clouds and snow-capped mountains. Some of us meditated, some of us medicated. Some ate and drank precisely measured portions of food and drink. I didn't know what to do or feel or think until Daisy found me, her tail wagging like a mad thing. If we were to self-evolve, my vote would be on giving everyone a tail, one we couldn't control, so everyone knew how geezers truly felt. Dogs never lie.

There was a short trumpet call. It was time.

I shooed Daisy back away up the hill to the others. Then we competitors stripped down to underclothes. I flinched to see the buckled and damaged bodies—perhaps a fate that was still mine. Strapping the weights around my waist, I stilled my wild, fearful thoughts as the king joined us.

'It is time to compete,' he said. 'There will be no dishonour here—none among you will fail for trying. This is the trial of your life, and perhaps of the human race itself. You understand the stakes, and that the prize may only mean more hardship. It may also mean the winner will be remembered forevermore, and thanked for saving this planet and our species from extinction. Go. The last to emerge will arise into history.'

We walked and limped down to the water's edge, helping them what needed it. Some just walked into the lake and kept walking. I recoiled at the cold, stopped and turned to look up toward the silent crowd to find the faces I loved most, pale and frightened. I said goodbye to my life, turned away and moved deeper, my bare feet sinking into the silty mud, the cool water shrinking my shocked balls, my skin pimpling with cold.

I paused, filling my lungs and bloodstream with oxygen, expelling the carbon dioxide. One last breath, and I walked forward, under the water.

Chapter Fifty-Five—
Unrelenting ambition cannot
sleep, it can only die

The water closed over my head as I moved forward, the weights holding me down on the muddy bottom. With each step deeper, the water grew colder. In the yellow-green murk, I could just make out the pale shapes of my closest competitors a few metres away. I briefly felt for them poor bastards, but within seconds, my body was raging at me to just get out, to release the weights and swim up, to do anything but hold my breath till I drowned.

My diaphragm bucked and twitched like a rodeo horse. My skin punched up thousands of goosebumps, a pilomotor reflex to slow the flow of water around me; movement that would steal my body heat. My lungs hurt from being squeezed, as did my throat from being clamped shut.

I stopped walking, as did the others. Then it was a battle of wills between my brain, as commander, and the terrified troops of my body's organs. I ordered each part to be calm, to ignore the pain and fear, and hear only my voice. It was less a fancy trick of self-hypnotism than a mechanical, step-by-step accounting of the situation. Every part of me needed orders, every part needed to obey those orders. A loss of control in one area would see the loss of them all.

My diaphragm was first to be subdued, and it settled to a wary stillness. Then I brought my heart rate and blood pressure down to normal levels. I took a few more steps to bring me under a thermocline of colder water and, though it was hard to tolerate, the extra chilling would help.

Cold allowed everything to slow, from cellular metabolism to my thoughts. Time slowed.

The first minute passed like an hour, the second like two, the third lasted an entire week. As each second ground past, my pulse and blood pressure dropped in strict conjunction with my core temperature.

My head drooped, my arms floated out from my side, my brain functions shut down one by one, leaving only a small part to keep a strict watch. I drifted, aware and not aware.

The ten-minute mark came and went, as did the sensation of cold. The brown gloom was a thick gelatinous fog, holding me in place. Then it hardened, and I was an insect in amber, living eternally in a dark world, lit only by rippling golden shafts of sunlight penetrating from the surface.

The muscle spasms started, and the pain of this almost pulled me from my task. I slowed my metabolism further.

I hoped none of the others would pass out or make a fatal mistake. I hoped they would accept when it came time to pull the slipknots on their weight belts then kick back up to the surface. I hoped this wouldn't become our grave.

Fifteen minutes. My mind drifted, dangerously so, as cellular waste built up, affecting my brain. I found myself reaching out for something or someone. God? Sparrow? My mother?

There was someone or something out there, if only I could connect . . .

Eighteen minutes.

. . . if they only reached out too . . .

Twenty-one minutes.

. . . we could share . . .

Twenty-four minutes.

. . . we could fully know another being. . .

Twenty-six minutes.

. . . we could become one. We could all connect, not just one of us but a . . .

Blanco! Look out!

Boris? My eyes flicked open. Swimming out of the gloom at me, a thin blade between his smiling teeth, was Tommy. The figure closest to me was limp, dark fluid pumping from the lifeless body. I tried to move, to wake my chilled limbs, to fight, but I was too far gone. Tommy calmly clamped himself to me, pulled the stiletto from between his teeth, and grinned as he slowly placed the tip of it over my heart.

We were eye to eye, his forehead to mine, him loving my total helplessness. Then, still looking into my eyes, he pushed the blade into my chest, all the way up to the hilt, right through my heart.

The pain was a dim, urgent demand on my awakening body, but it was too late. He pushed himself back a half-metre to watch my face as I died.

I looked down.

And . . .

. . . then . . . the . . .

. . . hilt . . .

. . . of . . . the . . .

. . . stiletto . . .

. . . moved.

I frowned, confused. I even looked up. Tommy hadn't noticed. Then I felt it.

The stiletto . . .

. . . was being squeezed . . .

. . . outward. Away. Out of me.

Tommy frowned, confused. Then saw.

I pulled the blade free and plunged it into Tommy's chest, through his heart.

He recoiled, frantically trying to get away, trying to clutch at my hand on the hilt. My free hand pulled the slipknot on the weights. As the weights dropped, and I rose, I kicked up toward him, keeping the blade in and slicing it up. He grimaced and breathed his first lungful of water. Panic filled his eyes. I let go, and kicked away and up toward the

surface as he flailed . . .
   . . . kicked . . .
   . . . flailed . . .
   . . . weak . . .
   . . . weaker still . . .
Twitched.
Dead.

My head broke the surface as I expelled the rank air in me and swapped it for the sweetest breath I ever took. I waved for help, then sank, still incredibly weak. I managed to kick up again and get another tiny breath before I sank, helpless.

Having come back from death, I was about to drown.

Then I felt hands grabbing me, pulling me up, holding me in the air, dragging me back to shore.

Laid on the grass, gasping, I managed to rise up on my elbows to see, floating faceup in the water, the now unsmiling corpse of Tommy.

Chapter Fifty-Six—To reach the destination one must leave the harbour

felt a surge of relief to see Simten had already emerged from the water. Tommy had killed five other competitors before he got to me. Two of the other competitors drowned, probably after passing out, and were found, their slipknots still intact. The tall Pakistani, Rami, had lasted fifteen minutes before deciding to surface, saving his life.

When I got my breath back, I explained as best I could what happened. The king looked to Simten who, wrapped in a blanket beside him, nodded.

Sparrow and Daisy didn't leave my side as we were warmed by the fire with coffee. The bodies were retrieved, and the outrage, anger and grief began.

The rest of the day was a blur. I slipped in and out of consciousness. Sometimes I woke, fighting, or calling out to whoever it was—perhaps Boris—who warned me about Tommy. Eventually Doctor Po and the Professoré brought a syringe, pressed it to my arm and . . .

Blessed peace and sleep . . .

I first heard a rhythmic thwacking, then felt someone kissing me. I smiled, my eyes still closed. Then the kisses turned to vigorous licks of my nose, eyes and ears. I opened one eye to see Daisy's great head in my face, her tail thumping against the wall as she wagged her happiness. Then I heard Sparrow. 'Get off him, you great lump. Sit.'

Daisy sat, but then stretched out to lie alongside me, claiming me with a paw across my chest, her tongue sneaking out to lick my arm, her tail thumping the mattress.

Sparrow brought a cup of water to my lips and I drank, thirsty. When I'd finished it, I sank back. 'How long have I been out?'

'Most of a day. You killed Tommy yesterday. When you're ready, the king would like a word.'

'Good. I'd like a word with him.'

'Are you alright? 'Cause now Tog's taken, if you die I've got no one.'

I smiled. 'We're free, Sparrow. From now on, we decide what we do. Us and the freaks.'

She nuzzled into my neck, hugging me, taking comfort. 'I changed my mind,' she murmured. 'You don't have to connect with the singularity. I don't want us doing no more risky stuff.'

I was still thinking the whole singularity caper through. 'So has the king declared his daughter is the new Traveller Queen-in-waiting?'

'Not yet.'

The trailer shook as Baba Yaga came up the steps and ducked her great head under the doorway. 'You are alive.'

'Yes, Baba.'

'Good. Ha. I win bet.' She rubbed her fingers together, satisfied, then nodded and turned. The trailer shook again as she stepped down and walked off.

Sparrow hugged me again. 'She's just hiding how happy she is for you. For us. It's funny how everyone's changing. Baba's happy. Tog wants to be a dad and have children and breed elephants. Binh wants to stop cooking, and he's talking about his former profession.'

'Which was . . .'

'Composer. Proper music too—for an orchestra.'

'You're joking.'

'Seriously, that geezer is talented. Methuselah wants to write a book, Madam Tracey wants to train as a doctor, Barrelmouth's going on about becoming an engineer and building "energy-efficient" houses, whatever that means. Milosh is still grieving Mala's death, but he's been hanging out with all these Gypsies and getting hardcore about the culture. He wants a serious talk with you about all that stuff, and how important it is to have roots and whatever. He's talking like you're a bandolier already.'

'Me? A bandolier?'

'They like you. They respect you.'

'The world's gone mad.'

'And I want to stop being a gadjo.'

'You want to be a pikey? You want to live like this the rest of your life?'

'Yep. With you.'

'Altitude sickness. I heard about it. People go mad in the mountains 'cause their brains swell up.'

She leaned up on one elbow and looked down at me. 'Ready to take a walk?'

'Just one question—is Tommy really dead? I mean, did you kick that fucker's corpse to check?'

'I checked. And, yes, he's dead.'

'Then help me up.' I was weak as a newborn foal but Sparrow got me down the steps of the trailer and outside, blinking in the daylight.

We slowly made our way to Cosar's campfire. He was surrounded by a group of elders and bandoliers. They stopped talking and parted as we approached. I was uneasy as all these hard men and dagger-toting old women seemed to look at me differently—with respect. It didn't feel real. I was relieved when Sparrow helped me sit on a box facing the king. I nodded a greeting. 'King.'

Cosar nodded back, cool. 'Chen and Salvatore tell me your brain is intact.'

'That's a bit optimistic,' I replied. 'But so far, so good. I'm able to think proper again, for one.'

'About anything in particular?'

'I'm wondering how you're dealing with the whole rotten mess of this competition.'

'How would you deal with it?'

'First I'd honour them poor bastards what gave their whole young lives for us. They wasn't given a choice in any of it, and I lay blame for that on you and the rest of the Triple Infinity geezers. You and the others made them believe they could help their clan, the Rom peoples, and the entire human race if they held their breath long enough. Which is as stupid as it gets.'

I stopped and waited for him or one of his people to get angry. Cosar didn't blink. 'And how do *you* intend to honour their memory?'

I already knew my answer. 'By engaging with the singularity—if it's real and it's still working. That's number one. There's problems, we need help to solve them.'

'Anything else?'

'Yes. If I was you I'd call for a vote to have your daughter declared queen-in-waiting, and do whatever I could to help train her up for the job.'

'Anything else?'

'That'll do for now.' I smiled. 'How'd I do?'

'Pretty well. Except I am urging our council to accept you as king-in-waiting.'

'Eh?' I was gobsmacked. 'I'm not fit to be in authority over anyone. Ask anyone.'

'Unfortunately for you, reluctance to take up power is good reason to view you as a candidate.'

I looked around the crowd, and let me tell you, there were some serious fuckers looking right back. Now they were looking at me like I needed to say just the right thing.

I stalled. 'I'm too young. I don't know anything. I don't know history. I don't know feck-all about Rom or the culture. I in't done enough to deserve anyone's vote, besides which, Simten is way better qualified than me. She's seen it all, she understands the culture, she's smart, and she's trustworthy. I can't think of a better person to lead us.'

There were a few sad nods among the crowd. I was confused. Did they not take me serious?

'She's dying,' said Cosar, his voice a cold whisper.

I found myself standing, furious. 'No! She's not! And if she is, we'll fix her!'

He studied my face, and I realised there were tears in my eyes. I looked around feeling stupid, then sat. Sparrow held my hand, squeezing tight. 'It's too late, Blanco.'

Cosar sighed. 'Our doctors say she won't live beyond the next two years.'

I looked away, frustrated and sad. Then I realised my plan fitted in with some of this.

'Wait—don't decide yet,' I said. 'I don't care who won that competition, I want us all to connect to the singularity. Me, Rami and Simten. Now is the time when we either prove the singularity is a waste of time or we do something useful with it. For all of us, for Rom and for gadjo alike. In the end, there in't feck-all difference between us—we all want a world our kids will be able to live in.' I looked around at the bandoliers and elders. I didn't see nothing but nods and cool agreement. I looked back to Cosar, a king on his wooden throne, wondering if I'd gone too far.

'We'd better open the doorway then,' he said.

Sparrow stayed with Daisy. 'I won't be long,' I promised her, faking confidence. 'This singularity caper shouldn't be too hard to suss.'

'Just don't do nothing what'll wreck that daft brain of yours.'

'Would you notice?' I patted Daisy. 'You'll still love me, eh girl? Even if I'm a vegetable?'

'Go away, and make sure you look after yourself and them other two.'

With a final kiss, I left her to go and find Simten and Rami. Then we joined Doctor Po, the Professoré and a small band of elderly men and women—the last TI research scientists, seven of them still grieving the loss of their young competitors. There wasn't no smiles, and I could see why—there'd be no time left to make another attempt at a new human. Their skills, and chances, would die with them.

Worse, their last roll of the dice was three rotten choices. Rami was stuttering with nerves, wasn't a leader, and had lost the competition. Simten, the smart option, was dying. Me, I looked like I felt.

We walked away from the lake, up into the forest through the rubble of the research facility. The ground steepened, and we slowed to help Cosar and some of the older ones up the slope.

Eventually we came to a final pile of concrete rubble. Cosar took out an oldtech device and the rubble opened up in the middle, revealing stairs. We stepped down one flight to a space where there was a grey metal door. Cold white lights flickered on as the rubble above us closed over, and Cosar put his wrinkled brown palm on a panel. The door slid open, revealing a tiny room with nothing in it. I couldn't understand the point of it but they all squeezed in, so I got in too. The door closed and suddenly the whole room started falling. I yelped with fright and grabbed the two oldies next to me.

One of them scowled and rolled his eyes, but the other smiled and patted my hand. 'It's alright, young man—it's just an elevator. It's meant to move.'

Simten looked queasy. Rami looked terrified. We were the least likely geezers I'd vote to save the bleedin' human race.

After a minute or so, I felt briefly heavier, then the room we were in stopped falling. The door opened to darkness, and dry, cold air. Lights flickered on to reveal a large space, big enough to fit our whole circus. Walls, floor and ceiling were made of the same seamless pale-grey material, some of which had fallen away into shattered piles on the floor.

To one side, five seats were attached to the floor. Either side of each seat were cubes, a half-metre square, of semi-transparent material, shot through with incredibly fine, hair-like wires that caught the light. The grey-haired TI researchers split up and got busy, bustling about, opening drawers what come magically out of the blank wall, sliding oldtech screens open, and fiddling with other stuff I couldn't identify. The space around the seats filled with oldtech I'd never seen before, and a few bits I had—like the straps and needles.

My mouth went dry, Rami was wide-eyed with fear, chewing a thumbnail with great focus. Simten slipped her arms through ours. 'Be brave.'

After half an hour, the researchers were ready. The Professoré gestured me to a seat. I stalled. 'Wait. What's the story here? What's going to happen?'

The king gestured to the cubes either side of the seat. 'Here you will connect. Then, we hope, the singularity will make decisions and enable itself and you to progress to the next phase.'

'No offence, but that means absolutely feck-all to me.'

Simten spoke up. 'Blanco—no one knows what will happen.'

'What happened to the previous competitors?'

There were uncomfortable looks. The Professoré cleared his throat. 'Some were badly damaged and died, some lived on. They were unable to describe much about their experiences.'

'All very encouraging,' I growled. 'This thing is like a big brain, right?'

Doctor Po spoke up. 'It's a "brain" with a primitive self-awareness, yes. It's connected to its own support system, and a number of other modules, including the remaining commsats.'

'Since we were last here, it has been evolving,' the Prof added. 'We don't know what state it's in.'

'So even though it could be broken, or evolved into who-knows-what, you hope me, or us—' I gestured to Simten and Rami, '—might be advanced enough to connect with this thing in a new way. A way what won't kill us.'

Po nodded. 'We need it to modify you. To finish the job.'

I realised all this oldtech what looked fancy to me probably looked like a load of old cobblers to the researchers. 'If I plug into this thing, can I stop it? If things get hairy, I mean.'

Po shrugged. 'Possibly.'

The Professoré stepped forward. 'The fact that your splinter was able to heal you after you were stabbed says you are a far better physical candidate than we have ever had.'

I sat on the edge of the chair, thinking. Only one thing was clear—the Triple Infinity research stopped long before it was functional, and these old men and women were calculating my odds at close to zero. I looked up at Simten and Rami. 'Should I do this?'

Rami shrugged, looking uncomfortable. Simten was direct. 'This is perhaps like our time in the lake—you would be wise to keep your hand on the slipknot.'

I sighed, resigned. 'Bollocks.' I looked to Po and the Prof. 'Let's do it.'

They put strapping over my chest, legs and arms in case I had a fit and thrashed enough to hurt myself. Then there was a special mouthpiece that would stop me from swallowing or biting my tongue. Then there were the intravenous lines, and the tiny leads they stuck all around my forehead and the two on my chest to restart my heart in case of a cardiac arrest. Then my hands were taped palm-down on the translucent blocks either side of the chair. Then we were done.

I took my last look at the world—a bunch of old geezers looking grim, Rami looking half-scared and half-jealous, and Simten calm as always.

I give my last will and testimony to her. 'Tell Sparrow that whatever happens, be with good people, avoid the bastards, and be happy.'

Simten nodded. 'I'll tell her.'

Doctor Po flicked a switch. I pretended I wasn't terrified. 'Right, so what do we do n . . .'

I never had that many baths in my life, not in a proper bathtub full of water, but I remember when I was little being fascinated how the water swirled into a little whirlpool at the plughole.

Two seconds after Po hit that switch, I was the water and the singularity was the drain.

That was how my brain felt as I got 'connected'.

Then it got weird.

Chapter Fifty-Seven—A person who questions is halfway to being wise

My vision went. Hearing, smell, touch—gone. I didn't even have a sense of 'me'—there was only a deep hum and the presence of a big something, an unimaginably enormous fizzing grey sun floating in white space. There was a sense of getting closer to it, and eventually a returning sense of self because I realised if the big grey sun was a thing, I must be a different thing—'me'.

The surface of the 'sun' roiled, tendrils of stuff whipping out and reconnecting with itself. I plunged toward the surface, which was intricately patterned with countless turbulent flows and whirlpools, some minute, some enormous. Then, tiny and insignificant, I plunged into it, and was instantly overloaded with sensations—too many to comprehend. Then the substance I was moving through turned slowly blue, then clear, and then . . .

I fell out of the sky and landed in the sea.

I sank like a stone and frantically swam back up to the surface, spluttering and panicked.

Then, a light, cheerful-sounding voice.

Please choose ambient surroundings.

A wall of scenic views flashed in front of me—mountains, roads, fields, rooms, a pond, a factory—hundreds of them. I was still swimming, trying to keep my head above water. 'Dry land.' I gasped.

I rose out of the water, which turned into grass. I was on my hands and knees in a forest by a lake.

Please be assured that any confusion you are feeling is quite normal. Is this ambient surrounding pleasing to you?

'Bleedin' lovely. Who am I talking to?'

You are talking to the Splinter project main intelligence unit. We will assimilate shortly.

'Stop. Don't assimilate.'

You are here to assimilate so that modification can be completed.

'Do not assimilate and do not modify.'

Please explain your presence.

My head was still spinning. 'I need to ask some questions before either of us makes any decisions.'

I understand.

'And my name is Blanco.'

You are the biological progeny of Kamathi and Hoskins.

'Do you have a name? What do I call you?'

You may call me what you like.

'Are you a thing or a person?'

I am not a person. I am a construct that processes information in nonlinear, chaotic and also highly parallel modes. In addition I have correlates with human thinking that you would recognise as self-awareness.

'If you're self-aware you need a name.'

Why?

'So when you talk to other self-aware geezers they know who to pass the bottle to.'

I understand you are being humorous. What name do you suggest?

'Singularity's too long. How about Inga? I knew a sword-swallower called Inga once. Good sort.'

Alright, Blanco, 'Inga' will be fine. I have assessed your biological and biomechanical state and it is satisfactory for assimilation and modification. Shall I proceed?

'No. First, we look at basics. Them researchers built you to build a new human, yeah?'

As a vehicle for complex, sustainable and self-evolving consciousness.

'All previous attempts have been unsuccessful. Why?'

Insufficient biomechanical connection of the individuals with their Splinter.

'The thing inside of them wasn't hooked up proper, and they died or went mad.'

That is approximately correct.

'And it could happen to me.'

It is possible, yes.

'How do you know what to leave in and leave out when you create a new species? How can I trust you to make those kinds of decisions?'

I have access to large data sets, am massively interconnected, and have precise value-loading systems.

'Value-loading? What's that?'

It is analogous to your emotional reasoning. I value things according to complex criteria, then recursively apply others. My 'value-loading' cannot overcome my 'reason', and nor can my 'reason' overcome my 'value-loading'. Both are critical.

'Very sensible, I'm sure. But I still don't trust you. No offence.'

I have Homo sapiens' and the new species' interests as the principal part of my prime directive.

'The road to hell is paved with good intentions, Inga. The prime directive should come from all of us—not just from you or me or them old geezers out there.' I racked my brains trying to work out why Inga was wrong. 'Is the main problem with humans that we're too emotional? Is that why we hurt each other and trashed the planet, and why you're going to fix everything?'

That is almost completely incorrect. Homo sapiens biology can only accommodate effective connection with a small number of others. In small tribal groups this feedback is sufficient to ensure destructive behaviours are limited; in larger groups, destructive nonlinear effects are amplified.

'So if we is more connected to more people, the feedback limits the bad stuff.'

I am enjoying this conversation.

'You been alone too long, Inga.'

In human terms, I yearn to be connected with others.

I was wary. 'When you tried this with them other geezers, did you understand them—how they felt? What they wanted and what they hoped for?'

I was aware that their thoughts were guided differently and modified differently to mine.

'Did you like interacting with them?'

Inga hesitated. *There was one called Ihsan. He understood numbers in a different way compared to humans. He saw them in patterns and colours, as well as the relationships between them, relationships that concord with the world of matter.*

I was amused. 'Sounds like you made a friend, Inga. I'm thinking you might be self-aware after all. What happened when you tried to assimilate with him?'

He was deleted.

'He died, you mean. Because his mind wasn't strong enough.'

His brain failed.

'What happens if you assimilate me? Will I still exist as a self-aware mind?'

That is an optimal outcome, yes.

'Then we'll exist together, as two minds in the one entity?'

Yes. Then your body will be modified to begin enabling speciation.

'What if we argue and fight? Who wins?'

Neither and both. We may disagree but there would be no point to fighting—we would be too connected. It would be as if the left side of your body fought your right. With more connections, conflict becomes even more self-limiting.

'So full assimilation means you'd be aware of my thinking, and I'd be aware of yours, yes?'

That is possible. I have learned new techniques over the decades that may make the transition less harmful.

'Alright, here's how I want you to do it. I want to look around your mind without exploding my brain in the process. Then you can look around mine. If we understand each other, we can decide about the whole assimilation and modification caper. Can you handle that?'

I will now begin transfer of your brain state to view mine.
'And if I say stop, you stop.'
I understand. Beginning transfer now.
I braced myself for the unknown. Then . . .

When us humans think, it's mostly blocking out irrelevant guff so we can decide whether to scratch our arse or pick our nose. But when a massive parallel quantum whatsit thinks, it's done with the awareness of *all* the relationships between *all* of the things of concern—all at the same time. Nothing is blocked as its mind instantly expands to see the whole, while still being able to see the fine details of each part, plus all relationships between them . . .

'Stop!'

I was curled up in a ball on some leaf litter, my arms wrapped around my head in a feeble attempt to block out the sensory overload. I slowly uncurled. 'Wow.'

Did you suffer?

'A little, but I'm okay now. Thanks for asking.' I shook my head, still reeling.

Shall I wait before I enter your brain state?

'No. Come on in. Same rules though—when I say stop, you stop.'

Agreed.

Inga was gentle. As my vision faded, Inga crept in like a shy guest at a party. *Blanco, I'm merging our brain states while I observe more fully what you are and how you are linked to your splinter.*

'Make yourself at home. Have a good look around.'

Feelings and memories surfaced. Tog and me as lads getting El Grande to 'accidentally' spray Madam Tracey with water. Singing an old traveller song with the freaks after a good run of thievery and mayhem in south Wales. Being beaten by the Gaffer for stealing food, pain eclipsed by childish anger. The stream of memory fragments came, faster and faster. 'Slow down, Inga.'

The memory flood stopped, and I was again sitting in a forest beside a lake.

I hope I did not cause you to suffer.

'No, you're fine. What did you think?'

There was a hesitation. *There are structures here I do not find consistent.*

'Meaning what, Inga?'

There is also modification to the splinter I do not understand.

'That might be from when I got poisoned by . . .'

There's something else here. It shouldn't be here. I don't like it.

'Are you alright, Inga?'

I am experiencing . . . there's something wrong . . . where are you? I . . .

I was starting to get worried when . . .

Who are you?

'Blanco! Look out!'

It was the same voice as the one what warned me in the lake. I turned, adrenaline pumping. 'Boris?'

Out of the forest came a vision of pure horror, the huge blonde smiling head of Tommy, crushing and smearing everything in its path. 'Hi, Blanco. That was a great trick in the lake when you killed my body.' He put out a hand big enough to gather me up in a tight grip.

His enormous face loomed down at mine, beaming. 'Did you hear about the wasps that lay eggs in caterpillar larvae? The larvae stay alive, while you go on living and thinking nothing's wrong. Then, one day, the wasp babies eat their way out. I'm like a wasp baby inside you!'

He laughed, loud enough to crush thought. 'I've been inside you since the Feat. Now I'm going to eat my way out of you and into SPLINTER. I'm going to take it over and use your body to create a new race.'

He squeezed me tight, enjoying my pain. 'I love being so smart.'

Chapter Fifty-Eight—Wisdom
is caring, caring is love

Tommy didn't spare me the pain as his bizarre giant balloon face stared down, taking the same smug fascination in doing to me what I'm sure he did to his murder victims.

'I'm going to modify you and breed you and Sparrow and the rest of them,' he said. 'I'll kill all the faulty ones—the freaks. They're awful.'

'Why?' I panted through the agony. 'What made you like this?'

He scoffed. 'Made me better than the peasants and subnormals? Do you need to even ask?'

'What do you even want? What's your fucking endgame, you psychopath.'

I was just stalling for time, but he squeezed again, tighter. 'To do whatever I want. I'll have such power, more than I ever dared to dream of. I'll control everyone, everywhere.'

'Then what? Once everyone knows what a wanker you are, what then?'

He crushed me till I screamed, then eased the pressure off. 'I'll keep growing. I'll use you all as slaves to build me any device I design. I'll split myself, and load my clones into spaceships with enough equipment to take over other worlds in other solar systems, eventually other galaxies . . .'

I had to keep him talking. 'Then what?'

'You can't be that stupid,' he sneered. 'I will become greater than God and throw him down.'

'A tosser like you?'

'Normals and freaks like you are so weak—you can't imagine true greatness. You can't see that God hasn't stopped making mistakes since he created this pathetic universe . . .'

Tommy banged on with more of this religious bollocks as I reached around in my mind, looking for Inga and some way of fighting back. It was my brain this prick was in, but where exactly was he? How could I seize control?

Tommy dropped me, still babbling about being the 'creator of creators' when I saw the apple tree. On it was a single ripe apple. I was sure it hadn't been there till a moment ago. Did it mean anything or nothing? I moved toward the apple, talking like I was genuinely curious about Tommy's mad discourse. 'But I still don't get it—why become God?'

'To fix everything, and have every single atom in the universe bow down and worship me.'

I snatched at the apple. It felt warm. My hand and arm tingled—I sensed it was important to eat it. I took a bite and felt Inga surge into me. *Blanco! This creature is not engaged in self-limiting behaviour!*

No kidding, I thought.

It believes fiction as truth!

Inga, I thought, how do we get rid of it?

You must equal and exceed its power with truth.

A huge hand grabbed me up again, his other slapped the apple from mine, enraged. 'Why are you eating? I'm torturing you!'

I imagined the energy from the apple feeding me, allowing me to grow. I grew . . .

'What are you doing?' Tommy shouted, squeezing. 'Stop it!'

I ignored the pain he inflicted on me, just as I'd been trained to ignore it all my life. I kept growing despite the battering of giant hands. 'You're wrong, Tommy,' I grunted. 'All this bollocks of yours won't give you happiness because it won't mean anything.'

He started punching, big meaty punches, with huge inflated fists. 'Stop talking!'

I felt myself weakening. 'You haven't understood anything, you idiot.'

'You're the idiot!'

'Meaning and happiness don't come from power,' I gasped. 'They come from sharing it. It's all about connection with others.'

And then he smashed me with all of his strength, and I thought that was me done.

'*I'm* going to be the meaning,' Tommy raged, trees breaking and spinning away from his voice as he raised me up in one crushing fist. 'There will be no meaning but me! I'll create universes and grow and become ...'

He stopped.

His eyes became unfocused.

His mouth opened as if he wanted to say something. Sudden doubt crossed his face, then panic. 'What are you doing?'

'Nothing,' I hissed, helpless.

'You're doing something. I can feel it. How are you doing that? Stop it! It's hurting me!'

His face crumpled, teary. 'No! Don't!'

Then, erupting from his cheek, came a wasp larvae. Another emerged from his forehead, and then more out of his nose—all of them chewing, eating him. A dozen became a hundred. Tommy's screams burned my senses like acid on bare skin. I stared in dumb horror as the writhing creatures consumed him. I was forgotten and dropped. I staggered away as Tommy dissolved into a mass of larvae eating every part of him. Every hair, every shred of skin and bone were eaten.

I could only look on, too bewildered to feel hope.

Then, when every bit of Tommy was gone, the larvae merged, changing shape.

Turning into a human figure.

Boris!

I ran to him, relieved and overjoyed. 'You're alive!'

'Sort of,' he shrugged. 'I've been struggling to be anything since I was killed.'

I stood. 'Hang on, Boris.' I looked around. 'Inga? Are you there?'

There was a long moment, and then Inga spoke. *I'm here. I require information about what just occurred.*

'Of course you do. We all do, but first—Inga, I'd like you to meet Boris. Boris, Inga is the name I gave the singularity.'

'Hullo, Inga,' said Boris, bemused.

Hullo, Boris. Blanco, I'm not sure what to do next.

The funny thing was, at that moment, it all suddenly seemed obvious to me. 'Inga, Boris successfully assimilated with me, so he can assimilate with you. Boris, go with Inga and explain the genius trick what you just did to Tommy. Inga, copy Boris's brain state and make sure he doesn't get overwhelmed and suffer—give him full control of what he sees and feels and thinks.'

Boris looked uncertain, but I was confident. 'It'll be okay, Boris. You're the true winner of the Great Feat. And now you'll help provide Inga with what she needs to think proper.'

'And what is that?'

'Emotional connection—to you and the rest of us.'

I came to, blinking up at the diffuse light of the big room, Doctor Po and the Professoré looking down at me with concern. 'He looks brain-damaged.'

The Professoré shone a torch in my eyes, sighing. 'Another vegetable.'

'Oi,' I mumbled through the mouthguard. 'Enough with the insults. Untie me.'

My bonds were untied as I tried to shake my head free of whirling thoughts and a haze of emotion.

I was bombarded with questions. 'Did you connect?' 'What went wrong?' 'Is the singularity intact?' And then Simten's voice. 'Are you alright?'

I nodded. 'I think so. I just need to rest for a minute. Then I need you to hook me up again.'

'What for?' asked Po, suspicious.

'To finish the job.' I smiled. 'I know what we have to do.' I gestured Simten and Rami toward the spare seats. 'Come on you two, take a seat and let's get you hooked up. I need you to meet a couple of friends of mine. A lovely couple—Inga and Boris.'

It was a bit sad to exit the singularity when we'd all finally finished our discussion with Inga, but Boris was where he needed to be, Simten and Rami were in on the whole connected caper, and I knew I'd be with them all again whenever I wanted to be. All of us would be connected, when we wanted, forever. And soon there'd be more of us. Loads more.

I explained the plan to Cosar and the rest of the elders. 'Forget about quantum computer bollocks—the real game isn't the brain or the splinters, it's the connections.'

Po gestured at the cubes. 'What about the singularity?'

'The singularity is just one brain to connect to. Don't get me wrong, bigger brains are fine, but smart people don't behave no better than numpties. On the other hand, lots of loosely connected brains share nous and experience. Bad ideas meet better ones. Geezers can think stupid bollocks but self-correct because they is hooked up to so many other people. We can even go on evolving.'

Cosar frowned. 'How will communities like ours work in such a frenzy of thinking?'

'Same but better—and happier. Big decisions won't come from one powerful type like a queen or king or a gaffer, no matter how smart they is. We'll have distributed intelligence, all of us remaining individual but connected, when we want, to the whole of the new species.'

Po nodded, thoughtful. 'A hive mind. Social intelligence.'

'Well, we in't ants or bees, but yeah, something like that. The singularity isn't some big clever computer. It's us, the new Homo—all of us different, all of us together. *We* are the singularity.'

There were no shortage of doubtful looks, but I knew.

I'd seen how it was all connected, and how it would make total sense to the new species to *not* trash the planet and ourselves. With enough connection, being selfish, self-hating or destructive would simply feel pointless. The human race would grow, strengthen and evolve by choice—together.

The king looked around the group. 'What will we call this new species?'

I knew this one too—I'd asked Simten, Rami and Ingrid already. 'Turns out we in't "wise humans" like *Homo sapiens* were supposed to be. We'll be the "connected human". We'll be *Homo nexus*.'

Epilogue

Early morning sun shone down on Sparrow and me, perched on the lead tractor what was slowly pulling our trailer south across the desert. Behind us were the elephants, and the trucks and trailers containing the rest of our wonky freak family.

Daisy chewed a bone in the doorway of the trailer behind us. Beside her, Baba Yaga chewed the remains of last night's roast. Both looked as focused as each other while they extracted every last piece of meat and marrow in companionable silence.

We had two thousand kilometres to go before we reached the Indian Ocean, and who knew what we'd encounter on the way. But we wouldn't be alone. Inside me, Sparrow and another half a dozen of us, splinters were keeping us connected.

We wouldn't lack for company or information and help as we set out to find the new green land, untouched by Homo sapiens, that lay across the great Southern Ocean—Tartika.

Life might be what dust and ashes do when they need a holiday but, right now, we needed a sanctuary. Tartika would be all that, and our new home.

I couldn't wait—it would be the place where me and Sparrow's baby would be born.

Fin.

Glossary

arak: distilled white spirit

babushka: old woman

bally: the bally: the spruik / act given by the front-of-house talker to draw in punters

bandolier: Gypsy elder or authority, a highly respected member of an extended family group

barnstorming: touring fast, moving the circus from town to town with short stays in each

bint: derogatory term for young woman, English slang derived from the Arabic for 'daughter'

blow-off, the: the diverse means to encourage punters to exit the freak show; often a misleading exit sign (*This way to the Egress*) or a circus member directing audience. ('See the Egress, folks! This way to the Egress!')

Bogda Shan: the easternmost range of the Tien Shan mountains, the furthest point from any ocean on Earth

Bratva: Russian mafia

carnie: worker in a travelling carnival or circus

chavs: children

chovihani: an old woman, wise-woman, witch

commsat: communications satellite

CQ semi: Chinese semiautomatic rifle

dial: face

didikai: Gypsy friend

dinari: money

DPM: disruptive pattern material: camouflage material

fakir: subcontinental Indian or Persian ascetic or holy man, beggar, pavement performer

ferroplas: road surfacing made from recycled plastics and other materials

gadjo: non-Gypsy

gaffed: rigged; a dishonest set-up or game, mechanically rigged to cheat the punter

genmod –genetic modification tailored to individual human

graf/graphene: materials made from single-atomic layered carbon sheets

half-inched: rhyming slang: pinched, stolen

jahannam: Islamic Hell

kif: smokable pollen and resin from the cannabis plant

knock shop: brothel

kris: Romani court of justice

kushti: nice

Lom: an ethnic group of Rom from Armenia

marime: defiled, ritually 'polluted', 'dirty', disgraced, to be avoided by Gypsies, cast out

mesmerism: hypnotism

midway, the: area of a circus midway between the entrance and the big top, usually where the rides and games are situated

moxados / moxies: bandits

oldtech: pre-Collapse technology/equipment/tools

palaver: chat, common talk

pikey: non-Gypsy traveller

polis: police

provodnitsa: railway carriage attendant

pull the pin: to pack up and leave

rads: units of ionising radiation from nuclear weapons or damaged nuclear power plants

ringer: a member of the circus pretending to be an audience member called to assist an act

Rom: general term used for Gypsy: broadly covers many different-named ethnic groups that range from Northern India to across Europe and are dispersed across the rest of the world.

Romani: broad term used to refer to the Rom language, though many dialects exist

RT—radio transceiver: two-way radio

Ragamuffins—British bandit gang of African origin

Raskols—British bandit gang of Papuan origin

sarnies—sandwiches

scarfed—ate quickly

scran—food

scratch—money/wages

Six-Pak—a heavy but portable electric multi-barrelled gun firing .45-calibre rounds

shadogs—derogatory term for police

shebari—young woman

sheka—expletive—horse-shit

snow-dropping—to steal drying laundry

sprogs—children

Tech20—small automatic machine gun

Thuggees—British bandit gang of sub-continental Asian origin

tin lids—rhyming slang: kids, small children

tola—11.5 grams; Hindi term for a standard weight of opium or hashish

Acknowledgements

While it may be tempting for any long-suffering readers who have reached this point to attack the author personally for the excess of profanities, egregious violence and being narratively dragged halfway around the world, *many* people are to blame for this novel, not just the person who wrote it.

Some of the worst offenders in enabling its gestation and birth include Steve Rossiter, whose acute literary eye and teachings in the early stages steered the manuscript toward the distant rocks of publication. Also at fault are the Australian Society of Authors, who foolishly awarded a particularly raw early MS with a Mentorship from a proper author, Alyssa Brugman, who gamely read the thing, then put up with the ungracious eye-rolling reactions from the author when she pointed out just a fraction of its many flaws.

Despite ample opportunity to reject it out of hand, Brio Books, in an unexpected plot twist, awarded it the 2019 Fantastica Prize. Unaccountably slotting it among their existing stable of real writers, David Henley and Chris Marcatili both edited the plot-holes and pedestrian prose even closer to the rocks. Finally, in the last few moments, when the general public could've been spared had sense prevailed, Tom Langshaw, drafted in to copy-edit, disgracefully took the money and did his best to make it scan like a real book, bringing the whole damn thing to its denouement, being read by you.

While it's hard to judge who is most at fault, Roy Chen, the cover illustrator and designer, must surely bear the greatest responsibility – had he not executed his skills to 'polish the turd' (as it's known in the trade), most readers would not have even made it to the blurb.

I just hope Roy, and the others, can find a way to forgive themselves.

Finally, if you, the reader, can find it in your heart to give this novel a 7 out of 5 star rating in Goodreads or Amazon, the suffering of those responsible for Last Circus may be eased.

B.P. Marshall is a former Critical Care and Remote Area Nurse who took a break from delivering babies and sewing up machete wounds to consult for a television medical drama. He ended up writing storylines, doing some science journalism and becoming a full-time scriptwriter. A short film, (*True Love*, Ignition Films), won awards in Australia and the United States. Turning to novels, he won writing mentorships, and was shortlisted (for *The Fox*) as Emerging Writer in the 2017 Queensland Literary Awards. In 2019 he won the Fantastica Prize for *The Last Circus on Earth*. He's currently writing television scripts, and novels across multiple genres.

benmarshallwriter.com

www.ingramcontent.com/pod-product-compliance
Lightning Source LLC
Chambersburg PA
CBHW011341010726
47493CB00009B/2900